JARRETT'S
JADE

JARRETT'S JADE

A Novel by
FRANK YERBY

THE DIAL PRESS · NEW YORK

For
GEORGE JOEL

PROLOGUE

JADEWOOD, THE HOUSE itself, as opposed to the plantation—since the name is used by the Jarretts to refer to both—sits in a liveoak grove on the outskirts of Atlanta. From it, the family maintains an uneasy truce with that bustling metropolis, by which Atlanta half-heartedly agrees to cease and desist from her efforts to engulf the plantation, while the Jarretts, on their part, with total lack of enthusiasm, agree to keep the peace.

It is easy to understand the Jarretts' stubborn clinging to their green and pleasant sweep of earth. "We were here first," they insist—and with perfect truth; for the plantation is more than fifty years older than the town. But age aside, that demi Eden is worth the struggle. Jadewood is nothing like most Southern manors. In style, it is chastely Georgian rather than Neo-Grecian; when it was built, that imitative flowering of an alien idea had not yet taken hold. Its red brick, kiln-burnt from native clay by slave artisans, has never known whitewash or paint. But time has dealt gently with Jadewood; in the few places where the ivy has not covered the walls, the raw red which clashed with the endless greenery around it when the house was new, has weathered into a rose-grey patina whose loveliness is absolute.

The ivy is the final touch in Jadewood's accidental perfection. The green—of lawns, of shrubs, of trees—has won. Jadewood, one says now with comprehension. Green as Jade. That explains it, of course. When Jarl Jarrett came here for the first time in 1783, he must have—

But, did he? In the great hall, his portrait stares down at his more civilized descendants with an expression halfway between pity and contempt. That smile is out of joint. Below the jut and flare of the Jarrett nose, one lip corner curls higher than the other. The painter was skillful. It is what people call a speaking likeness. To gaze at it is to wait—

For words unspoken. But not unthought. They are almost visible there behind those eyes.

Jarrett's Jade, he called it. And so, for that matter, do his descendants, nine times out of ten. It was his wife, Millicent, who added that graceful fancy of—"wood." The Jarretts, in their oblique, disjointed fashion, leave the impression that Jarl's name for his home had a deeper, even tragic meaning; but there, quite maddeningly, they halt, leaving that, like so many other things, unanswered and unsaid.

Perhaps there are no answers. At Jadewood, the questions duplicate themselves endlessly like images in a hall of mirrors; and the answers flicker out of time like candles plunged in wind, drowned in moving air. Turn away from Jarl; look upon the sombre countenance of his father, James, and answers begin to suggest themselves; but even they are framed as questions still. The two faces are marvelously alike, and yet—so different. The Jarrett nose is there in James' face, but it is even more imperious, closer to the Jarretts' primordial quality; and that thick hedgerow of an eyebrow flares across the face without a break, so that both eyes stare out from beneath a single line. But though the mouth has that same oddly sensual fullness duplicated in his son's, it is not sardonic. Grim. Controlled. But without irony—or humor. Living with James Jarrett as wife or son or slave was undiluted hell, as the Jarretts cheerfully admit, without ever stopping to say why. If, indeed, they know. Which, given the Jarretts' turn of mind, is doubtful.

There are no whys. Among the Jarretts, there is only the sweep of naked force like the sun-bright arc of a claymore's blade. They are not metaphysicians. They are Jarretts. Which is their reason for being; their justification.

But, enough of speculation. Look upon him. Upon James, the first American Jarrett, clad in kilt and tartan still, the bagpipes slung about his shoulders. Broadsword in hand, target on his forearm. Highland Chieftain, warrior, man. The first of the Georgia Jarretts. The Founder of the clan.

Or rather, its savior.

JARRETT'S
JADE

CHAPTER ONE

HE, TWO YEAR old James Jarrett, came crawling out of the sod-hut into the square between the clachan of three houses. At two, he should have been able to walk, of course. But he couldn't. In his two years of living, he had never had enough to eat for his legs to grow strong enough. His black hair was long and matted. He wore a shirt and nothing else. Beneath it, his body was a skeleton with distended belly, alive with vermin, covered with sores. He whimpered a little. He didn't have strength enough left to cry aloud.

He was looking for his mother. At two years of age, he was still breastfed. No other sustenance was available. There was no gruel, no porridge, no nothing. James Jarrett crawled on. Found his mother. She was stretched out on the ground between the houses. He crawled up to her, rooting at her breasts like the small and savage beast he was. They were dry. He went on rooting. Then he sat back on his haunches in the dirt and howled. Not from grief, but from hunger. He was too little to realize that Annie MacDugan Jarrett had starved to death. So had the women in the other two houses in the month-long absence of their men, gone to raid the Lowlands for food to keep the clan alive. Seventeen-seventeen was, for Clan Jarrett, the worst of the bad years. More than enough to kill women, the lean black Highland cows, the very raincrows in the trees, and any manchild not a Jarrett.

Eighteen hours later, Jonathan Jarrett, Chieftain of the Clan, came hallooing into that Highland glen, driving his herd of stolen cows before him, his bearded, kilted warriors whooping at his side, and saw the two figures on the ground. He stopped the infernal racket with a lifted hand. Bent and picked up his son. Rent the very heavens with his cry: "Alive! Alive, by God!"

He sat there on a log, holding the fevered mite, with the great, hot tears dripping through his fiery red beard into Jaimie's face, while the clansmen milked the cows. He dipped a filthy tartan rag into the hot, rich milk. The child sucked at it noisily. Vomited. Patiently, Jon Jarrett fed his son again. This time the milk stayed down. Little Jaimie Jarrett slept.

Then the clansmen attended to the burying of their dead.

When that had been done, Jonathan Jarrett, Laird of Clan Jarrett, stood over the cradle, hewn out of half a log with a broadaxe.

"Jaimie, boy," he whispered, "ever a fool I was; but, no more. At Sheriffmuir, the fighting was right glorious, but the truth is that we lost. And for the whiskey dream of putting the Stuarts back on the throne of England, I robbed you of yon angel. No more! Ever have we starved in the Highlands. When you're bigger, my son, my boy, it's taking you I am down to Londontown. To learn the English tongue instead of our wild Gaelic. To make a merchant of you. Mayhap there's pride in being the son of a bonnet laird—a man so mickle poor he has to wear a bonnet like a tenant croftsman instead of a hat like a gentleman; but such honor makes a slim diet, doesn't it, lad? May the mickle old black devil rot my soul before I'll raise up the Clan again!"

First in the morning of his tenth birthday, James Jarrett was awakened by the crowing of the cock, perched as always, along with five or six hens, atop the canopy of his rude bed. He rolled over and stared into the bony face of the cow, who likewise occupied the single room of the house that Jonathan Jarrett, with conscious irony, called his "castle." With irony, and with pride. For Laird Jonathan had built the house with his own two hands, digging the stones from the hillsides, piling them up, plugging the chinks with mud and heather, thatching the roof with reeds, throwing a net over the thatch, and weighting it down with stones to keep the highland winds from blowing it quite away—as once in a while they did—stones or no. In one thing only did it differ from the other houses in the clachan, as the village was called in highland Gaelic: it boasted a chimney. The others were "black houses," which meant that they had only a hole in the roof to let the smoke from the fire escape—and everything within them bore an inch deep layer of soot. But to young James Jarrett, who had never known or even seen a better, his was indeed a castle and the finest house on earth.

He rolled from the bed, wide awake at once, and ravenously hungry.

"Judy!" he howled; "my breakfast!"

The blowsy slattern of a maidservant straightened up from bending over the black iron pot hung on chains above the fire in which she was boiling his porridge.

"Wist, bairn, but ye hae no patience fer a fact!" she snapped. "Come and get it. Ye grow more like yer father iver living day!"

Shivering, James raced for the fireplace. He was clad only in a night-shirt, and the house was plagued cold. Greedily he began to lap up the thick, steaming mess Judy served him, making a good bit of noise in the process. In two minutes he had finished it, and passed his wooden bowl over for more.

"Blessed if ye don't be a greedy one!" Judy complained. "A body would think ye'd not eaten this last se'en night. . . ."

"Hold your tongue, and fill my bowl," James commanded. To his prickly Jarretts' pride, Judy's eternal grumbling seemed perilously close to insolence. He was a Laird's son, and he knew it, unwashed face, wild tangled hair and all. He'd have no lip from his inferiors. And here of late, he thought, this wench keeps her place but ill. . . .

He had no way of knowing upon what her so-called insolence was based. He was too sound a sleeper, and too young, to realize that she performed other services for his father in the night.

He went on lapping up his porridge. He had never tasted wheaten bread. He did not, in sober fact, realize that elsewhere people did not dine on oatmeal, watery porridge and skimmed milk—or even that in the Lowlands, yeomen farmers gained more from their broad acres in one year than the members of his clan could scratch from the thin, poor soil covering the floor of the deep, straight-sided valleys they called glens, in twelve. Nor was he concerned about the many things beyond his ken. He knew he was a Jarrett, and that was enough and more.

"You've a proud heritage, son," Jonathan had told him all his life; "the best. 'Tisn't every lad who can look forward to one day being Laird of Clan Jarrett. . . ."

It never occurred to James to question what difference that made in a land where a clan chieftain who gained twenty pounds a year in rents from the miserable tenant farmers, called "crofters," was considered rich beyond all dreams of avarice. The answer was simple: little, if any. For Laird Jonathan did not gain twenty pounds a year from his crofters. In a good year, he made ten. His average was five.

But to Jaimie Jarrett, it did make a difference. Imperiously he forced the children of the crofters, with whom he played, hunted, went curling upon the ice in winter, to accord him his due respect. He never tired of listening to his father's stories of his family's history; part lies, part legend, and part truth.

"The first Jarrett was named Jarl, you ken, my boy," Jonathan would begin. "He was knighted on the field at Dunstane, by Duncan, himself, for his valor in the battle in which that evil monster, Macbeth, was slain. 'Twas then that we became Lairds. . . ."

"What were we before?" James demanded, just as though he had not heard the tale a thousand times before.

"Honest yeomen, and warriors all. No Jarrett in history has ever died in bed. A stout family of men, such as they breed not oft these days. Why, with their claymores, our forebears could cut a man in two at the waist—"

"You mean broadswords, don't you, Father?" James said.

"Nay, lad, claymores. A broadsword's a puny toy in comparison. Nine foot of blade they had, and a two-handed hilt, so that a man could swing them full lustily, I tell you—"

"But, Father, what were we called? Not—just Jarretts, I ween?"

"Aye, and that was enough. We were only a family; but a proud one, even then. For that matter, all clans were merely families in the beginning. After Jarl was knighted, of course, we grew into a clan, acquired retainers, tenant croftsmen, and liegemen armed with claymores, targets, and pikes—"

"Father," James said, "were we—rich?"

"Nay, lad," Jonathan said honestly; "never in three hundred years has any Jarrett made or kept more than tuppence at a time. Our history was hard and bloody and glorious—and more oft than not, right gloriously we starved!"

"But I thought it was the Rising of Fifteen that cost us our lands and goods—"

Jonathan's eyes clouded with old, but still bitter sorrows. He looked away from his son. How could a man put into words the feelings the phrase, "The Rising of Fifteen," brought leaping into anguished life? Or how could he explain to Jaimie that witches' brew of reasons which had made him, an Episcopalian by conviction, raise up Clan Jarrett in 1715 to put the Old Pretender, James Stuart, a devout Roman Catholic, upon the throne of England and Scotland?

Jonathan didn't really know the reasons, himself. The Stuarts were Scotch, thus giving Jacobitism a national coloring. The Episcopal

Church, respected and tolerated in England was outcast and despised in Scotland. And, like nearly all Highlanders, Jonathan believed that the Campbells, leaders of those clans loyal to England's German King, George I, were bloody well begging to have their comeuppance given them because of their arrogance.

Memories of the cruelties of Oliver Cromwell's Roundhead Troopers had something to do with it, of course. His native Highland love for a good, rousing fight; the belief that the Stuarts, restored to the throne, would give Scotland back her independence, reluctantly surrendered in the Union with England of 1707.

Reasons there were in God's plenty. But did they—any of them—make sense? An independent Jacobite Scotland—if they had won. But, by definition—a starving, backward, weak kingdom; and, what was worse, from Jonathan's point of view—a Catholic one. He'd raised up Clan Jarrett, in part, to gain the freedom to worship God according to his lights. But when, in all of history, had Papists ever granted anyone the right to dissent? He'd looked forward eagerly to seeing the Campbells humbled; but John Campbell, the Duke of Argyll, at Sheriffmuir, had fought their Jacobite army of eight thousand men to a standstill by his skillful use of the only thirty-five hundred troops he had had under his command. And the Jacobites' chosen leader, the Earl of Mar, had proved an inept bumbler. Clan Campbell, the Dukes of Argyll, owed their preeminence to their talent and their skill. And jealousy be damned—in the world of hard reality, the better man always wins.

So they had lost. Or rather, they had given up little by little. In the long wait after the stalemate at Sheriffmuir, their very temperament, that characteristic highland want of patience, had defeated them. The clans began to desert. Night after night, their numbers dwindled—until when James Stuart, the Old Pretender, the would-be James Third, by God's withheld Grace, of England and Scotland, finally appeared, months too late, there were only a handful left to greet him. Jonathan had stuck it out that long; but when he saw the man he had been fighting for, he deserted in a sick rage. A worse bumbler than Mar; a man without grace, talent, or kingliness; essentially a foreigner—and totally unfit to rule men as proud and virile as Highlanders.

A fool's errand, that Rising of 1715. A monstrous folly that had cost him the lands he had planted to flax year after year, cost him his dearly-clung-to dream for the salvation of his clan: the fine, hoped for, lovingly planned linen manufactory—for his knowledge of both

flax and cloth making was considerable—that he would never be able
to open, now—all his worldly goods, in fact; and even, gallingly, the
simple right to wear his native dress, the tartan and the kilt, reduced
abruptly by their impulsive, unthinking act, from the emblems of manhood to the badge of traitors. That had cost him, finally, by the starvation his losses had brought him to, his wife.

"Father," James said again, "Wasn't it the Rising that made Argyll
rob us of our lands and goods?"

"Aye," Jonathan said morosely. "We were better off before—though
not much. And now, let's not talk on it further, lad. . . ."

He had told James the story again, a fortnight ago, just before his
departure upon one of his mysterious excursions down into the Lowlands. He should be back soon, the boy thought wistfully; and mayhap
he'll even bring me something—a smallsword or a toy—

Which was deuced unlikely. If Jonathan gained even a shilling, he'd
drink it up, and come home empty-handed as usual. James slammed
down his bowl and stood up.

"My tartan, Judy!" he said. Grumbling, Judy brought him his tartan,
kilt, knit stockings, weskit, and his shoes. Chilly as the morning was,
she brought no underwear. Like all Highlanders, under his kilt James
Jarrett wore only his manhood, and his pride.

Dressed, he picked up his bagpipes, and sallied forth into his world.
He stood before the door of his "castle," his eyes at first unadjusted
to the matchless light of a morning in the Highlands after the smoky
darkness of his home. Then they cleared. He looked out toward the
rounded crests of his native hills, for the Highlands are not craggy
mountains, but gently rolling hills and sweep of heather and of moor.
High they are, but they are also quite often flat. His dark eyes squinted
into the light, following the endless hills as they purpled with the distance. It was early in the Spring of 1725, and the air still retained its
wintry bite. He stood there without moving, dreaming on how it would
be in August when the heather turned a purple unmatched by the
art of man; smelling the fresh budding greenery, letting the wild beauty
of it enter him.

He was waiting for his father to come back and begin the "Lifting."
The word was damnably exact. After having been confined all winter
in the houses upon what fare was available, the bony highland cows
had to be quite literally "lifted" by the brawny crofters down to the
pasturelands in the glen. After a winter-long diet of sternly rationed
straw, which, among the Jarretts, always gave out completely two

weeks or so before the final thaw, the cows were too far gone to walk.

While he waited, he lifted the mouthpiece of the bagpipes to his lips, and began to play very softly, fingering the touch holes of the shortest pipe with real skill. From the four pipes, each of a different length in order to vary their tones, a wild caterwauling rose. Jaimie pressed the bag with his left elbow, forcing out a greater volume of air. He hadn't meant to play loudly, but the tune was his favorite: the warsong of Clan Jarrett, and, despite his good intentions not to disturb the neighbors at such an hour, that wild, keening chant took hold of him. He surrendered to its stirring music, playing with verve and skill, as his father had taught him to. Which was not to say he made lovely music: at their very best the pipes sound like a chorus of amorous tomcats.

Judy sailed forth from the house, blood in her eye.

"Gimme that!" she spat. "Ye want to have the whole clachan up in arms?"

Frowning, James gave her his beloved instrument. Ordinarily, he would have invoked a pox upon Judy's head and refused to surrender it; but today was—special, somehow. He had a feeling that something was going to happen, something so grand that putting Judy in her place as usual was completely wanting in importance. Judy took the bagpipes and went back inside, grumbling to herself.

Jaimie started to move off, to seek companions for a game; but then, at that very moment, he saw his father coming up out of the glen, driving a new cow before him. The beastie was sleek and fat. The minute James saw it, he knew Laird Jonathan had gotten it by open, blatant thievery. The fact did not shock him. Stealing Lowlanders' cattle was an honorable and accepted occupation among the Highlanders. But for their occasional raids into the more favored lands below, they would have starved more often than they did.

"Hoot, father!" he called. "A fine one for a fact! You've come back to start the liftings?"

"Nay, lad," Jonathan said soberly. "Tether the beastie for me. I've a thing to tell you. . . ."

James stared at his father. Laird Jonathan, oddly enough, wasn't drunk. And this tone was new. James could see that his father was laboring under the strain of badly suppressed excitement.

"Well, father?" he said.

"Today's your birthday," Jonathan said; "and all the way home I was regretting the fact that I have naught to give you. Then it came to me that I could, mayhap, give my son the finest gift of all—a future. . . ."

"A future?" James whispered; "but I have a future, father. One day I shall be Laird, and—"

"Fine future, that!" Jonathan laughed bitterly. "Nay, lad, hear me out. I've raided the Lowlands full many a time and oft; but, until today, I never truly looked at them—"

"So?" James said.

"So we go down to Edinburgh tomorrow, once I've told the crofters what to do. And, once there—"

"What?" the boy said wonderingly.

"We'll see," was all his father said.

Aye, Spring was fair in the Highlands when ten-year-old Jaimie Jarrett and his father left them forever. Not that they knew it would be forever; for the thing itself was then no more than a dream in Jonathan Jarrett's dreaming head.

They set out for Edinburgh, for them the gateway to the world. Right briskly they marched, father and son, following the new road that General Wade, Commander of the English Army of Occupation after the Rising of Fifteen, had built from Inverness to Perth to Fort Augustus to Crieff, ending the blighting isolation of the Highlands for all time. They drove the sum total of their fortunes before them: the stolen Lowland cow, whose price in the markets of Edinburgh would keep them until—

Beyond that "until" Laird Jonathan did not go. Though he mulled over the past long and deeply, about the future, he habitually thought in truncated phrases. A man did not tempt fate, he held, by thinking on it too precisely.

But Jaimie Jarrett did go beyond that until. He'd already learned that the past was a cruelly accurate measure of the future. And he knew very surely what his father would do with the money they'd get for the miserable beastie. Drink it up. Then they'd go hungry again, and sleep in the streets. At ten, he was wise beyond his years, accepting the world as it was with weary resignation.

"Father," he said; " 'tis true there are no weefolk in the thorn trees of the dene? Parson Williams says—"

"Wist, Lad!" Jonathan Jarrett laughed; "the good parson is a Lowlander and English bred. There are things beyond his ken. Myself, many's the night I've heard the Water Kelpie roaring in the spate, coming home at the dark o' the moon across the ford . . . Fairies there be. And a man is wise to be wary of them for a fact. In my father's time, we always lit the Beltan fires and danced them round to keep the wee ones pacified—or else they'd slay the cattle in the byre—or steal the children, and leave changelings in their places. Of warlocks and witches, let us not speak. And may our new English parson be spared the sight of the muckle black de'il climbing the northkirk wall. That would surely chill his Lowland blood for fair!"

"The parson says," James said stubbornly, " 'tis all nonsense. And d'you know what, father? 'tis thinking I am, he's right!"

Jonathan rolled his eyes piously skyward.

"May the Lord protect thee, my boy, from modern influences," he said. "Come on!"

"Father," James said, "What are we going to do in Edinburgh?"

"I have a wee bit of money saved," Jonathan said. "If we get a good price for this fine beastie, 'tis on to Londontown, my boy!"

"And there?" James growled. He was nothing if not a realist.

"I put thee out as 'prentice to a good master of a trade," Jonathan said soberly, "and find myself a job of work."

"But, father, we're lairds!"

Jonathan smiled at his son.

"Aye—that we be," he said, "but when in our lives has it filled a belly? We're neither Campbells, nor Mars. To be a great laird is a fine thing, son; but the life of a bonnet laird is another matter altogether—"

"Still," James said stubbornly, "a laird's a laird for awe that, bonnet or tricorne . . . But I do wish we weren't so mickle poor—"

"But we are," Jonathan said morosely. "And if it's thinking you are of your sainted mother's death, when haven't we Highlanders starved? Too much rain—or too little, an early frost, a bad crop, and we're done. Why, in King William's time, whole clans died of hunger. In some counties, no one was left to bury the dead, who rotted unshriven above ground. Nay, lad—I've had my fill of it. I'll swap my laird's bonnet for a journeyman's apron, and gladly—"

"But, father," James said with impish humor. "What work do you know aside from stealing Lowlanders' cattle?"

"None," Jonathan said; "but what I set these hands to can be learned. Besides, before you were born, I put the land I lost to flax year after year. 'tis thinking I am that a linen draper would not find my knowledge ill . . . ."

They fell silent. The heat was on the day. And they were leaving their homelands, now—putting everything familiar, cherished, loved, behind them with every stride. They trudged on, the boy beating the hedges with a blackthorn club, while his father idly swung the Scotch broadsword without which any Highlander would have considered himself positively naked.

They lay in a field and ate the bread and cheese while the black cow grazed. Then they pushed on. It took them three days, but they got there at last. In the full light of morning, they came striding through the streets of the tallest town in all the world. But, James saw, the height was man made. Because of the uncertainty of the times, and the fear of further Jacobite uprisings, Edinburgh hadn't dared spread beyond its ancient limits. Therefore the only direction it could grow was up. Canongate and High Street were jammed with filthy tenements ten storeys and more in height. The average Edinburgher wearily trudged more miles up and down stairs than he ever walked on the level.

The boy gazed with open mouthed wonder at the throngs filling the streets of this, the first city he had ever seen. High Court Judges strove mightily to walk as straight as befitted their dignity despite the heavy ballast of port, stout, claret, ale they carried amidships. Rough Highland porters swore in Gaelic as they forced a passage for the sedan chairs in which they bore their gouty Lairds. Keen eyed caddies, without whom business in the mazy winds and stairways of old Edinburgh would have come to a dead standstill, because each flat was considered a house, and no house bore a number—thus leaving the exact location of every family guarded solely in the peerless memories of the caddies, who served as guides, ran errands, and carried messages for hire. Above the teeming confusions, the redcoats of the small garrison of the Castle on the Rock looked down upon the turbulent city, fretfully wondering what species of riot, political, religious, or economic—not to mention those arising from plain Scotch cussedness—they'd be called upon to quell next.

It was young James' day of days. He missed nothing. From Holyrood Palace, that ancient seat of Scottish Kings, to Tron Kirk, the head church of all Presbyterianism, his eyes took in every detail. And, being a sensitive lad, he soon became aware that his father and he were being stared at in their turn. For many years now, the wearing of the tartan and the kilt had been banned, as a sign of royal disfavor at the Highlanders' part in the late Jacobite uprising. Now, of course, the rule had been relaxed. But the sight of a kilted Highlander, complete with broadsword and target, driving a black cow up High Street, followed by his small son, dressed in miniature duplication of his father's garb, wasn't the commonest sight in the world, even in a city as filled with sights as Edinburgh. The stares, the nudges grew; to be replaced by grins, and these by open laughter. James' small face flamed scarlet.

"Wist, you dunces!" he squawked. "Pox upon your laughter!"

But, at that precise moment, his luck turned dismal. Far above his head, a woman leaned out of an upper storey window and cried: "Gardy-loo!"

She was being most elegant. She was, or called herself, speaking French. Since Edinburgh was a smugglers' paradise, above half its revenue coming from the French wines brought in by every ship, the fashionable affected that tongue. What milady shrilled out was her Scotch burr's distortion of "Gardez l'eau!" "Watch out for the water!" And she was being polite—before flinging the contents of the collected nightjars of her entire family into the streets, as the custom of Edinburgh was, she was decently warning the passersby.

"Haud yer han'!" the crowd roared back, and scattered, running with humped shoulders to prevent their vast and expensive full-bottomed wigs from being put out of action by a cataract of filth.

But neither Jonathan nor James understood the cry. They stood there glaring. And were thoroughly splattered. A yard or two away from them, a sedan chair borne by two stout porters came to a halt at its occupants' command. The gorgeous red-haired lady, as richly dressed as any queen, opened the door, the better to see the sight. With her was a girl of eight or nine, obviously her daughter, for her hair was as sunburst red as her mother's, and her clothes as rich. The two of them sat there and shrieked with helpless laughter.

Which was a wee bit too much for a laird's son to gnaw upon. Nobody had ever taught James Jarrett that he had to be gallant with ladies. In two strides he closed the distance between him and that sedan chair, leaned in and boxed the maiden's ears right lustily.

Then everything happened at once. The porters laid brawny hands upon young Jim. He countered with his hawthorn stick. Jonathan Jarrett loosed the cow, unlimbered his broadsword, voiced the warcry of his clan, and charged the porters.

And all hell broke loose in High Street.

When it was over—and it took the timely arrival of the City Guard with their ancient Lochaber broadaxes, plus a detachment of soldiers from the Castle on the Rock to quell the riot—blood had been shed on both sides. Both Jonathan, Laird of Clan Jarrett, and James, his son, found themselves guests of the City of Edinburgh, securely, if somewhat uncomfortably, lodged in the High Street Gaol.

And some bright, enterprising citizen had made off with the cow.

CHAPTER TWO

FIRST IN THE morning, the turnkey knocked them up.

"On yer feet, ye smelly blackguards!" he growled. " 'Tis a visitor ye have. And a gentleman from his looks, I ken. So haud yer tongues, ye Highland rogues, and speak respectful to yer betters!"

"I have no betters!" James flared; but Jonathan caught his arm. The two of them followed the turnkey out into the common gaolyard. The gentleman waiting for them there, was a sight to see. Never had young James laid eyes upon such finery. The visitor was taller even than Jonathan; and his fullbottomed wig was snowy. The pigeonwing curls at its sides were dressed with exquisite skill. His plum-colored coat, cut *à la française,* was long and full; and his vest, beneath it, reached to his knees. His knee breeches were pale green, fitting flawlessly into his green leather spatterdashes and spur leathers. He wore a tricorne, embroidered with gold lace that matched the broidery on his vest. White lace exploded out at throat and cuff. He opened a golden snuffbox, applied a pinch to his nostril, sneezed; then offered the box to Jonathan with a steady hand.

"Thank you, my Laird," Jonathan said respectfully.

The man laughed. His laughter was deep and pleasant.

"No, friend," he said, "I am no Lord. 'Tis a mere merchant you see before you—my Lord. For you, I'm told, have some right to that title. . . ."

"Aye," Jonathan said morosely; "for all the good it does."

"I take it you're in straitened circumstances then, my Lord?" the merchant said gently.

"What Highland bonnet laird isn't?" Jonathan said flatly. "But that is neither here nor there. To what, Sir, do we owe the honor of this visit?"

"The name, if you will, my Lord, is Andrews—Beverly Andrews," the merchant said. "On yesterday, you and your boy were involved in a fracas in High Street. The lady who more or less caused the uproar is—my wife. The lass, my daughter."

"Oh!" Jonathan said.

"So I've come to see you freed. By my lights, Trudy and Maebelle behaved most ill. If you want my apologies, you have them."

"Thank you," Jonathan said softly; "and you have mine. I'm afraid I've let the lad grow up untrained since his sainted mother died. It never occurred to me to instruct him to take the laughter of females in good part. And—" he smiled gravely—"we must have been a sight!"

"And they say that Highland Chieftains are rude men," Beverly Andrews said. "By my troth, I like you, Highland Chief! You'll dine with us this evening?"

"In these splattered rags?" Jonathan said. "I'd gladly accept, for, to be honest, I have not a ha'penny; but—"

"But nothing. Come home with me now. I'll see that you're provided with clothes. And maybe we'll find a way to mend your fortunes. . . ."

Jonathan stood there. The muckle black devil is not more proud than a Highlander. But what had pride ever got him? Perhaps the nightjar of the skyward-dwelling shrew had been the shower of fortune, after all.

"I accept, because I have to," he said; "and stand eternally in your debt, Squire Andrews."

"It is my pleasure," Beverly Andrews said.

That afternoon, James Jarrett, after having suffered, protesting loudly, the indignity of the first all-over bath he had had in all his life, came down to join the others. He was dressed like a young lordling, complete with bagwig, that is, a wig whose queue was gathered into a small bag of silken cords, smallsword, and a habit *à la française* of sumptuously studied cut. The clothes fitted him almost perfectly.

When he entered the dining room Trudy Andrews turned to her husband, her blue eyes bright with tears.

"Oh, Bev!" she choked, "he is so like! Oh, dearest, can't we keep him, please?"

"Hush, Trudy," Beverly Andrews said. "The lad is nothing like our

John. It is the effect of the clothes, and the similarity of stature. But a bonny lad he is, for a fact. Come in, my boy. . . ."

"Aye," Jonathan growled. "Come in, my boy, and beg your humble pardon of this maid. For, if you knew it not before, now you do: a lad never strikes a lass, no matter how gross the provocation. Come—offer her your hand, and tell her you are sorry."

James took a step forward, his dark eyes bright under that jutting hedgerow of a brow that swept across his forehead without a break even above his axeblade of a nose. I didn't know, he thought wonderingly, that a mere lass could be so bonny, and smell so good! He took her hand.

" 'Tis right sorry I am, milady," he declared, "that I used you ill. But then, I know not how to treat with lassies. 'specially when they have the look of angels!"

Maebelle stared at him.

"You are bonny, too, Lord James," she whispered; "especially out of skirts. Now you may kiss me, if you like. . . ."

James hung there, frozen.

"Go on, my boy," Beverly laughed; "buss her a good one!"

And James Jarrett, aged ten, kissed his first, never to be forgotten love.

By nightfall it was all settled: Jonathan Jarrett, on tomorrow was to go down to Londontown, armed with a stout purse and letters of introduction from the princely merchant. The letters were enough to give him a new start in life. And his knowledge of linen and its making was indeed considerable. Beverly Andrews was sure that any one of the great houses of drapers with whom he did business would gladly welcome the Scottish Laird as an employee.

"The pay won't fatten your purse, you understand, Lord Jonathan," he said; "not at first. Which is why I ask you to leave the boy with us. Selfishly, he will make up to us somewhat for the loss of our own. But, beyond that, we're in a position to give him the care, studies, training— even the love and attention that you just won't be able to until you've established yourself—which may take a fairish stretch of years. Come, my Lord, what do you say?"

Jonathan looked at his son. His eyes, James saw, were already heavy and dull from the amount of claret and sack he had drunk. Leave me! the boy thought hotly; for you will never establish yourself, father.

You'll drink yourself out of job and lodgings and even sense, just as you have ever since my mother died. . . .

"You're right, Squire Andrews," Jonathan said slowly; "still, Sir, 'tis a hard choice. The lad has been the comfort of my life since his sainted mother died. I—I don't know. Suppose we leave it up to him?"

James could feel all four pairs of eyes turned upon him. And the choice, which had seemed so simple a moment before, became hellishly difficult. He saw his father as he was: an aging man, bowed down by sorrow, by privations, by loneliness. He had a child's pitiless impatience with his father's known weaknesses, and his faults. But he loved the auld fool for all that. He was quite sure that without him, Laird Jonathan would go to rack and ruin. No. It was not possible.

He cleared his throat to speak—and a small, hot hand stole, unobserved by the others, into his. Childish fingers sought his and gripped, hard.

"I'll—stay," James Jarrett whispered. And the thing was done.

CHAPTER THREE

JAIMIE JARRETT, fifteen years old in that Year of Our Lord 1730, measured his opponent's stone with a practiced eye. Then, in one long graceful sweep, he sent his curling stone flying across the ice. Before it, his teammates raced, frantically smoothing a path for it with straw brooms. But the huge curling stone, with its crooked wooden handle, hardly needed their help. It crashed into the opposing stone and sent it skidding obliquely out of bounds, at the same time continuing on, following a studied diagonal caused by the impact, to cross the goal line.

The broom wielders threw their homely implements into the air, ripped out a loud: "Hurrah! We've won! That does it! Three cheers for Jaimie Jarrett!"

"Nay, lads," Jaimie smiled. "It was but luck. I couldn't do it again in a hundred years. . . ."

"But next Saturday evening you'll have a try, eh, Jaimie?" Eugene Gilbert, his best friend, said. "For, if they've more curlers in the Highlands such as you, I think we'd best import them all!"

"Aye, but he is a bonny lad, your Jaimie," Laura Gilbert sighed to Maebelle Andrews from the bank. "'tis lucky you are, Mae, to have such a brother!"

"'Tis lucky I am, all right," Maebelle said impishly; "but you know in what that luck consists, Laurie, mine? That Jaimie is *not* my brother! Else I should have to leave him to your clutches, which, Saints be praised, I don't have to!" She turned toward the pond.

"Jaimie!" she cried; "it grows late, lad! And mother will be in a fret, that's sure. . . ."

"Coming, Lass!" James Jarrett called.

He came skidding across the ice, and took her arm.

"The top of the evening to you all, my friends!" he called, and led her away from there.

"Jaimie," Maebelle whispered, as they were crossing the snowy Grassmarket, "give me a kiss, will you?"

Dutifully he pecked at her cheek.

"Call that a kiss?" Maebelle hooted scornfully. "What ails you, Jaimie Jarrett?"

"Don't know," Jaimie said morosely; "or rather I do. But why should I burden you with it, little sweetheart? A man should keep his troubles to himself, and—"

"Even—from his goodwife, Jaimie?" Maebelle said.

He turned and stared at her. Mischief sparkled in his black eyes.

"I don't recall the day that we were wed," he chuckled; "but since it seems we were, let me be about my husbandly duties at once, fair wife!"

"Jaimie, you're horrid!" Maebelle cried. "You know full well I only meant that I feel like your goodwife, not that—"

"I aim to make you feel more so, still," Jaimie grinned. "Come on!"

Maebelle stamped a tiny foot.

"Stop it you forward devil, or I'll tell mother!" she cried.

"And I that her modest lass begs for kisses upon any and all occasions," Jaimie crowed. And then he saw her tears.

"Aye, lass," he rumbled, in a voice already at fifteen, deepening into a bass; "I'm sorry. I shouldn't plague you, thus. 'tis a brute I am, a wild croft from the Highlands and—"

"Nay," Maebelle whispered, smiling through her tears; "you are none of those things, Jaimie. One day I will be your goodwife in truth, and forward enough to suit even you. But, 'til then, we have to wait— as patiently as we can. I know that father has not the slightest objection, nor mother either. I overheard them talking on it. But you have to go up to the University yet—where I know you will do well. You're quite a scholar, Gaspard says. . . ."

"Poor Gaspard," Jaimie sighed. "A pox upon all Papists!"

"Nay, Jaimie," Maebelle said gently; "you are not just. Much have the Catholic families suffered here in Scotland. That the French persecute the Protestant Huguenots such as Gaspard—strange that a stiff Huguenot should be a fencing master, isn't it?—is ill. But have we

Protestants done better? In olden times, they hanged the poor Papists here upon this green. . . ."

"You're right, lass," Jaimie said gravely. "Strange that men should kill each other over questions of faith—when they all profess the religion of the Man who bade us sheath the sword. But the Frenchies did me a good turn, when they forced Gaspard to flee to Scotland. Else I'd never have had him to teach me French and swordplay. He's a capital chappie, for a fact. And come to think of it, Capelli, my dancing master, is Italian and a Papist, yet I like him full well. While my Dominie, Keith, I cannot stand!"

"Nor I. He should learn better his anatomy, then he would know that one cannot absorb learning through one's hide! But then he is Presbyterian, and the way we Episcopalians live smacks to him of luxury. Yet father says he's an excellent Latinist. . . ."

"He is. And he has forgotten more Greek than any man in town ever knew. I am lucky to have him. If only he were not such a dour beastie!"

"Jaimie," Maebelle said tenderly, "tell me what was troubling you when you came off the ice. It hurts me when I think that you guard secrets from me. . . ."

"I know. But 'tis a thing you cannot help, my Mae. It's father. I've had no word from him in above a year. . . ."

"I think he's ashamed to write you," Maebelle said. "He went down to London with such high hopes—"

"Which, knowing him, I never shared," Jaimie said grimly. "He is a good man, my father; but—weak. And my mother's death unmanned him, quite. . . ."

"Jaimie—" Maebelle whispered, "what would you do, if I were to—die?"

"Die, too," he growled. "What would life be without you, Lass?"

"Oh, Jaimie!" she cried, and kissed him, hard. "But you mustn't, Love. Promise me you will not. If anything happens to me, promise me you'll wed Laurie Gilbert, who worships the sod where your feet tread."

"Nay," he said furiously, "I'll make you no such promise, Mae! In all this world, there is but one lass for me, as you know full well. Now, come on!"

When they came up the stairs—for the Andrews had bought three entire flats and combined them into what in other cities would have been a townhouse, a thing that Edinburgh lacked, and would go on lacking for some years—they found Trudy Andrews talking to a stranger. They did not then regard this man as a cloud upon their horizon. He resembled anything in this world except a cloud, weighing, as he did, James guessed, above twelve stone. What he looked like was something closely approximating a mountain of refuse. His vast wig, of old-fashioned cut, was a perfect sparrows' nest, with wisps of dirty white hair sticking out at all angles. Tobacco juice drooled from both lip corners; on the vast expanse of his waistcoat showed the remote reminders of every meal he'd eaten in the last twenty years. And even from the doorway, their nostrils informed them that he was totally estranged from soap and water. As he followed Trudy toward them, his gait was shambling, like that of a dancing bear.

His face, smooth shaven some days before, showed a pepper and salt stubble on its various chins. His lace was limp and dirty grey, and his face—

Aye, that would be scanned. It was round and pink and as lineless as a baby's. Only no baby ever had eyes like those. They were tiny black pinpoints, stabbing into a body, probing, seeking—what?

But Trudy was speaking, now.

"Children," she said uneasily, "this is Squire Pitcairn Hogg, an old friend of your father. . . ."

"No, good lady," Hogg rumbled. "I do not presume so much. Say, rather, an old business associate. I was your father's representative upon the continent in the old days when—But your tender years preclude your knowing about such things as that! My bonnie lass, young sir, your servant!"

James took the fat, soft hand Hogg offered him with an inward repulsion close to nausea. Hogg, he thought; the name's most appropriate. It fits you jolly well!

Hogg had scarcely resumed his seat in Beverly Andrews' favorite chair, which no one ever dared to touch, before the merchant himself, came home. James waited hopefully for his foster father to damn Hogg roundly out of his private throne; but, instead—

Beverly Andrews hung there in the doorway, and his fine, florid face yellowed slowly into parchment. James did not know what was in Squire Andrews' eyes, then; though afterwards he would. It was—death.

"Hogg," he whispered. "I—I knew one day you'd appear. Bad pennies always turn up, men say. Shall we go into my study, and discuss— your price? 'tis not a fit subject for the ears of my family. Come!"

"Hogg," James Jarrett said to Maebelle after the newcomer had gone into the study, "is a hog!"

"Aye," Maebelle answered; "we'll be well rid of him. I like him not. There—there's something in his eyes that makes my blood run cold. Oh, mother, how could father have done business with such a man?"

"I know not, child," Trudy Andrews said.

But they were not to be rid of Pitcairn Hogg. He took his place among them as though he had a perfect right to be there. And, Jaimie Jarrett found, behind that broad, bland face, lurked a mind as subtly dangerous as a Medici's. It took young Jaimie exactly one day to find that out.

He came downstairs to have his daily lessons in French and fencing from Gaspard, that lank Huguenot refugee whom Squire Andrews had hired to teach his foster son. But Gaspard was not alone. With him were Capelli, the dancing master—and Pitcairn Hogg.

Jaimie stopped dead in the doorway. Then, seeing they had not noted his presence, so deeply were they involved in their conversation, he took a silent backward step, a quick, sidewise spring, and flattened himself against the wall, just outside the door.

Hogg was asking questions—and about the Andrews. That much was clear. Ever and anon, he or one of the others, pronounced the name. But what made Jaimie Jarrett almost weep with chagrin, was the fact that Hogg was asking those questions in French. And not in the stilted schoolboy French Jaimie had learned right well; but in a patois so different it seemed another language entirely. Jaimie had no way of knowing that this was the racy street argot of Paris, filled with thieves' and smugglers' slang, so different from polite French, so much more vivid and alive, that, as far as the boy was concerned, Hogg might as well have spoken Greek.

Jaimie listened with all his mind. It seemed to him he was getting the hang of it, when Capelli interrupted with a question in his native tongue. Whereupon Hogg switched into a Tuscan pure as Dante's, with no more accent than his thieves'-market Parisian had had.

And Jaimie was lost. His eavesdropping would do him no good now. When he had time to think about it, later, he realized that by then it already had. For, from that moment on, he ceased to underestimate Pitcairn Hogg. But then, because there was nothing else to do, he marched boldly into the room, cutting Hogg off in full Italianate flight.

"You speak Italian well, Squire Hogg," he said dryly; "but I do believe that your French is even better."

Hogg's smile was utterly bland. It was impossible for the boy to tell if his words had had the desired effect of convincing this vast, untidy monstrosity that he had understood the conversation—which, of course, he hadn't.

"Yes, lad," Hogg boomed. "I have the gift of tongues. And ever have I found it valuable. See that you attend these good masters well."

Then he bowed and left them there.

That evening, at supper, Hogg treated James to yet another lesson, though, by then, he hardly needed one. Furiously determined to get the better of his enemy—because he knew even then that there must be war to the knife between them—James ventured a cutting Latin tag at the table. He should have known better. For those little reptilian eyes fixed him gravely; then the huge man growled:

"Nay, lad, the sentiment's just but the Latin's bad. Fools we have with us everywhere, that's true enough. But, *'Stultorum plena sunt omnia,'* is what Cicero said; Not *'Stultorii.'* Remember that. And I give you yet another tag: *'Fortuna favet fatuis.'* "

Fortune favors fools. What did this gross swine mean by that? What else but that he had caught James' implication that he was a fool—which was a piece of youthful pique, for the boy, himself, did not believe it anymore—and was warning the lad not to be too sure of the assumption. And that offending such a fool as he, might prove dangerous when the day came that fortune favored him.

Hogg got up then, with a grunted, "Sirs, Ladies, your servant," and took his leave. The silence after his going was absolute. Trudy Andrews opened her mouth, wailed: "Oh, Bev! I can't stand that man! Must we have him here?"

"Yes, Trudy," Beverly Andrews sighed. "We must." And that was that.

But, in the months that followed, Gertrude Andrews' emphatic declaration that she could not stand Pitcairn Hogg, became, in the eyes of more than one member of the family, distinctly doubtful. Hogg was one of those entirely repulsive men whose success with women is mysteriously sure. And only the more marked, the finer and gentler the women are. James labored to deny, and then to explain the uncontrovertible evidence of his eyes. But how does one explain the black arts of a Warlock, as the Scotch called a male witch? Why does not the wee sparrow take wing at once, instead of sitting still and trembling before the slow approach of the serpent?

Or wasn't it, perhaps, a thing more mundane than dark magic? Certain phrases that Squire Andrews had used—"Shall we go into my study, and discuss—your price? 'tis not a fit subject for the ears of my family . . ." indicated that this slovenly monster had some kind of a hold over him. And Trudy, in reply to Jaimie's bitter remark that she was losing her dislike for Hogg jolly fast, had whispered desperately: "I have to be nice to him, Jaimie! I have to. For if I don't, he'll—"

"What?" James had demanded.

"Never you mind," Trudy said. "Now, no more of this, for here he comes!"

One thing was sure: the bottom had fallen out of his new world; and there was no security anywhere.

He came running up the stairs to seek his foster mother for some reason he never afterwards would be able to remember. To beg a guinea, perhaps; or to ask permission to ride out with his friend. It did not matter. It would never matter again.

Trudy was in her dressing gown. Hogg was sitting across the room from her—in that bedroom where he had no business being, either in the presence or the absence of her husband—and Beverly Andrews was absent on a business trip to Glasgow. Hogg was fully dressed, of course, and negligently dipping snuff from Squire Andrews' own golden snuff box. There was—nothing. Yet the whole scene vibrated with intimacy—old, accustomed, sure. James hung there in the doorway, his mouth opened, unable to utter sound. Neither of them noticed him.

"Come here, Lass, and give us a kiss," Hogg wheezed; and slowly, like a sleepwalker, Trudy got up and came to those monstrous arms.

James whirled and fled down those stairs, his eyes tear-scalded, blind. At the landing, he met Maebelle.

"Jaimie!" she gasped. "You're crying! Tell me what—"

"Out of my way!" he snarled. "Women! Cheats! You're faithless, one and all!"

She fell back before his fury. She could not, in her innocence, imagine what she had done to earn so bitter a denunciation. The answer was simple: nothing. She had merely had the misfortune to be an accidental witness of real tragedy: the shattering of an ideal. For James Jarrett worshipped his foster father. All Bev's joys, hopes, ambitions, had become his own. So, likewise, this injury was his, too; as keenly felt as though he were, personally, the victim of Trudy's faithlessness. As, in a way, he was. And, at fifteen years, the phrase "a broken heart," is far from an empty one.

That night, Squire Andrews returned from Glasgow and took his accustomed place at the head of the table. He looked, James thought, a trifle tired; but nothing more. His fine, florid face was grave, but pleasant. Only when he looked at Hogg, shoveling food into his gullet like a whole litter of his namesakes, did his mouth tighten with disgust and pain.

He picked at his food.

"Eat, Bev!" Trudy cried. "You'll fall into a decline, if you don't put away a man's share. . . ."

"Yes, Lass," Squire Andrews sighed; "but here of late, my meals have sat uncommon ill. 'tis strange. In my wanderings about the Kingdom, considering what our native inns are like, I've learned to digest carpet tacks. But—no more. Everything I eat seems to unsettle me. . . ."

Jaimie's knuckles, gripping the edge of the table, were white. He stared at Pitcairn Hogg. Then, with one swift motion, he snatched his foster father's plate from before him, and exchanged it with his own.

"What the devil's got into you, boy?" Beverly Andrews growled.

"Nothing, Father Andrews," Jaimie said quietly. "That plate, being mine, will cause you no harm, I'm sure. How this one will sit with me, I don't know. But I mean to find out."

Then he speared a cut of meat with his fork, and thrust it into his mouth.

Pitcairn Hogg threw back his vast, untidy head and laughed aloud.

"Eat hearty, Lad!" he roared.

Beverly Andrews' face was a thunder cloud.

"Jaimie!" he thundered, "would you mind telling me what this comedy is all about?"

"Nay, good Squire," Hogg chuckled. "Permit me first to carry our little farce one act further. Jaimie, lad, will you be so kind as to exchange plates with me?"

"This has gone far enough!" Squire Andrews said. "Are you all mad?"

"No, Squire," Hogg said peacefully; "all of us, even the lad, have our wits about us. He is being brave. Even gallant. You see, he thinks you're being poisoned. And he is willing to sacrifice his young life to save yours. Such a touching demonstration of filial devotion is not to be depreciated, Squire. Aye, right rare it is in this world of ours. Jaimie, you blithering young ass, give me that plate!"

Wonderingly, Jaimie passed it over.

With everyone's eyes upon him, Pitcairn Hogg forked up a double mouthful, and masticated noisily.

"Tell me, Squire," he said, "just what do you find wrong with this food?"

"I—I don't know," Beverly Andrews said weakly; "but here of late, it seems to have a foully bitter taste. . . ."

"I taste nothing amiss, Sir," Hogg said solemnly. " 'tis your system that's awry. Let's have one of the good Doctors from the University in. . . ."

And that, again, was that. Life at the Andrews' became what was at best an armed truce. Trudy stared at her foster son with fearful eyes; and James kept away from Pitcairn Hogg. Betimes, doctors came and went with their philtres and powders and eternal blood lettings. And Beverly Andrews sickened very slowly out of life.

Despite Giovanni, the new Italian cook that Hogg himself hired. Despite food so exquisitely prepared that people all but fought for invitations to the Andrews' table. Despite the fact that to reassure the dying man, Hogg always tasted his food before the eyes of all the family each time it was given to Squire Andrews.

" 'tis folly," he grunted, "but if it relieves his mind, I'll play royal taster to the king!"

"That fat Warlock's got a talisman against poison!" Jaimie Jarrett howled to his stepmother. "Even if father has not the strength to kick him out of here, you should! To sit and see your husband murdered, and not lift a hand! No, I'll not stand it! I'll kill—"

"Hold your tongue!" Trudy Andrews snapped. "You have the vapors for a fact. No man ever took finer care of the sick than Pitcairn takes of Bev. I tell you, Jaimie, a truer Christian gentleman than Squire Hogg never drew breath. With all he stands to gain by Bev's death, he—"

The black eyes were fire's self beneath that single jut of brow.

"All?" he grated. "I think he's gained all now. Yes, all! Though why a man his age should put such valuation upon mere female flesh as to murder to gain legal title to what he enjoys already, I'm sure I do not see!"

"Jaimie," Trudy whispered, "I have but to repeat your words to Bev

—and 'twill be you, you ungrateful Highland churl, who'll leave this house forever!"

"Then let's put the matter to the test," Jaimie said flatly. "Come, let's go tell him exactly what I said—and now!"

Trudy hung there, her face white.

"You dare not?" Jaimie howled. "Does that take more courage than to play your husband false?"

"Jaimie!" the weak voice called. The two of them stood still.

"He heard you!" Trudy hissed. "May Satan blast your soul, James Jarrett, if you have caused him pain!"

"Amen," James whispered; "if I have hurt him, I deserve it. And you? For my sin consists of—words. Mere words. While yours?"

He turned then, and went toward the curtained alcove where Beverly Andrews lay.

"Jaimie," the sick man whispered, "I am dying, lad. So, my boy, one promise—"

"No, father!" Jaimie wept, "don't talk this way! You'll have your three score and many more, I tell—"

"No, son. I cannot live. Promise me that you'll not desert Trudy and Maebelle, no matter what you have to suffer to stay. They'll have need of you, my boy. You're a fiery lad; but hold your tongue and wait! The time will come that you—"

"Can avenge you, father? Before my God, I swear it!"

"No, lad. Vengeance is the Lord's. In His good time, He will repay. Listen, Jaimie. In my youth, I killed a man. A royal customs guard who—"

"I don't want your secrets, father!" Jaimie cried.

"'tis no secret. Hogg was there, and witnessed it. We were smuggling; of that he was as guilty as I. But it was my hand that fired the shot. And for that knowledge, he is bleeding me white. Which is why this idea of yours, that he is poisoning me, makes no sense, lad. Why should he shut off, forever, the source of his income?"

To gain it all at one fine stroke, you fool! James thought. But he did not, could not say what he was thinking then.

And miraculously, it seemed, the next day Beverly Andrews began to recover. He got better and better, until he and his beloved foster son could ride to the hounds again, go golfing once more on the Grassmarket green. He seemed his old self: assured, forceful, gay.

But on Jaimie Jarrett's seventeenth birthday, Beverly Andrews ate a piece of the birthday cake that some fifty guests had eaten along with him, clutched his middle with two hands, sat back in his chair—and died.

And not until the day after her father's burial did Maebelle Andrews rise far enough out of the stupor of her grief to tell James that Hogg had served Squire Andrews that particular piece of cake with his own soft, grubby hands.

Three months from that date, Maebelle burst from her mother's bedroom, ran down the stairs, screaming: "Jaimie! Jaimie! Where are you, Jaimie? Answer me for the love of God!"

James put down his fencing foil, tore off his mask without so much as a by your leave to Gaspard, and sprinted up the stairs. He collided with Maebelle on the landing. She clung to him with desperate strength, breath gone, sobbing.

"Jaimie, Jaimie, Jaimie, oh, Jaimie!" was all she said.

"Easy, Lass," he whispered. "Calm yourself and tell me—"

"Oh, Jaimie, I want to die! I can't live anymore, Jaimie! I—cannot —live—"

"Mae!" he thundered.

"And father not cold in his grave!" she sobbed. "How could she? Tell me, Jaimie—how?"

She twisted in his arms, and her face, in that moment, was frightening. "Mother!" she screamed. "You have no daughter! From this hour on, you have no child!"

"You mean that she—that she—" James whispered.

"Has married Squire Hogg? Yes, Jaimie, she has," Maebelle Andrews said.

CHAPTER FOUR

NOR DID Pitcairn Hogg let a full fortnight pass before he showed his hand. It was the Andrews' pleasant custom to have the Episcopal Rector, Reverend MacCuddings, dine with them every Sunday afternoon. But the first Sunday after the monstrous marriage that rocked Edinburgh like a storm, Squire Hogg met the good pastor at the door.

"You'll find no welcome here, Sir," he boomed. "This house is mine now, and I'll allow no Papists in it. Not even demi-Papists that you Anglicans are! Begone, Sir, and the devil take you and your too high Kirk!"

Jaimie, who witnessed it, whirled upon Hogg like a young tiger.

"You filthy swine!" he began; but that was as far as he got. The next thing he knew, he was on the floor, looking up and cradling in his hand a jaw he was sure was broken.

"Let that be a lesson to you, you nameless Highland crofter's churl!" Hogg thundered. "You are in my house, and upon my sufferance. See that you govern yourself accordingly. For caning you, you whelp, would suit me mighty well!"

James Jarrett sat there, staring up at Pitcairn Hogg. He wanted to kill the huge man, then. But he was afraid. And he knew it. And that was the worst of all: that consciousness of fear.

But, as he got slowly to his feet, another thing hit James like a blow between the eyes: the way that Pitcairn Hogg was dressed. His fullbottom wig was new, and snowy. His brown suit, cut in the sober fashion affected by Lowchurchmen, Presbyterians, and Dissenters, was of absolutely superb materials. And he had been freshly shaved. There was about him the faintest hint of lilac scent. For the first time since James had known him, his person was entirely clean.

But, beyond that, there was a thing in this that lay fathoms deep beneath the surface. Well did James know how bitter, in that intolerant age, religious conflicts were. Not only did Protestants and Catholics slaughter each other upon every conceivable occasion, but even among the different Protestant sects there was dissention that stopped just short of actual war. In Scotland, a man could be High Church Episcopalian only at the cost of surrendering the major part of his political rights. No Highchurchman could hold public office, and popular resentment against him not infrequently reached the point where he ran the risk of physical mistreatment by the surly mob.

That much was clear. But what had the opaque quality of High Street mud after a rainstorm was Hogg's sudden taking of sides in the age-old dispute. Never, since James had known him, had Pitcairn Hogg so much as set foot in the Kirk. To all outward appearances, his indifference to all kinds of religion was complete. But now—

James turned on his heel and went to look for Capelli, the dancing master. Capelli would know the answers. No one in the Andrews' household had been closer to this devious monster than the Italian, child of a faith that Hogg now revealed he hated. Yes, Capelli would know, could explain—

But Capelli was not in his room. And the room itself had been stripped bare. All the dancing teacher's clothes were gone. Wonderingly, James sought out Gaspard. He found the Frenchman packing, his face white-lipped and tight with rage.

"Now, what the devil?" James growled.

"I've been sacked," Gaspard snarled. "Capelli, too. He left last night. . . ."

"Name of God, Gaspard, why?"

"We have become Presbyterians, here at the Andrews," Gaspard said. "So, my boy, no fripperies! A Presbyterian, it appears, is a peaceable soul. He has no need for skill in the use of the smallsword. And dancing, though you know it not, Jaimie, is a deadly sin. Poor Capelli. He was dreadfully cut up over this. He was sure that Squire Dirty Pig was fond of him."

"So was I," James said. "But the Squire isn't dirty anymore. Have you seen him today?"

"Yes. Now he has become Squire Dandy—or almost. I have remarked him well. That suit looks the sober garb of a Lowchurchman, but it isn't. He's skirted the edge of foppishness as closely as he dared. Quite changed, is he not, your new foster father? But one thing, my boy, has not changed at all—as a poseur, he remains the grand master of them all!"

"Then," James said slowly, "he didn't sack Capelli because the poor fellow is a Papist?"

"*Morbleu!*" Gaspard swore. "Far from it! Squire Hogg gives less than a tinker's damn about religion. The blasphemies I've heard him utter! He is truly a freethinker, *mon* Jaimie. He told Capelli in my presence that all faiths whatsoever are childish nonsense—"

"He said *that?*" James gasped.

"Of course. What makes you think he wouldn't have?"

"He just showed Reverend MacCuddings the door, on the grounds that Anglicism is only Catholicism in disguise."

"That doesn't surprise me," Gaspard said quietly. "Squire Hogg has what might be called a Machiavellian mind."

"So?" James said.

"So, considered in that light, everything he does makes good sense, my boy. A man can only proceed in a straight line towards honorable goals. But when a man pursues unearned wealth, and his benefactor's wife—ah! That is quite another thing! Fat as he is, his imitation of a snake is perfect. Deviations, meanderings, and indirection. But he arrives. *Sacre bleu!* As an *arriviste,* our gross Squire has no peers!"

"And now," James growled, "he has arrived, eh, Gaspard? So, Master Poser, off with the old disguise! Reveal yourself as you are. . . ."

Soberly Gaspard shook his head.

"Not so fast, my boy," he said. "That, too, would be scanned. Never as he is. Rather as he wants the world to think he is. He boasted as much to me, very nearly outlining his plan of action, so sure was he that I can do him no harm. And in that, he is right, I think. Who would take the word of a former employee, sacked for—of all things!—incompetence, and naturally, therefore, disgruntled? Oh, yes, of me, he's sure; but not yet of other things. You see, it's Squire Hogg, now, since he's acquired Squire Andrews' lands as well. So now he must live his new rôle to the hilt, become the very picture of respectability. He knows full well that Anglicism doesn't sit well on a Scotchman's stomach. Still less the freethinking which fits best his insidious mind. He has the scandal of his too impetuous marriage to Madame to live down. Then there must be those among the late Squire's friends, who've entertained—as I confess I have—the suspicion of—murder. So he is not sure, our fine Pitcairn Swine. His footing's shaky, yet. But given a year or two of thrice-weekly attendance at Tron Kirk, generous contributions to the poor, a sound response to every question, framed upon his knowledge of how a Scot thinks—ponderous nonsense uttered with weighty gravity—and they'll forget, or revise their opinions, say: 'Mayhap we were wrong. Squire Andrews was given to unseemly levity. Foppish in his dress. And High Church—only an inch or two below the Pope in Rome. While good Squire Hogg—' Yes, Jaimie, boy, he'll fool them right enough. Ever do men mistake girth for dignity, and lies for truth. . . ."

James stood there, staring at Gaspard.

"You're right," he said. "Tell me, Gaspard, what will you do, now?"

"I am a Frenchman, remember," Gaspard smiled. "Our minds work fast. I saw our parvenu coming long before he arrived. So, knowing one day I should have to leave this house, I called upon Colonel Gilbert. I have had these several weeks the post of *maitre d'armes* in their house waiting for me—I shall tutor your friend Eugene in the art of fencing. . . ."

"Good!" James said, and put out his hand. "Then I shall not lose you entirely. I'll visit Gene often and bring my smallsword. . . ."

"If he lets you keep it, which I doubt," Gaspard said darkly. "But, no matter; I have foils to spare. *Au'voir,* my boy. Go carefully, and with God."

The silence in the house, after Gaspard's departure, was unbearable to James. Any place he could go would better suit him than here. The green, then. He went down to the hall closet to seek his clubs. A round of golf would clear the worries from his mind. . . .

He bent to pick up his golf clubs. He had, by then, become a master of that game so ancient that the Caledonians played it before they had been mislabelled Scots, and the name Scotia still belonged to Ireland. He straightened up, turned, and stared into the face of Pitcairn Hogg.

"Your dress is unseemly, James," Hogg growled. "Go and change it. I've had a suit of decent brown made for you. I doubt not but 'twill fit; for 'twas cut upon the pattern of one of these la di da french things you wear. Without the fripperies, of course. 'tis laid out in your room. Go you and put it on."

"Brown," James flared, "is the color of mud, and dung. And of the hearts of those who wear it!"

Hogg looked at him a long, slow time.

"I don't recall having asked your opinions," he said evenly. "Nor have I intention to heed them. Go. We're all but late for services at Tron Kirk now. . . ."

"Tron Kirk!" James got out; "but you know well, Squire, I am no Presbyterian!"

"Aye, but you're going to be. You and all my house. We've had enough half-Papist sophistry here ere now. You hear me, go!"

James made one more attempt. At seventeen, to admit that one is afraid is unthinkable. But he was. Afterwards, he could never quite define the quality of that fear. It wasn't physical—at least not entirely. He was a Jarrett, of that stern Highland race who had repeatedly marched out to certain death with a song on their lips, to the tune of the bagpipes' squalling. Knowing that he was going to lose would never, in itself, have stopped him. Rather it was a thing in Hogg, a deep, miasmic thing that seemed beyond the natural, normal aspects of life. James told himself proudly that he was over his highland superstitions: that he no longer believed in Warlocks, but, somehow, effortlessly, Pitcairn Hogg made him less sure. He had seen Hogg bend Trudy Andrews to his will, as though she were a wax doll instead of a proud and lovely woman who ordinarily would not so much as have spat upon this gross slug. He was terrified and incensed by the fact that Maebelle, herself, showed certain signs of a diminution in her hatred for the man who had almost surely murdered her father.

"He can be gentle, Jaimie," she insisted. "He talks to me most kindly —and even takes far more of an interest in me, in what I think and hope and want and believe than father ever did. It's just because he's fat and ugly that you—"

"It is not!" James had howled. "It is because I *know* he is a swine!"

Now, with Hogg's strangely reptilian eyes upon him, he realized at long last what he was up against: a master actor, a true genius in the art of dissimulation and deceit. That Pitcairn Hogg could deceive the townspeople who knew him only slightly, was to be expected; but now James saw, his skill in hypocrisy was so great that subtly, slowly, calmly, he was beginning to convince Maebelle and Trudy he actually was the fictional character he had created for himself. And knowing this thing, facing it, seventeen-year-old James Jarrett was powerless. What could any lad, even a Jarrett, do against this all but consummate artistry?

Still James made the attempt. Dug deep for that pride overtopping Lucifer's; said:

"You go to the Kirk, if you like, Squire. As for me, I'm going golfing. . . ."

Silently Hogg stretched out his thick white hands. They were clean, now, the nails cut square and freed of grime. But they were as repulsive as ever—or more so, moving like creatures of dark and dampness, smelling, it seemed to James Jarrett, through the lilac scent, of decay, of the grave. Hogg did not speak. He had no need to. He simply took the golf bag from the boy's hands, without using force, removing it almost gently from those young arms bereft suddenly of all strength, gone nerveless, cold.

Then one by one he broke the clubs over one huge knee, taking all the time in the world about it, silent and intent. James stood and watched it without a word or sign.

"Go change your clothes, Lad," Hogg said quietly. "It grows late. . . ."

And like a wooden puppet, hung on loosened strings, young James Jarrett went.

The next two years were purest hell. Ceaselessly James Jarrett fought; effortlessly Squire Hogg won every contest. The Italian cook, Giovanni, too, was sent packing back to his native land. The Andrews and young James appeared in sober brown. Gave up attendance at the horseraces on Leith stands, cockfighting, curling, and attendance at dances. Endured the four hours of fire and brimstone in the Kirk. Forgot completely how to smile.

Betimes, Edinburgh rang with Squire Hogg's praises: He endowed an orphan home; opened a hospital for the poor; was named an Elder of the Kirk, sat weightily—in both senses—in the Grand Assembly of the Scottish Church. His severity in judging the cases, both ecclesiastical and moral, which by Scottish custom appeared before that body instead of the civil courts, won him wide approval and renown. The story became current, delicately let slip—or even, James was inclined to believe, implanted wordlessly in the minds of his fellows by those black arts which Hogg seemed master of—that his hasty marriage to the Widow Andrews had been based upon the good Squire's giving way to pity at the sight of her nervous distraction. By the Spring of 1734, it could be said in all truth that Squire Pitcairn Hogg had indeed arrived.

But, at the Andrews' house, the silence lay fathoms deep. Trudy moved through life like a sleepwalker, uttering disjointed phrases, which seldom, if ever, made any sense at all. Once, on the landing, she caught her stepson to her in a desperate embrace.

"Jaimie!" she whispered. "You were right! Oh, laddie mine, how right you were!"

James became increasingly convinced that his stepmother was losing her mind. Unable to keep his new trouble to himself, he sought out Maebelle. She listened absently while he told her his fears, plucking at a loose thread in her skirt with nervous fingers. When he had finished she sat there still, and her expression had not changed. Quite horribly it had not changed.

James stared at her. And the sudden chill that entered him struck to his very heart.

"Mae!" he got out, his voice choking, thick, "you haven't heard a word I said!"

"Aye, Jaimie," she said with a calm that was more awful still. "I heard you, aright. You're saying that mother—is mad. She is. And, d'you know what, Jaimie? So am I."

"Mae!" he thundered.

"That would explain it," she went on evenly.

"Explain what?" he howled.

"Last night. And I didn't cry out. Nor fight. Not really."

"What the devil are you talking about, Lass?" he whispered.

"You've hit it," Maebelle said, and got up. "The devil." She walked to the door, opened it. Stood in the doorway, looking at him out of eyes he had never seen before. The eyes of a stranger.

"Out of hell," she added, and was gone.

Nor could he get any clearer explanation out of her. On the morrow, she denied flatly having uttered those words, though he repeated them to her verbatim.

"Jaimie," she said gently, with a look of idiot's cunning that shattered his very flesh, "don't you think you'd better go lie down, lad? You're feverish for a fact. . . ."

James argued with her for an hour, so long that he was late for his classes at Edinburgh University. Strangely enough, Squire Hogg had made no objection to paying his fees there; but had sternly stipulated that James study for the one profession on earth for which any Jarrett was most unfit: the Presbyterian ministry.

Grimly James kept his mouth shut, and spent his extra hours studying both medicine and law. That morning, filled with desperate trouble, he set out at a lope for the University. He had to walk now, for Hogg had sold the horses, holding them a sinful luxury.

"I'll run away!" James muttered. "Make my way to London; find father—"

The very thought was idle, and he knew it. He would never leave Maebelle. Especially not now. He had to save her. But—from what?

In the months that followed, he came no nearer to answering the question that tormented him. Maebelle became a changeling there before his eyes. One minute she was her old, gay, laughing self; the next, a stranger, brooding, silent, sad, looking at him with eyes dark with pain—nay, more—with anguish.

Which was not to be borne. At nineteen, he was all Jarrett, and all man. His voice was a booming bass; he had to shave twice a day. And that axe blade of a Jarrett's nose, jutting from beneath a single brow that ran across his forehead without a break, made his age a matter impossible for anyone who did not know it already to determine.

So it was that he was able finally to surrender to his desperation without being questioned. One Spring night he did a thing he had never done before. Having had the pitiful example of his father to instruct him, he had always avoided spirituous liquors like the plague. But now he deliberately sought out a dramshop, and tried to drown his sorrows. That he had the money to do so was due to his stepmother. Though Hogg's frugality made even his notoriously tight-fisted fellow countrymen seem spendthrifts by comparison, he was always generous with Trudy. And she, in her turn, tried to ease her children's lot by being, secretly, of course, as generous as she could with them.

But, as far as James could tell, the wine he drank had not the slightest effect upon him. His puzzlement, his grief, his pain, were stronger than any wine. Yet his first drinking bout did affect him, though he knew it not. In part, it accounted for what happened next. He came home very late. He felt both sick and weary. But, passing Maebelle's room, he heard her crying. It went on and on in bitter, hopeless grief. James stopped dead. He pushed open the door. Came to her bed. Sat down upon it.

"What ails you, Lass?" he said.

"Oh, Jaimie!" she wailed. "Oh, darling, hold me! I have such a need of comforting!"

He took her in his arms. But he was nineteen years old by then. Maebelle was eighteen. Their bodies, their instincts were mature. The

kisses got out of hand. That night Maebelle Andrews loved her Highland Laird without reserve or shame.

And not that night only. Since everyone considered them brother
and sister except themselves, they were not too closely watched. They
were young and in love. They managed to be together and alone as
often as they liked. Which was to say very nearly nightly. Nor
did they conceive of their lovemaking as a sin. They meant to wed as
soon as James was of age and no longer needed Squire Hogg's consent. James was, of course, all for having the matter out with that fat
monster at once; but Maebelle would not hear of it.

"You can't, Jaimie!" she sobbed. "He'll only refuse—that's one
thing. But what's worse, he might even—"

"What?" James growled.

"Nothing," Maebelle wept. "I don't know what I was about to say.
Oh, Jaimie, hold me!"

The wonder of it all was that they got away with it as long as they
did. But in the early Spring of 1735, the inevitable happened. Dame
Nature was not to be cheated nor denied.

"We'll wed at once," James said when she told him. "Have you said
aught of this to—mother?"

"Nay," Maebelle whispered. "I didn't dare. And, Jaimie, you must
not marry me. Flee Edinburgh. 'Tis better that—"

"You're mad," James growled. "Why should I do such a shameful
thing? What reason on earth is there that I should not take you to
wife, loving you as I do?"

"There is a reason," she murmured. "You see, I'm not sure—"

"That you're with child? You told me that you were!"

"It's not that. I know I am. Only—Oh, Jaimie!"

But she could not say her trouble. Not then.

Pitcairn Hogg, newly master of the house, listened very quietly as
Jaimie talked.

"So, Squire Hogg," the boy concluded, "it seems to me that the
wisest course would be that we wed at once. That we have sinned, I
know; and right sorry we are for it. But to inflict the consequences of
that sin upon the head of an innocent child is neither meet nor just.
Which is what we came for. Not, by my troth, to either grovel or beg
pardon; for, sin though it is, it is yet a natural thing, and one that
wants remedying—not—"

Before that pinpoint gaze, the boy's voice died.

"Jaimie," Hogg growled, "go and call for my chair. And you and the lass attend me before the door. . . ."

"But—where are we going, Sir?" Maebelle whispered.

"To the Kirk, where else?" Hogg said.

"But, Sir," Jaimie said happily, "we'll need witnesses and—" Then he saw Maebelle's face. Snow, itself, was not whiter.

"Mae!" he got out; "what ails you, Lass?"

"Not—" she choked, "to see us wed, Jaimie! You know him so little, still? Nay. To sit us up upon those high stools before all the Kirk, clad in those horrible blue gowns like gaberlunzie beggars, while the Minister preaches to the congregation about our sins! And not one Sunday, merely—but twenty in a row, until all Edinburgh knows I have been yours without ring or veil or lawful authority. You thought he would be kind, Jaimie? You believed that these dour Presbyterian beasties know the meaning of mercy?"

"Hold your tongue, Lass!" Hogg thundered.

"Their minds work like that, Jaimie mine," Maebelle whispered; "for they were born without either youth or joy. They'll take the thing we had—that lovely, tender cherishing of each other, and make of it a nastiness! The minister will describe our acts—describe them, Jaimie! —one by one, in language that would bring a blush to a soldier's face, in words that a Canongate strumpet would scruple to use—"

"What else," Hogg snarled, "can a strumpet expect, gently born or not? Or this mannish Highland beggar's churl, having been your partner in your whore's sty? Come, both of you! You have disgraced my house; so upon your heads be it!"

Maebelle faced him, then; and what was in her eyes was a thing that Jaimie had never seen there before.

"Disgraced it?" she whispered. "*Your* house? But that is not possible, Squire! You have the gall to say that—to me? You? You'd condemn me for loss of innocence, when you know full well how and when and where—and with whom—I lost it? What honor has this house, Squire, that can be disgraced? My father murdered; my mother corrupted, and I—"

Then she felt, more than saw, Jaimie's eyes upon her.

She whirled, caught his arms, hid her face against his shirt front, wailing:

"Oh, Jaimie, darling, I—"

"Don't weep, Lass," Jaimie growled. "Before I'll see you shamed, I'll kill—"

Hogg stared at him.

"You once tried laying hands upon me, Lad," he said quietly, "to your sorrow. I have had such a life as has taught me to break men like brittle staffs across my knee. Mind you, I said men. A stripling such as you would not raise up a sweat upon my brow. You heard me, come!"

Jaimie took a step forward, his eyes bleak.

"Nay, Jaimie!" Maebelle wept. "We have trouble enough. And fighting is not the way. Let us outface him! Him and all the world! I have no shame of loving you! Say what they will, they cannot make of it an ugliness. The joy we've had of each other is no shameful thing, but rather, husband mine, a source of pride!"

Which was easily said. But outfacing the crowds come to gloat over the spectacle of their shame, in practice, proved another thing. For, though there have been in human history, systems crueler than the Scottish Kirk's open exhibition of a sinner's private shame, their cruelty was physical, which, in a way, is easier to bear. This savage mental cruelty, however, was a new thing in the world. It can be submitted, with some justification, that young James Jarrett did not survive it. That some time, during those twenty Sundays in a row he had to sit and watch Maebelle weep, hear the Parson dwell with that lip smacking delight which is the truest pornography in this world over such expressions as: "In their nasty sty of lechery!" "Sinful dalliance o' the flesh!" "Clipping and playing!" something in him died. His love of living. The joyousness of youth. The innocence that no such youthful, tender encounters such as theirs has ever yet destroyed. And the iron entered in his soul. The black hell that was to unman his enemies until the very end of his life. The hardness. The utter lack of mercy, having been granted none.

On the twentieth Sunday, Maebelle failed to appear. Parson Creighton suspended services while the City Guard was sent to find her. Then the entire congregation sat in grim silence from early morning until nightfall, when the Guards returned.

Bearing her with them. She looked like a half-drowned kitten.

On the way back, her clothes had dried; but they were mudcaked, showed traces of sea salt. Her eyes were wide and wild in her small face; but what was in them was another thing: a kind of desperate resolution that stopped the beating of James' heart.

The Captain of the Guard saluted by touching the haft of his Lochaber axe.

"She were for drowning herself," he growled. "We tracked her north to Leith and e'en beyond. Caught up with her just as she walked out into the waters of the Firth of Forth. Aye, and hard the battle was that this wee lass put up before she was subdued. Well, good Parson, we return her to yer hands."

The Minister's face hardened into granite.

"So, Lass," he boomed, "to the sin of fornication, ye would add self murder? Think ye that to escape your proper punishment at our hands, it was the wiser course to embrace hell?"

"Aye!" Maebelle flared suddenly; "the muckle black devil is no whit crueler than you who call yourselves men and Christians!"

"Silence!" the Minister roared.

"I'll not be silent!" Maebelle cried. "For myself, I could endure it. I loved yon bonny lad with all my heart, and all my body, too—which is what the Good Lord gave me a body for, I ween! I'd have wedded him to be his goodwife all life long, except—"

Her voice smothered, broke. Then it cleared again. "Except I have not hypocrisy, nor cant, nor deceit enough to lay upon yon innocent shoulders the burden of another man's child!"

James Jarrett came upright then, inch by terrible inch. To say what was in his face then wants a new language with words not worn oversmooth from too much use. For it was a new thing, never there before. And it would stay with him. Forty years from that day, men would quail before it still.

"Aye, Jaimie!" Maebelle wailed. "Don't look at me like that! I've loved no other but you, my Lord, my heart! That the child is not yours, is true; but only because I was forced—by spells and witchcraft of a warlock; by brute strength itself! By the intrigues of a madman, who dares to witness while you suffer for his sins! As God is my Judge, I—"

He held her with his eyes. Stopped, with a look, her speaking voice. Said but one word; and that right quietly:

"Who?"

"Jaimie!" she wept, "I can't tell you that! For you'd—"

"Who was it, Maebelle?" he whispered. His voice was almost gentle.

Maebelle straightened up, then. She seemed to grow a foot in stature. Her finger, pointing, did not even tremble.

And every eye in the Kirk, turned to gaze at Pitcairn Hogg.

Nobody moved. No one spoke. There was death's own stillness in the Kirk. It was broken by James Jarrett's cry. By agony given voice.

Then the boy was down from his stool. Plunged, head down like a battering ram into a guardsman's belly. The man went down with James on top of him. When the boy came up, he had a flintlock horse-pistol, torn from the guard's belt, in his hand.

The congregation exploded into motion. People scattered, shrieking, knocking over pews in their efforts to get away. They need not have fled. Black death, himself, was not more sure than James Jarrett, then.

He put that ounce of lead into Pitcairn Hogg's fat paunch from no more than a yard away. Hammered that vast head with the barrel of the gun until all the full-bottomed wig was red. The guardsmen came alive, their clumsy poleaxes in hand. James faced them, howling like a timber wolf. Hurled the horsepistol into the face of the nearest one. Overturned a pew beneath the feet of the rest. Fled the Kirk untouched.

Outside, they heard a horse dance as he mounted. Then the drumroll of hoofbeats, rising, driving, going on. And James Jarrett, who came into Edinburgh without a ha'penny, driving a stolen cow before him, left it in the same condition, riding a stolen horse. But one thing had been added to lend him stature.

Now there was a price upon his head.

CHAPTER FIVE

SOME TEN MILES south of Edinburgh, James Jarrett, wanted
criminal, pulled up his stolen mount, and sat there, thinking.

I've two choices, he thought. Either I take to the hills, and shake off
all pursuit—and surely starve—or I stick to the road, and risk being
taken. Rum business, both. On the road, I can beg food, or work,
which will slow me down—and leave this Jarrett's face of mine fixed in
the memories of all and sundry. Who wouldn't mark this beak of mine?
Or recall it when asked? And how many men have this great brush of
eyebrows with no separation, even over the bridge of the nose? Aye,
right well they'll mark my villainous features—only—

Only the choice is not so bad as it seems, I think. Pursuit? Knowing
Edinburghers as I do, it'll take them a week to organize it. They'll
call the City Council together to vote funds. Mayhap even the Grand
Assembly of the Kirk, since sacrilege is involved. In Scotland, 'tis not
considered meet to shoot a man in the Kirk. Nor pound his skull into
a jelly, either. And they'll need a special warrant from the Crown
Bench, or the constables of the other towns will not lift a finger. If
they will, even then. In Scotland, each town's an island, jealous of the
rest . . . The road, then; I'll chance it. And once across the Tweed—

He'd be safe.

He pushed on. He was a month past his twentieth birthday, a fine
broth of a lad, tall and strong; and the villainous face he complained
of, was less villainous than exciting. It was, indeed, a face that people
remembered. Particularly when those people were young and female.
Which, in part, was to be his salvation.

And of salvation, physical at least, he stood in dire need. In the years at the Andrews', he had forgotten what it was like to go hungry. He had not a farthing in his pockets, not to mention a ha'penny. And his stubborn Highland pride forbade his begging. Besides, both his looks and his clothes were ill designed for the rôle of mendicant. Sober though it was, his suit was well cut, and of good materials. He wore his own black hair, clubbed into a queue, that is, gathered into a pig-tail braid and tied with a brown satin ribbon. And nobody would ever mistake that imperious jut of nose and brow for the face of a commoner. James Jarrett looked like what he was: a Lord. And he would have looked the part, beyond all possibility of disguise, had he been clad in rags.

He made the forty-odd English miles to Kelso, in something under two days. His route followed the valley road through the Southern Uplands. Looking at the gently rounded hills, covered with grazing sheep, recalled to him the Northern Highlands of his childhood. Those Southern Uplands, which have kept England and Scotland apart for centuries, were but a gentler version of the hills in which he had been born. Here were the same moor and heather, the same rolling hills purpling away into the distance. For the first time since he had left it, James felt a tinge of nostalgia for his ancient home.

Which, be it said, did not last long. For, in those two days, not a crust passed his lips. He quenched his thirst at the streams that came down from the hills into the valley, discovering painfully that water, while marvelously good for thirst, has no effect at all upon hunger.

But he had his antidote, at the beginning, against that age-old curse. Ever and anon as he rode, he raised his brawny fist to dash away a tear. He had but to murmur, "Maebelle" and the rumbling in his belly fled before a far deeper pain.

Yet, on that journey, he soon proved to his own satisfaction that he was both a Highlander and a Jarrett still, despite the baneful years with Hogg. Faced by starvation, he brought his native canniness to the fore. Outside Kelso, on a farm where he spent the night in a haystack, he encountered a plump and blushing milkmaid. From fair Rose he managed to obtain a vast meal of cold cuts, which she stole from the manor, and even provisions to see him some days further on his travels. For all of which, he paid her with a kiss. He might have in-creased the payment considerably, for plump, blonde Rose was a win-some lass, but the memory of Maebelle was still too fresh to permit him further dalliance.

With canny Scotch frugality, he husbanded the rations Rose had given him. It was well that he did, for the route from Kelso to Carlisle did not follow the dales or valleys where he might have found work, or food, but climbed up over the hills, themselves. Upon another occasion he would have been moved by the beauty of this part of the Southern Uplands; but now he was too driven to even notice it. His supplies lasted him past Carlisle, Penrith, Kendal, almost to Lancaster, enabling him to ride through the lovely green valleys without having to think about anything but his broken past, and his unknown future. He still had food left as he approached Lancaster, then capital of England's woolens' industry; but his frugality had been excessive: he was forced to throw the last of it away for it had spoiled.

He did not tarry in Lancaster; but neither did he, as he had with the other towns on his route, circle around it. Lancaster was big enough for people to pay scant attention to a hatless, cloakless, bootless rider. From that public indifference he took comfort. In a city the size of London no man would ever find him.

But, by the time he got to Preston, he was again faint with hunger. He saw a pack train on the outskirts of that town, which did not surprise him. All over Scotland and England, the roads were still so bad that the only feasible means of transporting heavy goods were the canals and pack horses. Loaded wagons sank to the hubs in the mire after every rain. But the sight of the pack train did give him an idea. He rode boldly up to the leader and said:

"Could you, good sir, use another man and a horse? I have to travel south—if that be your route—and, to tell the truth, I have not tuppence in my pockets. . . ."

So it was that young James Jarrett, gentleman rogue, trudged the distance from Preston to Manchester afoot, leading his protesting barb who liked not at all the weight of pottery upon his back. But James found the journey pleasant. For one thing, he ate regularly, though the food was both coarse and poor. For another, walking cured his saddle-soreness, and strengthened his legs. And the jingle of the shillings in his pocket made a most pleasant sound.

In Manchester, he slept in an inn, damning the expense, so greatly did he long for a bed by then. And he was weary enough for not even the bedbugs, with which even the best of inns in those days were over well supplied, to keep him awake. In the morning, he enjoyed the blissful luxury of an all-over wash, and a shave; and set out to seek his fortunes anew.

Nor was he long in finding them. Some miles out of Manchester, he rode into a village on the very day of the village fair. He was still fresh from his bath and shave, and many a side long glance from the village maids met his bold gaze. To tell the sober truth, sad though it is, the ache in his heart was growing a wee bit dull by then. And he was a Jarrett. He stared at the maids, voiced a gallantry or two. The smiles and blushes he obtained were reward enough. He was still a driven man, with no time for more.

He hitched his horse to a tree and wandered among the exhibits of blooded cows, farm produce, and fine needlework of the farmwives. He lost tuppence at a game of chance, which, under his present circumstances was roughly equivalent to losing a pound. But then his luck changed, and that fortune, which, as Hogg had said, favors fools—especially young fools—smiled on him.

For a little man was standing in the middle of the square, bawling:

"Come one, come all! Who'll try a feat of strength against Tim Hodges, Village Champion? Fer a pound! A pound, me friends—think of it! The cherce is yers! Catch as catch can! Pugilism—or single stick! Who'll try? Who'll try?"

James stepped boldly forward. He knew better than to attempt to either wrestle or box with the giant roped all over with muscles that Tim Hodges was. But the single stick was another matter. During all the years he had spent at the Andrews', he had had daily lessons in fencing. And, since the beginning exercises in swordplay were always given with the stick before passing on to the more dangerous foils, James could manage that plebeian weapon very well indeed. More than very well. For he had enjoyed working with the sticks so much that he had continued the devilish play with them against his friend, Eugene Gilbert, long after the need for such practice had passed. Big as he was, strong as he was, Tim Hodges hadn't a chance.

Twenty minutes later, James Jarrett rode wearily out of town, his fingers all but crushed by Hodges' grip, and twenty lovely shillings jingling in his pocket.

Enough and more to end his troubles for the rest of his journey. In 1735, his prize was a princely sum; there were families who lived right well on twenty pounds a year. But, if now he could eat regularly and dispute the occupancy of the beds in the inns with their original inhabitants, the bugs, he was yet to be supplied with one more piece of purely gratuitous excitement.

En route, he fell in with the Manchester-London coach. And as the barb was beginning to show signs of wear, James paced his mount by riding behind that lumbering vehicle. That was one reason. Another, unexpressed, but no less real, was the fact that he had now entered the backbone of England, the Pennines—a high plateau of gritlands, moor, heather, wooded valleys, and limestone, through which the streams cut, making their water both hard and unpalatable to the taste — and the loneliness of the landscape had its effect upon him. He had no intention to bespeak the people travelling in the coach; but, somehow, their very presence was a comfort to him. He kept his distance behind them, aware that the guard on the high seat beside the driver had turned, and was watching him.

But, almost at once, the stage pulled to a halt, and the guard climbed down, blunderbuss in hand.

"What be yer business, young sir?" the guard growled. "We like not being followed by a horseman!"

"Don't be a fool, man," James snapped. "Can't you see I am not armed? The fact is, on this lonely road, I want the protection of that cannon that you're carrying. . . ."

"Ye do seem a gentleman, I'll allow," the guard said grudgingly; "though to ride without hat or cloak is right strange. . . ."

"I was robbed of them in the last inn I stopped at," James lied smoothly, "and a goodly sum in sterling to boot. Up with you, my goodman. I'll not trouble you."

"Begging yer pardon, sir," the guard said, "but with all due respects, I got to be sure. Ye'll not object to a search for concealed weapons?"

"Not at all," James said, and dismounted.

The guard ran his hands over his slim body. Stood back and touched his hat.

"Begging yer pardon, again, young Sir," he said soberly, "but this road is fair infested with highwaymen. We've been robbed three times in a fortnight. I trust the young gentleman will understand I meant no disrespect?"

"No offense taken," James smiled. "I've often been told I have the face of a rogue. You don't mind, then, that I follow you? I have not a penknife, because those thieves got my horsepistols, too. And having your blunderbuss at hand would be a comfort. . . ."

"Follow if you will," the guard said. "A pleasant journey to you, Sir."

Jogging along behind the coach, James let his mind wander. He had all the Scottish capacity for introspection; and a new problem was troubling him now: his single stick contest with Tim Hodges. The savagery of his attack upon Pitcairn Hogg troubled him not a whit; but the beating he had given Hodges was another thing. He had all but blinded the big man, taken ferocious delight in slashing him bloody. He had never been consciously cruel before, but now—

But now he had turned murderer, however great his justification. Changed into a shameless rogue to whose lips lies came more readily than the truth. Taken out upon the hide of a completely innocent stranger the festering rage he felt toward all the world.

A rotten show. But—why not? The world was what it was—a jungle. A man had but two choices in it: to be a tiger—or a jackal. And he was a Jarrett, scion of a race of warriors. Toward the weak, the defenseless, society was merciless. And Christian virtues be damned! Men had a healthy respect for fang and claw. So be it. Strike first, and ask questions later—or else submit to being ground into the mud, with every man's boot upon his face. . . .

Nay, mine the boot that does the grinding! Mine the pitiless denial of all compassion, the dirty advantage taken, the crushing blow!

He had, within the hour, the opportunity to put his new-found philosophy into action. For, as the big coach crawled southward, three riders dashed out of a covering of trees. They, all three of them, were quite obviously highwaymen: black three-cornered hats, greatcloaks trailing behind them as they galloped, black masks hiding their eyes.

And unarmed James Jarrett sat there and watched it. The driver whipped up his eight-horse team. The coach careened into flight, jolting over the ruts, threatening to overturn at every instant; the screams of its passengers audible above the groaning of the tortured wood, the thumping of the springless axles. In full flight, its speed was not above a horseman's canter; the highwaymen flanked it on both sides, firing. The guard got off a blast with his blunderbuss, with miraculously good results, considering the heaving platform from which he aimed. One of the highwaymen caught the charge of scrap iron from the bellmouthed handcannon full in the belly, reeled from the saddle, dead before he hit the ground.

But the others bore ten or twelve pistols in their belts and shoulder straps, so that in a day when repeating firearms did not exist, they managed to keep up a running fire. The guard had two horsepistols in addition to the blunderbuss. He used them bravely; but to hit the side of a barn with a flintlock horsepistol at twenty paces, even while standing still, elevated a man, in the seventeen hundreds, into the ranks of marksmen. The guard missed cleanly with both his remaining shots.

Helpless now, it being demonstrably impossible to reload a flintlock with powder, ram home a ball, put a pinch of primer into the pan, while keeping one's seat atop a coach that was duplicating all the motions of a storm-tossed vessel, the guard sat there stoically and awaited death. Which was some time in coming. Even from the two- or three-yard range to which they had closed now, the highwaymen discharged most of their weapons before they succeeded in gunning both the driver and the guard down.

Then one of them spurred his mount forward, leaped from the saddle onto the back of the left lead horse, pulled him and his team mate to a sudden stop, so that the coach, with no hand to set the brakes, slammed into the rumps of the tail team, grinding, jolting into a long, slow halt.

James had already been some distance behind the coach when the attack began. And he had prudently reined in his barb, allowing the distance to become greater as the running gunfight sped along the road.

If, he thought soberly, I had an ounce of sense in my head, I'd take to the woods. But there are women in that coach. And those black-guards haven't seen me. If they had, they'd have taken me for an outrider, and killed me first. As for arms, that poor devil of a guard has supplied me well. I have only to rob the dead highwayman, and—

With a savage grin James Jarrett dismounted, approached the dead highwayman. The cadaver was a bloody mess. What that half pound of rusty nails, bolts, nuts, and pieces of scrap iron had done to him wasn't pretty. But James had the Jarrett stomach as well as the family looks. Methodically he possessed himself of all the dead man's pistols which had not yet been fired, unbuckled his swordbelt, wiped the blood off it and from his own hands with the highwayman's cloak. Belted it on, leaped into the saddle, turned the barb off the road, skirted through the trees.

When he came up to the coach, the highwaymen were busily en-gaged in robbing the passengers. One of them held a pistol upon them, while the other snatched purses, tore rings from dainty fingers, clawed necklaces from slim, and not so slim necks, collected watches. . . .

If, James thought happily, I ever take up this interesting trade, I'll be more refined. I'll kiss all the bonnie lassies, and thank them nicely as I relieve them of their trinkets. . . . But now to take these rogues, as soon as I study how. . . .

Both of the highwaymen had their backs to him. Having robbed a dozen coaches with impunity upon this lonely stretch, the last thing in the world they expected was attack. James climbed down, strolled up behind them with all the casualness of a man upon a Sunday morning promenade. He prayed the passengers would not cry out, for they could see him. His luck held good; the victims were too numbed by then to cry. Besides, seeing that Jarrett face of his, they made the normal assumption: took him for another bandit, perhaps even the chief.

James drew the late highwayman's sword. He had absolutely no faith in pistols. For one thing, he had seldom fired one; for another, he was too well aware of their damnable habit of either missing fire completely or throwing a blind country mile to one side of the intended target, and leaving the shooter helpless. But he dearly loved and trusted a blade.

He leaped in, slashing. And one highwayman stood there, staring at his severed hand, still holding the pistol, lying on the ground. The other whirled, dropped his loot, went for a pistol, drew it, yanked the trigger, and the flint flashed futile sparks into the pan. In his haste, the bandit had drawn a weapon he had already fired.

"Nay, friend," James laughed. "No gunplay! Mustn't frighten the lassies overmuch. Your sword, man! Let's play this out like gentlemen!"

The highwayman drew his broadsword. The blades, meeting, made hot, bright sparks. The bandit was no novice; but he was facing Gaspard's pupil—a lad who had spent nearly ten years in the daily exercise of fence. James could have killed him any time after the first feint; but he was young enough to be aware of his audience, and the streak of cruelty in him was growing deep.

He parried his opponent's thrusts with laughing ease; engaged him in terce, passed into quince, locked his blade beneath the basket hilt of the highwayman's sword, gave a contemptuous flick, and the man stood there staring at his empty hands.

"Ye win," he croaked. "I surrender!"

"Nay, lad; pick up your blade." James smiled. "You see, I mean to kill you. . . ."

The bandit's face went grey. He hadn't a chance, and he knew it. He scurried to his fallen weapon, bent, picked it up, turned—

And his wounded companion came alive. He had been sitting propped up against one wheel of the coach, trying to staunch the flow of blood from the stump of his arm with his filthy cloak. But seeing how his fellow fared, visions of the gallows dominated even his weakness and his pain. Craftily he drew a loaded pistol with his left hand, steadied it with his maimed right arm—and fired.

James felt a whitehot iron run along his skull, under his softly clubbed black hair. He hung there dizzily, feeling the weakness and the shock and the first slow drip of the hot stickiness of his blood. Then all his Highland furor entered him. He leaped, roaring, upon the wounded bandit, drew back his sword, put the point against the man's throat, tensed his arm to thrust home, when:

"Look out, Sir!" a woman cried.

James whirled to meet the other bandit's blade, tossing a snarled, "Disarm him!" backward over his shoulder. The male passengers fell upon the wounded man, stripped him of his arms, dealing him, in the process, a plentiful supply of kicks and cuffs.

James set to work in deadly earnest now. It was less easy than he had thought: the highwayman was consciously fighting for his life. But James parried once, deliberately thrust wide, forcing the bandit's parry to leave his body exposed. Again—a trifle wider still. And now, in terce, out, out—then, like simmering summer lightning, his blade flashed in; he leaned forward, graceful as a dancer, his foreknee bent almost to the ground, his right leg extended backward, locked and stiff; and the blade went into the highwayman's middle, to come out thirty inches on the other side.

James straightened up, withdrew the blade; turned to the frightened passengers, the half fainting women; saw among them a man in clerical garb.

"You might say a prayer, good Reverend," he said icily. "The man has, presumably, a soul."

The driver was still alive, though badly hurt. James went about bandaging his wounds. The women jostled each other to supply him with strips of cloth from their petticoats. Then he turned his attention to the other bandit he had maimed. The man had lost a frightful quantity of blood. James was sure he was dying, that he would not make it to the next town. But he bandaged the stump just the same, and the men lifted the highwayman to the top of the coach, making room for him and the wounded driver amid the luggage.

James stood there, swaying a little, staring at the three corpses.

"Seems ill to leave them here like this," he growled. "Could not you gentlemen organize a burial party?"

As he spoke, he half turned; and a deuced pretty lass let out a shriek:

"Oh, Sir; you're hurt! Your face—it—it's all blood!"

"A scratch," James muttered; but his head ached as though all the fiends in hell were hammering at his skull.

"Now sit you down!" the young woman cried; "and let me tend to you!"

James dropped wearily to the ground. Slim, perfumed fingers moved amid his hair.

"Oh, La!" the young woman gasped. "It's open to the bone!"

"Let me have a look at it, Jane," a big man growled.

Her husband, damn it! James decided; then: what's the odds? I'll profit from her gratitude in spite of him.

The man examined the wound.

"Bad," he muttered; "wants stitching. I'll have to shave your head, young sir. A pity; but you've too damned much hair."

He climbed up atop the coach and sought his bag. Another passenger fetched water from the waterkeg. When they got through, James Jarrett looked more villainous than ever. But a wide strip of Jane's petticoat improved his looks a bit, though otherwise it didn't help matters much at all. As her husband had said, his wound wanted stitching; and that could only be managed if there were a doctor in the next town.

They were some time in moving off. Sick as he was, James again insisted upon their burying the dead. Then the business of the redistribution of the stolen goods caused more delay and occasioned some bitter arguments as to whose watch was whose.

People! James Jarrett thought. You are one and all blood brothers to Squire Hogg. . . .

Then there arose a discussion as to who would drive the coach. It turned out that there was not one decent whip among them.

"All right," James growled disgustedly. "I'll bring you in. Will one of you gentlemen be so kind as to tether my mount behind the coach?"

"Fred," the woman named Jane commanded, "you ride up there beside him, to see that he doesn't fall off. He looks terribly pale and—"

"All right," her husband grunted. "Pass me over those pistols, young sir. I'd best load them and have them ready. It's not rare to be attacked two and three times along this road. . . ."

But they were not attacked again. The trip was grim enough without that, however. James was as sick as a dog; but he well concealed his weakness and his pain. They did not find a doctor until they got to Sheffield. And brave though he was, when the doctor cauterized the wound with a red hot iron, James Jarrett fainted. He was three days abed. Which, short of putting him in irons, was as long as the doctor could keep him there. To get up when he did was pure folly. With a furrow ploughed along his skull, lifting a five-inch splinter of bone, a month's repose was the minimum indicated. But James was a Jarrett, than whom there was no more stubborn breed.

To a man, the passengers refused to go on without him, though a new guard and another driver had been engaged. James was about to revise his opinion of human nature for the better, when he learned that due to public indignation, the wounded highwayman had had a summary trial and on the morrow was to be hanged.

For every one of them who waited to see me up, James thought, there were three who wouldn't miss the fun. Poor devil—crippled as he is, he's had punishment enough. I wonder if I said a word—

Which did no good at all. The guard had been slain. And the driver died while the bandit was standing trial. James Jarrett was sufficiently a part of his age to attend the execution. It wasn't an edifying sight. The wretch was dragged to the gallows, bodily, shrieking and begging mercy. The executioner was clumsy—or cruel; he made the knot too loose. Instead of breaking the felon's neck cleanly, the robber's victims had the keenly felt pleasure of watching the maimed man kick and choke for eight long minutes, while his tongue protruded, his eyeballs bulged from their sockets, and his lean face turned slowly purple.

And seeing the avid countenances of his fellow spectators, James Jarrett revised his estimation of human nature downward once again.

But on that journey down to London, he conceived sufficient respect for Frederick Perkins, Esquire, to decide to leave his wife alone.

Which was, all in all, one of the wisest decisions he had ever made.

CHAPTER SIX

AT THE ENTRANCE to the greatest city in all the world, James Jarrett shook hands with his new-found friends and took his leave. He was, of course, showered with invitations to visit and to dine. He pocketed their cards with grim mockery.

If you hold your lives and goods worth no more than the recompense of a meal, he thought, I can but agree with you. If, indeed, they're worth that much.

He became aware, then, that Fred Perkins was staring at his face. Already, James had come to like Perkins very much, which was not strange. Frederick Perkins, Esquire, was a fine figure of a man, large and square, of middle years, with a hearty, healthy red face that, without actually resembling it, reminded James of Squire Andrews'. His imposing bulk, despite the fact that he had obviously passed his fiftieth year, was nearly all muscle, not fat. He looked the archetype of the Country Squire, a thing he was not at all. Mr. Perkins, actually, was both a city man and a banker.

"I like not your look, my boy," he said now with grave kindness. "To me, you appear uncommon ill. A head wound's not a thing to trifle with. So I'd like to make a suggestion. We have a dwelling in Bloomsbury Square. Why don't you stop with us a fortnight, or even longer, if you will? Time enough to let your hair grow out again, and put some color in your face. Our fare's plain but 'twill put some covering on your long bones. And of that, by my troth, you have some need!"

"Oh, yes, please do!" Jane Perkins said.

James looked at her. The offer was tempting. The trouble was that

Jane Perkins was even more tempting. She was younger than her husband by at least twenty-five years. Her blue eyes were soft and candid. Her well coiffed chestnut hair made James' fingers fairly ache to reach out and stroke it. And her figure—

No. Fred Perkins was far too good a man.

Besides, James had a thing to do. He had guarded in his mind the address in East Cheap, from which his father's last letters had come. Lodging with the Perkinses would not, of course, impede his search. But if he found Jonathan? And in the state he'd likely find him? He couldn't bring a whining, witless drunkard to the Perkins' house. And, having gained their liking, and their respect, he'd damned well rather that they didn't see the auld fool at all. . . .

Slowly he shook his head.

"I thank you most kindly, Sir—and Madam," he said formally. "I'd gladly accept, but it so happens I cannot. You see, there's a thing to be done that cannot wait. I'm in search of my father, who disappeared here in London some years ago. . . ."

"In that I can aid you," Perkins said; "my acquaintances are wide, and—"

Paradoxically, perhaps even quixotically, James Jarrett told the truth:

"Do they extend to East Cheap, Sir?" he said sardonically; "or even to Alsatia? I've had letters from both those quarters, sent by him. . . ."

"Alsatia no longer exists," Fred Perkins said. "The barristers in the Temple protested so strongly at having that den of thieves at their doorstep, that it was abolished. About 1725, if I recall well. The name persists, of course; but 'tis an honest tradesman's quarter, now. You need not be ashamed if your father lives there. . . ."

"I know not where he lives. I haven't had a line from him since 1728. But, truthfully, Sir—I know my father. The only reason why he ceased to write me is that he must have fallen upon evil days. He—he had a weakness for drink—"

"I find this strange," Jane said, wrinkling her saucy, uptilted nose. "You have the look of a gentleman, so how—"

"A Scottish gentleman, milady," James said quietly. "My father was Laird of Clan Jarrett. Which means that never in his life has he seen twelve pounds in any one year. We Highlanders are an uncivilized race. A title and wealth don't go hand and hand as they do here in England. . . ."

"Not even always here," Fred said. "But come with us. 'Tis true I have no connections in the places that you mentioned. A banker naturally deals with the monied classes. Yet, since you've waited all these years, a fortnight or two will not change matters. Your search will be better conducted without a broken head. . . ."

"Thank you, good Sir," James said. "But no. I didn't come before, because I couldn't. But now that I'm here, I'm impatient to begin."

"All right," Perkins said; "I'll not insist. But if I may presume upon the fact that I have twice your years and more, I'd like to ask you one question, with no offense meant: Have you any money, my boy?"

"Plagued little," James laughed, "but I'll manage—"

"Allow me to advance you twenty pounds or so," Fred Perkins said gravely. "You may consider it a loan, if you like. I know you Scots; the devil, himself, has not a more prickly pride. . . ."

"I've had to learn," James said, "that pride makes a lean belly. And to prove how well I've been ridded of my own, I'm going to ask you an even greater favor. . . ."

"Name it," Fred Perkins said without hesitation. "We stand eternally in your debt."

"Which is a thing I'd rather not trade upon," James said. "Accepting recompense ill becomes a gentleman. What I'd like of you, Sir, is a thing which I feel I can maintain my end of the bargain full well: a job. I was, until recently, a student at the University of Edinburgh. I write a fair hand, have a respectable knowledge of the law. My Latin's more than fair, which, I'm told, some use in legal documents; and I can total sums with as few errors as any man. . . ."

"Could I find clerks with so many accomplishments," Fred Perkins said, "half my troubles would be over. Consider yourself engaged, young Sir. Here's my business card. My bank is upon the Strand. If you'll meet me there, tomorrow—"

"By your leave, Squire Perkins—" James began.

"I am no Squire," the banker growled. "I began life as an honest Yorkshire yeoman. The Squire bought my father out, and to London we came. With the money gained, my Guv'ner set up in trade. All his life he'd given honest work for an honest penny. And not being inclined to change his ways, we prospered. In a town where the shoddy and the cheap abounds, people marked the difference, so—"

"So you're growing old, Fred!" Jane laughed. "Think you a young Lordling has any interest in the story of your life?"

"Aye, much!" James said; "for my empty title is a thing I've clean forgot, milady. I mean to follow in your good husband's footsteps. And all I can learn of him, I will. . . ."

"Then I'll expect you tomorrow," Fred said decisively.

"Begging your pardon, Mr. Perkins," James said; "if you will grant me the liberty, I'd like to postpone my employment until I've found my father. I can hardly work and search at the same time."

"I'd forgotten that. But you will accept the twenty pounds?"

"Gladly—but only as an advance against my wages. And, by your leave, I'll call upon you from time to time, to report my progress—"

"You'll be most welcome," Jane Perkins said. "You're a handsome lad—and I have among my circle of friends more than one fair spinster who—"

"Matchmaking again, Jane?" Fred Perkins laughed. "Don't you women ever tire of that?"

"No," Jane said mischievously; "having found so much happiness with you, good husband, a spinster's plight moves me to pity. Besides, when you consider that Grace Lawson has above twenty thousand pounds; Sue Merrick, twelve; and Ruth—"

"Wist!" James laughed. "And what think you, milady, that I have to offer spinsters of such imposing wealth?"

"A bold, exciting face," Jane said gaily; "a well turned leg; an aspect of devil-may-care that would delight any pale London Miss's heart. And a title—do not forget that, milord. In London, among the pushy commercial classes, like ourselves, that has an astonishingly high market value. Not that you need it, I think. You'd have only to flash that devilishly crooked smile of yours, and half the girls I know would faint outright!"

"You turn my head, good Lady," James said. "I'll call upon you, and soon. But remember that we Scots are a romantic breed. So present me the prettiest one first, and hang her bank account! I think I'll accumulate one of my own, ere long."

"I think you will," Fred Perkins said judiciously, and offered James his hand. When James gripped it, he felt the texture of folded paper. Big and bluff though he appeared, Fred Perkins had that much delicacy. No one in that crowded London Street could tell that money had passed between them.

"Young Sir, your servant!" Fred Perkins said.

"Nay," James said quietly. "I like not that word even as a form of courtesy. For you, good Sir, were not meant to be the servant of any man. Nor your fair lady, either. Now I understand why England is the greatest land on earth; for if she be populated with such as you, she can only grow greater still. My respects, Sir, Madam—and my heartfelt thanks!"

He felt shockingly alone when he had taken his leave of the Perkinses. His head ached damnably. Though he did not realize it, to rise from his bed after only three days, and submit himself to the jolting of the coach for all those miles, had been an act bordering upon idiocy. To which he proceeded to add a greater folly still. He found an inn, stabled his horse, and lay down until the hammering inside his skull subsided a bit. Then he went out, bought a hat and cloak; the hat to cover his shaven, bandaged head, and the cloak to make him look less like a mendicant. He entered a barber shop where he submitted to being shaved. In the process, the barber managed to bleed him as effectively as any surgeon. Swearing, he left the shop, and searched until he found a cutler's. He went in, and bought a pair of razors, and a strop. In another store he purchased a shaving mug, soap and a brush. Then he went back to the inn and deposited his purchases there.

He took his noonday meal and left it scarcely touched, for a wave of nausea all but overcame him. Then, instead of going to bed as he should have, he set out to look for his father.

He walked, not feeling up to managing the ill-tempered beast he had stolen in the crowded streets of London. He was feverish and sick. He did not realize the gravity of his wound.

"A stone's not harder than a Jarrett's skull," he muttered and plunged on. But he was wrong. It was true that the great gash running along his head was not deep. But it had lifted a splinter of bone out of his skull. And though it had not penetrated, its effects were grave enough. His brief, desultory dipping into medicine at Edinburgh served him not. He knew nothing about impact or concussion. Under his skull, a clot was forming on his brain. Had he gone to a surgeon then, he would have been trepanned, and probably killed. But he did not go, stubbornly underestimating his illness. What he suffered now could well have finished him. It so happens that it did not. What it did do was only a trifle less tragic: It changed him—completely, and forever.

The streets through which he moved presented an aspect that, happily, in twenty more years would have vanished from London's life. What caught his attention first, probing through even the pain-fogged dullness of his brain, was the number of funerals he encountered. In

1735, the birthrate of the town was only beginning, slowly, to overhaul the rate of deaths. And for that state of affairs, which did not terminate until 1751, when a wise new law taxed it beyond the reach of the poor, one short word was responsible: Gin.

James had never heard of Hogarth; but had he had the skill, within the hour he had gathered the materials for a masterpiece equalling that savage master's own. Men bawled out at him as he passed:

"Come in, my fine young Gent! Here you kin get drunk for a penny, dead drunk for tuppence!"

James turned aside in sick disgust. Aye, he thought, 'tis sure I'll find my father here!

His foot struck something soft. Looking down, he saw a maid, not seventeen years of age, lying in the mud. Her clothes were rags. Her not uncomely face had not known soap and water these several years. James caught the particularly insupportable odor of unwashed female flesh; the reek of sweat. But topping them, overmastering them, was the sodden stench of gin. She lay there in the mud and snored right blissfully. James Jarrett stepped over her with a shudder, and moved on.

In two short blocks, he lost count of how many insensible drunkards he saw lying in the mud. They were of both sexes and of every age from children below the age of puberty, to toothless, ancient slatterns with wild white hair. Beggars came whining up to him:

"A penny, milord! I have not had a dram in these two days. . . ."

James shouldered them aside with considerable force. He came to a flight of stairs, started to descend, and all but stepped on a naked baby of about a year, howling lustily. He stooped, picked up the child, averting his face from its smell. Turned, and saw its mother, a filthy slattern like all the rest, sitting there rocking back and forth and crooning tenderly to her empty arms.

He gave her the child.

"Thank ye, milord," she croaked, as she extracted one grimy breast from amid her rags, and applied the child to it. Only, James saw with grim wonder, she had made a slight mistake: the child went on howling like a tiny fiend, while his sodden mother pressed his besmeared bottom to her breast and his dangling head turned purplish red.

James took the child away from her again, and righted matters.

"Heads it is, Lass," he growled; "not tails. . . ."

"Thank ye! Thank ye kindly, Sir!" the slattern grinned. " 'Tis hard to tell the difference with 'em both bare!"

Behind him now, the howling stopped. Wearily he shook his aching head. No wonder they are drunkards all, he thought, since they imbibe gin with their mother's milk. . . .

He came to the address from which his father's last letter had come. A stout landlady, a trifle less drunk than the rest, met him at the door.

"What be yer pleasure, good milord?" she cackled. "A room? I have a good one, fer a fact; though by yer looks, ye're used to better than any ye'll find hereabouts . . . Still, a young gentleman can be out o' pocket for a spell. Come in. I'll show—"

"Nay," James croaked wearily, feeling the sickness in him down to his very bones. "I have no need of a room, Mistress. I am looking for a man. Know you aught of—Jonathan Jarrett?"

The woman's face went red with sudden rage.

"Aye, that I do! The drunken sot! Owed me half a year's lodgings when they took him away from here!"

"Took him?" James whispered.

"Aye—took him! He was in debt to half the town by then! Every farthing he got his hands on went fer drink. Now I be not one to scorn a dram or two, but enough of a thing is enough. Right fine he were, with the manners of a lord—and smart, too, I vow. Only he could not keep employ. A week here, a day there—"

"I know, I know," James said tiredly. "But I pray you, Mistress, just where did they take him?"

"To Fleet, where else? I'll wager ye he stayed sober there!"

"Fleet?" James said wonderingly.

"You're no Londoner, be ye, Lad? Fleet Prison, the debtor's gaol. Good riddance! From yer talk, ye're Scotch, so ye know not English law. A creditor can secure the person of a man who owes him money, by flinging the debtor into gaol. So—if ye'd find that drunken fool, since ye're of a mind to, go there, me fine lad—"

"Where is it?" James croaked.

"In Fleet Street, where else? Corner of Farrington Road. Wait! Ye have his look! Ye be—ye be his son!"

"Yes," James said simply. "I am. Why?"

"Then dig up the—" she swept her gaze over his clothes, shrewdly estimating their cut, the cost of the materials—"the twenty pounds he owes me, me boy! Or I'll call the constable instanter!"

James stared at her. He was not a Scotsman for nothing. At the sum for which rooms were let in this quarter, his father could not have accumulated a debt of twenty pounds in so many years. Not unless she had loaned him money. And her face was enough to demonstrate the total unlikelihood of that. This viperous shrew wouldn't extend a farthing to a starving beggar. Not to mention the fact that she'd surely never had a pound in her hands in all her life, not to mention twenty.

"Call him and be damned!" he said flatly, and strode away from there.

It was a long way to Fleet Prison. When he got there finally, he was utterly weary. And so sick that his words came out with the heavy Highland burr he had not spoken since his childhood.

"I don't catch yer meaning, young Sir," the gaoler growled. "Be ye sick or drunk?"

"Sick," James whispered. "Listen, man! I'm seeking my father. He was incarcerated for debt. . . ."

"Now, I get ye. Ye're from out of town. We have no debtors here. Nor in any other prison that I knows of. Ever since 1729, when Gen'l Oglethorpe started dipping his bill in things that was none of his business, trying to get poor Bambridge and Huggins hanged—"

"Get to the point, man!" James snapped.

"They've all been freed. Act of 1729. Ten thousand of 'em was let out at once. Poor devils! I'll allow their lives in gaol wasn't no bed o' roses; but here they didn't starve—which is what they've been doing ever since. The talk is that Gen'l Oglethorpe is planning to gather 'em all up, and ship 'em off to a place called Georgia—in the West Indies. He bloody well should! 'twere all his fault anyhow. Don't hear of him doing nothing for poor Bambridge and Huggins, and they've been out o' work since then!"

"Who the devil are Bambridge and Huggins?" James growled.

"Ex-gaolers. Bambridge o' this here gaol, and Huggins of Marshalsea. The Gen'l were fer hanging 'em out o' hand. Seems a few prisoners died, and—"

James looked around him and shuddered.

"A few?" he whispered, "or a few hundred?"

"Wasn't more'n twenty. The Gen'l charged abuse and ill treatment. Now it stands to reason that a gaoler ain't agoing to kiss his blinking prisoners' hands. And a man what can't stand a few kicks and cuffs, ain't no man nohows, to my way o' thinking. . . ."

"Have you," James said quietly, "a list of those who died? Or a record of the whereabouts of those who were freed?"

"No," the gaoler growled. "Who kin keep up with them vermin?

They come; they go; they live; they die—what's the odds? What good be they to anybody?"

"But you know where Bambridge lives?"

"Yes. In—" Then the gaoler saw James' eyes. "What d'ye want it fer?" he croaked.

"To repair the General's omission," James said flatly. "For, if my father died in this hole, Bambridge had better say his prayers!"

"Then I'll not tell ye!" the man snarled. "And out with ye, me fine lad, afore I treat ye to free lodgings here, yerself! Threatening a man's life be a crime in England!"

James' hand shot out, caught the stuff of the man's shirt. Sick as he was, the rage in him lent him strength. The muscles of his arms bulged; and the gaoler found himself in midair, staring into a pair of pitiless black eyes.

"Call the guard, if you will," James whispered. "Mayhap he can serve as pallbearer for your corpse." He opened his hand and let the gaoler drop. "I'd best go wash," he sighed; " 'tis a filthy business, man-handling swine!"

Then he turned on his heel and strode out from there. The quaking gaoler stood there without a word, and watched him go.

But that, too, was a mistake. The hammers inside his skull set up a renewed pounding. He reached Chancery Lane before he saw he wasn't going to make it. With all London performing a slow and stately dance about his head, he stepped to the edge of the road and hailed an open landau which bore the sign, "For Hire."

He gave the driver the address of the inn, and reeled into the vehicle. When they got there, the driver had to lift his unconscious body down, and carry him inside. And he was fortunate in that his estimation of human nature was not strictly, or at least not entirely, correct. By and large, eighteenth century Londoners were a kindly lot. The innkeeper paid his fare for him, and he and the coachman carried James up to bed.

Where, for a fortnight, he lay and raved, alternately blessing and damning poor Maebelle. At times he seemed to be in hell, being tortured by a legion of fiends all of whom wore the face of Hogg. At other times, a racking sense of shame tore him. He screamed aloud, calling himself coward, accusing himself of not having had the nobility of soul to forgive his Mae, nor the courage to stand beside her, risking the gallows for her sake. Delirious, all the fears, feelings of guilt, con-sciousness of his unworthiness assailed him. His defenses down, lacking even the protection of a rational, functioning mind, he descended, almost literally, into the Inferno; and in no poetic, Dantean sense.

But, he was not alone, albeit he knew it not. For during that fortnight that he wandered among shades and shadows, smelling the brimstone, his eyes glaring red with the very fires of the pit, Bess, the innkeeper's fat, matronly wife, scarcely left his side.

It is quite probable she saved his life.

CHAPTER SEVEN

JAMES JARRETT TOTTERED to the mirror and stared at his reflection. The reflection stared back at him, eyes sunken in their sockets, cheeks hollowed, mouth all but hidden by a brush of mustache and two weeks growth of beard. His skin was drawn tight over the bones of his face, and a wide red line, through which no hair would ever grow again, arched through the porcupine quills which had sprouted on his head.

"Hoot, you brigand!" he chuckled: "Think you that any man would let you in a bank without calling the guard?"

He turned, walked carefully over to the washstand, poured water into the basin, got out his razor, brush, and soap, and began to shave. His hands trembled wildly, but, even so, he escaped with only four or five cuts. When he had finished, he stared at his face again.

The face that gazed back at him was still the face of a brigand, but an infinitely more subtle one. He smiled, and his white teeth flashed out of the native brownness of his face in a purely wolfish grin. He noticed, suddenly, that even smiling, his eyes had not changed. He smiled again; but they went on boring out of that reflected image, dead level, still, penetrating, icy.

"The eyes are the mirror of the soul, men say," he murmured. "Aye. And what a soul have you now, my friend!"

He ran a hand over the wild brush atop his head. Something will have to be done about this, he thought. He picked up the brush and comb, tried combing his hair to one side to cover that hideous scar. It sprang erect at once, each time the comb and brush passed through it. Swearing, he turned back to the washbasin, gathered up a piece of soft soap. He kneaded the soap into his hair. This time his hair stayed down. The scar was hidden. He had a more civilized aspect.

Still, he looked odd enough. In 1735, men wore their hair long, or even covered it with a powdered wig. Accustomed all his life to seeing his head well thatched by his deep-waved black hair—clubbed into a queue at the back—his head looked singularly small to him. And his great, bushy single brow jutted ferociously out of a face curiously emphasized by his still short brush.

No, he decided, I won't call on the Perkinses just yet. Let this heather of mine sprout a while longer. The way I look now would throw a gentlewoman into a screaming fit. And, besides, I still have father to find. . . .

He went back to the washstand, stripped off the nightshirt that the Innkeeper had put upon his thin body, and washed all over, shivering at the water's icy touch. But it revived him greatly; and his great Jarrett's nose no longer wrinkled at the smell of sodden fever stench and sweat.

In the closet he found his clothes, cleaned, pressed, his underwear and shirt snowy. Bless them, he thought, and dressed.

As he came slowly down the stairs, Bess, the Innkeeper's wife, let out a glad cry.

"Josiah!" she shrilled, "our boy is well again! Look at him, how fine he looks! Praised be all the Saints!"

"I take it that you attended me, kind Mistress?" James said. "For that, my heartfelt thanks. . . ."

"Aye, that I did, my poor boy," Bess said. "You were like to die. What happened to you, Son? Were you set upon by bandits on your route?"

"Yes," James smiled; "or rather, it was the other way around; 'twas I who attacked them. . . ."

Josiah Martin, the Innkeeper, came puffing up the stairs from the winecellar.

"You've had our prayers, my boy," he said. "You were in a bad way there for a spell. Hadn't been for Bess, here—"

"I know," James said, "and I thank her and you for it, Sir. For that, and one thing more: 'tis good to know there are people in this world who've not forgot how to be kind. . . ."

"You're not leaving us?" Bess said anxiously.

"Nay, Mistress," James said. "I'll stay on for yet a while. Speaking

of that, the night I fell ill, I had a sum about me. You must have un-
dressed me, Sir. Tell me, did you—"

"Aye, I found your money right enough," Josiah Martin said. "I
keep an honest house. Here it is: nineteen pounds, five shillings, and
eight pence. But, if I were you, I'd take only what you think you'll
need for the day. Leave the rest with Bess. London abounds with
pickpockets, and even armed robbers. And I don't believe you have
strength enough yet to fight to guard your purse. . . ."

"Your advice is well taken," James said. "Give me a pound and
keep the rest. I know it's plagued late, Mistress; but I'm hungrier than
a wolf. Could you get me a bit of breakfast?"

"In two minutes," Bess beamed and scurried off.

Well fortified by a bowl of steaming coffee with hot milk, buns,
marmalade, eggs and bacon, James Jarrett set off about his search.
He was more careful with himself, now. He husbanded his strength.
He searched for two hours among the roaring drunkards in the "gin
lanes" of London. Then he came back to the Inn and rested. By the
end of the week, he was strong enough to wander daylong through the
streets. But, by then, one thing had become abundantly clear: to find
a lone man among London's teeming population, even to encounter
one drunkard in a city whose drunkards could be counted by the tens
of thousands, was a task in comparison to which the hunt for the
proverbial needle in the haystack paled into almost total insignificance.

Nay, he thought grimly, 'tis a thing that wants the hand of a professional. I'd best go take my place in the bank, and hire a runner. I
could search for twenty years, and pass some crooked lane, a thousand
times, some hidden blind alley, in which he mayhap lives, without
ever seeing it. I need must hire some arrant rogue who knows the
poorer quarters of London like the palm of his hand. Yes, to Perkins,
now. Only, with my hair still so plagued short. . . .

To that, there was an easy solution. He entered a wigmaker's, and
came out with his head decently covered. To that good artisan's astonishment, he insisted that the wig be left unpowdered. Since, in that
day, fine wigs were made of human hair, sold by maidens fallen upon
destitution, he had no difficulty in finding one black enough to match
his Jarrett eyebrow.

Then he set out for Bloomsbury Square. He stood before the house,
staring at it. The Perkins' house was new and it had been built by
a master. The architect's taste was impeccable: every line of that elegant Georgian mansion displayed fineness and restraint. James had

never seen a lovelier dwelling in all his life. Standing there, he memorized every detail of it.

When I get back to the Inn tonight I'll make a sketch of this, he decided; I have but a clumsy hand with a quill, but, by God, one day I'll build the like. 'Tis in such a dwelling that a man should bring up his sons!

He went up on the low stoop, and brought the brass knocker, shaped into a lion's head with a ring in his mouth, down smartly. A liveried doorman appeared. He stared at James a long moment before he spoke.

"What be your pleasure, Sir?" he asked uncertainly.

Not to rob the house, as you surely believe, James thought sardonically. "I'd like a word with Mr. Perkins, or his lady," he said evenly. "You may tell them that James Jarrett waits without. They'll know the name. . . ."

His tone, his mode of speech, belied his brigand's face. The manservant's eyes cleared.

"Have the goodness to come in, Sir," he said. "You may wait in the vestibule. Mr. Perkins is not at home; but Madame will receive you, surely. If the young gentleman will follow me. . . ."

James stared around him at the furnishings of the house. The ceiling was moulded with Grecian motifs in low relief. The walls bore their like, but touched with gilt. The chairs were slender, graceful; urns stood in niches in the walls. The drapes were of maroon satin; a Persian rug covered the floor. On the mantel above the fireplace, were figurines: the Nike of Samothrace; a Venus de Milo, Apollo Belvedere. . . .

Compared to this, the Andrews' home had been humble. He thought wryly of his father's "castle," with the cow sharing the one room with them and the chickens perched atop his bed. This, this was how a man should live! Not in a stable or a sty. Nor even in the overcrowded rooms of the Andrews' flat, where five or six periods and styles of furniture warred silently with one another. This was taste, all the more striking because it was so quiet. He memorized the waiting room, too.

The clatter of high heels interrupted his reverie.

"Lord James!" Jane Perkins cried; "how glad I am you've—"

She stopped short. Her eyes were suddenly very wide in her face. Wide and—shocked, James decided. No. More than shocked—frightened. Then her impeccable good breeding came to her rescue. She picked up her phrase in midflight. But, even so, her voice had dropped to a near whisper. There was the faintest hint of a tremble in it.

"—come at last," she got out. "We were beginning to despair. . . ."

James bent and kissed her hand with studied grace.

"Tell me, milady," he said quietly, "have I changed so much?"

"No," Jane began uncertainly, "it's just that—"

"The truth, Jane," James said, holding her with his eyes.

She stood there, staring at him.

"The truth," she whispered, "is often difficult to put into words, Lord James. You haven't changed at all, in one way. In another—totally. You're just the same—except that you're dreadfully thin. But, it isn't that—"

"Then, what is it?" James said.

"Your—your eyes. I—I shouldn't want you for an enemy, now—"

"Small chance of that," James smiled.

"Ah, that's better!" Jane Perkins laughed nervously. "When you smile, you become—almost—the gallant gentleman that I knew. . . ."

"Almost?" James said.

"Oh, how you seize upon things!" Jane wailed. "Yes, Lord James, almost. Your eyes, again. Not even when you smile do they change. They're the eyes of—"

"The devil?" James suggested.

"No. Of a soul in hell, maybe. Or rather, of a soul who has been in hell and emerged victorious, but not unmarked. I've the feeling that everything—well, soft, gentle, compassionate in you—has been burned out. La! How I talk. I must have the vapors, for a fact!"

"I think not," James said easily. "You're right. I've made my grand tour of the Inferno—and with no Beatrice to help guide me, either. But I beg you not to be overfrightened of me, now, milady. . . ."

"You called me Jane, before," she said suddenly.

"I know. Presumptuous of me. Am I forgiven?"

"I liked it. I wish you'd go on calling me that."

"I will—if your good husband does not object. . . ."

"Fred? Lord, no! He's not the jealous type. I've never given him reason to be. . . ."

"And think you that you never will?" James mocked.

She looked him straight in the face, and said it, softly:

"I *know* I never will. Men like my Fred are rare, Lord James. But tell me, why have you taken so long to visit us?"

"I could not come before," James said. "This Jarrett's skull proved

less thick than I thought it was. I've been more than a fortnight
abed. . . ."

"La!" Jane said, "but you look fit enough, now. But so awfully,
dreadfully thin! You'll not escape without sitting down to supper. Besides, Fred won't be home 'til then. Come. I was talking about you
when Jenkins brought in your name—"

"Speak of the Devil—" James grinned.

"That doesn't work," Jane laughed. Her voice had lost its former
nervousness, James noticed with relief. People could get used to him
now, after all. "For, if it did," she went on gaily, "you should have
been here long before now. Besides, you're hardly the Devil. And you
couldn't have chosen a more opportune moment to appear. I was
having tea with friends, girls whose names I believe I mentioned to
you, before: Grace Lawson and Sue Merrick. They're all a-twitter to
meet you. . . ."

"They'll be sadly disappointed, I fear," James said. "And, if you
don't mind, milady, I'd rather not. At least, not at the moment. I'm
plaguedly ill dressed; and this villainous face of mine would frighten
them out of their wits, I'm sure. . . ."

"You know," Jane said seriously, "I rather think it will. But 'twill
be such a fear as women often like. I'm quite sure they won't notice
how you're dressed. They'll be too busy staring at that bold rogue's
face of yours, and wondering what horrible plans you have in mind
for them. Frightened speechless at the thought that you might well
drag them off to your lair and—"

"Ravish them?" James said bluntly.

"Well—" Jane faltered, "the phrase is hardly suited for a woman's
lips, is it? I hadn't thought on it so precisely. No woman ever does,
not if she's gently bred. But—to be honest—something like that,
vaguely. . . ."

"All the more reason, then," he said, "that they should be spared—"

"No! You didn't let me finish what I started to say. They'll be
frightened, all right. But they'll be even more—intrigued. You see,
Lord James, a maid's heart is compounded of nine parts curiosity
to one of all the other emotions, which, being a maid, she doesn't
even know she has. That ugly phrase you used has no exact meaning
for them; but, you may believe me; they're plagued anxious to un-
cover its real meaning. La, how I talk! That's your fault, too—the
new you, I mean. You seem to bring out effortlessly the things in us
we spend our lives decently hiding. . . ."

"I'm glad," he laughed. "I like to get to the root of things."

"You do—and it's disturbing. In any event, I mean to present you. However frightened they may be of your wicked good looks, they'll be even more disappointed, I fear, if you don't at least attempt—"

"To ravish them?" James said again. "Happy to oblige, milady!"

"Oh, you!" Jane said. "But seriously, milord, one favor. They're sweet, innocent girls, both of them. So—don't, please. With Grace, there's no danger. None at all. But with Sue—"

"I just might succeed? My thanks, dear Jane. The information's useful."

"You are a monster, aren't you? But come. They're probably having the nervous vapors by now!"

The two young women stood up as he entered. James saw at once that Jane Perkins had been both perceptive—and right. The taller one, a blonde, stiffened. And the fear in her eyes was plain. But the other, a short, distinctly chubby brunette, stared at him with an expression compounded in equal parts of excitement, interest, pleasure—and even dawning hope. He made them a bow with style.

"Miss Lawson," Jane said, nodding toward the blonde; "and Miss Merrick," indicating the brunette with a slight and graceful gesture of her hand. "Girls, may I present Sir James Jarrett, Laird of Clan Jarrett, the proudest tribe in the Scottish Highlands. . . ."

"You do me too much honor," James smiled. "One, it is my father who is Lord of the Clan; two, I shall inherit the title only upon his death, which, God willing, will not be for many more years. Three, 'tis proud we are, all right; but I know not what of; your footman, milady, is both better dressed and fed than any Jarrett born."

"I think she does you too little, milord," the plump and pretty brunette said. "There are some things which cannot be bought with money; and you, Sir James, have them all!"

"Sue!" the tall blonde gasped, "must you always be so outrageously forward?"

"Small good it's done me so far," Sue Merrick chuckled; "but, after the languid beaus of London, to look upon a man plays havoc with my good resolutions to be more ladylike. You'll forgive me, Sir James?"

"You have scant need of forgiveness," James laughed; "with me, you're free to speak your mind plainly. But, upon one condition—"

"What condition is that?" Sue said.

"That you drop this business of Sir and Lord, which, in my case, is so much nonsense. I've come to enter into Squire Perkins' employ.

You see before you an humble banking clerk. Ladies, your servant!"

Grace Lawson was studying him with wide blue eyes. She was, James saw, close to thirty. She was table flat both before and aft, and her face had the curiously horselike elongation seldom found outside England. Still, she was not ugly. Twenty thousand pounds, James mused, should surely have been inducement enough for some hungry chap to discover whether or not she whinnied in the night.

"I think," she said, with that near rudeness that the titled and the rich seem to think the prerogative of their position, "that you don't look like a Lord at all, Sir James. . . ."

"So I've been told," James smiled. "I've often been mistaken for a highwayman. . . ."

"The comparison's apt," Grace said frostily. "I shouldn't like to encounter such as you in a dark street at night!"

"*You*," James said with biting mockery, "would have absolutely nothing to fear, milady."

"Touche!" Sue cried. "You've never seen, Sir—"

"James to you, Milady," he said.

"No. James is not enough. Ah, I have it! I hereby christen thee Beau James!"

"Sue, I never—" Grace Lawson said.

"Let her talk, Miss Lawson," James laughed. "She's deuced amusing. And plagued pretty, too, I think. . . ."

"In spite of all this embonpoint?" Sue sighed. "I try and try; but tarts, jellies, candies, flummeries, fools, and trifles just will not leave me alone. . . ."

"Especially fools," Grace Lawson snorted, "of all orders and classes. Forgive me. That was unkind. I try not to behave like an aging, disappointed spinster; but that, Sir, is what I am, I'm afraid. . . ."

James stared at her. And what he saw, was, in a strange way, pleasant. Her seeming rudeness was but a part of a rather painful honesty, which, he saw now, she applied as unmercifully to herself. Perhaps even more unmercifully.

"La! But he's turned your head!" Sue laughed. "I've never heard you be so frank with a stranger before, though you're frank enough, God knows. I started to say—"

"James," he supplied.

"No, no! James sounds like a footman. I'll stick to the name I gave you. I started to say, Beau James, that you've never seen a girl so plagued choicy. She could have wed a hundred times over—"

"Fortune hunters," Grace snapped. "I know only too well how I look. The ones who seek you out, Sue, have at least other things in mind. . . ."

"The wrong things, I sadly fear," Sue sighed. "But, if Grace will ever let me finish a whole phrase, I'd like to tell you that she isn't really impolite. It's because she's so infernally—and I think unnecessarily—on the defensive, that she's formed this ugly habit of striking before she's struck. Will you behave yourself, please, Grace? Can't you see he's nice?"

"Interesting," Grace said judiciously, "even—exciting. But nice—no. Far from it! That face is positively satanic. I'm sorry, Sir. Sue is right. I am quite often rude."

"Girls, please sit down!" Jane Perkins said. "Our friend was badly wounded in our defense; and standing there you impose upon his courtesy to remain afoot. Sit down, all. I'll ring for more tea. . . ."

James dropped gratefully into a chair. He turned to Grace. "I take it, then, Miss Lawson," he said gravely, "that in a suitor, you insist upon a man whose fortune matches your own?"

"No. But that his means be respectable enough that the question be not over pressing," Grace said. "I ask too much, I know. Most girls nowadays are not so scrupulous. . . ."

"And you would not make an exception in my case?" James said lightly.

Grace Lawson stared at him. Slowly she shook her head.

"No," she said quietly; "*especially* not in your case, Sir James."

"Grace!" Jane protested. James silenced her with a lifted hand.

"Why, especially, milady?" he said.

"I should not like to marry you upon any condition," Grace said slowly; "even if you had a fortune of an hundred thousand pounds, I think I'd surely refuse. . . ."

"Grace," Sue wailed, "there are limits!"

"Hear me out," Grace said sharply. "My reasons do me credit and are not insulting to Jane's new friend. First of all, I should be afraid of you, Sir James. I am afraid of you. There is something about you never found in the commonality of men. An excess of vital force—and, I'm afraid, a want of pity. You're not unattractive, by my troth. Rather, I find you too attractive. And I know myself. However foolish it may be to answer thus seriously what you ask only in jest, I know I should be miserable with such as you. For I am not woman enough to match such a mate. I doubt such a woman exists. And since, even unattractive as I am—"

"You're not—" James began.

"Don't interrupt! Since unattractive, by my troth, as I know I am, I insist upon wedding only for love. I should be jealous. And you, within a week, would be bored. Crashingly, thunderously bored. I'd never submit to neglect, nor to the fashionable London practice of a secret flat, with a loose female in it, on the other side of town. There! Have I answered your question, Sir James?"

"Too well," he smiled. "I've been eliminated. I bow to your decision, Miss Lawson. . . ."

"Good!" Sue laughed. "For if you care to pay me court, Beau James, I care not if you have a farthing, or no!"

"Girls!" Jane cried, "I confess I never expected this of either of you. You're embarrassing our guest frightfully. . . ."

"Nay," James said, "I'm not embarrassed, milady. As a wild Highlander, I was simply gathering useful information about London life. But I must say that I think Miss Lawson's right. Any man who'd marry for money, is no man at all, to my way of thinking."

"You mean," Sue whispered, suddenly grave, "that if you grew fond of a maid you'd let her fortune stand in your way?"

"Exactly," James said. "The poor dear would have to wait, I sadly fear, until I had risen far enough in life for my means to stand on equal footing with her own."

Sue turned to Jane, her penny-brown eyes alight with mischief.

"What was that orphanage you were telling me about that needed endowment?" she said. "I've suddenly become a philanthropist. By tomorrow I'm going to be so poor that I'll have to sell flowers in Piccadilly!"

"In which case," James chuckled, "in a se'enmonth, you'd be as rich as ever. For I doubt not all the blades in London would line up to buy your posies, and give you a pound a blossom. . . ."

"You have a flare for gallantry, have you not, Beau James?" Jane Perkins said. "With Sue's permission, I shall call you that, too. It fits you. But to change this dangerous subject, tell me: Have you found your father?"

"No," James sighed. "And, what's more, I've come to believe I cannot. The task wants a man who knows London well, which I don't. So I've decided to begin work, and hire a runner to seek him out. . . ."

"A capital idea," Jane said, "and one in which Fred can help you. He has a man in his employ who is charged with finding people who disappear without paying back the money they've borrowed from the bank. He's named Tom Morris; but everybody calls him The Ferret. He never fails. If anyone can find your father, he can. . . ."

"Good," James said. "I'll put him to work at once. . . ."

The hours flew. Before Frederick Perkins came home, Sue Merrick had managed to hint that her father would not be adverse to finding James a more lucrative employment than being a mere bank clerk; and had invited him to dine. James declined the invitation politely, pleading lack of time until he should have become accustomed to his work. The truth was that after Maebelle, he had no great desire to wed. Beyond that, Sue didn't appeal to him as prospective wife.

She'd make a man a deuced fine mistress, he thought; which should be easy, only her mind's full of matrimony, and that's the cardinal drawback in a mistress. No, for gentle pastimes of that sort, I'd best look elsewhere. . . .

Fred Perkins returned at eight; at which time, reluctantly, both girls took their leave.

"I'll have to open an account in the bank," Sue sighed, "and come every day to watch my money. If not, I'm afraid I'll never see you until some slender maid has snatched you off, Beau James!"

"I care not," James said carefully, choosing his words so as not to offend Grace, "whether a maid be thin or plump. If her heart is good, and company pleasant, her curves or lack of them are unimportant. Love involves many more things than mere bodily charms, my dear. . . ."

"I like those sentiments," Grace said. "D'you know, you're the first man I've ever heard utter them, Sir?"

"That's because he is a man," Sue said, "and not a dressed-up fop. Goodbye, Beau James. I'll see you soon, whether you will or no!"

"So," Fred Perkins chuckled, after they had gone, "you've been playing the gallant, eh, my boy? Tell me: how fares your search?"

"Not at all," James said sadly. "I've all but given up hope. But your lady has what seems to me a fine idea. . . ."

"Jane's full of ideas," Fred said fondly, "most of them utter rubbish. Come: we'll talk at supper. I've had a long day, and I'm plagued hungry. . . ."

At the table, the talk was long and good. Fred Perkins was a man

of mature wisdom. James' story of his visit to Fleet Prison led him
into a discussion of the career of General Oglethorpe.

"A fine man," he said; "all heart even though he comes from a
family of domned Jacobites. The early, military part of his career is of
little interest; nothing noteworthy until about 1722, when he dropped
out of the Jacobite movement, took over the family estates, stood for
Parliament as Member from Haslemere, and, finally, in Twenty-Nine,
displayed his compassion by freeing the imprisoned debtors through
that celebrated investigation of his. . . ."

"Which," James said, "I'm glad he did—in one way. But in another,
I'm right sorry. For if he had not, I should have found my father
easily—as it was certain he was in Fleet Prison for debt."

"Never you fear, my boy," Fred Perkins said. "We'll find him. I'll
give orders to The Ferret tomorrow. . . ."

But the task proved difficult, even for The Ferret. Betimes, James
took his place in the Bank upon the Strand. He was good at figures,
intelligent and alert. Within a month, he was given more important
tasks. Upon Frederick Perkins' orders, he became an habitue of
Windsor Coffee House at Charing Cross, where the news of European
trading reached London first. In that pleasant room, one could pick up
many a profitable tip, and the *Haarlem Courant* was translated from
the Dutch as soon as the mailboat came in. He likewise frequented
William Lloyd's Coffee House in Lombard Street, where a pulpit had
been set up for auctions and the reading out of the financial news.
Lloyd's was growing more important to the business world every day,
and was already on its way to becoming Lloyd's of London, of all
but universal fame. . . .

James saw Grace Lawson no more, but Susan Merrick proved
another matter. A small speculative flier having netted him two hundred
pounds, James took lodgings in Ely Place; visited a fashionable tailor;
and started to play the beau in fact. Under the circumstances, he could
hardly have avoided Sue, as that determined maiden threw herself
constantly in his path. He began to squire her about, knowing all the
time that it would end badly. It did. But, curiously, not in the way he
thought.

The first time he asked her up to his flat, having let the decent
interval of a fortnight pass before broaching the subject, she looked
at him out of her great, penny-brown eyes without saying anything.
She didn't move. She sat there in his hired rig a long time, looking at

him, and letting those eyes which he had come to like full well, fill up very, very slowly, with tears.

Fury entered him. Maebelle had cried, too. Maebelle had sworn undying devotion, and then had surrendered without a struggle to that gross swine, Hogg. To hell with it, he thought; to hell with all manners and conditions of women!

"James," Sue whispered, "I—I suppose this is a sort of an ultimatum, isn't it? If I don't come with you, now, I'll never see you again, shall I?"

"And," he snarled, "mayhap even if you do. That depends upon your capabilities."

"Oh!" Sue gasped, "don't you even know the meaning of—pity, Beau James?"

"No," he said flatly, "not in the sense you mean, my dove. But in another, I know it ruddy well. 'Tis the excuse fools employ to excuse their fatuity."

"Is—that—all you want of me?" she quavered. "I'd thought that you were—"

"Beginning to care for you? I do. Especially for this, and this, and this. You're well supplied with charming attributes, fair Sue. They should prove useful."

"Oh, James!" she wailed.

"Oh, James!" he mocked. "What the devil d'you think I am? I'm a man. Prick me, and I bleed—real blood, not tea or lemonade. Jarrett's blood—the best brand that there is, I vow. So hot 'twould scald you."

She didn't answer. She sat there crying very quietly.

He swept her into his arms. And there had been a music hall girl or two by then. A waitress at a local pub. Even one of those gentlewomen whose names are bandied about at coffee houses like Will's or White's—the kind whose gentility only lasts until dark. His kisses were expert. His bold hands even more so.

She pushed against his chest with her two hands.

"Let me go now, James," she whispered.

He turned her loose.

"Then it's goodbye, Sue?" he said indifferently.

"No," she said sadly. "I'll go with you. I'll never be able to see my face in the glass again without shame. But I'll go. It's—horrible. But giving you up is—unthinkable. You've won, Beau James. And I hope you're very proud!"

"Of what?" he said flatly. "Think you that tumbling one maid more or less makes a difference? I care not if you go or stay. It's up to you. . . ."

She stared at him.

"You—you've become a—a monster!" she whispered. "Jane said you were gentle before. . . ."

"Jane didn't know me before," he said flatly. "Still, she's right. I was once a soft fool. But I was taught the exact value of a woman's virtue by an expert. So now I esteem it at its worth: tuppence or less. Mayhap not even a farthing."

"James," she said, smiling through her tears, "you're sorry you started this, aren't you? So now you're trying to shock me into my senses?"

"If any," he grinned. "No, Sue. A night with you would suit me mighty well. And, what's more, 'twould suit you, too. Fact is, I don't think you'll find it horrible at all. Dame Nature's not unkind, y'know. For, if she were, we'd never repopulate the world. . . ."

She stared at him.

"There's—that, too," she whispered. "Oh, James—if that happened, father would kill me!"

He tightened an arm about her soft shoulders. "About that detail, you need have no fear," he laughed. "A monster I may have become, but a cad, not yet. Makes the matter a bit more sporting, doesn't it? That way you snare me into matrimony. Otherwise, no. I'm not the marrying sort. Fair enough?"

She laughed then, suddenly, gaily.

"That makes the game worth the price," she said. "Next Spring I'll be stationed before your door with a little monster in my arms and father beside me with his blunderbuss. Come on!"

"You're a game lass, aren't you?" James said soberly; "but you'd better pray that you escape unhallowed maternity. For if ever I do wed, God pity the poor maid who shares my bed and board! For if there be such a thing as hell on earth, she'll see it, ere she dies. . . ."

They turned into Ely Place. James hitched the hired nag to the rail, and helped Sue Merrick down. As he did so, she clung to him.

"I'm glad I came!" she whispered fiercely. "I wanted to, all the time!"

He unlocked the front door. Tiptoed with her, up the stairs. Bent to insert the second key in the lock of his flat, and saw the warm lamplight flooding out from beneath the door.

He stood there, staring at it. Then he tried the knob. The door wasn't locked. And he'd left it locked. It wasn't the sort of thing he forgot, ever.

He pushed the door open. Entered. Stood there staring at the ratty little man who jumped to his feet.

"Tom!" he growled. "Now what the devil?"

"I've found 'im," The Ferret grinned, showing his ugly, yellowed teeth; "and, since he's all shrove up, yer landlord were kind enough to let us in. I've put him in yer bed. He bloody well needs a wash; but seeing as how he's yer guv'ner, I thought—"

Then Tom Morris, The Ferret, stopped dead.

"Oh, I say, Sir!" he got out, "I'm bloody sorry! Didn't know you had a laidy with you! I'll go—"

"And take my father with you?" James said quietly. He turned to Sue. "Get out," he snarled. "Take the rig. If you know not how to drive, find yourself a hack. Or walk. I care not—only go!"

Sue hung there, her round face very white. And Jonathan Jarrett came tottering through the door of the bedroom. He was a dreadful sight. His clothes were rags. Filthy rags. He had not been shaved in a se'ennight. His hands trembled like a man with palsy. But what stabbed into James like a blade, was his apparent age. He looked seventy. No—eighty. And on that summer day in 1735, Jonathan Jarrett, actually, had not reached his fifty-sixth year.

"My boy!" he croaked, and the great tears spurted from his eyes. "Wist, lad, how fine you look! You've become the English gentleman for a fact—"

Wordlessly, for he did not trust his voice, James swept his father into his arms. Stood there, holding that frail skeleton, loosely covered by far too meagre flesh. Supported that beggar's smell, which was rank. Felt, at long last, Jonathan stiffen.

"You've wed, then, my boy?" the old man quavered. "Hoot, and a fine lass you've chosen, I'll vow! None of these skinny wenches for us Jarretts, eh, lad? Always did like 'em well covered, myself. Turn me loose. I claim a father's privilege to kiss my new daughter. . . ."

James released him. Stood there smiling with satanic glee while Jonathan brushed Sue's cheeks with his dirty grey bristles.

"You're not in the family way, are you, lass?" Jonathan said. " 'Tis happy I'd be to live long enough to bounce my grandson on my knee. . . ."

"No," Sue whispered; then with a flash of malicious mischief, "not yet, father. . . ."

"Soon, I hope," Laird Jonathan whispered. "I have not long to live, you ken. The doctor says—"

Then, suddenly, as if to make his meaning clear, he began to cough. The sound of it was the ugliest thing in all the world. It racked him, tore him, doubled him in half. He groped blindly in his pocket, came out with the tattered, filthy rag that served him as a handkerchief. In the lamplight, James saw the dark stains upon it. Recognized them. Observed the new stain, red and bright, when at last, Jonathan drew the rag from his mouth.

"'e's a lunger, now," Tom Morris whispered, quite unnecessarily. "Caught it in Fleet. They mostly does, there. Ain't one in ten what comes out alive. . . ."

"You'd best be off to bed, father," James said gently. "Come, I'll help you—"

"But," Jonathan croaked, "you've but one. Where'll you and the lass sleep? I'll not deprive you—"

"The lass," James said cruelly, "will sleep at home, well guarded by her sire. We are not wed. You'd not have me buy a pig in a poke, eh, father? Pays to sample the goods before hand, you always said."

"Oh, James!" Sue wailed, "did you have to tell him?"

"Wist, lass!" Jonathan chuckled feebly; "be not ashamed of following the ways of nature. Many's the one before you who's trod the primrose path. And there'll be many more right up to the crack of doom. . . ."

Then he saw her face. Laird Jonathan was not an insensitive soul.

"And he's done wrong," he said angrily. "You're not that type. You're a good lass; that I can see. . . ."

"You say that," Sue whispered, "even finding me—here?"

"Aye, I do! What I see in those bonny eyes is love. All women are powerless afore that. And this caddish whelp has taken advantage of your fear that you'd lose him—"

"Not yet, father," James grinned ruefully. "Your arrival was a trifle inopportune. . . ."

"Hold your flip tongue!" Laird Jonathan roared. He went up to Sue and took her hand. "Don't worry, Lass," he said gently. "I'll see that he does not molest you this way again."

"Only see," Sue whispered, "that he does not leave me, Father Jarrett."

"Aye. You've my word. For to have such a lass as you for a daughter, would make me rightly proud." He turned then toward his son, every inch the Lord, despite his rags. "See the lass home, Jaimie," he commanded, "and blast ye for a mannish churl, behave yourself on the way!"

"Yes, father," James said gently, "but first I'd better—"

"Nay. Tom will help me off to bed. Show him where your razors be. I've played the beggar long enough. Now I'll go wash and shave. I'll not have this bonnie lass ashamed of the family into which she comes. Be off with you! Good night, my Lass. . . ."

"Good night—father," Sue murmured. Then suddenly, impulsively she kissed him.

She did not say a word all the way home. James helped her down. Said:

"'Tis sorry I am you saw the old goat before I had a chance to clean him up. He's not a bad sort, really—"

Sue whirled upon him, her round face furious.

"Bad sort!" she snapped. "Among all the other things you are, Beau James, you disappoint me most when you show yourself a fool! The boot's on the other leg, quite. Think you that his rags and dirt make him any less the gentleman? For that he is, and to the manor born. While you—"

"While I?" he said mockingly.

"Are still a monster. Even a little bit of a cad. Oh, I hate you! I hate, loathe, and despise you, Beau James!"

He stood there, looking at her. Then he took her in his arms. She struggled furiously. Freed one hand; brought it across his face in a stinging slap.

He laughed then, clearly, almost joyously. Twisted his long fingers into her dark hair. Yanked her head back, back, bent and found her mouth. Kissed it until he had the response he sought.

Then, abruptly, contemptuously, he released her.

"Goodbye, Sue," he said.

"James!" she wailed, "don't go! I didn't mean—"

"What woman ever means anything?" he said wearily. "Good night, my dear."

"You'll come again?" she whispered tremulously.

"Yes," he said flatly; "but upon the same conditions as before." Then he turned on his heel and left her there, standing in the moonlight, crying.

CHAPTER EIGHT

BUT, FATHER," James protested, "you're in no condition to undertake a voyage to the West Indies. Have you any idea what it's like to travel by sea?"

"Aye," Jonathan croaked, "I have. 'Tis a rum business. But I care not. I'm going to die. And it matters little if I die here, at sea, or in the new colony of Georgia. But I want to go out with a peaceful mind. And I won't, leaving you here in London!"

"Father, for God's sake—"

"Hold your tongue. Look at you! Sir Fop, Beau Dandy, Esquire, the typical London Rake, Seducer of—"

"Would-be seducer," James said dryly. "You took care of that matter deuced nicely, thank you. She won't even go for a drive with me in broad daylight, now. . . ."

"Good. There be lassies and lassies, you ken. And that one is one of the best. Not a toy for your appetites. A true woman—"

"Oh, hell!" James said wearily. "Hearing you talk, a man would think you'd studied for the priesthood. I happen to know—"

"You know nothing. And if you're about to throw my wild youth in my face, I won't have it. Wild I was, all right; which is not unfitting in a man. But I knew how to pick and choose. And no man can say of me that I took unfair advantage of an innocent maid's fondness—"

"Nor did I," James mocked, "thanks to you. . . ."

"Hoot, ye muckle young de'il!" Jonathan exploded. "You do as I say! Go see General Oglethorpe today. He'll receive you. I was ad-

mitted to his rooms, though I was dirty and in rags. I hear he plans to
sail again next month. There's not much time—"

"But to live in a wilderness, among savages—"

"Aye, in a wilderness! Better that. A broadaxe in your hands or
following a plough might be the making of you. And, as for savages,
I have met the good redskin Tomochichi at the Georgia offices. Would
God I had had such a noble companion in my youth. But you, no doubt,
prefer the Rakes and Blades at White's. . . ."

"I do," James said evenly; "more my sort, father."

"I doubt it not. But not the sort I'd planned for you. We've been
brought low, we Jarretts; but we'll rise again. And not, my boy, in this
thieves' business of money and trade. Upon the land, as a gentleman
should. In a new country, with the future shining before us like a
star. Away from dram shops and coffee houses. With an ocean between you and lisping fops, whom a body has to look twice at to see
whether they be men, or maids in masquerade. You heard me, go!"

"But, father—" James began. Then Jonathan began to cough. James
was sure that he could induce these seizures at will, as his ultimate
weapon. But they were, nonetheless, terrible to witness. And this one
was the worst of all. James lifted the frail, grey figure onto the bed.

"All right, father, I'll go," he said.

It was a grey day in August. A sullen drizzle made the cobblestones
glisten. The weather accorded perfectly with James Jarrett's mood. He
missed Sue damnably. Though he refused to admit it, even to himself,
he was more than fond of her. Another month like this, he thought
glumly, and I'll find myself asking her hand. Ye Gods, what a piece of
folly is a man. Now she's sweet and plump and soft. But, at forty, she'll
weigh twelve stone. Nay, boy, keep a check rein on. There're lassies
enough in London to suit any man. . . .

He moved on through the rain. Father's more than half right, he
thought; spend my life here, and what have I gained? I'll rise in the
bank, right enough. One day, then, I'll be Fred Perkins' image: stout,
slow moving, filled with dignity—a city man, part of this teeming
metropolis of fogs and mists and rains, with the youth gone out of
me, and—

He bent his steps toward the Georgia Office. There, his fine dress
served him well. He was admitted to the General's presence after but
ten minutes' wait. The General wore a great, flowing wig of old fash-

ioned cut. His nose outdid James' own. But his small eyes, set in his elongated face, were intelligent and alive.

"What may I do for you, young Sir?" he said.

"Now that's plagued hard to say, General," James smiled. "My father insisted that I seek you out. He has some mad dream of our emigrating to Georgia—"

"A dream, yes," the General said softly; "but hardly, mad. 'Tis there that the future waits, my boy. You're Scots, are you not?"

"Yes, Sir," James said.

"A party of Highlanders, all of them, unfortunately, implicated in the Rising of Fifteen, will set sail from Inverness in October. Mayhap you and your father would like to join them?"

"My father would be delighted. But I can't say I share his views. Frankly, the motive for his voyage is to get me away from the coffee houses and the maids. . . ."

"Ah, youth!" the General smiled. "There'll be maids enough in Georgia, Mr. Jarrett. And fresher, fairer than the ones you know here. The climate's better, for one thing. Warm, sunny—"

"Say that I decided to go," James said suddenly. "Could we sail with you? 'Tis a long way to Inverness; and you're leaving soon, I'm told, Sir. . . ."

"Of course. We're introducing a new class of settlers into Georgia, now, Mr. Jarrett. Our first group—especially the debtors, did not work out as well as we had hoped. I suppose the characteristics that made them debtors in the first place, persisted. So now, we're hoping to find a more ambitious sort. Hence we've opened the lists to Adventurers, in which class, by your dress and speech, you properly belong. . . ."

"Adventurers, Sir?" James said.

"People of some means and substance. By definition, a man capable of paying his passage and that of ten indentured servants. We need a servant class, too; because I've seen to it that the hideous blight of African slavery shall never be introduced into Georgia!"

"But ten servants, Sir!"

"That requirement is not absolute. An adventurer must, however, be capable of paying his own passage. 'Tis to his advantage to bring the indentured servants, though; for the amount of land granted to him depends upon the numbers in his employ. With ten, you'd receive five hundred acres. Quite an estate, Mr. Jarrett."

"Aye," James laughed, "but I fear my dress has deluded you, General. I am a banking clerk, no more. And my father was in Fleet for debt—"

"Jarrett?" the General mused. "Of course! Jonathan Jarrett, a Highland Laird. An unfortunate weakness for drink—and bad lungs. I'm afraid, young Sir—"

"But," James said, "wasn't your colony founded to aid the released debtors?"

"Yes. Such of them as could get quitclaims from their creditors. And they must be sound of health. Your father can meet neither condition, my boy. Therefore, your only way of joining us would be to find the money for your passage, and his. A pity. You'd surely do well, there. . . ."

"Or," James said lightly, as he stood up, "to bind myself over for seven years to one of your Adventurers. . . ."

"Nor that. You're not the type. Our Adventurers are mostly married men. And few of them would be willing to have that bold rogue's face of yours constantly in the company of his wife. But surely you have friends who have means enough to advance you—"

"I have," James said quietly. "But I have also my Highlander's pride. 'Twas only by forgetting his that my poor father fell into debt. I fear me I shall have to postpone my voyage. . . ."

"A pity," the General said again; "we sail late in October. If, by then—"

"Small chance," James said; and, bowing, took his leave.

The rain had grown harder. He moved through the streets towards the bank, morose and frowning. His life was plagued empty. No Sue—no Maebelle—no one. And the company of the Rakes and Fops at Will's and White's was beginning to pall upon him. The other night, a young Lord, much too exquisite for James' tastes, had persistently invited him to dine at his diggings. James had politely refused; whereupon the Lord had flown into a pet.

"I know your sort," he cried, his tenor rising into a soprano; "gross brutes—with no understanding of the subtler ways of life and love—"

James had stared at him wordlessly; certain talk he had heard coming crystal clear in his mind. This was one of—those, then. The type which—

"Yes, milord," he'd said with dangerous quiet, "I am a gross brute, for a fact. Now leave me, before I prove well just how gross a brute I am!"

He remembered, suddenly, the Highlands, with the heather blowing purple on the moor. The hills blue with the distance. The little talking wind, blowing gaily through the glens. . . .

Aye, mayhap the feel of a broadaxe in his hands would be good. Perhaps, in a new land, he could build one day such a house as the Perkins lived in—the house he loved so well that ever since he had carried the drawing he had made of it around with him, always in his pocket like a good luck charm. Make it the seat of a dynasty of new world Jarretts. Become there—the first Jarrett. The stern patriarch of his clan, rather than the last offshoot of a family sunk in ruin—as he was here. . . .

He moved on through the rain. The very city seemed to be waiting, crouched in the darkness like a shapeless monster. He felt a cold sensation between his shoulder blades. His skin roughened as though from—fear. The night was alive with dark expectations; there was an electric quality in the air. Something's going to happen, he mused; I feel it in my bones. And it damned well won't be good. . . .

Then, as if in answer to his thought, he was jerked, physically out of his reverie. Rude hands clapped down suddenly upon his shoulders. He whirled to face three men, armed with tipstaffs, pistols and an air of authority.

"Ye'll come along quietly," the leader growled. "Aye, look upon him, lads! How fine he is. Profitable business, highway robbery. . . ."

"Just who the devil do you think I am?" James snarled.

"I don't think. I know. Ye're Walt Blackstone, highwayman deluxe —and there be a price upon your head, so come!"

"One moment, Constable," James said evenly; "I take it you can read?"

"I know my letters, ruddy well. But enough of this. Come along!"

"Nay, wait," James snapped. He pulled out of the pocket of his coat, letters, papers, accounts, all upon the stationery of the Bank. A memorandum from Fred Perkins, addressed to him. He passed them over.

"My name, for your information," he said icily, "is James Jarrett. I work, and have worked, for some months at Perkins, Limited, a banking establishment on the Strand. If you care to accompany me there, Mr. Perkins, himself, will identify me. In any event, take your filthy paws off me, and at once!"

The Constable stared at him. Then he ran his eye over the papers James had given him.

"Turn 'im loose, boys," he said at last. "We've made a mistake. I'm right sorry, Sir. But, damn it all, ye do look like a highwayman!"

"So I've been told," James smiled. "Mayhap I'll take it up, one fine day. Betimes, I'll go on struggling with ledgers and accounts. My papers, please!"

The Constable passed them over.

"Ye're not a bad-looking lad," he said. " 'Twas not that I meant, young Sir. Ye doubtless cut a swath among the maids. But ye have the look of a fine roguery about ye, fer a fact. And were I owner of a bank, the minute a broth of a lad with a mug like yours entered it, I'd surely call the guard!"

James threw back his head and laughed aloud.

"Plague take it, but I like your frankness, man," he said. "Have a pint of stout and bitters with me tonight, when you come off duty. I'll meet you at Will's. . . ."

"Tonight, I can't," the Constable said; "but I'll meet ye there tomorrow, if ye be still so inclined—"

"Done," James said. "I want to learn how a man sets himself up in the business of highway robbery. Since everyone persists in thinking me a rogue, I might as well begin—"

"Ya jest," the Constable said. " 'Tis a rotten calling, me fine lad. Stick to yer bank. There ye can be assured of dying in bed of peaceful old age, instead o' choking yer life out upon the gallows. Th' top o' the afternoon to you, young Sir. And me apologies—"

"Think no more on it," James said. "A natural enough mistake. 'Til tomorrow night, then?"

" 'Til tomorrow night," the Constable said.

The day wore on. James' mind wandered. Five hundred acres! What a quantity of rye and oats a man could raise upon that. Fine horses, too —a cross between gaited English and barb. A house like the Perkins'—

He made mistakes, had to do each column of figures over several times. When he came out of the bank, it was already dark, and the rain still fell sullenly.

Will's or White's? he mused. Neither. I couldn't stomach the chatter—the endless shredding of feminine reputations. The thing itself is ruddy pleasant; but to talk about it, afterwards? What are they trying to prove? That they're really men, and not of his lordship's persuasion? Rum way to prove it. A man does what he must, then keeps his blinking trap tight shut. Thank God I've never been guilty of that kind of talk. . . .

The evening stretched out before him, blank and vacant. People moved through the mists, like dream shapes, distorted by the darkness, their footsteps ringing hollowly on the wet stones. Now and again, the lights of a tavern illuminated their faces. Suddenly white, above the shadowy silhouettes, they seemed to float disembodied upon the darkness.

Such was his life: to wander in the rainwet night, peopled by the ghosts of strangers . . . Georgia was warm and sunny, General Oglethorpe had said . . . But ten servants! Five hundred pounds, at least—mayhap a thousand. And he'd jolly well blown the two hundred he'd gained by his lucky stroke. Blown it upon loose maids, drink, gaming, and reckless companions. . . .

Small chance, he sighed. I'd best go home and see after father. He'll be deuced disappointed when I tell him—

Nor that. Mrs. Murphy, the fat Irishwoman he had hired to take care of Laird Jonathan, was competent enough. What he needed was to sit and talk—with someone. Someone who found his company pleasant. Someone who cared about him—if there were such in all the world. . . .

Jane Perkins. But he was rather a bit too fond of Jane. And she was married to a fine man, in many ways his benefactor. Best to leave her be. . . .

He stopped short, frowning. In all London, in all that sprawling, rainwhipped town, there was not one soul with whom he could sit and chat upon a plane of gentle fondness. No one at all, except, mayhap—Sue.

He turned at once and hailed a cab. Sue lived in Westminster, a plagued long way from here. And he knew not whether she'd receive him or no. Still—he was alone and the night remained an aching void. He gave the cabby the address.

A manservant took his card. He had to wait an abominable time, before the man appeared again.

"Pray come in, Sir," the footman said.

Sue was sitting in the living room with her father. He was tall and stern, a military man, obviously. He looked like a greying lion.

"Father," Sue whispered, "this is James Jarrett, of whom I've spoken to you once or twice. . . ."

Bruce Merrick stood up, put out an immensely strong hand.

"Welcome, young Sir," he growled. "Sue tells me you're a Lord?"

"Not yet," James said. "My father is, though—"

"I see. We were talking about that subject when you came. Seems I've made the King's Honors list. From here on, 'twill be Sir Bruce Merrick, Bart. Fat lot of good that does me, with only this chit of a girl to inherit . . . Sit down, sit down. You look half frozen. Rum August, what? Some brandy to warm your blood?"

"Thank you," James said, his eyes upon Sue.

"Don't fret, Sir James," Bruce Merrick boomed. "I'll leave you two alone to talk, after a bit. But first, tell me: how is life in Scotland, these days?"

"I don't really know, Sir," James said; "I've spent most of my life in Edinburgh—which is more English than Scotch. My father took me away from the Highlands as a child—"

Bruce Merrick sat and sat. It was growing plagued late. James began to fear he'd have to go without having a chance to talk to Sue at all. She had changed. She was much thinner—almost slender. It didn't become her. She was one of those girls who was meant to be plump. Her eyes were blue-ringed. They looked as if they'd often been employed in weeping.

"Father!" she said suddenly, desperately, "will you leave us? I've some things to say to Beau James—"

"Things unfit for my ears?" Bruce Merrick growled.

"No, father. They're fit enough—only they're a maid's things, and I—I couldn't say them before you. . . ."

Bruce Merrick stared at James.

"Sue tells me you're ruddy poor," he said bluntly.

"She tells the truth," James said. "I have but my wages at the bank."

"Oh, father!" Sue wailed.

"And 'tis true," Bruce Merrick said, "that you told her you'd never marry wealth?"

"Aye, I said that, right enough," James said evenly; "and I meant it. I'm not such a man as to live upon a woman's sufferance."

"Noble sentiments. I like you, my boy. You've a look about you that I thought no longer existed. An antique Roman look. Come and see me at my offices tomorrow. You know where they are?"

"Yes. Sue has told me."

"Good. You're not too proud to accept a bit of aid in mending your fortunes? A few names—a suggestion or two, that's all. The achieving of it will be up to you. . . ."

"Upon that basis," James smiled, "I am not too proud. . . ."

"Good!" the new Sir Bruce said again. "Good night to you, young Sir. Don't keep my daughter up over late. . . ."

But, after her father had gone upstairs, the silence between them lay fathoms deep.

"Sue," James said at last, "you'll pardon me if I tell you that you look like ruddy hell?"

"I know," she whispered. "And it's your fault, Beau James. I can't sleep; I've no appetite at all—and crying's hardly good for the eyes. . . ."

"Look, Lass," James said morosely, "you mustn't be that fond of me. I'm not at all worth it."

"I know you're not. You're cruel, heartless, selfish, and a wicked cad. But, somehow, it seems I can't help it. . . ."

"Oh, damn father anyhow!" James growled. "If he hadn't shown up when he did—"

"I should hate you, now," Sue whispered, "instead of—of loving you. As I do. With my whole heart. Fine lot of good that does me!"

"I don't think you'd have hated me," James grinned. "When it comes to that gentle pastime, I—"

"I should have hated you," Sue said flatly, "and despised myself. You're mistaken, quite, Beau James. I doubt not that—that loving you would have been—pleasant. Mayhap, even wonderful. That has nothing to do with it. That changes not at all the fact that you consider me a—a convenience to be used, for a night or two, then tossed aside—a trifle soiled. That nothing about me interests you enough for you to want to have those nights as long as we both should live. . . ."

"Look, Sue," he growled.

"Those nights," she whispered, her eyes bright with sudden tears, "and all my days as well, which is a thing you men never think of. The being beside you—comforting you, cherishing you. Listening to your hopes, your dreams. Telling you mine, though I doubt that you would listen. Doing things for you—all the little things that warm a woman's heart each time she does them for her man—sewing buttons, say, mending, making some favorite dish, instead of leaving it to the cook, who wouldn't make it—with love. Even—mothering your sons. There is, Beau James, ever so much more to love than bedding with one's partner! Which is why, in my heart, I pity you—"

"You pity me?" James growled.

"Yes. You're like a blind man in an art gallery. Or a deaf mute at a concert. You miss so much, so much! All the little, delicate, subtler things: a smile, an accidental touch of a hand bring you no joy. You don't even know me. You look upon me with your vision distorted by—lust. An ugly thing. I—I hate it, Beau James! I don't want to be just desired; I want to be loved. . . ."

"Mayhap you will be," James whispered; "even by—me, given time—"

"No," Sue said, and stood up. "You see only—my body. My plump, attractive body. But my body's not me, Beau James. I dwell in it, like a person in a house. But it is not me!"

"Quite a house, I must say!" James laughed. "Deuced decorative!"

Sue stood there, staring at him.

"Good night, Beau James," she said. "Thanks for calling. . . ."

"And if I come again, you'll receive me?" James said.

"Yes. I am always—polite. But I'd rather that you didn't."

"Why?" he said.

"I am not strong. One day, I'd come to accept you upon—your terms. Accept the crumbs of your affection, instead of the feast. So father's right to regret not having a son—"

"So that he could call me out in your defense?" James said.

"No. Because a son would be strong enough to live up to the motto father's chosen for his new coat of arms. It's Latin, and I can't say it right, so I won't even try. But what it means in English is: 'Death before Dishonor.' "

"Damned sententious!" James laughed.

"You have a gift for mocking noble things, haven't you?" Sue said bitterly; "or sneering at them. Which is another thing about you I don't like. In fact, I don't believe I like you at all. As a person, you're absolutely insufferable. Only I happen to be in love with you. Not a reasonable emotion, what? I'm trying to get over it. And, if you'll have the decency to stay away from me—providing you have any decency about you at all, a thing I doubt—I will get over it. Otherwise—"

"Otherwise?" James prompted.

"I'll be like that phrase father is so fond of quoting from Sir Francis Bacon: 'Who can see worse days than he that yet living doth follow at the funeral of his own reputation?' But I suppose you'll call that sententious, too. . . ."

"It is," James said. "But tell me one thing, Pigeon: You really want me to stay away from you?"

"No. I don't want you to. I desire your absence, Beau James, as little as a person desires—death. For it will be that for me: a kind of death. But I—I need it. I need a long, empty, peaceful time—to recover my senses, become my own mistress, learn to live again, instead of existing upon my beggar's diet of forlorn hopes. What I want is unimportant; what I need is—vital."

"You've got it," James said flatly. "Goodbye, Sue—"

"Oh, James!" she wailed.

"You're right: I haven't a spark of decency about me anywhere; there is nothing too base for me to do, now. I could become a murderer or a thief. But I do have a rather adequate substitute for decency, a thing that's mayhap stronger: my pride. I have never set foot in a house where my welcome's equivocal. I never shall. So—fare thee well, Pigeon! It's been jolly, quite!"

"James—" she whispered.

"Yes, Sue?"

"Nothing," she said bitterly. "Goodbye!" Then she turned, and fled up the stairs.

The footman showed him out. The sound of the door's closing was curiously loud in the silence. To James, it seemed that it closed upon his youth.

He went off through the rain, walking ever faster, muttering a phrase from Plautus: *Homo homini lupus!* "Man's a wolf to man!"

Georgia, then. In that sunny clime, he could begin again. Become a master of men, instead of one of the crowd. And, once arrived, men would not ask by what route he had come, no more than they had put that query to Pitcairn Hogg. Oh, no. They'd bow and scrape, and court his favor. Human nature could be depended upon.

I'll keep that appointment with the Constable, he thought, flashing a wolfish grin. Aye—the world owes me a debt; and, by heaven and hell, 'twill pay!

CHAPTER NINE

THE LONDON-LANCASTER coach thundered down the road at a hard gallop. On the tossing, jolting seat, the guard leveled his blunderbuss, fired. But the masked rider wasn't there. He went over sidewise, hanging from his horse's neck. Passed the coach. Drew abreast of the right hand lead horse. Put a pistol against the racing animal's head. Pulled the trigger. The horse went down, his teammates falling over him. There was a horrid screaming of broken-legged animals, the splintering of wood. The coach ground to a stop.

The lone highwayman dismounted, sauntered leisurely up to the coach, a fresh pistol dangling negligently in his hand. Below the black mask, his mouth curled into a sardonic smile.

"Ladies and gentlemen," he said easily, "will you have the kindness to descend? I'll not detain you, long. . . ."

The frightened passengers scrambled to the ground.

"You, too, my good man," the bandit said to the guard. "Have no fear; I have a certain repugnance against killing people. That scruple can be overcome, if you insist. So, I pray thee, don't insist. We shall both regret it, if you do. And, mayhap, your widow will regret it even more—at least for a fortnight. After which, human nature being what it is, she'll console herself with the driver. Better to avoid that, what?"

The guard climbed down.

"Now, ladies," the bandit said, "be so good as to pass me over your trinkets. As you may have noted, I'm a man of many scruples—even of a certain delicacy. Far be it from me to rudely snatch your baubles; even in this sad business, one can maintain a certain tone, if one really tries, don't you agree? There, that's a good lass! Milady, your servant!"

Then the highwayman bent and kissed the woman's hand.

He repeated his theatrical, mock gallantry with each of the women passengers whom he robbed—until he came to the last. She was a tiny blonde, some eighteen years of age, and pretty enough to make the angels chant hosannas. She stood there, weeping as she stripped off her rings, brooches, necklace, bracelet.

"Ah, you melt my heart!" the bandit sighed. "Tell me, milady, hold you your trifles worth—a kiss?"

"Y-y-y-yes!" the little blonde sobbed. "They're gifts from Papa—and from Tom. . . ."

"Tom, I take it, is your promised?" the bandit said.

"Y-y-y-yes," the girl wept.

"Lucky, lucky man!" the highwayman said. "I hope he will not begrudge me my kiss. . . ."

Then he bent and touched her lips, lightly as a breath.

"Nectar and ambrosia!" he exclaimed. "Here you are, my pretty maid—all your baubles. What I have robbed you of, I value more. I have not often the opportunity to press the soft petals of so fair a flower. . . ."

With the men, he was almost equally as polite, constantly repeating: "Thank you, kind Sir!" Or: " 'tis a pleasure to do business with such gentlefolk; that's the real reason I took up this trade. Otherwise, my chances for association with my betters would be sharply limited, you understand? And a man must live. Your servant, gentlemen!"

Within a fortnight, London rang with the praises of "The Gentleman," as the new robber came to be known. Broadsides about his feats were scattered about. A starveling bard composed a Pindaric ode in his honor. His victims were lionized.

"I tell you, dearie," the women sighed, " 'tis distinctly a pleasure to be robbed by him! Such address, such grace! Not even a courtier could make a finer leg. And when he kissed my hand, la! The shivers fairly raced up and down my spine. . . ."

The coaches went heavily guarded by outriders, now. But, at a wayside inn, a gruff, stout old gentleman, with white hair and a most imposing belly, invited the outriders to a round of claret. The riders drank, and one by one slumped to the floor, fast asleep.

"Curious," the gruff old gentleman said. "We were better tipplers in my youth. . . ."

Then he went outside, pulled the pillows from beneath his waistcoat, stripped off his white wig, wiped the grease paint from his face, donned his black mask and rode off.

Half an hour later, "The Gentleman" robbed the coach again.

The guard was doubled, supplied with their own ale in leather bottles. "The Gentleman" changed his route and robbed the London-Oxham coach. More guards. The next time it was the Edinburgh coach that fell an easy prey.

All England rocked with laughter. Well do men love a bold and gallant rogue.

And in the Bank upon the Strand, James Jarrett sat upon his high stool, scribbling industriously at his ledgers.

It was economically unfeasible to supply outriders for every coach that left London. "The Gentleman" seemed to know beforehand which ones would be guarded, and which ones not. At times, he changed his tactics: fell upon a stage guarded by no less than three riders, outpistoled, and outfenced all three, dealing them trifling wounds in the process; forced one at gunpoint to bind his fellows to the wheels; bound the last, himself, and robbed the coach with his usual neatness, efficiency, and dispatch.

Time was growing short now. The good ship *Simmons* floated on the tide at Cowes. The emigrants were coming aboard daily. General Oglethorpe gave a farewell dinner at Pontack's for all his friends and the Trustees of the new colony, on September 25th. On October 14th, he took his leave of the Queen and set out to join the vessel. James Jarrett almost despaired; but that same night the winds began to blow with gale force. The Captain refused to sail. Week after week, the bad weather held, and the ship lingered at Cowes. The General, himself, was bedridden of a fever. James Jarrett took hope.

One more good haul, he thought, and we'll make it!

But that one last good haul proved very nearly fatal. He performed the feat at the very gates of London, at ten o'clock at night. Fled, hotly pursued by the guards, through the streets of Westminster. His barb had received a pistol ball, and was losing strength steadily. At that hour, there were no crowds among whom he could lose himself. There was but one thing to do, so, reluctantly, he did it.

He rode up to a certain wall, stood up in the saddle, and vaulted to the top. Leaned down and gave the poor wounded beast a slap on the rump. Hit the ground hard in a long soaring leap. Hid his loot beneath the back stairs. Then he climbed the trellis to Sue's room.

She sat up in bed, her eyes wide and frightened. He clapped a stern hand over her mouth.

"Don't scream," he grated. "I'm being pursued. Only you can save me, if you will. Otherwise, Lass, it's—the gallows. D'you hate me enough for that?"

Dumbly Sue shook her head. He took his hand away from her mouth.

"Good!" he grinned. "Now hide me. They may trace me here. . . ."

"Go down the hall," she whispered, "to father's room. It's the last on the left. He—he's not at home—"

James' eyes were suddenly very bright.

"Lock yourself in," Sue went on. "And, Beau James—this door will be locked, too, since I'm sure I read your eyes aright—"

"A pity," James mocked; "but as you will, Pigeon—as you will!"

"James—what are you being pursued for?"

He smiled at her.

"Robbery. Highway robbery—of which I'm ruddy guilty. You've heard of 'The Gentleman'?"

"Oh, James, no! You're not—"

He made her a deep, sardonic bow.

" 'The Gentleman,' and your humble servant, milady!" he said.

"How horrible!" Sue wept. "Oh, Beau James, how could you?"

"Easily enough," he said; "there's nothing to it. I point a pistol at the men, kiss all the lassies, and the thing is done. Besides, it's your fault, anyhow, Pigeon. . . ."

"My fault?" Sue gasped.

"You made me decide that London, vast as it is, was not big enough for both of us. I—I missed you damnably, Sue. So I'm bound for Georgia, once I've accumulated my passage—and father's—"

"Oh, Beau James! I—I want to die!"

"Rubbish, Pigeon. There'll be some likely lad for you; and better far than I'll ever be. . . ."

"But—" Sue began; then they heard the pounding on the door.

James made a dash for the closet.

"No!" Sue hissed. "They'll look there first of all. Off with your things, and get into bed!"

He stared at her.

"I'll say you've been—with me—since eight. That I told you father was—away. Is eight enough time?"

"Plenty," he grinned. "I robbed that coach at ten!"

He stripped off his boots, cloak, and hat. Hesitated a moment. Growled: "Turn your back, Pigeon!"

Sue turned her face away from him. A moment later, he hurled his clothes over a chair, and leaped into bed. Sue covered him up. The knocking came again, louder now.

"Just—just a minute," Sue quavered.

She went to the door, opened it a crack. The footman, clad in night-cap and robe, stared at her with frightened eyes.

"They say—there's a robber in the house, milady!" he croaked. "They were pursuing him and—"

"Tell them to search, then," Sue said evenly.

"We will," the Constable growled. "And begging yer pardon, milady—we'll start right 'ere!"

Roughly he shoved by her into the room. Sue stared at her foot-man's face.

"Aye, boys! 'Ere 'e is!" the Constable roared. "Snug as a bug in a rug. Wimmen! I ask you!"

Sue turned away from the footman's gaze, her eyes sick with shame.

James Jarrett came up on one elbow, blinking sleepily. He was naked to the waist.

"Oh, Miss Sue!" the footman choked, his voice humid with tears. "Yer poor father!"

"That," Sue said coldly, "is not the man you seek. This, gentlemen, is James Jarrett, an honorable employee at Perkins' Bank—and, quite obviously, my lover. Runyon here, has seen him several times here at the house . . ."

"My Lady speaks the truth," Runyon, the footman, groaned.

The Constables hesitated.

"Well now," their leader growled; "we don't want to make no mis-takes. False arrest can cost a body dear. Still, young Sir, if ye be who the lady claims, Mr. Perkins, himself, can identify ye, now can't 'e?"

"Yes," James said.

"Then if ye be innercent, ye'll 'ave no objections to coming along to 'is diggings. Ye aren't under arrest, mind ye—just in temporary custody 'til 'e clears the matter up. Fair enough?"

"Quite," James said crisply.

"Then up with ye, me fine lad," the Constable said, "and come with us."

"Turn your back, Sue," James said.

"Rather late for modesty now, isn't it, Beau James?" Sue said bitterly. But she turned her back just the same.

As bad luck would have it, Tom Morris, The Ferret, was just leaving the Perkins' house, as James, surrounded by the Constables, arrived. Alone of all Fred Perkins' employees, The Ferret had the right to call upon his employer at any hour of the night, if he deemed his information of sufficient urgency. The very nature of his work, tracing fleeing debtors, demanded that. There were times, when, had he waited until morning, the fugitive might well be permanently out of reach.

So the chance encounter at nearly midnight was not strange. But it was unfortunate. For Tom took one look and jumped to conclusions. Rushed off to tell Jonathan Jarrett his son was under arrest. The results were very bad. In fact—they were fatal.

Fred Perkins had already gone up stairs. He came down again in slippers and a dressing gown. Naturally, under the circumstances, his mood was hardly jovial.

"James!" he growled, "what the devil have you done?"

"Nothing," James said easily. "Which is why we're here. But first, Sir, permit me to beg your pardon for this intrusion. Unfortunately, it cannot be helped. These gentlemen are laboring under the odd misapprehension that I am 'The Gentleman', that notorious rogue of celebrated ill fame. . . ."

"How perfectly ridiculous!" Jane Perkins said from the stair. She had, of course, followed her husband, especially since she had caught the butler's whispered words: "Your clark, Sir—young Jarrett. Under arrest, it appears. Fair surrounded by tipstaffers!"

"One minute, my dear," Fred said. "I'd like to get to the bottom of this. Would you, Constable, be so kind as to tell me why you believe my clerk is a highwayman?"

"Well, Sir," the head Constable said uneasily, "it were an 'onest mistake, 'specially since ye've already identified 'im to my satisfaction. In the first place, 'e looks just like the blinking 'ighwayman—"

"Rubbish," Fred Perkins snorted. "Hundreds of people look alike. You'll have to do better than that, Sir! Arresting people on trumped up charges is actionable under the law!"

"I know, Sir," the Constable said. "Which is why 'e ain't under arrest. 'E was, 'e'd be in Newgate by now. No, 'e come along voluntary to prove 'e ain't who we thought. . . ."

"I see. But why in the name of everything unholy did you think a thing like that?"

"We chased the real 'Gentleman' into Westminster, Sir. 'E jumped a wall into Sir Bruce Merrick's garden. So we surrounded the house, but 'e must 'ave jumped another wall into somebody else's place. Anyhow we caught this young Sir in the house—seems 'e was taking advantage of 'is Lordship's absence; 'cause, begging yer lady's pardon we found 'im in the girl's—bed—"

"Oh, James!" Jane Perkins gasped. "How could you!"

"Easily enough, it appears," Fred said tartly. "That little Sue always did have—well—a certain look. And amatory escapades are hardly a crime, my dear; not when both parties are unmarried and of age."

He turned back to the Constable.

"I take it you're satisfied then, my good man?" he growled. "For, if you're not, I can tell you that this lad once saved myself and my wife from being robbed by just the sort you've accused him of being. Fought like a tiger, he did. And, if you should bother to think about it, answer me this question: Why should a man with the opportunity before him daily to embezzle hundreds of thousands, stoop to the rather inelegant pursuit of highway robbery?"

"Now that's a fact," the Constable said admiringly; "but I don't 'ave to go so far, Sir. All that was needful was for ye to identify 'im. Now that ye 'ave, 'e's as free as a bird. . . ."

Which, it proved, was not so free after all. For when James finally got back to his lodgings, after wandering nightlong through the streets, thinking on the enormity of the thing he had done to Sue, trying to decide what, if anything, he could do to compensate her for the sacrifice of a spotless reputation to save his worthless neck, he found Mrs. Murphy bowed down in tears.

"Yer poor, poor Guv'ner," she wept. "He was took off sudden like . . . Kind of a fit—after that fool Tom Morris told him you was in gaol. Ranted 'n raved sumpin' awful—betwixt fits o' coughing, that is. Abegging and apleading with you just like you was here—to leave London—to go to the Indies—to some place called Georgia. . . ."

"I know," James whispered.

"But, at the end, he was calm. Made me bring out his bundle, and spread that funny woman's dress you Scotsmen wear across the foot o' his bed. Said you was to put it on. ''Cause not even that wild whelp,' sez he, 'would dare dishonor the tartan of his clan!' Then he got worse. Tim had him took to the Charity hospital, but 'twere too late. He was dead afore they got him there. . . ."

James left her, stumbled into his bedroom, stood there looking at his father's plaid tartan and kilt with tear-blinded eyes. Stripped off his well cut suit, dressed again in the flowing Highland garb. Made his way to the hospital. Knelt before that silent figure on the marble slab. Said:

"You're in heaven, Father, and at peace. While I'm alive. Alive in hell! On borrowed time, lent me by a maid who gave up for my worthless sake what she valued more than life. You're right, Father; I cannot dishonor the tartan of my clan. And 'tis a fitting garb to perform the act I now must do!"

But he did not seek out Sue at once. The sad business of arranging a decent burial for his father detained him some two days. Then there was the further matter, of collecting and disposing of his hidden loot. For, though he hated the sight of it by now, the hard fact remained that the fruits of his crimes were the only means by which he could carry out Laird Jonathan's dying wish. All of which took time. He had to proceed with extreme caution. He was not at all sure that the Constabulary did not suspect him still; and if he were seen entering the door of a known or suspected receiver of stolen goods, the whole matter would burst wide open again.

So, on the pretext of needing a rest, he journeyed to Liverpool, and disposed of his ill-gotten wealth there, receiving for it far less than he would have in London. Then he came back to the capital—too late.

For, even as he descended from the stage, he was stopped cold by the voice of a newsvender bawling in the street.

"Great scandal!" the man was shouting. "Bart's daughter 'n a lowly banking clark! Surprised by the Constables! Read all about it!"

James thrust a ha'penny into that grimy hand. Took a sheet. It wasn't a newspaper as he should have known it wouldn't be, but a badly printed broadside. Initials had been substituted for names. Sue was called Lady S. He was not even identified beyond the phrase "an humble employee at a respectable local Banking House." The broadside was not signed. The writer of this distorted account, filled with thinly veiled obscenities, had skirted the edge of the libel laws with care and skill.

James stood there, death in his heart.

"That goddamned blabbermouth of a constable!" he muttered through set teeth. Then he turned and hailed a cab.

"Sir Bruce Merrick's!" he snapped. "Westminster—if you're the one person in all London who doesn't know where it is by now!"

Runyon met him at the door with stern and disapproving face.

" 'Twould be wiser, Sir," he said stiffly, "if you went away. Sir Bruce is set to pistol you!"

"He's quite right," James sighed. "I came to give him the opportunity. I richly deserve it, Runyon. But, if he will hear me out, I mean to undo the harm I've done, as fully as I can. I think I can serve him rather better as a son-in-law than as a corpse, what?"

Slowly Runyon nodded.

"Yes, that would be best, wouldn't it, Sir?" he said gravely. "I'll tell Sir Bruce of your intentions. Mayhap he'll cool off a mite. And, Sir—I trust you'll be good to Miss Sue. After all, she saved your life. . . ."

"I'll worship her on my knees, lifelong," James growled. "Runyon—"

"Yessir?"

"For your own good comfort, she lied. She's as spotless as the day she was born. I reached her room not five minutes before the runners. . . ."

"God, Sir! She did *that* for you?"

"Aye, she did. Now go and announce me," James said.

Bruce Merrick received him frostily.

"Were it not for my baby," he growled, "I'd not deprive myself of the pleasure of shooting you, you Scottish dog. Only that would remedy nothing. You've my deuced unwilling consent. Where would you like to go? Sue damned well can't live in London, now. I've branches in Scotland, Ireland, Wales—"

"Ireland," James interrupted. "I've had enough of my native land. . . ."

"More likely they've had enough of you!" Sir Bruce snapped. "Ireland it is, then. But if you ever abuse or mistreat my daughter, I'll—"

"You need have no fear of that, Sir," James said.

"Good. I'll send for her now. And leave you alone with her. Even a proposal of this sort merits privacy. And because a maid's honor cannot be lost but once, she's in no further danger. Good day, Sir. We'll work out the details after you've talked with Sue. . . ."

She came slowly into the room.

"Good day, Beau James," she whispered.

He took a stride forward, stretched out his arms. She leaped backward as though he were a snake.

"Don't touch me!" she shuddered. "Your touch would dirty me, now, Beau James, I think!"

"Sue—" he groaned.

"No, James. Father tells me you've come to ask my hand. To—remedy the—the damage that you've done. As if you could! What remedy will bind a broken heart, Beau James? What sort of cure know you for shame?"

"None," he said honestly; "but I should like to try. For you, Pigeon, are an angel out of heaven!"

"For God's sake, James, don't call me Pigeon. You've lost the right. Reserve your quaint endearments for the wenches in the taverns where you thieves hang out. You must have your share of that sort. And it suits them rather better than it does me. . . ."

"Sue, I swear to you there's no one else—"

Her eyes cut him short.

"And that there's never been, Beau James?" she said.

"That, no," he said soberly. "I've sins of the flesh enough upon my soul, I'll admit. But, no more! As long as I live, I'll never look upon a maid again, save you. . . ."

"Look all you like," Sue said tonelessly. "It's all the same to me. I don't propose to join the wide circle of your strumpets in actual fact, though I seem to have already joined them in name. . . ."

"Sue, for God's love!"

"No, James. You see, I don't love you anymore. I rather despise you—which is a pity. I'd thought I could hate you; but I can't. You aren't even worthy of so fine a thing as hate. I—I couldn't see you hanged, that was all. So, now go away from here with your gratitude! I'd never take a man upon that basis. I—I still insist upon being loved. As Grace says, there is no other acceptable basis for a marriage. . . ."

"But Sue," he almost wept, "I love you, now! God in Heaven is my witness that I do!"

"Don't blaspheme," she said dryly. "For, even were you telling the truth, as I see you think you are, my answer would be the same: No,

James. Very quietly and simply—no. I can stand the pointing fingers, the whispers, the life of loneliness and shame I've taken upon myself for your sake. But, Beau James, Gentleman Thief, by heaven and hell, I could not stand being married to such a thing—as you!"

He hung there, his face grey, death in his heart.

"Goodbye, Beau James," Sue said simply. "My best wishes to your father. He, at least, is a man. I wonder where he got you from!"

"He *was* a man, Sue," James whispered, the tears bright and un-ashamed in his eyes. "I—I could not e'en hold his hand, and bid him godspeed when he—went. I was—in custody. And he died—knowing that. . . ."

"Oh, my God!" Sue whispered.

"So," James went on bitterly, "now I am alone—in a world peopled with the ghosts of my sins. My father's life—and your reputation—these, these were the price upon which my freedom's based! Think you I'll ever be free?"

Sadly she shook her head.

"No," she said. "I think you never will."

"Sue," he said with desperate urgency, "I need you! Not for merely saving your reputation, but for my own sake! Without you I'll live out my days in hell. You've done so much—cannot you do this little more?"

She stood there, staring at him. Then she said it, very softly:

"No, James, I'm sorry, but—I can't."

So it was that when, finally, on December 3rd, 1735, the good ship *Simmons* weighed anchor and crawled out of the harbor of Cowes upon a freshening wind, a young man leaned over the aft rail, staring at the fading shore. A young man, the passengers judged, from the way his broad shoulders filled his tartan, and the sturdy, well turned legs beneath his kilt—until he turned and they saw his eyes.

They were as old as time.

CHAPTER TEN

THE VOYAGE WAS terrible. From December 8th, 1735, the day they dropped the shores of England behind them, until February 5th, 1736, when the *Simmons* sighted the coast of Georgia, the periods of calm could only be counted in hours. Not a man aboard her, in his heart of hearts, believed they would reach the colony alive. Not even James Jarrett. But between him and his fellow sufferers from the torments of seasickness, there existed one fundamental difference: he rather hoped they wouldn't.

Two days out, during one of those rare intervals of calm—which was to say only that the *Simmons,* instead of standing on her beams' ends, and alternately pointing her prow at the heavens, and attempting to plunge straight for the ocean's floor, was rolling but at a moderate forty-five degree angle, and pitching at something around fifteen— James was standing at the lee rail watching that devil's dance of wind and water with a grim smile on his face. He was enjoying the tumult. It accorded with his mood. Then he saw a young man coming towards him. He knew who the young man was: John Wesley, who, along with his brother Charles, had come along to take charge of the religious affairs of the colony.

Before young Wesley even reached him, James had his Highland dander up. He could not have, even to himself, defined the emotion that gripped him. It was, actually, very simple and endlessly complicated at one and the same time. James Jarrett was protecting the line of his retreat. He was, after all, a Highlander—of a race fundamentally devout. And he knew beyond all possibility of doubt that his sins had no pardon on earth or in heaven. So, having become an outcast from the comforts of the spirit, he reacted as outcasts always do: he sought to obtain some kind of status by rejecting in his turn what he knew he could never more obtain. Hence, he instinctively saw in the young founder of Methodism an enemy. His response to John Wesley was the age-old response of outlaws to pillars of respectability, the maintainers of social order: wild, unreasoning hate.

"I say, Brother Jarrett," young Wesley began. That was as far as he got.

"Brother?" James snarled. "I was not aware, Sir, that my late father's amorous activities extended so far afield as Yorkshire. In fact, I doubt they did. And I doubt even more that a canting, pious maid would have interested him in the least!"

John Wesley stood there, his face very white. Then, with truly Christian resignation, he bowed before the insult direct.

" 'Tis but a form of address, Mr. Jarrett," he said quietly. "If Mister suits you better, I'll call you that. . . ."

"It does not," James snapped. "You may address me, if you must address me at all, as Sir James. Or milord. Sir James Jarrett, Marquis of Argyll, Lord and Chief of Clan Jarrett, and *not* your servant, Sir!"

"I'm sorry," John Wesley smiled a little pityingly. "I was not aware of your rank, Sir James. My purpose in addressing you is, in any case, a friendly one: I wanted to invite you, personally, to join our morning and evening services. . . ."

"Thank you," James mocked; "but I must decline, Sir, as I am not of your Faith. . . ."

"That does not matter. All Protestants are welcome—and even Papists, too. I have converted a number of the latter to the true way. . . ."

"I belong to neither band, Reverend," James said flatly. "Your scope is not wide enough to include the likes of me. . . ."

"I take it that you're a freethinker, then? Even so—"

"I'm not a freethinker," James said sardonically; "in mine own way, I'm most devout. But to save you from prying further: I, Sir, am a devotee of the Devil!"

"The Devil?" John Wesley gasped.

"Aye. Lucifer, Mephistopheles, His Satanic Majesty—call him what you will. The true Master of men, before whom, in secret, even you pious ones bow. And, to return the compliment, I'll invite you, come Michaelmas, to join the Black Sabbath, and prostrate yourself before our cloven-hoofed Lord!"

"Sir James!" John Wesley got out.

"Leave me," James said brusquely. "My stomach's occupied enough
with wind and wave. And it ill supports cant even on dry land!"

To his credit, be it said that John Wesley tried several more times
before giving the task up as hopeless. Even then, the other good men
of the cloth aboard, Charles Wesley, Francis Moore, Benjamin Ingham,
David Nitschmann, and John Andrew Dober, all took turns in the
attempt to convert the "Devil Worshiper." Naturally, in so small a com-
pass as a sailing vessel, James' mocking, and completely false declaration of faith was noised abroad. Poor Mrs. Welch, the wife of one of
the emigrants, already great with child, ran and hid each time she saw
him coming, at least until the dreadful weather and her increasing
heaviness confined her to General Oglethorpe's cabin, which that gallant gentleman gave up for her sake.

"He hath the evil eye!" she wailed. "I want no Satan's hoofprint
on the forehead of my child!"

She did not realize that, far from having any intention to cast a spell
upon her, James scarcely realized she was alive—and cared even less.
He was concerned only with maintaining his brooding solitude. The
company of his fellows, male and female alike, had become anathema
to him.

Most of all, he avoided the General. For that great man's behavior
was a living reproof to him. Without being obviously religious—his
negligence of services was only a little short of James' own—the General
gave a practical demonstration of daily Christian charity that put the
Ministers aboard to utter shame. Not only did he surrender his comfortable cabin to Mrs. Welch, but he ate only the coarse salt fare of
the sailors, so that his portion of the fresh provisions might go to the
sick. He visited the sufferers constantly, full of tender compassion and
fatherly advice. When he discovered that the crew were scanting the
few debtors aboard in the distribution of water, his wrath was Jovian:

"Aboard this vessel," he thundered, "all men are equal, and are to
be treated alike!"

Moreover, he forbade the crew's intent to subject the passengers,
landlubbers to a man, to the rough horseplay in worship of King Nep-
tune. It is probable that his orders would have been disobeyed had it
not been for James Jarrett. Seeing the crewmen, a trifle worse for grog,
laying rude hands on Charles Wesley, James promptly stretched their

leader out senseless upon the deck. Then he turned on his heels and went his way, having settled that matter for good and all.

That, and even another he didn't even know about: for, as the voyage wore on, attended by bad weather without let-up, the more superstitious aboard began to attribute the all but unbearable hardships of their passage to the Job-like presence among them of a trafficker in demonism. And the suggestion that heaving him over the side one dark night might help matters passed in whispers from man to man. Only, having seen how James had served the sailors who had attempted to haze Charles Wesley, a volunteer to do the actual heaving proved impossible to find.

On the morning of February 5th, at long, long last, and to the vast relief of every manjack aboard, save alone James Jarrett, they sighted Tybee Island like a greenish brown haze low down on the horizon. The Wesleys organized a thanksgiving service at once. Every man, woman, and child aboard knelt upon the deck—except James. He stood in the prow, gazing at the island growing very slowly before his dark eyes as the vessel crawled toward it.

A new world, he thought darkly. A new life. Ha! That I doubt. For certain 'tis that I have brought myself with me. . . .

A statement which, within the next forty-eight hours, he proceeded to prove to the complete conviction of everybody.

That night, as they lay off Tybee, the emigrants were startled by a sound unlike any other under heaven. It sounded like a legion of amorous tomcats wailing at the same time. Then it rose to the shriek of a banshee, warbled high and shrill upon as inharmonious a note as ever assaulted human hearing. To a man, the passengers rushed aft toward the sound. Came to an abrupt halt. Stood there, spellbound, before the spectacle of Laird James Jarrett, clad, as always, in tartan and kilt, playing his father's bagpipes.

He had but scant practice at it. He had not picked up the traditional instrument of the Highlanders since he left his native hills as a child. But that made little difference. To the untrained ear, the bloodcurdling wails produced by the greatest master of the pipes alive and the fumblings of an utter duffer are completely indistinguishable from one another.

He ignored his audience as though they were not there. Went on playing, frowning and intent. There was, under all the caterwauling, a recognizable fragment of a tune. It was the warsong of Clan Jarrett. He played it in memory of his father. And in defiance of the world.

The next day, February 6th, 1736, he marched ashore, again playing that wild tune, but somewhat more surely, and with a certain verve. It cut through the thunder of the twenty-one guns that were being fired in the General's honor. Then he lowered the mouthpiece from his lips and looked around. Savannah, he decided at once, was neither Edinburgh nor London. But it was, he had to admit, a cut above his Highland home. It was a rectangular clearing, with rude frame houses set in precise squares. It was perched atop a high bluff. To get to it from the river, one had to climb forty half-log stairs. Lining the bluff was a rail fence, placed there, James was sardonically sure, to prevent the drunkards from falling into the river. At one corner of the clearing, close to both the bluff's edge and the dense forests that surrounded Savannah on every side, was the fort. Above it, the Union Jack fluttered in the breeze. And that was it. That was all. A man could cover the greatest metropolis in Georgia with one long sweeping glance.

The people, however, proved more interesting. There were Salzburgers, Moravians, talking together in their guttural German tongue; Swiss, French, and a group James recognized as Highlanders at once, though they did not wear their native dress. The expedition that had set out from Inverness in October, doubtless. . . .

And the General had been right about one thing: the maids were more than fair.

When he thought that, James stopped short, his great Jarrett's eyebrow gathered into a frown. Have you not had enough sorrow of the lassies? he told himself. And have you not dealt them enough in your turn? Have done, lad! You're young yet. The founding of the New World Clan Jarrett can bloody well wait a while. . . .

He turned his gaze toward another group, whose identity he was unable to recognize. The men were all heavily bearded and wore sidecurls. They had on hats with low, rounded crowns and broad brims. These were Savannah's Jews, whom the General, with a breadth of view the world two hundred years later had still to match, had defended stoutly against the colonists who wanted to expel them.

But it was the redskins who, more than any other group, caught James' eye. That Savannah was free from Indian attacks throughout her early history was due to General Oglethorpe's diplomacy and skill. The Creeks literally worshipped him. And his wise act in taking Tomochichi and seven other chiefs to London with him had but cemented the peace. After a four months' stay, the redskins had come home filled with awe at the power and wisdom of Englishmen. Their descriptions of the wonders of London had spread even to the Cherokees, so that even that much more warlike tribe had been brought under the General's sway. Which was a good thing, what with war with the Spaniards, sitting behind their mighty fortress at Saint Augustine in nearby Florida, threatening to break out momentarily. . . .

Despite all his good resolutions—for he was quite correct in his belief that he had brought himself with him—James' gaze strayed back to the laughing, chattering group of maids. Under that bold stare, the laughter and the chatter died. There were all complexions and shapes of lassies in that little crowd. Then he saw the girl—some eighteen years of age, he guessed—standing at the center of them all, and the rest of them, for James Jarrett, vanished abruptly out of time and mind.

She was like a flower. There was no other way to describe her. A delicate early Spring blossom, fragile and fair. Endlessly ethereal. The palest blonde, with lips of soft shell pink and eyes whose blue was that of the very edge of a summer sky, where the deeper azure of higher up fades into a color nearly white. They did not absorb the light as darker eyes do, but threw it back, so that every time she turned her head, they made reflections like still water touched by moonsilver. She was very slender, but the promise of the curves of maturity were beginning tantalizingly to appear. And the sweetness of her face was like a cry in the bitter darkness of his heart.

'Twould be a crime, he thought, to lay rude hands on such a lass! Then, instantly, he made up his mind to do just that.

So busy was he with staring at her, he failed to notice for some time that he was being stared at in his turn. The starers were close at hand: big Northumberland men, the brothers Knox. He did not notice then, that they were one and all gross caricatures of the blonde maid. If he had, mayhap his subsequent behavior might have been different. They moved toward him, ringed him round about. Looked at his kilt, and their broad grins spread.

"Tell me, friend," the eldest, Peter, said, "just what have you beneath yon skirts?"

James looked him up and down. Turned his gaze upon Cromwell Knox as well. Upon Henry, the youngest.

"You speak in jest, friend?" he said softly.

"Nay. Other than a Popish Priest, I've never seen a man in woman's dress before," Peter grinned. "What have you beneath them, friend? Lace?"

"I have beneath my feileadhbeag," James said, using the ancient

Gaelic word for kilts, "a stretch of noble Scottish hide. And more
blood and guts than exists in the whole race of Englishmen. To which,
friend, you'd better show the proper respect. And quickly! On your
knees, ye dogs!"

Peter's big hands doubled into fists. He swung right lustily. Which
was his mistake. One of the things he didn't know about Highland
Lairds was that they fought with their fists only when they couldn't
possibly avoid it. And never when there was a Highland dirk, or a
singlestick, or both, available. Voicing the warcry of his Clan, James
Jarrett drew his two-edged dagger, and proceeded to deftly notch
both Peter's ears and his nostrils like a sow's.

"Thus ever will you remember me!" he snarled, "each time you
gaze upon your ugly countenance in a glass!"

Roaring and splattering blood, Peter rushed forward. In another
minute he would have to kill the big man, James saw. Which would
be a rum way to begin his life in the New World. So he sheathed the
dirk. Picked up his hawthorn stick from beside his duffle bag. Sailed
into all three of them.

Four minutes later, all three were stretched out on the ground, blood
streaming from their cracked pates. James stood over them, holding
his hawthorn club ready to knock down again the first who attempted
to rise.

And the slim blonde maid he had been staring at before came flying
out from among the group of the other lassies.

"Oh, you horrid beast!" she cried. "You've hurt them! Oh, I'll—"

Then with her slender, almost angelic face gone white with rage, she
hurled herself upon him, pounding at his chest with two small, inef-
fectual fists.

James Jarrett's grin was the devil's own. He dropped the stick. Pinioned her in his mighty arms. Bent down and kissed her mouth, slowly,
lingeringly, with all his rakehell's skill.

The pounding stopped. She stiffened, froze. He went on kissing her.
Felt, very slowly, the thaw set in. The stiffness melting into spring
warmth, young, sweetsighing.

He turned her loose. Made her a deep and mocking bow.

"Permit me to present myself, fair lass," he said. "James Jarrett,
Marquis of Argyll, Laird of Clan Jarrett and—your future husband!"

"Oh!" the maid whispered, her face matching the pale shell pink of
her lips.

"And you, milady?" James said.

"Mary Knox," the girl said; then, even more softly: "And I think you're a dreadful man, Sir James!"

"I am," James said cheerfully. "Now off with you, my goodwife to be, and attend to yon gross louts. As little as I have need of such brothers-in-law, 'tis not meet to let them bleed to death. . . ."

He felt then, the hands clapped upon his shoulders. Whirled to face the Captain of the Guard.

"Ye'll come quietly," the Captain growled; "or be borne to the stockade bodily, ye wild Scot. The choice is up to ye!"

But the Captain had reckoned without another thing. There were thirty Highlanders present. And more than one of them had heard their ancient dress insulted. They gathered, muttering.

"Now look, ye Highlanders!" the Captain roared. "Ye rush me, and I'll give the order to my men to fire!"

"Wheniver hae that stopped a Scot," a Highlander cried. "Wist, lads! Forward and Hail Caledonia!"

James stood there, grinning. All the makings of a bloody riot were at hand. And, like all Highlanders, he dearly loved a riot.

But, as a score of Highland dirks glittered in the morning sun, and a broadsword or two was unsheathed, General Oglethorpe came marching sternly between the Scotsmen and the soldiers.

"Put up your arms!" he said with impressive quiet. "Lieutenant MacKay, what is the meaning of this?"

"It was like this, General," Lieutenant Hugh MacKay growled. "The Knoxes insulted Sir James' filabeg. And you know us Scots. Nane o' us will have the tartan and the kilt of our clans disparaged."

"Is that true, Mr. Knox?" the General said to Peter, who had stumbled groggily to his feet.

"It is, Gen'l," Peter said honestly. "I asked him if he wore lace under his skirts. . . ."

"The Highlanders' dress," the General said sternly, "is an old and honorable one, Mr. Knox. I'll not have it insulted. Far from implying effeminate weakness, it displays just the reverse. In England, we call these lads, 'the Ladies from Hell.'"

"I'm sorry, Gen'l," Peter Knox muttered.

"Apology accepted," the General said crisply, and turned to James.

"Sir James," he snapped, "the insult, while worthy of your resentment, was hardly sufficient to cause you to disfigure a man! Therefore, I hold it meet that you reflect upon your sins in the stockade for the next fortnight. Guards! Off with him. And, as for you Highlanders, let this be the last time you attempt to take the law into your own hands. Save your strength for the Spanish Dons. You'll find you'll need it, then!"

"Very good, Sir!" Hugh MacKay said, and saluted.

"Now you," the Captain of the Guard said to James; "come along!"

As he was being marched away, James saw Mary Knox staring at him with wide blue eyes. Gaily he blew her a kiss.

Such was his introduction to Georgia.

CHAPTER ELEVEN

THOUGH GENERAL OGLETHORPE did not realize it, he made a serious mistake in sending James Jarrett to the stockade. Because, for those with a naturally lawless bent, there is no better school than a prison cell. And James, bold rogue that he was, commenced his learning at once.

The stockade was exactly what its name implied, a high-walled enclosure, somewhat similar to the fort. In it were several log huts in which the prisoners slept. Not that there were many prisoners: two drunkards, noisily snoring away the effects of rum, and a tall, well made man of some forty years, whose look of devil may care, James liked at once. There was a look of strength and certainty about him that went beyond the physical, though his great thewed arms and legs showed he was to be reckoned with in a fight. But his face, square-jawed, composed, with just a hint of quiet humor about it, revealed that here was a man completely master of himself. He was almost as dark as James; but his black hair was lightened by patches of grey at the temples and the crown. Seeing his eyes, James discovered a certain mockery in them, a want of respect for mankind and its works.

A rogue, James decided at once; and a brother under the skin, or I miss my guess. But, despite the instinctive feeling of sympathy that one rogue senses for another, James did not address the man. Instead, he sat down on a log, drew from his pocket the drawing he had made of the Perkins' home, and fell to studying it.

A shadow darkened the drawing. James looked up and the tall man was at his side.

"Now, that I call a house!" the tall one said admiringly. "In such a dwelling, a man could draw a civil breath. I'm so damned sick of log huts and fleas that—"

"I mean to build this, ere I'm wed," James said. "I carry this drawing with me, always. It's become a sort of a talisman for me. And it'll remain so until it has been transformed into brick and mortar. But I suspect that 'twill call for a plagued lot of money, even here—"

"Especially here," the tall man growled. "Were we citizens of Carolina, 'twould be different. A pox upon the General!"

James stared at him. The tall man was the very first person he had met whose admiration of the General was somewhat less than warm.

"Tell me, friend," he said, "just what have you against General Oglethorpe? Is it because he clapped you into gaol? He served me in the same fashion, but I hold it not against him. In my case he could do naught else. . . ."

"Nor in mine," the tall one grinned, and sat down beside James. "But before we go into all what's wrong with the blinking General, we'd better exchange names, don't you think? Mine's Higgins, Timothy Higgins, at your service, Sir. . . ."

"Jarrett," James said; "James Jarrett. And now, Mr. Higgins—"

"Tim, to you, friend," Higgins said. "From the looks of you, you're very much my sort."

"Very well. And now, Tim, you say you don't hold the General's throwing you into the stockade against him—or at least that he could do naught else in your case as well. So?"

" 'Tis the way he runs the ruddy colony," Tim said. "He's not a practical man, Jim, my boy. . . ."

"Everybody seems content," James said. "Mayhap you'd better make your meaning clear."

Whereupon Tim Higgins did. Abundantly. The prohibition of Negro slavery—which just across the river in Carolina was making their sister colony rich. The General's insistence that they grow silk and indigo, both unsuited to Georgia's climate. That fiery old soldier's constant warlike gestures toward the strong and well armed Spanish colony of Florida. His refusal to let them grow rice and tobacco which were perfect for the lowlands near Savannah. His insistence that they plant indigo and mulberry trees for silk, which jolly well weren't perfect for the climate, which, in fact, would hardly grow at all. But rice and tobacco, Tim admitted ruefully, again demanded slave labor.

"Why?" James said.

"This just isn't white man's country, Jim. You wait 'til you've lived through a summer, here, and you'll see. The Devil turned over this outpost of his to the General and went back to hell to cool off. We aren't getting any richer, I can tell you. We try to work our lands; but come August, we just wilt. Now, if we had niggers—"

"Is that why you're in gaol?" James grinned. "Did you try to bring in a few?"

"No. I brought in something that's even more in demand: rum. Another idea in old Holier Than Thou's thick head: 'The sale of spirituous liquors shall be forever forbidden in Georgia.' Lord bless us, how he does love to forbid these things forever!"

"And given that August heat you mentioned, people get deuced parched, what?" James said, a wicked gleam beginning to show in his eye.

"Do they! You're a quick one, aren't you, Jim? How'd you like to throw in with me, once we're both out of here?"

"In the rum running business?"

"Exactly. Given two years of luck, you can build your blooming house!"

"You got caught," James pointed out. "Plagued risky business, Tim. . . ."

"No, it's not. I had rum luck, that was all. Overloaded me boat, and got stuck on a sandbar. Even then it was all my fault. Just couldn't bring myself to leave the boat and all that precious liquid gold. Had I done that, they never would have caught me. Anything happens, heave the stuff over the side. They can think what they ruddy well like, but, without evidence what can they do?"

"And your oarsmen?" James said.

"Niggers. Big black Gullah bucks, strong as mules and twice as dumb. I've outraced the General's patrol boats many's the time. . . ."

"But I thought you said—"

"That blacks are forbidden in Georgia? I did. Only I got a head for organization. I rent 'em from a down-at-the-heels planter in Carolina. Bring 'em back after every trip safe and sound. What do you say, Jim, boy? The two of us could really float Savannah so deep in rum that it'd bloody well drift off on the tide. . . ."

"Done!" James Jarrett laughed, and put out his hand.

"Great!" Tim Higgins grinned, and took it. "Tell me, me boy, how long are you in for?"

"A fortnight," James said. "I carved my initials in the hide of a gross lout named Knox. And cracked his brothers' pates for them. . . ."

"Why, bless you!" Tim Higgins said fervently; "were you a mite prettier, I'd kiss you, boy! I've been fair itching to do the same for years. . . ."

"Rum characters, what?" James said.

"The worst. They haven't a friend. Amongst them, they've whipped damned nigh every man in the colony. . . ."

"Including you?"

"Including me, though it took all three of them to do it. One time they kidnapped an Indian lass, and almost caused a war. Fortunately, the guards caught them before they harmed her. Tell me, how'd you manage to beat them. You're not that big. . . ."

"I'm not a fancier of pugilism," James smiled. "I gave the big one a few neat slices with my dirk, and then took my stick to them. Hardly improved their looks, I must say. But Tim, tell me what you know about them. Whether they will or no, I mean to wed the lass."

Tim stared at him soberly.

"Sure you aren't making a mistake, boy?" he growled.

"Of course I am," James said serenely. "To acquire three such louts as brothers-in-law at one time is mistake enough for any man."

"'Twasn't that I meant," Tim said. "'Tis the maid, herself, I'm thinking on. . . ."

James glared at him.

"What's wrong with her?" he snapped.

"Nothing—outwardly," Tim said. "She's a winsome lass. Only, she's all of nineteen and still not wed—"

"Nineteen!" James laughed. "The way you said it, a man would think she were eighty!"

"Amounts to damned nigh the same thing, here, boy. Hardly a maid gets past sixteen without being spoken for. Wives are plagued scarce in the colonies, Jim. So Mary Knox is three years overdue. And if she were a homely lass, 'twould be some reason for it. No—not even that. No matter how ill favored a female is, in Georgia, she can still take her pick. . . ."

"Mayhap, her brothers—"

"No, Jim. They'd be glad to see her wed and off their hands. The fact is, every bachelor in Savannah has tried and she's turned them down flatly. Not one of them who can say he's had a kiss from her—or even touched her hand. Cold as ice, I'm told. . . ."

"I," James chuckled, "can say both. . . ."

"You can! Why that ruddy boat only got here this morning and you claim already that you—"

"Thrashed the brothers Knox most soundly, and kissed their sister. Aye. In the presence of the whole town. . . ."

"Well, I'll be billybedamned!" Tim Higgins said.

"Tell me," James went on, "how are their fortunes? They don't raise silkworms, do they?"

"Hardly. Rough as they are, the Knoxes are nobody's fools. They're cattlemen. Got themselves a little ranch north of here. That's a good business, now. They ship hides and tallow back to London, and sell the meat here. I'd say that they're the only family hereabouts a body might call rich without straining the word overmuch. So naturally, they're ruddy conservatives. Tory as all get out. God save the King, and all that bloody rot!"

"I take it, then, you're not?" James said.

"Hardly. This land's too big to nestle under England's motherly wing. One day we'll be free—and a nation. Mark my words. . . ."

"If," James said dryly, "the Spanish don't take over, as you claim they're able to."

"They are. And they will if old Firebrand doesn't stop provoking them. I've seen Saint Augustine. Quite a place, my boy. A real city with stone houses, cobblestone streets, and a fortress the whole British Navy couldn't level. Walls ten feet thick, bristling with guns. But General Know It All thinks he can take them. In a year, boy, if he doesn't watch out, we'll all be unwilling subjects of the King of Spain. And, what's worse, going to mass on Sundays. . . ."

"For that, I care not," James said. "One faith's as good as another to me. I consider it most unlikely I shall go to heaven by any route. So, what's the odds? What I mean to do, Tim, is to make the best of this earth. That house I intend to build is a part of it—a fitting seat for a dynasty of men. You see, I am the last of my line—and, in Scotland, we were nobles. . . ."

"Blimey!" Tim croaked; "and me treating you so familiarly!"

"Which, pray continue. In Scotland, I am Marquis of Argyll; but this is not Scotland. Here, I have the feeling, it is not from whence a man comes, but where he is going, that counts. And, from this spot, it seems to me the only direction that one can go is—up. There hardly is anything lower than this wooden imitation of a gaolyard, what?"

"Hardly," Tim said. "Look, Lord Jim—"

"Jim, to you, my friend. Let us dispense with this ruddy nonsense of titles."

"That rumrunning business; you still want to go into it?"

"Of course. I'm in a hurry, Tim. Within a year or two I want to be able to wed Miss Knox, and sire the New World Clan of Jarretts. Better than the old—stronger, taller in their pride. And having something to be proud of: some green and pleasant sweep of earth—a house with memories enshrined within it. To achieve that, I'll run in your casks of rum, readily enough. Or traffick in slaves, if that's more lucrative. . . ."

"That, no," Tim grinned. "You can't drink a nigger, or keep him hid—not if you want to work him, that is. There's a movement afoot to have the law repealed. Heard that your future in-laws were at the head of it. . . ."

"They can count on my cooperation," James said. "I've never even seen a black; but, if that's the way to get rich, I'm all for it!"

Those two weeks in the stockade, despite the pleasant company of Tim Higgins were, for James, damnably hard to bear. He was not ill-treated by his guards, and the food, while plain, was plentiful. But his imprisonment gave him what he wanted least in all the world: an uninterrupted stretch for thinking. For remembering—which was worse.

For, what he had to remember wasn't pleasant: Maebelle standing in Tron Kirk, pointing a finger that didn't even tremble at Pitcairn Hogg. Himself kneeling, the damp earth cold against his bare knees under his kilt, beside his father's grave. Sue's voice, quiet and dry, full of an insupportable dignity, as she said: "No, James; I'm sorry—but I can't. . . ."

And the future. The future of an ex-highwayman, common thief, rumrunner to be! A man who had gained his passage to the New World from the sale of stolen goods. A criminal, who, upon the basis of still other crimes, meant to build the towering structure of his future: his lovely Georgian Mansion, respectability, sons.

He doubted profoundly that it could be built that way. But what other road was open to him? Take his plot of ground and bend his hands to the plough? He had no fear of, or dislike for, hard work; but one man alone could never hope to rise above the status of a simple yeoman, a small farmer—not in this peculiar colony with its damned peculiar laws!

Escape to Carolina? Hell and death! He'd spent his life in running from one place to another. No more. He was here, and here he'd put down his roots. Besides, this Georgia, which, at long last, he knew wasn't in the West Indies at all, but on the mainland of North America, was a rarely lovely place. And Mary Knox—

I've made my bed, he thought wryly; now to lie in it. But not alone, he added with a grin; for, Tim to the contrary, that ice can be thawed! I've already proved that much—

The morning he left the stockade—leaving Tim behind, as that worthy still had two more months to serve—the Captain, after having grudgingly given him back his arms, conducted him to the General's dwelling.

The interview was stormy. General Oglethorpe opened the engagement with a request, couched in terms practically indistinguishable from a command, that James take a commission in MacKay's regiment of Highlanders.

"You've proved abundantly, Sir James," he said, "that you have fighting blood. Of such men we have a sad lack—and with the French muttering away in Moville, and the Spaniards at Saint Augustine, we're going to need all the fighting men we can get. . . ."

"You are making a slight mistake, General," James said dryly. "I was not brought over at the expense of the Trustees, nor did I enlist in one of His Majesty's regiments. As an Adventurer, I have, I believe, certain rights. Among them is the choice of where, and under what conditions, I shall dwell. And I like not soldiering. I dearly love a fight, but on my own terms, and under the command of no one. We Jarretts have always taken orders with deuced bad grace, when we took them at all, which was seldom. So thank you very much, Sir; but no."

"Have you so little patriotism, Sir James?" the General thundered.

"None at all, Sir," James said cheerfully. "My loyalties are confined to Clan Jarrett. They go no further than that. If we are attacked, I shall enlist and fight—because I prefer even that fat Hanoverian swine who sits on the throne to being subjected to a Papist King. In other words, my personal interests, my tenure of land, and my own freedom will be involved, then. Now, they're not. And they won't be as long as you, Sir, refrain from provoking the Spaniards. You've been here three years, and not a shot has been fired in anger between us and them. They claim Georgia and the Carolinas—with some justice, you must admit, since their De Soto discovered both—while we claim Saint

Augustine. A moot point, which can well be left that way. But when you, Sir, start fortifying lands that damned well do lie within their territory, it is you, I insist, who put us all in danger. Believing that, I see no reason to embark upon military adventures to which I am most opposed—"

"You have your nerve, young Sir!" the General roared, "to address me, thus!"

"I only say aloud," James said serenely, "what every man in the colony whispers behind your back. Will that be all, Sir?"

"No," the General snapped. "Tomorrow, I, along with MacKay and his Highlanders, embark for Saint Simon's Island, which, as you probably don't know, is one of that long chain of islands just off the coast of Georgia, stretching all the way to Florida—perfect natural defenses against a surprise naval attack—to fortify it in our defense. A worthy project, Sir James, designed to protect even the lands you've not been granted yet, should the Spanish come—as they will. In *our* territory, which, despite all your arguments, extends at least to the Saint Mary's River, and mayhap to the St. John's. And since we're plagued short of strong and able bodied men, I'm formally requesting that you come along. . . ."

"And if I refuse?" James said quietly.

"You are within your rights. As I shall be within mine when it comes to deciding where the lands you're entitled to shall lie—and also as to when I shall get around to granting them. I'm a busy man, Sir James; and the interests of the colony at large occupy me to the exclusion of those of any individual. . . ."

James smiled.

"The thing I dislike most about the military mind," he said, "is that it, in one way or another, always finds ways to enforce its will. Even stooping to half-veiled threats. Very well, Sir. Since I am still a Jarrett, and since we never bow to threats from any quarter whatsoever, I shall have to sample the freer air of Carolina. A very good day to you, Sir!"

Leaving the General's outraged presence, James set out to explore the town. His principal object was, of course, to find out where the Knoxes' dwelling stood, and have, if possible, another word with Mary. Considering the size of Savannah, his chances of accomplishing the former were excellent. As for the latter, they were both very poor, and downright dangerous. For, having gazed upon his scarred countenance fourteen mornings in a row, listening betimes to the choice remarks of Martha, his ill-favored shrew of a wife, who, being what she was, let not one of ten thousand occasions to remark upon it escape her, Peter Knox's temper, vile at best, had already reached a state nothing short of murderous.

Which James might have suspected, if he had thought about the matter. It was characteristic of him that he didn't. He'd thrashed the Knoxes once. And he was prepared to repeat the performance as often as was necessary. But his easy victory caused him to make the grave mistake of underestimating them. Before, he'd held the advantages of surprise, and his skillful use of weapons. He would never have either advantage again. From then on, the Knoxes were on their guard and fully armed.

So, of course, was he. He carried his hawthorn stick. His dirk hung at his belt. And two skean dhus, the smaller fighting knives, reposed in their sheaths in his knitted socks, where a Highlander always carried them. He was cheerfully prepared for anything.

He found the house easily enough. Its identification, among all the other exact duplicates, was pleasantly marked out for him. Mary Knox was in the backyard, hanging out the washing. She had her back turned to him, so he was able to lean over the fence and gaze at her to his heart's content.

He liked what he saw. He had a feeling that he would go on liking it forever.

"D'you know, Mary, Lass," he chuckled, "that you look good from any point of view? Though I must say I prefer the sight of your bonny face. . . ."

She whirled, her pale blue eyes wide and frightened.

"You get away from here!" she hissed. "If Peter finds you're here, he'll—"

"Get another cracked pate, and a few more decorations on his hide," James drawled. "Come here, Lassie mine—it's been a long and cruel fortnight since I kissed you last. . . ."

"Oh, you!" Mary gasped, and bolted for the door.

James vaulted the fence. Raced before her. Got between her and the door.

"Come to my lonely arms, goodwife," he grinned. "This is no way to treat a doting husband."

"Husband!" Mary said furiously. "I wouldn't marry you, Sir James, if you were the last man on this earth!"

"Well, I'm not the last," James mocked. "I am merely the best.

What I am offering you, fair Mary, is a privilege long sought by a legion of pining lassies. See that you avail yourself of it before I change my mind. . . ."

"I said I wouldn't marry you—" Mary began again.

"If I were the last man on earth," James grinned. "Scant chance of that, my Dove! For, if I were, you'd be trampled in the rush. Now stop this ruddy folly and kiss me, quick. My lips are fair parched for that nectar and ambrosia of thine. . . ."

She scampered to one side, trying to avoid him. But she was attempting to escape a trained fencer, with a swordsman's legs. In half a minute flat, she was again pinioned in his arms.

"Let me go!" she wailed. "You hear me, Sir James? Let me go! I'll scream! I'll call my brothers!"

"Call them," James chuckled. "I can always whip them again. Though I'd much rather spend my time at pleasanter pursuits. . . ."

Whereupon he kissed her. A long time and very thoughtfully. She struggled in his arms like a captive bird. But he went on kissing her until her struggles ceased. That they did, made her doubly furious.

He drew away his mouth. Stood there gazing fondly into her slim, angry face.

"Ah, Lass, Lass!" he breathed, "you cure the black sickness in my heart!"

"Let me go!" she whispered. "Have you not shamed me enough? What think you that I am, Sir James, that you make sport of me, thus?"

"An angel," he said, his voice gone grave and tender; "with moon-silvered hair, a mouth like a heather rose, and eyes that outdo a summer sky. A little angel, sent down from above to heal and comfort me. That, Love, is your destiny. Why do you seek to avoid it?"

She shivered a little then, at the slow, deep rumble of his voice. She could feel the anger draining out of her. She searched his face with quick, darting glances. Each time her eyes moved, they made those reflections that had so intrigued him before.

"Know you, Mary, mine," he bassed, "that you've eyes like none other on this earth? They make summer lightnings as they move. And each ray's a blade, standing and quivering in my heart . . . What is it that you're seeking in my face?"

"The—the meaning of it," she whispered. "It's a horrid, ugly face, Sir James. The face of—of a villainous monster. Of the Devil. And yet—"

"And yet?" he prompted.

"When you say those things—about my mouth, my hair, my eyes —it changes. You—you're a sorcerer, I think. How can you make a face like yours seem fair?"

He laughed aloud.

"I'm no sorcerer, Lass," he said; " 'tis but your gentle heart instructing you. And the heart sees truly—always."

"But," she wailed, "you cut poor Peter up so terribly. And you hurt Cromwell and Henry—"

"I know. And I'm sorry that I did. Had I known they were your brothers, I'd have spared them. You have no right, my Dove, to hold against me the things that happened before you came into my life. Now, let's stop wasting time. When?"

"When?" she murmured. "When, what, Sir James?"

"Shall we wed? I'll go down to the Kirk and have the bans published this very day!"

"Oh," she wailed. "I—I'm all confused. I—I don't want to wed, Sir James. Not—not because of what you did to my brothers. Not even because you're—so strange—so terrible. Though that's part of it. The real reason's hard to say. . . ."

"Try," James said softly.

"It's—it's me," she said in a troubled voice. "Will you pardon me, and not think me—immodest, if I speak plainly?"

"You could never be immodest, Lass," he said gently. "Out with it; speak your mind. . . ."

She raised her hand, touched her heart.

"There's something here," she got out, "that sickens at—at being touched. I'm a country maid, Sir James. I—I've seen the animals in their seasons. Oh, Lord, what an awful thing to say!"

"Not at all," James said.

"A man weds—to have sons, does he not?"

"Aye," James said simply; "and my get of you would be most wondrous fair."

Her face was very pale, then. She shuddered.

"No, Sir James," she whispered. "I shall not marry you. You—nor any other man. . . ."

James looked at her, seeing the fear clouding those light-filled eyes. And he knew suddenly that his bold tactics had been both right—and wrong. Right, because they had advanced his suit more in a space of days than he would have been able to gain in months by gentler methods; wrong, because they had now gone too far, set up a reaction that was likely to impede further progress. And, being, above all things, a pragmatist, he abandoned them at once.

He turned her loose. Stood back.

"I think you will," he said quietly. "I know not what happened to you to make you have this unreasoning dread—of life. What you propose to do, Mary mine, is to exist half alive, to bury yourself, living. And 'tis wrong—monstrously wrong. What you have: this matchless, gentle beauty, is a thing that demands perpetuation. You see, Lass, I brought with me here, a dream. And I see in you the instrument of its fulfillment—"

"What was that dream, Sir James?" she whispered.

"To build here, in this new land—a race of men—a clan such as existed for centuries in Scotland. No. Better than that. Braver, gentler, finer. A breed of New World gentle men: the Jarretts of Georgia. And that requires that the female progenitor be selected with care—for she will be the mother, not merely of sons, but of statesmen, warriors, poets, Lords. I am the last of my line, Lass—with me, Clan Jarrett, the Marquises of Argyll will die, unless I wed and sire tall sons. Simple enough, you say? There are no lack of maids? You're wrong—"

"You *are* a sorcerer!" she said. "I was thinking precisely that. . . ."

"I know. And, as I said, you're wrong. There is a lack of maids. Because, my Mary, in all this broad and teeming earth, there is but one who can flesh my dream. And I—out of God's tender mercy, have found her!"

"Me?" Mary whispered.

"You. We're a wild lot, we Jarretts, as I have more than convinced you now, to my sorrow. We need that wildness tempered by a finer strain. My sons can't go hooting through life, flashing dirks, roistering . . . They'll have other things to do—grander things, Lass. A state to build. This vast land's destiny to guide with firm and capable hands. Strength and pride o'ertopping that of Kings, they'll get from me; but of gentleness, fineness, delicacy, they'll have need. Restraint, consideration for the rights of others, that true courtesy which is the hallmark of nobility—those things must be learned at their mother's knee. . . . The fear of God which is the beginning of wisdom, reverence before the Unthinkable, the Unknowable. All these, fair Angel, you and only you can give them—for these I lack. So think on it. I shall not press you—"

"I think," she said suddenly, oddly, "that you are not one man, but two, Sir James!"

"Two?" he laughed; "I, Lass, am legion!"

"Yes," she said seriously, "you are. You came off the vessel playing the bagpipes, and I—I remarked you, then; though you did not see me. Your dress, of course. I'd heard of it, knew from talk and books that in the Scottish Highlands men wore skirts. But seeing you dressed this way was still—a shock. And then I saw your face—"

"And were shocked even more?"

"Yes. And no. You have a monstrous face—sometimes, Sir James. . . ."

"Only sometimes?" he smiled.

"Only sometimes. For when you talk as you did just now—so gentle and so fair, I see that it's just a mask. That there are many things behind it. I think you put it on to overawe the world. Because, when you spoke a moment ago of your—dream, there were Michael's eyes shining out of Lucifer's face—the eyes of the morning star, so gentle and so bright. I—I like those eyes, Sir James. . . ."

"Thank you," he said gravely; "then I have some hope?"

"Oh, I don't know!" she wailed. "You get me so confused!"

"Long live confusion!" James laughed. Then: "I tell you what, my Mary. Suppose you give me a chance. Let me pay you court openly and honorably. You have naught to fear from me. To me, you are a treasure beyond all price. I'd die in my socks before I'd harm you. I promise not to drag you into my arms like a wildman, and kiss your mouth whether you will or no. That, now, is not enough. . . ."

"Not enough?" she snapped. "Methinks it is too much by far, Sir James!"

"It is not enough," he repeated firmly. "From now on, what ever kisses I have from you—few though they be—must be freely given, not snatched unwilling from your lips. For unwilling kisses are a mockery. I want your gentle heart behind them, Lass. So, now, go you and call your brothers. . . ."

"My brothers?" she faltered.

"Aye. I would make my peace with them; beg their pardons; crave the right to come as a suitor to this house. . . ."

"None of which they'd grant," she said right sadly; "the only thing they'd grant you, now, Sir James is—death!"

"I think not," he smiled; "and, in any event, they'll find killing me a monumental task. Get you and call them, Lass. . . ."

"I—I can't. They aren't here. They're out at our country place, tending the cattle. And, Sir James—"

"Yes, Love?"

"Stay away from them! There's been blood enough. If you fight again, some one of you might be killed. I—I shouldn't like one of my brothers to die—at your hands . . . Especially not at *your* hands—"

"Why especially not at my hands, Lass?" James said.

"Oh, I don't know! Yes, I do. And it's strange—"

"Strange?" he echoed.

"I—I feel as though I've known you a long, long time. That, despite your wild cruelty, you—you're a friend. And that makes it doubly horrible. And I shouldn't want—"

"One of them to kill me," he supplied. "Likewise, especially not one of them. . . ."

"Yes," she said simply. "I can't explain it, but that's the way I feel. . . ."

" 'Tis but your gentle heart that speaks," James said tenderly. "Let it, Lass. The heart hath its reasons, truer far than any other reasons in this world. But I shall see you? I must see you! Would you take away from me all sunlight, joy, and peace?"

"No," she said in a troubled tone. "I would not take away from you those things, Sir James. I—I take walks, sometimes. . . ."

"Alone?" he said.

"Alone," she whispered; "that is, if you promise to behave!"

"Upon my father's grave, I swear it!" he said fervently. "When will you next feel the need for a stroll . . . ?"

"To—tomorrow," she got out. "I—I have to collect some roots for Martha's rheumatism—"

"Martha?" he said.

"My sister-in-law. Peter's wife—the querulous, complaining thing! If ever I do wed, it will be, in part, to be rid of her!"

"Good riddance," James chuckled. "Now, Lass, kiss me goodbye, for I have a thing to do. . . ."

"What thing?" Mary said.

"I have to call upon the General—again—and tell him I have changed my mind. He all but ordered me to accompany the expedition to Saint Simon's Island, tomorrow. I told him before I'd take orders, I'd leave the colony, go to Carolina—"

"Oh, James!" she gasped, "you wouldn't!"

"Nay, Lass. Wrong word—I couldn't. For to leave you would be very death. . . ."

"Oh," she said again. "You—you mean you truly—love me, Sir James?"

"Beyond my fear of death or hope of heaven," he said quietly; "as I'd vowed never again to love a maid. . . ."

"There was some—sorrow in your past?" she whispered.

"Too much," he growled. "Now, kiss me, Lass. . . ."

"I—I couldn't!" she wailed.

"Why not?" he said.

"I—I've never kissed a man, before. Nor been kissed by any, save you. I'd be—too ashamed, Sir James. . . ."

He stood there, looking at her, as though to memorize her face. Then he sighed.

"Very well," he said, "as you will, Mary. About that walk tomorrow, forget it. I shan't be here. . . ."

"You shan't be—here?" she whispered.

"Nay. I go with the General to beard the Spaniards in their dens."

"When—shall you come back, Sir James?"

"A fortnight—a month. God knows. We have, it seems, a fortress to build. Mayhap a war to fight. . . ."

"A war! Then—then—you might—"

"Be killed? Yes, Lass," he said morosely. "What's the odds? My life is valueless as it stands . . . Goodbye, Mary. . . ."

He turned, took a step away from her. Another. Looked back. Saw, to his astonished joy, that she was crying. He whirled, took her in his arms—this time as gently as though she were made of fragile glass.

"Why do you weep, Love?" he rumbled.

"I—I don't know!" she sobbed. "Oh, you drive me out of my mind!"

He bent and kissed away her tears, brushing her cheeks with his lips, as lightly as a breath.

"Don't cry, Mary mine," he said. "I'd not have you spoil these bonny eyes—for me. . . ."

"Let me go, now," she faltered.

He released her again. Stood back, searching her face, her eyes.

"Oh," she whimpered, her voice a wild, piping dirge of desolation, "I wish—I wish I could kiss you!"

"Try," he said gently, and stood there, waiting.

She took a faltering step towards him. Another. Halted.

"I—I can't!" she breathed; "I have not the courage. . . ."

"Then I'll lend you it," he said, and bent and touched her mouth, cherishing it like a flower, hands at his side, not touching her.

He straightened, smiling. Her eyes were paler than an August sky. Wider. Filled with—wonder. With what was, or could become, tenderness. Then, wordlessly, she whirled, fled towards the house.

He watched her go. Stood there a long time looking at the closed door. A very long time, until the very pattern of the wood was imprinted on his brain.

Then he turned and started away from there, falling unconsciously into the Highlanders' marching step, his footsteps loud in the noonday silence.

But he could not hear them for the beating of his heart.

CHAPTER TWELVE

Mary Knox DROPPED the heavy oaken bar latch across the door, and, turning, leaned against the wall. She was trembling, but her eyes were soft and wide. She stood there, like that, without moving, until the savage cackle of Martha's laughter rode in upon her.

"Little Miss Mary, quite contrary!" Martha rasped. "Little Miss Touch Me Not, purer than snow! Aha, Mary Knox—the saintly Mary Knox—what have you to say for yourself now, you baggage!"

Mary stared at her sister-in-law.

"Only," she whispered, "that I hope you won't tell Peter. The hope's a vain one, I know. But, Martha, remember that—that Peter's not invincible. And if you cause him to attack James again, it might mean—donning your widow's weeds!"

"Think you, wench," Martha snarled, "that I care a fig for that? If your beskirted gallant would be so kind as to relieve me of the burden of your brother's goatish attentions, I'd be eternally grateful!"

"And if," Mary said softly, "Peter were to—to kill—James, what think you that I should be?"

"I care not," Martha said icily. "The griefs or the joys of any Knox whatsoever are a matter of indifference as far as I'm concerned. So that was your James! Sir James Jarrett, isn't it? Marquis of Argyll. Laird of Clan Jarrett—La! I shall have to be dropping you courtesies lifelong, now—if his intentions are honorable, which I doubt. . . ."

"They are honorable," Mary said. "He's already asked my hand. He wanted me to call Peter just now, in order to gain his permission for posting the bans. . . ."

"La! He does go fast, doesn't he? But his methods are somewhat

wanting in diplomacy. You can't expect Peter to be kindly disposed
toward your wedding—and bedding, for that snow is all on the surface,
isn't it, milady Marquise?—with a man who notched his ears and nostrils like a boar's. . . ."

"Oh, Martha!" Mary wailed, "must you always be so horrid?"

"A lesson I've learned from associating with the august family of
Knoxes," Martha said dryly. "I take it that your heathen in woman's
dress has already won your blushing, maidenly consent?"

"No—" Mary faltered, "I—I made him no promises—"

"But you'll give in, right enough," Martha cackled. "With benefit of
clergy, or without it, I ween. For you're a Knox, after all, aren't you?
With all the Knoxes' baser appetites, suitably hidden under that minc-
ing gait, that wheyfaced countenance of a gilt and plaster angel. I
should like to listen beside your door upon your wedding night! For,
I doubt it not, 'twill be he who cries for mercy 'ere you're done!"

"I won't listen to this!" Mary gasped. "I knew your mind was positively filthy, but—"

"But I mustn't put that filthiness into words, eh, my swooning virgin?
Mustn't confront you with the truth about yourself? La! You'll learn
it soon enough—without further words from anyone. Now go fetch me
my herb tea; if it hasn't boiled away quite by now. . . ."

So it was that James Jarrett never entered the temporary lodgings
assigned him by the General. Because, by then, Martha's viperous
tongue had informed the Knoxes fully. They rode off in a towering
rage to search for him. Which, of course, he didn't know. Not that
he would have been even slightly perturbed if he had. After his second
interview with the great man—an interview a trifle more cordial than
the other, he spent the rest of the day exploring the countryside near
Savannah, going always downstream, and paying particular attention
to the coves and inlets sufficiently sheltered to afford a haven for the
boats of an enterprising, if somewhat illegal, importer of rum. Which
there were, in God's own plenty. And the offshore islands, with the
narrow, crooked passages that divided them from the mainland, made
this coast a smuggler's paradise.

Tim, he thought gaily, had to be a ruddy ass to get caught in this
country! I'll not be. I've marked out seven possible landings now—one
for every night in the week. Never the same spot any two nights in
succession . . . 'twill be a lark! Two years, I said? By God, I'll build
that house in one!

So thinking, he turned back towards Savannah. It was fast growing dark. He did not quicken his pace because of that. He moved on, staring at the river and the sky, trying to discern the first pale twinkle of a star against the deepening dusk. It came, at last, a pin point of light directly above his head. To him, it seemed almost a benediction. He could feel in his veins the slow, soft stirrings of—peace.

Ah, Mary, Lass, he thought, this time I've chosen well. What a wife you'll make—gentle, fair—a good mother for my sons . . . And I—I'll be patient, doubt it not, sweet lass. For you must be won slowly, taught the meaning of ardor. With you, it must be consummation, not violation. No matter how long I have to wait, you must come willingly to my arms. . . .

He started walking again, faster now. After all, this raw new land did abound with savage men and beasts, and he was in no mood for a fight. He wanted to preserve his new found tranquillity. It was that, and not fear that drove him.

When he entered Savannah again, it was night. Here and there, the pine knot torches of the guards flared. But, beyond them, not a soul was in sight. He strode on, searching for the house to which he had been assigned—a plaguedly difficult task in a town where all the houses were identical. He found it at last, raised his hand to knock upon the door. But he never brought it down, for all the lights of heaven exploded inside his head. He felt himself going down, down into utter darkness. Heard, before his senses went out upon a black riptide, a voice, saying:

"Hit 'im again, Crom! We'd better make sure. . . ."

The lights, he was achingly aware, were no longer inside his head. He blinked his eyes; his vision cleared. A campfire threw grotesque shadows against the encircling trees. The shadows had the forms of giants, doubled over like antique fire worshippers, prostrating themselves before their god.

James turned his head very slowly. Nothing else about him could move. He could feel the bite of the leather thongs that bound him to the tree even through his clothes. He knew at once that to struggle against those thongs was useless. They had been put there by experts. He moved his head a little further around on his neck, convinced by now that it wasn't going to fall off, after all.

Then he saw the Knoxes. They were bent over the campfire, staring at something in it. Craning his neck, James could see what it was: an iron set into the end of a pole. A curious sort of an iron, hand wrought into the shape of the letter K. It was still black; but the edges of it were beginning to turn a dull, bluish red.

"Hell, it's hot enough," Henry Knox said.

"No it ain't!" Peter growled. "When I mark 'im, I mean to mark 'im good!"

"Look!" Cromwell spat, "he's come to himself! He's a watching us!"

"Good evening, gentlemen," James said mockingly.

"You'll see how good it is!" Peter spat. "Time we learnt you what it means to trifle with Knoxes. As if scarifying me wasn't enough, you—"

"Kissed your sister," James said pleasantly. "Again. In broad open daylight, on your very premises. Thoughtless of me, what? Only you weren't at home. . . ."

"And if we had been," Cromwell said, "you'd have been carried off, feet first!"

"Just as I was carried away from the public square?" James chuckled. "I think not, Cromwell, my boy. Because you're not up to handling me; no one of you, nor even all three. You might, I think, examine the difference between us. I took on all three of you at once, with your hands unbound. Now, you manage a show of courage—the courage of ambushers—of sneaks. 'Fore God, you make me almost change my mind!"

"Change your mind?" Peter growled. "About what, you heathen?"

"About wedding your sister," James said evenly. "I want not my sons to bear the blood of cowards."

"Cowards!" Peter roared. "I'll show you, you Highland dog! Cut 'im loose, Cromwell!"

"Now look, Peter," Cromwell said uneasily.

"You heard me, cut 'im loose!" Peter howled.

"Don't be a fool, Peter," Henry said coldly. "Loose him, and he'll take you apart, just as he did before. I didn't come here to display the ancestral valor, such as it is; I came to make ruddy sure this swine will never show his face in public again. . . ."

"That," James said, "is beyond you, Henry. Beyond all Knoxes, past, present, and future. Even if you succeed in burning my face with that cattle iron, I shouldn't hide it. For even though men look upon it and shudder, they'll shudder even more when they pass your tombs!"

Henry took a step toward him. He was the youngest of the Knoxes; and, now, as he came forward, James saw that he was far more graceful than his brothers; that, curiously, he resembled Mary to a startling extent. Even, James thought wryly, in a certain aspect of—coldness.

"Still you threaten?" Henry almost whispered; "let's see if I cannot close that mouth of yours!"

Then he brought his fist crashing into James' mouth, leaning upon the blow, putting all his weight behind it. James shook his head to clear it, tasting almost at once the heat and salt of blood.

Henry hit him again, harder, now.

"That's enough, Hank," Cromwell grinned. "You put him out and he won't even feel the heat of the iron!"

Henry stood there, his weak mouth twitching a little.

"Iron?" he snorted. "I have no need for irons—why with my bare hands, I—"

"You mean paws, don't you?" James grated. "That's what puppies come equipped with, I ween!"

Henry surged forward, his two hands curving into claws. They locked around James' throat. Savagely he banged James' head against the tree. The others made no attempt to stop him. James could feel his consciousness slipping from him. Grimly he held on to it, stretching his hands downward, downward toward the tops of his argyle socks. Because his two skean dhus, his fighting knives reposed there still. In the darkness, the Knoxes hadn't noticed them, had not, in fact, thought to look in a man's stocking tops for weapons.

But he couldn't reach them. The green leather thongs were far too tight.

"I'll kill you!" Henry snarled. "I'll—"

"Stop it!" The high soprano was a silver blade, cutting through the darkness. "Cowards! Cowards! Three against one, and you had to bind him! I knew you'd be here! The same place you dragged that Indian maid off to for your mischief and almost caused a war! Now this!"

She came flying down from her mount. In the firelight, James saw wonderingly, she was lovelier than ever.

She hurled herself upon James, sheltering him with her body. He could feel her trembling. Even under the circumstances, the sensation was a remarkably fine one.

"Get away from there, you shameless baggage!" Henry grated. "You've made us the laughing stock of all Savannah now, and—"

"And thus you propose to remedy it?" Mary whispered; "thus you'd show what men the Knoxes are? You show only how you fear him, I think! Cut him loose! I'll ask him not to harm you—and he'll heed me, I'm sure . . . Won't you, James? You'll not hurt these small boys playing redskins, will you?"

"Nay, Lass," James bassed, "I'll not harm them. Far be it from any Jarrett to soil his hands with the blood of cowards."

"That's damned well enough!" Peter roared. "Look upon my scars, Missy! See how he left me! For that, there is but one answer—this!"

He stooped then, and snatched the branding iron from the fire. It glowed redly in the darkness, casting a devilish light on Peter's scarred face.

Mary stood there, looking at her oldest brother. She didn't make a sound. James was not even sure when she began to move. But when she did, it was like lightning striking. Her leap was a red blur in the firelight. Her nails, clawing, brought blood.

Big as he was, Peter reeled backward under her attack. He dropped the branding iron. Drew back his big hand. The sound of its striking, open-palmed against her face, was a sick smashing, the loudest, cruelest sound in all the world. Mary went down upon the earth. Lay there.

"I don't know whether you're aware of it," James said quietly, "but for that, Peter Knox, you're going to die!"

Peter bent and picked up the iron. It had cooled considerably. He stood there, looking at it ruefully.

"Have to do," he muttered. Then Mary came alive. She reeled up from the ground. Grappled with Peter again. Cromwell and Henry sprang forward. Seized her arms—too late. She had already snatched the horsepistol from Peter's belt. She tore free of them. Stood there, leveling the heavy weapon at all three of them. It shook wildly in her hands.

"I'll kill you," she wept. "Touch him and I'll kill you!"

But, of them all, Henry knew his sister best. He came toward her, straight into the muzzle of that pistol.

"Shoot," he said evenly, "if you're capable of killing a brother for this swine. Shoot and be damned, Mary! Think you that you can live out your years, thinking on what you've done?"

Mary hung there. Henry took another step toward her. Suddenly, decisively, she jerked the muzzle skyward. Yanked the trigger. The report split the night apart, deeper than August thunder.

"There!" she whispered. "That will bring the guards!"

"Damn your soul!" Cromwell howled. "You traitorous little bitch!"

"Put the iron in the fire again, Peter," Henry said coldly. "Before those sleepy bastards get here, there'll still be time!"

"Oh!" Mary wailed. "You beast! I—"

"Come here, Lass," James said gently.

She whirled, flew to him. Cromwell started after her.

"Leave her alone," Henry mocked. "Let her gaze upon him while he's still pretty!"

"Mary," James whispered, "knives. Two of them—in my socks. Kneel down as though you were half fainting. Then put them in my hands!"

She stared at him barely half a second before she obeyed. She dropped to her knees, clung to him desperately, while she groped for those blades.

"That's damned well enough!" Peter growled; but she had had time by then. James felt the bone handles of the skean dhus slap into his numbed palm, just before Peter jerked her away from there.

Blessing the darkness, and the not inconsiderable distance he was away from the fire, James set to work. He'd always kept his infighting weapons sharp enough to shave with, and that helped. In seconds, his right arm was free. Slowly, cautiously, he cut the rest of his bonds, watching them all the time. But they were staring into the fire, watching the iron come to cherry-red heat.

Then they stiffened. Far off and faint, James could hear the sound of hooves, of marching feet.

"Now!" Henry shrilled, his voice as high as a woman's.

Peter jerked the branding iron from the fire, and sprang forward. Mary raced after him, but Cromwell and Henry were faster. They caught her arms; held her. She struggled wildly.

James smiled a little, then. Stood there, waiting, until the iron was so close to his face he could feel the heat. Then he moved.

Peter's roar was that of a maddened bull. He dropped the iron and stood there staring at his right arm, that James had ripped open to the bone from wrist to elbow. James watched him, narrowly. Any man with a wound like that should be hors de combat; but did Peter Knox know it?

If he did not, he learned soon enough. Even in the ruddy glow of the fire, James could see his face whiten as the pain and shock hit him. He took a backward step, groaned aloud. Sat down upon the earth, clutching his wounded arm.

Cromwell and Henry turned Mary loose. Dragged out their pistols. James came on in, the warcry of Clan Jarrett rocking the very night. Cromwell fired first. James saw the flash of the priming powder in the flintlock's pan and threw himself to one side even before the gun roared. He heard the whistle of the ball; then he was bent over low,

racing in with yard-wide, zig zagging leaps, calculated to throw Henry
off the mark. They did; but not enough. He felt a white hot iron sear
along one of his ribs; but it didn't even slow him. The wound wasn't
deep, but it laid his side open like a dull knife. Blood spurted from
it, sickeningly. A vein, he thought bitterly; pray God it's only a
vein. . . .

Then he was upon them, a knife in each hand. They fell back,
drawing their big hunting knives in their turn. But they were fighting
quicksilver, lightning. Within half a heartbeat, he had blooded both of
them.

How it might have ended, he never knew; for almost as soon as the
duel began, it ended. General Oglethorpe rode into the clearing at the
head of the guards. He said but one word, and that one right crisply,
uttering it out of the profoundest disgust:

"Again!"

Then he turned to the soldiers.

"Seize him!" he said, pointing at James.

"No!" Mary stormed; "he's done nothing! It was my brothers!"

"Nothing?" the General said dryly, nodding towards where Peter
Knox lay, soaking the ground with blood. "I call that a lot, Miss
Knox!"

"He had to, Sir!" Mary wept. "They—they had him tied—they—they
were going to—to brand him! In the face, General. . . ."

One of the guards picked up the still hot iron, held it up for the
General to see. Then, with his other hand, he lifted the cut thongs.

"I see," the General said gruffly, a ghost of a smile playing about
his lips; "but they forgot those knives you wild Highlanders wear in
your socks, eh, Sir James?"

"Exactly," James grinned; "and, General, begging your august
pardon, I'd like to say a word. . . ."

"Say it," General Oglethorpe snapped.

"I could have killed them, if I'd wanted to. So to a plea of self
defense, I can also add mercy. Peter didn't even know I had a knife.
I could have gutted him. . . ."

"I see," the General said again. "Now hear this, all! First, a detachment to take Mr. Knox back to town, stanching that wound before he
bleeds to death. That's it. Now, one other thing. I'll have no feuds,
Highlander or any other kind in Georgia. The first one of you—either
you Knoxes, or Sir James—I catch breaking the peace, will receive
sixty-nine lashes upon his bare back, well laid on! Is that clear?"

"Perfectly, Sir!" James said crisply. A trifle too crisply. He was beginning to feel weak and sick, the more so because his weskit was sticking to his side with his own blood. And the wound was beginning to ache damnably.

"And you, Messers Knox?" the General growled.

"Yessir," they chorused sullenly.

"That's all, then. Get you home. Especially you, Sir James. I mean to put that ferocity of yours to good use—and soon!"

"Very well," James whispered. "But first, Sir, before I go, I'd like a word with Miss Knox. I'd like to thank her for saving my life—or at least my manly beauty. Have I your permission, Sir?"

"Over my dead body!" Henry Knox howled.

"So that's the way the wind blows, eh?" the General growled. "It seems to me that Miss Knox is of age, and knows her own mind. Suppose we put the question to her. Miss Knox, have you any objection to Sir James' seeing you home?"

"None, Sir," Mary said firmly.

"And you, Sir James—the truth now, you rogue!—are your intentions towards this maid such as can bear public scrutiny?"

"I mean to wed her, Sir," James said simply, "if she'll have me. But 'tis plagued hard to have a friendly chat with these oafs forever in the way. . . ."

"They're bound to keep the peace—as are you, on pain of being whipped through the town behind a cart," the General said dryly. "And I, for one, approve most heartily of this match. A decent way of nipping your bloody feud in the bud, methinks. And if it produces a breed of fighters such as you, my lad, the whole colony can be grateful for it. . . ."

"Sir," Cromwell got out, "we don't approve—"

"I care not a snap for your approval, Mr. Knox!" the General said. "The days of the Montagues and the Capulets had been over two hundred years even when the Bard penned his immortal lines. I'll have no warring houses in this colony, thank you. Ye're not bad sorts, you Knoxes. Nor, by my lights, is Sir James. I'm ordering him to behave himself, and you to give him his chance. And I—even though it seems to me that you have not—have sufficient faith in your sister's decency to be sure she'll keep him in line. Now get you home, and leave these young swains in peace!"

She did not say a word as they walked along. Once or twice, James stumbled. He was losing a plagued lot of blood; yet he kept his mouth tight shut. He ached to take her in his arms, but he refrained. The silence was unbearable. It crawled along his nerves with a thousand, thousand tiny feet.

"Mary, Lass—" he groaned.

"You promised me!" she said, her voice tight with fury; "you promised you'd not hurt them—and now you've gone and all but killed Peter!"

"Sorry," he said flatly, "but that iron was a trifle too close to my face for comfort. Had to make sure he dropped it, and didn't pick it up again. . . ."

"I fear me," she choked, "he'll pick up nought else in this life. They are my brothers, Sir James! Cannot you for one moment remember that?"

"Would God I could forget it forever," James growled.

She turned and faced him, then.

"Goodbye, Sir James," she said icily. "I know my way home from here!"

"Mary, for God's love!"

"No, Sir James—not for God's love. I like not blasphemy. And I like even less having for a suitor a man who—cuts my brothers to pieces every time they meet!"

He stared at her, trying to make out her eyes through the darkness.

"This time, Lass," he said quietly, "I did not meet your brothers. I was knocked on the head before mine own door, and dragged off into the woods. Trussed up like a hog. Prepared for branding—"

"You scarred Peter's face horribly!" she said.

"Before I knew he was your brother. With his hands unbound, and able to fight. After he had struck the first blow. Which should make a difference, even to your curious little female mind. Apparently it doesn't—which makes me sorrier still. . . ."

She stood there, staring at him, and her eyes were luminous, suddenly.

"You're—you're right," she whispered. "I am being unfair. What they proposed to do was—horrible. Still—"

"Still we have the General on our side, now," James said huskily. "With his help, we can be wed. I ask you only to name the day, Mary—"

Slowly she shook her head.

"I shall not wed you, Sir James," she said.

"Why not?" he croaked.

"I—I've lived all my life among savage brutes," she said, "though it is ill of me to speak thus of my brothers. The man I wed, if such exists, must be both fair—and gentle. You are neither. I have a horror of fighting and of blood, Sir James. And with you, there'd be one thing I could look forward to, surely—"

"Which is?" he said faintly.

"The day they brought you home in your blood," she whispered, her voice hoarse with horror. "I couldn't stand that! I'd go out of my mind—or die. . . ."

"Because you love me, Lass?" he whispered, tenderly.

"No! I hate you! I think you're perfectly horrid!"

"So horrid," he chuckled, feeling the weakness in him down to the very bone, "that you came flying to my defense, threatened to shoot your own brothers, fought like a tigress—"

"I'd have done as much for any man," she began; but he held her with his eyes.

"Would you?" he murmured, and bent and found her mouth.

She stiffened, pushing against him. Her left hand slid along the thirteen-inch gash Henry's ball had opened in his side. She felt the hot stickiness, the wet. Drew back her hand, held it high. In the moonlight, the blood with which it was completely covered, showed black.

"Oh, James!" she wailed, her voice rising to a wild, high keening sound; "they—they've killed you! You—you're bleeding frightfully—and you never said a word! You—you aren't human! You're—all torn open there—there's no end to that wound, and you didn't cry, or complain—or even use this in your defense when I berated you for hurting them! Tell me, what manner of creature are you?"

"A man," he said serenely. "'Tis not strange, you didn't recognize the breed. There are not many left." He winced suddenly from a renewed stab of pain. Her involuntary push against the wound had opened it again.

"But I'm human enough," he added softly; "for now, I fear me I needs must lie me down—and die. . . ."

That last was pure calculation. The gash, while bad enough, was hardly fatal, and he knew it. But he knew even better how to use and press an advantage.

As he sank to the earth with theatrical grace, he could hear her screaming his name.

"James!" she wept, "don't die! Oh, my God, don't let him die! Please, God, don't let—"

"Goodbye," he whispered tenderly. "Fare thee well, my Mary; I go in peace, having known—you—"

She flung herself upon him, kissing his face, his eyes, his throat. Her ardor was too much for him. He had lost a fearful lot of blood, and he was dreadfully weak. Somewhere along the line, pretense slipped over into reality. The moon went out. The stars. Her face disappeared into the darkness. Only her voice came over to him, screaming.

She dug frantic fingers into his long hair. Lifted his head, clung her mouth to his, found it cold as ice. Released him, watched his head loll lifelessly to one side. This time her screams shredded the quiet night, splintered in crystalline slivers against the very stars.

And, more importantly, brought the guards. They picked him up, bore him home.

That next morning, the richest scandal in the whole short history of the colony rocked Savannah.

For Mary Knox refused to leave James Jarrett's side, all that long night through.

CHAPTER THIRTEEN

So IT WAS that James Jarrett did not sail away with General Ogle-thorpe's expedition to fortify the offshore islands. He was more than a week abed, during which time Mary visited him daily, to the tongue clucking delight of the gossips, male and female, with whom the colony was infested. Each time she came she brought more disquieting news about Peter's condition. James had never heard of a slashed arm killing a man—particularly not a man as big and strong as Peter Knox; but now, apparently, Peter's wound was threatening to do just that.

"He's awfully sick, James," Mary said; "and that's strange—"

"Why strange, Mary?" James said.

"Because, truly, his wound is no worse than yours. And you are nearly well, now. Besides, Peter has been hurt before. Once, on one of his trips down to Florida, the Seminoles left him for dead in the swamps. Yet he came home—with seven arrow heads buried in his flesh, burning up with fever, down to skin and bones—and recovered. Ordinarily, he'd have considered this cut a trifle; but now—"

"Inflammation's set in?" James growled.

"I—I don't know. Martha won't let me near him—which is stranger still. She has always pretended to despise him; and now she is nursing him like the tenderest, most devoted wife on earth. . . ."

"Women!" James chuckled. "All contrariness and contradiction. Take you, for example. . . ."

"I know. Only I've grown fond of you, James—"

"Merely fond?" James said. "Cannot you bring yourself to say, 'I love you, James'? 'Tis not a hard phrase to say. . . ."

She stared at him, and her eyes were troubled.

"I—I'm not sure I do," she said softly. "You're a dreadful man, Sir James. And if Peter dies—"

"It will be finished between us," James said bitterly; "because never could you bring yourself to wed your brother's murderer. . . ."

"I should not call you a murderer," Mary said. "After all, you fought in self defense, and could as easily have put that blade through his heart. But, beyond that, you're right, James: his blood would be upon your hands, unwillingly or no. That would be too much to stand forever between man and wife. I don't see how we could be happy under the circumstances. . . ."

"Then pray God he lives!" James said.

"Amen," Mary whispered. "Now I must go, before Crom and Henry find out I'm here. . . ."

"You mean they don't know?" James said incredulously. "Think you that in a village such as this, with nothing to occupy the people's attention but each other's affairs, your visits have not been remarked?"

"I know they have," Mary said; "but apparently no one has dared—"

"Rubbish!" James said; "they'd dare all right. . . ."

Mary stood up.

"I think you're right," she said. "I think they're pretending not to know. They're not really brave, the way Peter was—I mean is—especially not Henry. And they're not exactly longing for sixty-nine lashes on their bare backs—nor, for that matter, the necessity of facing you again. Can't say I blame them. As I said before, you're perfectly dreadful. . . ."

He swung his long legs down from the bed, and stood up. His face went white from the pain that effort cost him.

"James, you mustn't!" Mary wailed. "You—you look just like you're going to swoon!"

He laughed then, and took her in his arms. Kissed her mouth, slowly, lingeringly, tenderly.

"Still think I'm dreadful?" he growled.

"Yes," she began; but he stopped her words with his lips. Or tried to. Now they came out muffled, sweetsighing against him:

"Dreadful, dreadful, dread—"

He turned her loose.

"So wonderfully, beautifully dreadful!" she said, and fled.

She did not go home at once, which was a pity. For, had she done so, she might have discovered just how deep Martha Knox's new found devotion lay.

Martha came out of the house, and stood on the steps, darting quick, furtive glances about her. Sure now that no one was about, she crossed the yard with rapid steps, no trace of the rheumatism about which she complained so bitterly visible in her gait. She came up to the door of that homely, but useful structure with which all houses in that day were equipped. But she did not enter it.

Instead she circled around behind it, scattering the chickens from their noisome feast. From her apron pocket, she took out a roll of bandages. Bent down, holding her breath against the stench, and smeared the bandages against that befouled earth.

Forty-eight hours later, his arm blue with gangrene, his bull-like roars audible over half the town, Peter Knox died.

The pounding on his door awakened James. He raised his head, growled:

"Come in!"

The door flew open, and Tim Higgins stood there. His face was grey, his jaw tight.

"Up with you, Jim, boy," he whispered hoarsely. "I've a boat at the landing, manned with niggers. Thank God you're dressed! Now slip on your shoes and come!"

"What the devil's wrong now, Tim?" James said.

"You've hit it," Tim groaned; "the very devil's loose. Even in the stockade, I heard it. So I broke out last night and arranged things. Don't just lie there! Come!"

"You heard what?" James said wearily.

"Peter Knox died last night. So now the good citizens of Savannah are planning to make you the guest of honor at a nice, cozy little hanging. You heard me, get up!"

Slowly James swung down from the bed.

"I had no idea," he said quietly, "that friend Peter was so popular. . . ."

"He wasn't. Only, it appears that you're even less. That's one thing. Another is that in this dead hole, where nothing ever happens, a hanging would liven things up right smartly. Jolly idea, what?"

James sat down on the bed, began to draw on his shoes.

And Mary Knox, her young face white as death, flew through the door.

"James!" she wept, "you must go! They're holding a mass meeting right now, and they're talking about—"

"Hanging me," James said dryly; "I know, Lass. Thanks for warning me. And thanks even more—for not joining them. . . ."

"I couldn't," she breathed. "Peter was my brother; but you—you didn't mean to kill him—"

"Yet," James said bitterly, "he's dead. And now—"

"Now, what, James?" she whispered.

"Look, Sir, and Madam," Tim Higgins growled, "I'll wait outside. But for God's love, Jim, don't be long!"

"Now," James croaked, "I've lost you. Because of this—this thing I never meant to do. Mary, Lass—"

"Yes, James?"

"Come with me! We'll go to Carolina, or to some other colony where nothing of this is known. Far from here. And we'll leave all this behind us. Live out our lives in happiness and peace—"

Slowly she shook her head.

"No, James," she whispered.

"Mary, before my God—"

"No, James. For I should take with me far too heavy a baggage— of memories. Even should we flee to the earth's last end, each time I looked upon you, I'd see—Peter lying there on the ground with the blood streaming out of him. Or upon his bed last night, screaming, screaming . . . That—that nightmare would lie between us in the dark, rise up with us in the dawn, choke in my throat every crust of your bread I tried to eat. So—goodbye, Lord James! I—I'm sorry. I was beginning to—to entertain seriously the idea of being—your wife. . . ."

"Then entertain it still! I'll make you forget! I'll keep you so happy that—"

Again that slow, negating head shake, that silent denial, louder in his heart than any thunder.

He sat down again, very quietly, drew off his shoes. Stretched himself out full length upon his bed.

"James!" she shrilled, "they'll come! As soon as that meeting is over, they'll—"

"You may tell Tim he can go," James said softly.

"James, they'll hang you!"

"I know. But what is life without you, Lass?"

"James, please! Listen to reason! There are other maids! You'll find—"

"There is but one you, Mary mine," he said tenderly. "I prefer actual death to this death in life you'd leave me. Now go. 'Twould not be good for them to find you here. . . ."

She bent then, seized his arm. She was sobbing helplessly.

"Come!" she wept. "Before I'll see you hanged, I—I'll go with you! But God forgive you, James Jarrett, for this choice you've put upon me; for I—I never shall!"

James sat before the campfire, looking at her. They had made Ossabow, the nearest of the offshore islands, lying a few miles below the town, just before dark. Tomorrow, they'd head south, towards the Spanish territory of Florida. For Tim had advised against their going to South Carolina.

"The General and Governor Broughton," he growled, "are closer than two peas in one pod. You'd be seized and handed over to the Georgia authorities at once. Better to take your chances with the Dons. They'll let you stay, particularly if you pretend to be some kind of a political refugee—and display a leaning towards Papism. . . ."

But now James could see Mary, lying, covered with her cloak, a full five yards away from the campfire. He wondered whether or not he should speak to her. Then he decided against it. Better to go slow. She had not parted her lips since they had left Savannah.

Sighing, he stretched himself out beside the fire. His wound ached damnably; the night was chill and damp. He was utterly weary. And though he did not believe he could, he slept.

To be awakened in the greyish light of dawn by Tim's rude hand upon his shoulder.

"Jim, boy!" Tim croaked: "up with you! We'll have to search for the maid. She—she's gone. . . ."

James came upright at once.

"But where could she go?" he growled. "Ossabow's an island, is it not?"

"Damned right it is," Tim said worriedly. "I only pray God she didn't try to swim the channel to the mainland. That current's plagued swift and—"

James was on his feet, then, his eyes wild.

"Dear God!" he whispered. "Come on!"

The search took them all day. Ossabow was by no means a small island. But they found no sign of her.

"Get the blacks ready," James said flatly. "We're going back to Savannah!"

"Don't be a fool, Jim," Tim growled; "no maid whatsoever is worth getting your neck stretched for!"

"She is," James whispered; "but I don't mean to be hanged. We'll slip into a hidden cove, and you'll make the inquiries for me. Until I know she's safe, I'll never sleep another night through. . . ."

"Hold on, there, my boy," Tim said; "you forget that I'm an escaped prisoner with a price on my head. Show my face in Savannah, and I'll never get out of the stockade again!"

"One of the blacks, then?" James said.

"Still less. You know full well that niggers aren't allowed in Georgia. . . ."

"Oh my God!" James almost wept; "then I'll go! To hang me, they first have to take me, and that'll take some doing—"

"Jim, boy," Tim Higgins began. Then James caught his arm.

"Tim!" he hissed; "isn't that a fire, down there?"

"It is," Tim said. "Mayhap she's hiding out in that cove."

But she wasn't. The fire came from the chimney of a fisherman's hut. The fisherman's wife, a halfbreed squaw, faced them stolidly.

"Your husband?" James snarled. "Where is he?"

"Gone," the woman said.

"I know that, plague take it!" James howled. "But where?"

"Savannah," the woman said.

"Tell me, woman," Tim said, "did he go alone?"

"No," the woman said.

"Was there—" James whispered, "a woman with him? A white woman?"

"Yes," the woman said.

"Thank God!" James said fervently. "She didn't try to swim."

"Swim, no," the woman said. "Boat. My husband's boat. Give him pound for passage."

"That does it," Tim said tiredly. "Let's get back to camp, boy. Tomorrow we'll have to head south—"

"Yes," James said grimly; "but no further than Saint Simon's Island, Tim."

"Saint Simon's? Are you mad? That's where the General is!"

"I know. Which is precisely why I'm going there. I mean to throw myself upon his mercy. After all, Tim, I'm not guilty of murder. I gave Peter Knox a slash on his arm, nothing more, when I could have killed him easily enough. Murder involves deliberate intent to kill. All I can be charged with truly—is homicide, and self defense. The worst the General will do is to throw me into the stockade for six months or a year. If he does that much, which I doubt. He, after all, witnessed the circumstances surrounding that particular fight. And say what you will of him, you, nor any other man alive can accuse him of being less than just. . . ."

"That's true," Tim said grudgingly; "can't stand the old buzzard, but he's fair enough. Hell, what you're saying makes sense! That way, with some luck, we'll both live to carry out our scheme—which we can't with you in gaol, and me an exile in Florida. . . ."

"You mean to surrender, too, then?"

"Yep. I've only a month to go. The General'll probably add on another one—which I can stand—for my breaking out. Yep, makes sense, all right. . . ."

"Then come on," James said.

In his tent in the middle of the newly founded town of Frederica on St. Simon's Island, some miles south of Savannah, General James Oglethorpe listened gravely to their story.

"The fools!" he growled; "when will I teach them not to take the law into their own hands? I must say your behavior in seeking me out is commendable, Sir James. Did you not even fear that I might order you hanged out of hand?"

"No," James said calmly. "I know you better than that, Sir. Men have said many things about you: that your reforming zeal is foolish, your laws impractical and unworkable, and that you're as stubborn as the devil. All, to my mind, with some truth. But no man whatsoever has ever called you—unjust."

"I see," the General said dryly, a ghost of a smile hovering about his lips; "then 'twould be unjust for me to hang you, Sir James?"

"Entirely," James said stoutly; "me or any other man in my circumstances. Your knowledge of English law is both wide and profound, Sir. You know as well as I that homicide does not carry the death penalty—still less self defense!"

"You infer, young Sir," the General growled, "that you had no intent to kill Peter Knox?"

"None. Beyond the fact that a man as skilled in knife work as I am would have aimed for his heart and thus ended the matter at once instead of merely slicing his arm, what man whom you know, Sir, would

have taken such an asinine method of endearing himself to the heart
of the maid he plans to wed—as killing her brother?"

"Yet, you did kill him, unwillingly or no. Tell me, how goes that
affair of Mary Knox?"

"It is finished, I sadly fear," James whispered. "Well, Sir?"

"A pity," the General sighed. "You two would have made quite a
pair. Well, Sir James, what shall I do with you?"

"What you will, Sir—short of hanging. And if that be your pleasure,
at the moment I care not overmuch. . . ."

"It is not my pleasure," the General snapped; "as you said before,
I am always just. You are at liberty—both of you—because, Higgins,
your motives in breaking gaol were worthy, since they saved me a
fighter that I prize. That liberty, however, is conditional. . . ."

"Conditional upon what, Sir?" James said.

"Upon your doing what work you can here to aid the building of
Frederica. 'Twill be a great city one day, my friends, mayhap the grand-
est in the New World. And after that, I require your services upon my
expedition to the South next month. Serve me well, and your liberty
becomes complete. Is that fair enough?"

"More than fair, Sir," James whispered. "You are being most wondrously kind. . . ."

Saint Simon's Island, James saw, was a lovely place. It was crowned
with giant trees, from which the Spanish moss hung and shredded the
light. The air was balmy, warm—the soil endlessly rich. After a day's
exploration, for his still unhealed wound did not permit him to work
upon the rapidly rising fortifications, James sought out the General
once more.

"Sir," he said, "if it be not overbold of me, I should like to make a
request. . . ."

"You are always overbold, Sir James," the General smiled, "but,
like all Englishmen, I have a certain fondness for gallant rogues. Speak
your piece, young Sir!"

"As an Adventurer, I am entitled to one hundred acres. I'd be most
grateful, if I could have them—here."

"Delighted," the General said. "I've had the devil's own time getting settlers for this island. The only way I could keep this worthless
crew I have here from deserting was to put the food and the ale in the
first boat, so they had to keep up—or starve. Have you picked your
spot?"

"Aye, Sir. South of here—on the landward side to afford me some shelter from the storms. . . ."

"Good, I'll send Major Furness, my surveyor, with you tomorrow. I'm pleased with your decision. See that you make the best of it."

"I mean to, General. And Sir—any objections to my taking on Tim Higgins as my partner in the venture?"

"None at all, so long as the two of you confine your efforts to farming. I'd take it most ill if Frederica were suddenly flooded with—rum!"

"You have my word, Sir," James smiled, thanking all the stars that no mention had been made of a similar flooding of Savannah. He'd keep his word to the letter and beyond—as far as Saint Simon's was concerned. Bad business, he thought sardonically, to befoul one's own nest. . . .

On the Eighteenth Day of March, the expedition to explore the Southern waters set out. James had become aware that the General was considerably less of a fire eater than Tim had accused him of being. Considered calmly, his policy of building a chain of fortifications southward made good sense. For, as the General said, dryly:

"Which opponent does a powerful nation attack first, my boy? One which is weak and defenseless—or one that can match them gun for gun?"

The very existence of those forts would insure the peace. The weak invite attack. And whatever validity the Spanish claim of all the lands lying as far north as Port Royal, South Carolina had—which, James was honest enough to admit, was considerable, since the Spaniards had discovered and mapped out all this territory—they'd think again when the threatening war became less one-sided. With all his faults, the General, as a military man, was nobody's fool.

Along with them went the ninety odd year old Cherokee Chief, Tomochichi and forty braves, painted for war. Hugh MacKay and his Highlanders. Other officers and citizens.

James became aware at once that his popularity among his fellow countrymen had all but disappeared. Apparently the story of his refusing to join their regiment had been noised abroad.

To hell with it, he thought, and avoided them. 'Twould not do now to become embroiled in still another quarrel.

The expedition proved entirely peaceful. They left Hugh MacKay and his Highlanders—much to James' relief, because their snarling mutters as he passed had become deuced hard to take—on the north point

of Cumberland, another of the long chain of offshore islands, hugging
the coast of Georgia, there to build another fort, which would be
called Saint Andrews. Then the rest of the expedition proceeded south
to the mouth of Saint Mary's River; passing that, they discovered a
new island. Named it Amelia's Island. Went on. Came at last to
Spanish San Juan the last of the islands fringing the Georgia coast.
Found it deserted, its ancient fortifications in ruins. Entered the river.
Tomochichi began to chant his warsong; his braves danced the blood
dance upon the decks. But Oglethorpe restrained them.

"Nay, good Chieftain," he said calmly; "we come not seeking war—
but peace. . . ."

Then the General had his little fleet put about, and returned to San
Juan. There they spent some days repairing the ancient Spanish fortifi-
cation and left it manned. That done, they sailed homeward, without
having so much as having seen a Spaniard.

And James Jarrett found himself once more a free man.

But what to do with his freedom proved a problem. The land he
had been granted was endlessly rich; but no two men were capable of
working one hundred acres profitably. He and Tim went through the
motions, of course: planted fruits and vegetables; hunted wild turkeys,
hares, and deer—lived like Lords upon the fat of the land. But to really
work James' new plantation, they had need of hands—many hands.
And Negro slavery was forbidden in Georgia. That meant indenturers
—which cost money. And of that commodity, neither of them boasted
more than five shillings apiece.

To all of which, there was but one answer: rum.

Within a month, the arrests for drunkenness in Savannah increased
startlingly. The sleek black boats came slipping into the coves and inlets—each night at a different spot. In vain the General ordered the
whole river from Savannah to the sea patrolled. James and Tim landed
their liquid goods on Ossabow, or Jekyl, or one of the other islands.
Crossed to the mainland far below Savannah, hauled it to their buyers
in wagons by circular routes. The guards were called inland, to patrol
against the wagons. And the black boats swept into the coves again.

By September, they were operating five boats at a time, and the
oilskin-wrapped pound notes, the silver shillings, the golden guineas
buried in the garden they worked with such tender care—albeit somewhat sleepily—by daylight, climbed to formidable sums. And Savannah was on its way to becoming one of the wettest spots on earth. . . .

James had money enough now. By the Spring of 1737, he could begin. Build his Georgian Mansion, bring in indenturers, plant his lands to tobacco—the low lying marshes to rice. Build his dikes and flood gates, become the lordly country squire—

Only there was a void at the center of his existence. Though Frederica's rapidly increasing population contained many a fair and blushing maid, to whom, it seemed, his well publicized sins acted as a lodestone, James went his way, morose and sad. He was still laboring under the somewhat irrational misapprehension that nowhere under the blue skies of heaven existed a fitting substitute for Mary Knox. Such errors are common enough in the minds of twenty-one-year olds; the trouble was that James had no intention of giving himself time to prove how wrong he was.

That winter, the threat of war with Spain grew steadily more grave. James was sure that only General Oglethorpe's unexpected skill in diplomacy had held it off so far. The General, any man not prejudiced or blind could see, had done all he could. As early as February 19th, the day before the expedition to St. Simon's Island set sail, he had sent Charles Dempsey and Major Richards to treat with the Spaniards. In April, suspicious of Dempsey's continued absence, he had sent Mr. Horton and Major Richards once more to San Augustíne to look for him. All three men came back safely, accompanied by Don Pedro de Lamberto, Colonel of the Spanish Horse, and Don Manuel d'Arcy, secretary to the Governor of Florida, sent by the Spanish to make a treaty of peace.

James, whose friendship with the General had grown warm, was taken along to the ceremonies on Jekyl Island—chosen by the General because he jolly well didn't want the Spaniards to see his fortifications at Frederica and the new Fort St. Simon on the point of the island opposite it.

"What a showman our General is!" James told Tim. "First the salutes—you'd have thought every gun in this wicked world was being fired. And not only here. I'm told that as they passed every fort we've built between here and Florida the same thing happened. . . ."

"Too bad they didn't aim true!" Tim growled.

"Why?" James said mildly. "I thought you rather liked the Dons."

"I do," Tim admitted grudgingly. "As a people, they're all right. It's their ruddy religion I can't stand!"

"For that, I care not," James said softly. "I don't believe God is so narrow or so mean as to close all roads but one to His Grace. But no matter. It was at Jekyl that the General really staged a piece worthy of Covent Garden. We were having dinner with the Dons aboard the *Hawk,* Captain Gascoigne's sloop o' war. And Tomochichi and his braves burst aboard in feathers and paint, chanting their warsong, and threatening death to every Spaniard in this world for alleged crimes against the Indian nations. The General restrained them, of course, with much difficulty—just as if he hadn't put them up to it in the first place! Seems to have worked—the treaty's signed, presents exchanged —and now we can look forward to peace for at least two years. . . ."

But, in that, James was wrong. Learning that his royal commissioners had agreed to give up the territory north of the Saint John's River, the King of Spain invited Don Francisco Moral Sánchez, Governor General of Florida, home to Spain, and, upon his arrival, hanged him out of hand. And, in August, Don Antonio de Arredondo came to Frederica, having sailed post haste from the frowning city of Habana in Cuba, to present His Majesty's demand that all Englishmen evacuate Georgia at once, and retreat as far north as Saint Helena Sound in Carolina. . . .

There matters rested, broodingly. Any morning could bring the sight of Spanish sails upon the horizon, any night the thunder of cannon in the bay. But James cared not. He spent that winter building his house—which, due to the lack of brick, and his even greater lack of skill turned out to be but a sad caricature of the Georgian Mansion he had planned. Still, for St. Simon's, it was a most imposing house, two stories high, and painted white. What mattered it that no joist quite met its corresponding beam, and the winter winds howled through it without hindrance or let? Or that, come Spring, the flies, insects, and even an occasional snake used it for a parade ground? It was a house—a real house, perhaps the first such in all Georgia. All Frederica turned out to stare at it with admiration and ill-concealed envy. . . .

During that winter, James accomplished one thing more. One Thomas Hogan having died, James bought from his widow the services of some twenty indentured servants, since Mrs. Hogan, bowed down with grief, announced her immediate departure for England.

Now, indeed, he was ready, his broad fields being worked, his dikes built, his low lying marshes flooded for the planting of rice. Ready to begin his dynasty—his New World Clan of Jarretts, tall in their pride, gallant, fair.

But for that, he needed a bride. Which, to James, meant just one maid in all this world:

Mary Knox.

CHAPTER FOURTEEN

WHEN JAMES JARRETT came up the stairs from the landing at Savannah, a crowd gathered. They stood there, gaping at his new tartan and kilt, the feather sticking up jauntily from his Tam o' Shanter. They marked well, too, the pistols nestling alongside the dirk in his belt, the two skean dhus in his socks, the Scotch broadsword that hung at his side. He was, indeed, a sight to see; a brave, bold splotch of color in a drab, colorless world. There were those who muttered angrily, spoke darkly of the General's absence on a voyage to England where he had gone to procure munitions and troops against the threatened Spanish attack, suggested that without General Oglethorpe's protection, this beskirted gallant could fall into their hands easily enough, was, in fact, overripe for hanging.

Then they looked at his weapons, and his face, and changed their minds.

They followed him at some little distance as he marched boldly up to the Knoxes' house. This time, Cromwell and Henry both were there. Seeing his arms, they flew for weapons.

"Nay, lads!" James sang out. "I come in peace. . . ."

The brothers Knox reappeared, fully armed.

"There'll be no peace between us ever, Jarrett!" Henry shrilled.

"I think there will," James said calmly. "Even you, Henry, must admit I had no intent to kill your brother—"

"'Twas dark," Cromwell growled; "your aim was bad. . . ."

"My aim is never bad," James snapped. "I can cut a man's heart out blindfolded, have I a mind to. But enough of this nonsense. The General, himself, has accepted my views in that matter. I am right sorry about Peter's death. I would not have killed one of Mary's brothers for all the world. Therefore, you two are safe from me, so long as you do not presume upon my fondness for your sister over-much. I come to make what amends I can. I am prepared to settle a pension upon Peter's widow for life. That will not bring him back, I know—but 'tis an earnest of my honorable intent. Beyond that, I come formally, to ask your sister's hand in marriage—"

"Over my dead body!" Henry howled.

"Don't tempt me too strongly, lad," James grinned. "But, in this, it seemeth me that Mary, herself, has some rights—"

The door came open, and Mary stood there, draped in black. She was terribly pale, and painfully thin.

"I do, Sir James," she said with great dignity. "And though in addition to having taken my brother's life, you've also destroyed my reputation to such an extent that no man alive would have me now, my answer is still the same: No. Not even if you were the last man alive upon this earth!"

"You're not being fair, Lass," James said gently. "I ask of you but one thing: that you come and take a walk with me, now. Listen to my side of the matter—"

"Mary!" Cromwell thundered, "I forbid you to leave this house!"

"You need have no fear, Cromwell," Mary whispered. "I have no intention to. I should not like to be found dead in the company of this swine! Goodbye, Sir James. I hope you retain enough gentility not to trouble me again. . . ."

James stood there, looking at her a long, slow time.

"Nay, Lass," he said, "not goodbye—au 'voir. Because there will never be a goodbye between us until Death lays his seal upon my eyes. Wed me, you will—though all the hosts of hell stand between us, in my way. And the day will come that you shall glory in it. So now, adieu—until we meet again!"

He turned on his heel then and strode away. The rabble followed him. And Mary Knox stood there, watching him go, with sad and troubled eyes.

That night, she lay sleepless in her bed, and wept.

Why, why, she stormed, inside her heart, do I feel this way about him? He *is* a swine! He killed my brother! He bore me away against my will—so that all the town now calls me whore—though in that way he is guiltless of me. . . .

And, her heart whispered, he didn't mean to kill Peter. He was only defending himself. He made no move to harm me when I was entirely

in his power. He has always declared before all the world his desire
to make me—his wife. Lady Mary Jane Jarrett, Marquise of Argyll.
How fine that sounds! Still—

Still he is such a man as there exists not in this world his like. That
face—so ugly, and yet—so fair! That voice that can roar like an angry
bear, and a moment later frame such dulcet accents. There's not a
maid in all Savannah who would not leap into his arms. I—I've heard
them admit it, often enough. Grace Dugan says he's the most exciting
creature alive—and she's right. And I—who only need to open my
mouth, say one short word, or even nod my head like this—

"Good!" James Jarrett chuckled. "I'm glad you've changed your
mind!"

She came upright in the bed, gathering the coverlets about her,
her face gone white as death.

"James!" she whispered. "Get out of here! I—I'll scream!"

"As you are screaming now?" he mocked. "That was what I expected you to do; but you cannot, can you? For, however you think
that you should behave, your heart's my ally—in league with me!"

"Go!" she sobbed. "Oh, James—please go!"

"Aye," he growled, "I'll go a-right, but with you, Lass. Have done
with folly. You were meant for me, and all your denials serve for
nought. Now get you up and dressed. I'll turn my back. . . ."

"I said I'll scream!" she hissed.

"I think not," he laughed, softly.

Her head arched back, back, her mouth came open; but his big
hand clamped across it like a vise.

"I'm sorry, Lass," he said tenderly, "that you force me to this pass.
Still, I'll make it up to you. But time is fleeting, and Clan Jarrett must
go on—"

Whereupon he bent and scooped her up, coverlets and all, as though
she were a waxen doll. Soared through her window in a matchless leap,
struck ground, his long, powerful legs already in full marching stride.
Bore her away to the bluff, scrambled down it, some two hundred
yards above the stairs. Dumped her unceremoniously into the boat.
Snarled at the black oarsmen:

"Row, you inky images of antique sin! Goddamn your kinky heads,
row!"

The boat shot away from the bluff like an arrow. Far above her,
Mary could see the torches of the patrol. Even then, had she screamed,

she could have brought rescue. But, to her own vast amazement, she lay there at his feet—and did not make a sound.

He came marching up to the house in the first light of dawn. He did not know or even care that at the Knoxes', Henry and Cromwell snored blissfully on. Only Martha stirred fitfully in her sleep, her cries throat-locked as she stared into the pit of hell that nightly yawned before her. With all the black evil in her heart, she did not make a good murderess. She was very slowly going out of her mind from fear.

In James Jarrett's arms, Mary Knox sobbed pitifully. She knew only too well what interpretation the gossips of Savannah would put upon her disappearance. That James had not so much as touched her hand on that voyage mattered not at all, because no one would believe him innocent of her. Not ever. Nor, for that matter, her, of him.

James bore her into the house, into his bedroom. Put her down upon his bed.

"Compose yourself, Lass," he said gently. "I go to fetch Reverend Wesley. . . ."

She came upright, staring at him, and her eyes were wild.

"And when you come again," she said, "you'll find me dead!"

He sat there, looking at her. His eyes were very black.

"Then," he said very simply, "there is but one thing to do—"

His hand came out. Big fingers locked in the top of her nightdress. She heard the sodden rip of cloth, felt the dawn chill on her flesh. Opened her mouth to scream; but, then, she saw his eyes. What was in them was another thing than lust. Wonder. Awe. Something close to reverence. . . .

"James," she whispered, "why do you look upon me—thus?"

"Because it is so," he murmured, "that men should look—upon the miracles—of God!"

Then he took her in his arms.

When time was again, when existence came shuddering into being once more, she opened her eyes to find him gone. She looked down at the slim and silvery length of her body. Reached wildly to draw the covers up about her. Stayed her hand inches from them. Lay there staring at her form with what she didn't know was—pride.

Her mind was a maze of wonder. She had fought. He couldn't deny that! She had defended herself with teeth and nails, thrashing like a wild thing, raking him bloody, clawing for his eyes. But he—he had only laughed, and then—

The struggles had ceased. There had been death's own stillness; the sudden stab of pain. That went on and on until she'd thought she could bear it no longer. But she had borne it. Found amazingly that it was no longer pain.

She slapped her slim flanks now, stingingly.

"You're a traitor!" she wept. "You—you betrayed me! You and you!" she added, raising her fingers to her bruised and swollen mouth. The mouth that had ceased crying. That had clung and clung, insistently uttering wild, sweet, tender things. That had cried out at last, but not from pain—Oh, no, not evermore from pain!

The shame was in her now, bottomless and deep. I've played the whore! she wept inside her mind. He'll think—

What matters it what he thinks? I must go—escape him forever. Submit to this degradation no more—

She sprang from the bed, gathered her shredded nightdress from the floor, put it on. Stood there, staring at it ruefully. The sun stood high in the heavens, now. Even if she wrapped herself in blankets, she could never—

She raced to the closet, tore it open. Saw the tartans and the kilts hanging there. They were far too big for her; but she bound them about her as best she could. Flew to the door. Found it locked.

"Oh, you beast! You beast!" she wailed.

Then she saw the window. Crossed to it, looked down. A drain spout was at hand. A little courage and—

But she hung there, seeing that landscape flooded with sun. His lands, his! The giant oaks trailing silver moss. The tiny figures of the indentured servants moving down the furrows, sowing the seed, their bodies rhythmic in the ancient rites of Spring.

The channel, blue silver in the morning light. The high and cloudless sky. All beauty and all—peace. Such a house as any woman could love with her whole heart. A house where she could wait and —say it! Speak the truth—thrill to the sound of her man's footsteps returning in the night. Where she could croon her babies to sleep, watch them grow tall and strong with noses like a broadaxe's blade, a single jut of brow, eyes like young eagles, and a mouth—a mouth—

She could feel the weakness entering her. The slow, deep warmth. She raised her fingertips and touched her mouth. The hard, sweet, bruising heat of his kisses was upon it still. She stumbled blindly away from the window, stood there trembling. Heard the key turn in the lock.

"I've brought you a dress," James whispered. "Stole it from my manservant Stephens' wife. It's too big, but 'twill have to do. Quick, Lass, put it on. Though I must say you're deuced fetching the way you are!"

"Oh, James!" she wailed.

"Quick, Lass! The Reverend Wesley's downstairs. Tim. Both Mrs. Hawkins and Mrs. Welch for witnesses. I picked them on purpose as they have the foulest tongues in town. That way no doubt can ever be cast upon—"

"I won't marry you!" she stormed; "I'll die first! I—"

"Will go home and bear the son I've probably given you," he chuckled, "unshriven and alone? Nay, Mary, you can't escape me, now. . . ."

"Oh, James—" she whispered; "a—a child—a son! I—I hadn't thought—"

"Well, think now," he said gravely.

She turned away her face. Bowed her head. Then, suddenly, wildly, she turned. Flew to his arms.

"Oh, James! Oh, my darling—I hope it's so!" she said.

So it was, that when Cromwell and Henry Knox stormed ashore at dusk of evening, armed to the teeth and surrounded by friends and retainers equally armed, Mary met them on her new doorstep, her arm through James', her eyes like stars.

"Put down your arms, my brothers," she whispered gently; "for we —are wed . . ."

"I don't believe it!" Henry howled. "It's a trick! I'll—"

"You may go ask Reverend Wesley, if you like," James said calmly, "or Mr. Higgins, Mrs. Hawkins, and Mrs. Welch. They witnessed the ceremony. Look in the register in the Kirk—"

"Then," Cromwell Knox roared, "I'll make you a widow so damn fast—"

"Hold on there, Crom," John Filbert, one of the men who had come with them, said. "What's to be served by that? I came to rescue an abducted maid from her seducer. But Lord Jim's righted matters, it appears to me. All right, he kilt Pete—but in a fair fight, when your brother was trying to brand 'im. And maybe he did besmirch your sister's name a mite. But damn it all, man, for that he's provided the best remedy in the world!"

"Thank you, friend," James said gravely. "I want only peace from here on in. In proof of which, I'd like to invite you all to my wedding supper. There's ale, wine, stout, bitters, claret—even a tun or two of good Scotch whiskey. Turkey, duck, chicken—a baron of beef—"

"Done!" John Filbert roared. "I accept! What say you, lads?"

"Lead us on!" the crowd chorused. "Let's get drunk as Lords, and kiss the blushing bride!"

The Knoxes stood there apart, glowering. Mary stretched out her hands to them.

"You, too," she said wistfully; "please, Henry, Crom—"

Cromwell's face slowly cleared.

"Right," he said. "I would not have had you for a brother-in-law, you heathen Scot; but, since you are—here's my hand!"

"You, Henry?" Mary whispered.

Henry stared at her. Drew himself up proudly.

"I am not such," he said, "as to spit upon my brother's grave!"

Then he turned upon his heel and left them there.

Thus it was, and under such auspices, that James Jarrett, Marquis of Argyll, Lord and Chieftain of Clan Jarrett, took a wife.

Which had, of course, its consequences.

CHAPTER FIFTEEN

THEY HAD A YEAR of very nearly perfect happiness. Mary made him a lovely, enchanting wife. The coldness of which Tim Higgins and others had accused her, was conspicuous by its absence. James Jarrett lolled through life, filled with a complacent content that was almost comical.

If it hadn't been for the indentured servants, he would have had nothing in this world to complain of. But Tim's estimation of them proved damnably accurate. They managed to spoil the rice crop completely, and the tobacco was so scant as to be scarcely worth the harvesting.

He and Tim put their heads together.

"I vote we go back to rumrunning," Tim growled. "That way at least we'll—"

"No," James said. "Now that I'm married, I mean to set my sons a sterling example. Respectability, Tim. I can't go on being an outlaw all my life—"

"You mean she's already—?" Tim said.

"Of course," James said complacently. "We Jarretts are a fertile tribe. So rumrunning's out, Tim. What think you of cattle?"

"Excellent," Tim said. "We've got enough money left to buy the beginnings of a herd. I'll go over to Carolina and—"

"You don't have to. I've already spoken to Cromwell. He's willing to part with seven cows, and lend me his prize bull to service them."

"Seven's damned few," Tim said.

"I know. But there are any number of brush cattle loose south of the Altamaha—escaped from the Spanish farms. We'll take ourselves a trip down there . . ."

"You're crazier than usual!" Tim groaned. "What with the General in England raising troops to fight the Dons, we'll probably get shot on sight!"

"I think not," James said calmly. "Besides, I have still another venture in mind, first—a trip upriver to Fort Augusta to set us up in the fur trade. Ever noticed that every respectable fortune in Georgia has been made in either cattle raising or fur trading?"

"That's true enough," Tim said judiciously. "Only, Jim, boy, none of those fortunes could hold a candle to the money we could make right here if we had us some niggers. . . ."

"Well, we haven't," James said, "and we won't have until after the General gets back. You've signed the appeal to withdraw the prohibition of slavery, haven't you?"

"Me and everybody else except the blinking Salzburgers and your ruddy Highlanders. What about you?"

"Signed it, of course. My fellow countrymen have had no love lost for me since I refused to join their regiment—so I've no need to court their favor. The appeal's a forlorn hope, anyhow—the General's stubborner than a mule, and he's got the Trustees in the hollow of his hand. We'll have to get along without blacks for a good many years yet, Tim—"

"Mayhap until the General dies, what, boy? Rum old customer for a fact; but, damnit, you can't help but like him!"

"The General's a good sort, Tim. Even when he's wrong—as he often is—he's wrong for the right reasons. Well, what say you to our trip up to Augusta?"

"Fine. But that ain't the question. The real trouble is: what is your lady going to say?"

"Oh, she won't mind at all. She's at the stage now where a husband's damned superfluous. . . ."

"All the same," Tim said, "she ain't agoing to like it. Have you told her what you mean to do?"

"No," James said. "I'll tell her today. But I don't expect any trouble from that quarter. . . ."

Which proved how little he knew about women still.

"You'd leave me—like this!" Mary stormed. "Gross and helpless! Oh, James, I was right! I should never have married you! You're horrid, beastly, selfish, and—"

"Now, now, Lass," James laughed. "Stephens and his wife will take care of you. And though you know it not, it's because of you that I'm going. . . ."

"Because of me?" Mary wailed. "I know I'm troublesome, now! But all women are, I'm told, when they're like this. And I'm not pretty anymore . . . That's it, isn't it, Sir James!"

"My precious idiot," James said fondly, "you're prettier than ever. So round and rosy. I confess I find you deuced fetching this way. . . ."

"Fetching?" Mary wept. "Being sick in the mornings? Crying at night? Aching all over, and quarrelling with you every time you open your mouth, no matter what it is you say? I think not, James! The truth's quite obvious: you're already tired of me!"

He seized her gaily, sat her on his knee.

"Never shall I tire of you, Lass," he said softly. "And you've the right to be as troublesome as you like. It's not that. Don't you see, Mary, that we have to stop thinking about ourselves at last, and start considering the future of our son?"

"What has running off into the woods among savage redskins, and mayhap getting yourself killed got to do with our baby?" she sobbed.

"Everything. I was wrong not to take you into my confidence before, Lass. But the fact is that the crops have failed. And little James damned well can't grow up in poverty. You wouldn't want that now, would you?"

"No—" she whispered tremulously. "You mean that by going into the woods, you can make enough money to see that our son grows up like a gentleman?"

"A blessed lot. And it will only be this once. My idea is to set Tim up as my agent in the fur trade. That way we'll always have funds, no matter what these stupid louts do to the crops. . . ."

"But I thought you said that cattle—"

"That, too. In three or four months we'll have the beginnings of the finest herd in the colony. Now be a good Lass, and don't worry about me while I'm gone. . . ."

She buried her face in the hollow of his throat.

"I shall worry," she whispered. "That I cannot help, James. If anything happened to you, I should die!"

"Nothing will happen to me," he said stoutly. "The redskins are friendly enough. And as angry as the Carolinians are over the General's policy of licensing the fur traders, they'll hardly declare war. After all, both colonies are English. . . ."

"You're right," she murmured. "Our baby must have the best, mustn't he? But, James, Love, do hurry back, I pray you!"

He was to remember her words. In fact, he did remember them, often. Because the trip to Fort Augusta proved much too easy. There was something disquieting about that fact. The only regret James had upon his return was that he had chosen his lands too soon. St. Simon was lovely—but the countryside about Fort Augusta was nothing short of glorious. Over the years, a man and his sons could clear themselves a thousand acres—ten thousand acres—half a world! Really become lords of the earth up there . . . Well, it was too late now. He had his plantation for good or ill, and there he'd have to abide.

The journey was entirely successful. Tim secured his license as a trader. In that year, 1738, Augusta was the greatest fur trading post in North America. In three trips, Tim made back twice what they had lost with their ill-fated crops. Successful, too, was their expedition into Spanish territory to secure strayed cattle. They returned with a hundred head, more or less. On that journey, they did not see a single Spaniard, and the Seminoles were friendly enough to be pacified with trinkets. Fortune had indeed favored them.

Which, curiously, worried James. Few things in his life had ever come to him easily, and when they had, as in his early years with the Andrews, they had soon gone bad. On the surface, it looked as if his luck had changed; but luck, as well he knew, was a fickle jade, not apt to abide with a man. Besides, he had a Scotchman's conscience, deny it though he would. What had he ever done to merit all he'd gained? His hands were stained with blood: Hogg's, that highwayman's, Peter Knox's. He had destroyed Maebelle Andrews' future, not to mention Sue's. His presence in the New World was due to his activities as a thief. And how had he begun life here in Georgia? By running in contraband rum!

Yet, his affairs continued to flourish. Even the indentured servants were working fairly well. The crop, this Fall would be, if not good, average. Why then was he worried? Mary was plump and rosy, her health good, the discomforts of her early pregnancy passed, her temper sweet and serene. . . .

The wages of sin, he told himself mockingly, are overwhelming success!

But by September 18th, of that Year of Our Lord, 1738—the day that the *Blandford,* protected by the Man o' War, *Hector,* and shepherding five transports packed to the gunn'ls with troops, appeared on the horizon, bringing General James Oglethorpe back from England—James Jarrett had all but forgot his not entirely unreasonable fears. Mary was blissfully sunk in that curious placidity which is nature's protection for women great with child. Her health and her appetite were both remarkably good. In fact, she was rather a bit too fat; but neither of them gave that matter the importance it deserved. The child, by their deuced uncertain calculations, was due early in December. Mary sat in the sun, heavy and content, busily knitting tiny things. James turned his hand to making a cradle. It turned out a little better than the house had, but not much. As a carpenter, Laird James made an excellent swordsman.

He was relieved to find that Mary made no objections whatsoever to his proposal of spending a few days in Frederica with the General. The plain truth was that he was bored with so much peace. His private war with Mary's brothers seemed to have ended for good and all. Though neither of them had become really friendly, Cromwell, at least, was prepared to help his sister's husband all he could—because James was her husband, not because of any sudden change of heart. But Henry maintained his wall of frozen hostility.

Ah, well, James thought, as long as he leaves me jolly well alone. . . .

The morning that James set out for Frederica, about four miles distant from the farm he had not yet learned to call a plantation, the peace between him and the Knoxes was suddenly confirmed, perhaps for all time.

He was breakfasting with Mary in an antechamber, when Stephens, the oldest of the indentured servants, and the only married man of the lot, knocked upon the door of the little sitting room just off their bedchamber. Because of his age, James had retired Stephens from the fields, and employed him in the house in the capacity of a butler, while Elizabeth, his wife, served them as housekeeper and cook.

"Come in!" James called.

"Begging your pardon, Sir," Stephens said; "but Master Cromwell's downstairs. Wants to know if he may come up. He says it's important. . . ."

"Of course, Stephens," James said.

"Very good, Sir!" Stephens said.

Mary laid an anxious hand upon James' arm.

"You—you haven't quarrelled?" she whispered.

"Hardly," James said. "The last time I saw Crom was to pay him for those cows. Good beasties they are—four of them have already calved, and the other three are heavy. My talk with your brother was deuced friendly, Lass. Even a Knox rarely quarrels with a man come to bring him money. . . ."

"I'm glad," Mary said; but the knocking sounded on the door again.

James got up and opened it. Cromwell stood there, his face grey and working. He was clearly struggling with himself; just as clearly come upon an errand that sat plagued ill with him.

"Crom!" Mary gasped; "what's wrong?"

"It's Martha—" Cromwell said slowly. "She—she died this morning. We're burying her tomorrow. I—I thought about calling you two to the funeral, but in your state, Mary—"

They stood there, staring at him.

"But," Cromwell said heavily, "I didn't come merely to tell you about Martha's death. For that, a note sent by one of the servants would have sufficed. I'm a fair man, James Jarrett. I've come to offer you, in person, my apologies. . . ."

"For what?" James said.

Then Cromwell told them. All of it. How Martha had died raving, her mind broken by remorse and fear. Shrieking aloud the ugly details of the thing she had done.

"I got Reverend Whitefield, the new Minister, since your gossips here in Frederica have managed to chase both the Wesleys clear out of the colony," Cromwell said. "Of course, he did what he could; but I don't think she would have understood the Archbishop of Canterbury. Kept saying: 'It's no good, no good! I'm going to hell, I tell you—to hell!'"

"Poor thing!" Mary whispered.

"I should have known Peter's death was—strange," Cromwell said. "He was stronger than an ox. Remember how he came home from Saint Augustine, Mary? No mere cut arm would ever—"

"Oh, Crom!" Mary said, "I—I'm terribly sorry about Martha; but—on the other hand I'm glad! You don't know what a burden you've lifted from our lives!"

"So am I," Cromwell said gravely; "since James is family, now, I'd rather there were no more bad blood between us. And here's my hand on it. . . ."

Slowly James took his brother-in-law's hand.

"I'm not entirely guiltless," he sighed; "for if I hadn't slashed Peter's arm, he—"

"Would have burned your face!" Mary said hotly; "which was worse from my way of thinking!"

"Push the matter further back," James said dryly, "and you come to the fact that I scarred him first. Still further, and you arrive at the way we both were made. Go deep enough into things, Lass, and you ultimately stand face to face with God. Or the Devil. More likely the Devil, at least in my case. Look, Crom, I have to ride into town this morning. Would you like to come along?"

"No, thank you, James. Been some time since I had a chat with my wayward sister. Henry's quite worried about her. Says girls as small as she is have a bad time having babies. So I'd like to find out from her how she fares—"

"I see," James said. "Very well, I'll go alone, then. But, speaking of Henry, how'd he take dear Martha's confession?"

Cromwell frowned.

"He doesn't believe it," he said slowly. "Says Martha was out of her head and imagining things. Seems to me that hating you is a luxury he doesn't want to give up. . . ."

"Or a vice," James said dryly. "In any event, he can afford it, since I've vowed to keep my hands off any man of Mary's blood. Sit down, Crom. I'll have Stephens bring you up some coffee—"

But, before he reached Frederica, James was to have still another encounter. He had gone perhaps half the distance, mounted on his magnificent new Arab that Tim had brought him back from a Southern trip without any explanations whatsoever as to how he had obtained so fine an animal, when he saw another horseman coming toward him. The rider, he made out as they approached each other, was Lieutenant Hugh MacKay. James pulled the Arab up, and waited.

"Good day, Sir," young MacKay said stiffly. "The General's compliments. He sent me to find you. He'd like a word with you if you have the time—"

James smiled. Knowing the General, he doubted that the request had been couched in terms half so courteous.

"Go get me Jarrett," the General had probably growled. "I needs must have a word with him—and at once!"

"Very well," James said peacefully. "In fact, I was coming to call upon him. Lead on, Lieutenant. . . ."

MacKay put his black about. They cantered toward the town. Mac-Kay didn't say a word all the way. But James knew well what he was thinking. Such words as 'Traitor! Disgrace to all men of Scottish blood!' were running almost visibly through his mind. . . .

James found the General drawn and grey.

"Troubles, troubles, troubles!" he growled. "Why I sent for you, my boy. Mutiny's afoot—civil and military, blast it! Not to mention religious. Both the Wesley's gone. John—woman trouble. Charles, over-whelming ambition. Good riddance! Habersham turned businessman instead of attending to his preaching. And now, Causton, our fine bailiff and keeper of stores is misbehaving—robbing the colony blind for his friends like Noble Jones. Jones and his cronies are mouthing rebellion because they know I'm going to bring Tom Causton to book—"

"That takes care of the civil and religious," James said dryly. "What about the military?"

"Troops. New ones I brought over from Gibraltar. Rotten with Papist sentiment. Half of 'em Irish. Ready and willing to betray us to the Spanish because of their precious religion. Had to hang one bloke from the yardarm, and whip another—name of Shannon, William Shan-non. Had him drummed out of the regiment. A mistake. Should have stretched his neck, too. Now he's vanished. Rumor has it he's taken refuge with the Creeks, there to do what mischief he can—"

"What do you want of me, Sir?" James said. "If I can, I'm willing—"

"Act as my bodyguard. The blackguards are threatening my life. I know you don't see eye to eye with me over that business of rum—with which you and Higgins have flooded the Colony, and the question of Negro Slavery; but I know I can trust you for all that. Will you?"

"Of course," James said. "I'm at your service, Sir."

"Heard you've finally married Miss Knox, and that she's with child," the General growled. "That won't prevent—?"

"No," James said. "My son's not due until December."

"Plagued sure it's going to be a boy, aren't you?" the General laughed.

"We Jarretts always get what we want," James said.

So it was that he spent the next five days with General Oglethorpe in Savannah. The expected storm over the dismissal of Causton—for that clever individual managed to conceal or destroy all evidence on which a criminal charge could be based—blew over with nothing more than mutterings. But James served the General well, presenting him the colonists' complaints over the lack of rum, the prohibition of slavery, the laws of inheritance, and even—with the slowly growing prosperity of Georgia—over the sumptuary laws.

As he expected, the General rejected all complaints out of hand, exhorted the colonists to return to their all but disastrous silk and indigo planting, and commanded them to cease such new-fangled ideas as the planting of cotton, which that keenly mundane religious man, James Habersham, had already begun.

From there, James accompanied the General southward to Cumberland Island, where the strengthening of Fort Saint Andrew was the next item on the program. As it turned out, it was a good thing he did.

For the very next morning after their arrival, one hundred troops, in full battle array, marched upon the General's tent. The General received them calmly. But calm was not enough. The troops were plagued ugly. They demanded their back pay and full subsistence. Whereupon characteristically, General Oglethorpe damned them roundly as mutineers. Which was a mistake. Two of them opened fire, missing him by a hair.

An even greater mistake on their parts. For James Jarrett shot one of the would-be assassins dead upon the spot; put his dirk against the other's throat, and ordered the mutineers to lay down their arms on pain of seeing their companion die, too.

Even so, that moment lasted a nerve-crackling age; but then Hugh MacKay came charging out of the woods at the head of his Highlanders, and the revolt was over.

"My thanks," the General said gravely to James, "for having saved my life. MacKay, take this mutinous beggar to the nearest tree and hang him!"

James stood there, watching it, the taste of nausea at the back of his throat. Of all the unpleasant ways to die, hanging was the worst—except, mayhap, burning, which, thank God, he'd so far never seen.

The disarmed troops were drawn up in parade formation. On the left, the Highlanders' Pipe Major loosed the bagpipes' hideous cry. White-faced, young MacKay nodded to the drummer. The kettledrum's roll was long, drawn out. At an almost imperceptible signal from MacKay, a kilted Highlander jerked the General's campaign table, upon which the soldier stood, out from under him.

The man kicked once or twice, and that was all. The hangman had made his knot with skill. The mutineer's neck broke very cleanly.

Two more lives upon my soul, James thought grimly. Oh God, I—

It was then he heard the sound of running feet. He whirled facing the shore.

And Tim Higgins' bellow cut through the heavy silence like a bass-horn.

"Jim!" he roared, "you've got to come! Your wife, she—"

James whirled to face him.

"What's wrong, Tim?" he said.

"She's in labor, boy," Tim panted. "Way ahead o' time! And Lord Jesus—she—"

"She's what?" James whispered.

"I'm afeared she's—dying, boy," Tim wept. "Lord bless her sweet little soul! I've seen suffering and suffering, but—"

"Come on!" James spat.

"Wait!" the General snapped. "Mr. Fergurson; you're hereby detached! Accompany Sir James to his home and do what you can!"

"Yes, Sir!" the Highlanders' surgeon said.

"It started yesterday morning," Tim groaned, " 'bout dawn. Missus Stephens sent me for the midwife. She done what she could, but your brat's too big, boy . . . And Mary, poor little thing, tiny like she be—"

"Dear God!" James breathed.

"Damned brave," Tim choked. "Nary a whimper 'til 'most night. Then she started in to scream. That was when I left. Couldn't stand it any more. We rowed all night and half the day. Thought we never would get here. . . ."

"Thanks, Tim," James whispered, and, bowing his head, he began to pray. But he had the despairing feeling that his prayers did not mount above the mast. What availed the prayers of a killer and a thief? A despoiler of women? A rumrunner, blackguard? For that matter, what value had even the prayers of a Saint, now?

The boat seemed glued to the ocean. Roughly James pushed aside one of the Negroes whom Tim, as always had hired from a Carolina planter, as the prohibition against slavery in Georgia was still in effect. He took the oars himself. He doubled, straightened, pulling with all his strength. The boat shot ahead.

Still, it was midafternoon of the next day before they got back to Saint Simon's. The Negroes hung helplessly over the gunwales, bathed in sweat, their tongues out, panting. But James Jarrett leaped ashore, already running. Clumsily Tim and the surgeon followed.

There was no sound. At the door, James stopped, unable to move a muscle. He hung there, trembling, and Mrs. Stephens came out to meet him.

"Is she—is she—?" he croaked.

"Not y-y-yet," Mrs. Stephens sobbed, "but she's sinking fast. Been unconscious since last night, and—"

James shoved by her, went flying up those stairs.

Mary lay there on the big bed. Her face was the countenance of a woman dead of torture. Only when he leaned close, could he see her breathe.

Then Doctor Fergurson took over.

"Water!" he rapped out. "Hot! Tell me, Sir James, have you any rum?"

"Yes," James whispered.

"Send it up," the surgeon snapped; "and you stay the hell out of here! I've got to take that child. I'm sorry, but it's her only chance. . . ."

James hung there.

"Couldn't—couldn't you save them both?" he whispered.

"No," the surgeon said gently. "There's one chance in a thousand that I could save the child—at the cost of its mother's life. You want that, Sir James?"

"God, no!" James shuddered. "Save my Mary, Doctor—"

"For that, the chances are somewhat better," the Doctor said; "though, frankly, I can promise nothing." He turned to the midwife. "Go wash your filthy hands!" he spat; "then come back. Though what good you'll be, I'm sure I don't know. Had I my way, the whole tribe of you murderesses would be hanged out of hand!"

The next two hours were, for James Jarrett, purest hell. Finally the fat, slovenly midwife came down stairs.

"The Doc sez you kin come up, now," she said.

James stared at her.

"Your Missus is going to be just fine," the midwife said. "That Doc's all right, for all his rough talk. But the kid—"

"The child?" James croaked.

"A girl," the midwife murmured pityingly. "And dead, th' poor lil' thing. The Doc done all he could, even to blowing into her mouth. But 'twere no go. I'm sorry, Sir—"

James flew up the stairs.

As he came into the room, astonishingly, Mary opened her eyes.

He could see her lips move. He bent over her, gathered her into his arms.

"Oh, James," she sobbed, her voice so low that he had to strain to hear what she said. "I've failed you! Oh, my poor darling, I'm so sorry —so very sorry, Love—"

"Hush!" James croaked, his eyes scalded, blind. "You're alive and that's what counts. . . ."

"I'll do better—next time," she breathed. "I—I promise you—"

James felt the doctor's hand upon his arm. Afterwards, he never knew whether Doctor Fergurson had heard, or had merely guessed her words.

"Come outside a moment, my boy," the surgeon said.

James followed him out into the hall.

"There must never be a next time," the doctor growled. "The next one would kill her, sure!"

James stood there. Then he threw back his head and laughed aloud. That laughter was the bitterest sound in all the world.

"Clan Jarrett!" he choked. "Brave men all—tall in their pride!"

"Have you gone mad?" the doctor said.

"Nay," James said quietly; "not yet. But I shall. Mark this well, Doctor—I shall!"

Then he turned and went back into that silent room.

CHAPTER SIXTEEN

J AMES," MARY SAID fretfully, "don't tell me you're going away—
again!"

"Yes, Lass," James said quietly. "The General's invited me to go
along with him on his trip to Coweta, the capital of the Creek Nation.
It's terribly important, Mary. Because with our relations with Spain
growing worse daily, we'd better make sure the Creeks are on our
side. . . ."

"How far is it?" Mary said.

"About three hundred miles," James told her.

"Oh, James!" she wailed; "then you'll be away for months!"

"No more than two," he said reassuringly, "though it does depend
upon how long it takes us to come to some agreement with the
Creeks. . . ."

"James, I don't think I believe you! Old Tomochichi adores the
General. And ever since the Colony was founded we haven't had the
slightest trouble with the Indians. . . ."

"Look, Mary, things are different now. For one thing, the Dons in
Saint Augustine have been stirring up the Seminoles; and the Creeks
are too friendly with that Nation. For another, ever since that scoundrel
Bottomsworth married Mary Musgrove our relations with the Creeks
haven't been as good as they formerly were. . . ."

"I know all that," Mary whispered. "Reverend Bottomsworth is trying to steal all the best lands because Mary is a Creek princess. Claims
they belong to her, and that Tomochichi had no right to sign them
away. A matter which can be settled easily enough. What I want to
know is why are you *really* going?"

"I told you," James said lamely. "The General—"

"Rubbish. You spent a week in Savannah last December when they held those meetings about slavery, which I must say I'm glad the General rejected. To hold human beings in bondage is both a crime and a sin, James Jarrett!"

"Don't see where a bit more of either will make the fires awaiting me any hotter," James drawled; "and meantime we struggle on here with these worthless indentured scum—"

"Then," Mary went on angrily, "you went to Port Royal in April with the General on a trip that had no other object than to display his credentials as Commander in Chief of the troops of both colonies. Journeys up to Augusta with Tim—three, I believe. Another expedition down to Florida to get more cattle, although we have more than we need, now—"

"It's the future I'm thinking about, Love," James said.

"It is not! What you're thinking about is staying away from me as often, as far, and as long as possible!"

"Now, Lass—" James began.

"Now, nothing! You haven't so much as—as kissed me in more than three weeks, James. Not to mention—"

"What cannot be mentioned by a modest lass," James said dryly. "I know. But—"

"Is this the way you plan to arrange the future, James?" Mary whispered. "By denying me the child I want and need?"

"Mary," James said, his voice dark with anguish, "I wish you wouldn't inquire into my behavior. For me, it's been purest hell!"

"And for me," she said simply. "I like being loved, James. So, now, tell me—why have you taken away from me the—the joy of being your wife ever since I lost our baby?"

"Mary, for God's love, don't ask me that!"

"I do ask it. And not for God's love, my husband; but for thine. Tell me—why?"

"All right," James groaned. "I've been avoiding this subject like the plague. But you must back me up into corners. Sit down, Lass. What I have to tell you isn't very pleasant—"

With her great blue eyes upon him wonderingly, Mary sank into a chair.

"Doctor Fergurson says," James said flatly, "that another child would—kill you, Lass. Naturally, I—"

She sat there very still, looking at him. The summer light of her eyes changed, became crystalline, brimmed moonsilver on her pale lashes, spilled over, traced slow streaks down her cheeks.

"Don't, Mary!" he croaked. "Please don't cry!"

"You see only—the tears on my face," she whispered; "not those that—that run through my heart. They—they scald me, James. . . ."

"Lass, I'm sorry," he began; but she came up out of her chair in one wild rush, and hurled herself into his arms.

"I knew you were good!" she sobbed, "in spite of all your thunder and pretense. But how good you are, I did not know! I realize what having sons means to you, my James—and I—I've failed you forever. Because of me—of me!—Clan Jarrett must die. Oh, no, James! I can't let that happen! All my life long I'll remember that day you told me your dreams, explained why I must be your wife—because you believed I'd be the perfect mother for your brood—bring them up to be so gentle and so fair!"

"Hush, Love," James said tenderly.

"I will not hush! I want to howl like a child! To scream and roll in the dirt!"

"Which," he chuckled, "will arrange nothing, Lass. . . ."

She raised her eyes to his, then; and the light in them was deep and still.

"James," she whispered, "take me upstairs now—and love me to sleep!"

"Or better yet," he said dryly, "I could draw my dirk and plunge it through your heart. That would be quicker, Mary."

"James, doctors have been wrong! And I—"

"Fergurson is a graduate of Edinburgh, Mary—and that's damned well the most advanced medical school on earth. I've deaths enough upon my conscience now. . . ."

"I care not for what you have upon your conscience," she said, "but I will not have upon mine the destruction of unborn generations down to the end of time!"

"Listen, Mary," he said gravely, "nothing is to be served by this folly. You'd risk your life to give me the son I crave; but I cannot permit you this species of gallantry. For one thing, 'tis not a risk, but a certainty. For another, the likelihood is that your sacrifice would be in vain, because there are nine chances in ten that the child would die, too. So I shall go with the General. Away from you, not seeing you daily, my lot's much easier to bear. . . ."

"And mayhap," she said darkly, "away from me, you may encounter some maid who—"

His native sense of mischief got the better of him, then.

"And if I did?" he said mockingly.

"I think I should die," she whispered. "I know this is bad of me. I—I should understand; but I—I couldn't, James. The very thought of another woman in your arms, makes me sick unto death. . . ."

"Don't worry about that, Lass," he said quietly. "I told you once that there was no other maid for me upon all this earth. That still holds true. And it always will, sons or no. Besides, 'tis my fault, anyhow. . . ."

"Your fault? I don't see—"

"The things I've done," he whispered, "have no pardon on earth, or in heaven, Mary. Hence this—this visitation. The mills of God, men say, grind slowly; but they grind most exceedingly fine!"

The night of August 21st, 1739, James sat before the campfire in Coweta, watching the Creek braves performing their buffalo dance. But in reality, he did not see the howling, painted redskins. His mind was three hundred miles away—with Mary. For all his craggy looks and towering stature that made him look much older, he was still only twenty-four. He could look forward to forty or fifty years more of life. Forty years of emptiness, of vacancy. And with him, Clan Jarrett must die. . . .

Rebellion rose in him, hotly. 'Tis not just! he thought; not just! I've been a swine, all right; but the world is filled with swine, busily engaged in producing their litters, while I—

He bowed his head, feeling the salt sting of tears upon his lashes. And a soft hand stole out and touched his arm. He jerked upright, and stared into the face of a halfbreed maid. He already knew who she was. In his gruff way, the General had jested about the way that the Creek's interpreter, Loosaponakee MacTavish, had been staring at James ever since he arrived in this metropolis of tepees.

Loosa was very fair. From her Scotch father, a fur trader, she had inherited green-grey eyes, and a reddish tint to her long, dark hair.

"My father says," she whispered, "that the skirts the Scotch braves wear are a sign of manhood, Sir James. And those tears are the weakness of women. You must not shame your tribe this way!"

"Aye, Loosa," James growled. "You're right. But there are times when—"

"Why do you weep, Sir James?" Loosa said.

He started to answer her with some mocking quip; but the firelight was in those eyes, then. Watching him, they were grave and still—filled with—with tenderness. That. Almost surely that.

"I answer your question with another, Loosa," James growled; "Why do you care?"

"I know not," she said simply, "but I do. Mayhap 'tis the call of blood to blood. For we are both Scotch, you and I—though I am only half. . . ."

"You sound as if you regretted that other half," James said dryly.

"No," Loosa said. "My father always says that the Creeks are the finest of the Great Spirit's children. He loved my poor mother dearly. In proof of which, he wedded her not only according to the custom of the Creeks, but once again in your Kirk—travelling all the way to Beaufort Town to do it. I am glad to be a Creek. And I am glad to be a Scot—especially now—because you are here. Because my father made me learn your so difficult tongue, and I can talk to you. Because—perhaps, I can even comfort you—"

"For my grief," James said morosely, "there is no comfort under heaven. . . ."

"Why? Have you lost someone you loved, Sir James?"

"Nay, Loosa—and yes. For the one I've lost is a son unborn. I wept for him. For him, and all the sons I'll never have!"

Loosa stared at him.

"This is a hard saying, Sir James. And I am but a simple maid. I confess I do not understand it. To have sons, a man needs but to wed, and—"

"Nay, Lass," James said. "Sometimes he needs more—a wife sound enough in body to have them. . . ."

Loosa stared at him, her great eyes troubled—even sad.

"Then," she whispered, "you are already wed, and your wife—"

"Aye, Loosa," James said.

"She is—sick?" Loosa said.

"No," James said. "'Tis a hellishly rare business, Loosa—and one that I see no need to burden you with, fair lass. . . ."

"It would not be a burden," Loosa said gravely; "and I should like to know. Besides, talking helps sometimes, Sir James. . . ."

He looked at her. She sat there, waiting. He was a Scot, with all the proud silence of that race. But, somehow, he found himself talking, telling her the failure of his dreams. He poured out his grief, his pain.

And Loosaponakee listened to it all, without a word or sign. Then, very quietly, she got up and left him there.

He stared after her, in astonishment and pain. She had not said so much as fare thee well or even good night. She crossed the red circle of the firelight, beyond the prancing braves. Came to the door of her tepee. Stood there a long moment, like one lost in thought. Then she went on, beyond it, to the edge of the woods. She stopped then. Turned. Looked at him. A long, long look—as grave and tender as the night. As filled with meaning. Then she plunged into the utter blackness beneath the trees.

James sat there, frozen. Louder than the dogskin drums, he heard the sudden thunder of his heart. He felt his legs move, thrusting upward, powerfully. Oh, no! he groaned inside his heart; of all the swinish things on earth—

But he took a step forward. Another. Then suddenly, wildly, he began to run, straight toward the brooding silence of the trees.

Each morning during the month they remained in Coweta, he fought again his predoomed fight. Cursed himself, tortured himself with the remembered image of Mary's face. Heard again her words: "The thought of another woman in your arms makes me sick unto death—" Swore he'd go no more to that pleasant spot beside the little stream where the water talked with dark voices in the night. But at the dusk of evening, all his vows drowned in the torrents of his blood, were blasted out of time by the trumpeting of his heart. . . .

He lay in the pale light of the morning they were to go, once more at Loosa's side.

"You know, Loosa," he said, "that we leave today?"

"Yes," she whispered.

"I must go, Lass," he groaned. "When a man weds, he gives his sacred word—"

"I know," Loosa said.

He stared at her. The dawn light was in her eyes. And that smile, that smile—

"You seem glad to be rid of me!" he snarled.

Slowly she shook her head.

"No, James," she said. "I am not glad—not of that. . . ."

"Then what are you glad of?" he growled.

"Of—of having known you," she said; "of having had you for a

little while. It is not enough, but I'll be content with that. All my life
long, I'll think of you, and the very thought will comfort me. Besides—"

"Besides what, Loosa?" he said.

"Nothing," she whispered.

He peered at her, his eyes very black.

"What will become of you, now, Lass?" he said.

"I go to join my father. He's up north, among the Cherokees. He
writes that they, too, are a fine Nation. Civilized. They plant and sow
like you palefaces do. They live in houses and wear white men's
clothing—"

"And mayhap there, you'll find some sturdy brave—"

"No, James," she said gently; "that is quite impossible, now."

"Why?"

"No man could ever take your place, James," she whispered. "That's
one thing—"

"And another?" he growled.

"That one is enough," Loosa said. "Now get you up, and go from
here, before your fierce General sends men to find you—"

"Loosa—" he all but wept.

"Go, James," she said softly; "and quickly, while I yet can bear
it. . . ."

After he had gone, she got slowly to her feet. Went to the stream.
Entered it. Washed all over, her motions curiously ritualistic. Came
out again, donned her deerskin robe. Stood there a long, long time,
until the light of the newly risen sun was dazzling through her tears.

Then slowly, softly, sweetly, she smiled.

You have your wish, my James, she thought. Your tribe will not
die with you, now. And that beauty of yours—that face of thunder and
of storm will go on forever. . . .

She started back toward Coweta. Stopped again.

"Great Spirit," she prayed, "father of all. Make it a man-child—a
warrior—with eyes like night, a tomahawk for a nose, a black brush of a
brow and—"

Then she started running, toward the sleeping town.

When they reached Fort Augusta, the shame was in James still. I
cannot face Mary now, he thought bitterly; she'll look into my eyes
and see—

Then he saw the runner coming toward them. The General pulled
up his horse and waited. James and the others did the same. The Creek

brave raised high his message stick for them to see. Between its fork was a roll of paper. The Indian runner held it up to General Oglethorpe. The General took the scroll, unwound it. Read it quickly. James could see the sparks in his eyes, the smouldering, the blaze. Slowly the great man turned to them.

"Gentlemen—we are at war with Spain," he said.

CHAPTER SEVENTEEN

IT WAS, James realized, the outbreak of war that had saved him from giving himself away to Mary. Upon his Scotch conscience, the burden of his guilt was heavy indeed. But in the bustle and the excitement of the preparations for battle, the reasons for his sad silences could be well concealed. Besides, Mary had other things to occupy her mind. She could see widowhood looming up before her; she had a painful knowledge of how rashly brave her Highland Laird was. Beyond that, beneath it, ran a deeper, subtler fear, which she never put into words: With the destruction of all his hopes, what was to prevent her James from deliberately seeking death, hurling himself into the thick of the fight in the vanguard of a Highlanders' charge?

She wept herself to sleep nightly in her lonely room—for she had acceded to James' entirely reasonable request that he occupy another, now—during that month and a half that the war held fire.

Betimes, James occupied himself with many things. On October 6th, he followed the bier of the ancient chief Tomochichi, dead at last at ninety-seven years of age, and buried, at his dying request, among his white friends in Percival Square in Savannah. Beyond that, James sat in the counsels of War; refused the command offered him on the realistic basis that his knowledge of military tactics was nil; enlisted for the duration under Lieutenant George Dunbar in the Second Highland Regiment; soberly made his will, leaving everything to Mary—

And, on November 16th, 1739, this slow-fuse war burst finally into fire.

It was Tim who brought James the news. He came ashore at the landing before the plantation, his sunbrowned face hard and still.

"It's started, boy," he growled. "The Dons have taken Amelia Island near St. Augustine. Killed two Highlanders—unarmed by all accounts —and hacked their bodies to pieces. . . ."

"Tim," James said wearily; "you ever see a Highlander even go to bed without at least one skean dhu tucked into his socks?"

"Well—no," Tim said, "but—"

"But the ear of that smuggling scoundrel Jenkins wasn't enough," James said, "albeit we've converted him into a peaceful trader instead of the demi-pirate he was. Public enthusiasm for our General's imperialistic designs upon Florida is somewhat less than delirious, friend. The Highlanders are well liked, and to elevate them from mere soldiers fallen in the line of duty, to noble martyrs to our cause just might provide the necessary spark. The General is not overscrupulous with the truth when it suits his purpose not to be. . . ."

"Spark, hell!" Tim grinned. "He's got himself a whole bonfire, now, boy! You're wanted in Savannah. His Nibs, himself, sent me to find you. . . ."

"We leave at once, Tim?"

"No. We'll have to drill and puff and make speeches for a day or two. Give the poltroons a good show, what? Some of 'em might be charmed into enlisting, that way. . . ."

"I'm glad we don't sail today," James sighed. "I'm just not up to tearful goodbyes at the moment. Don't mention what your errand's about to Mary, Lad. I'll prepare her for my departure as gradually as I can. . . ."

They came up the stairs from the river to find Savannah echoing with noise and excitement. They moved through the roaring crowds to the General's office. When they came out again, having been placed on active duty, they saw a man flying before a mob—led, James was not at all surprised to note, by his valiant brothers-in-law, Cromwell and Henry Knox. The man was already bloody, and, as James watched, Henry pulled him down. The others ringed him round about, kicking.

James drew his big horse pistols slowly. Calmly looked to their priming. Crossed to that ring of would-be murderers. Cleared his way to the center of it by the simple process of cracking the heads of all who were in his way with the barrels of his guns.

A moment later, Tim was at his side, his pistols likewise in his hands.

"You Highland dog!" Henry howled; "why you—"

"Shut up, Henry," James said quietly. "I promised Mary I wouldn't kill you, but I said nothing about breaking your filthy bones. Now hear me, all. I know not what this man's offense was—"

"The yellow rat won't enlist!" Cromwell snarled; "one of them damned Dutchmen, James—those Moravians who claim their religion's against killing—"

James smiled. In the General's office he had seen the enlistment rolls, so he knew perfectly well where he stood.

"And you, Cromwell?" he said tartly, "is your faith also against it?"

"Well—" Cromwell spluttered, "I just haven't had time, yet—"

"I see," James said. "Busy crew, aren't we all? Henry, who hid out every time the recruiting officer came to call. Jonas, who had to go trapping out of season; Philips, whose wife—a sturdy lass if I ever saw one—was suddenly taken ill. The whole blinking lot of you! I've seen the enlistment rolls, friends—the General showed them to me half an hour ago. Bit of a case of the sinless casting the first stones, what?"

They stood there, with hangdog looks, muttering.

"So, of all men present," James went on calmly, "only Tim and I have the right to kick this poor devil. A right which I hereby waive for us both, with Tim's permission—"

"Yep," Tim growled. "It ain't him I want to kick!"

"Because," James said, "you all knew where the Moravians stood. For years now, they've undergone abuse, insult, physical attack, in defense of their beliefs—all without raising a hand in their own defense. In this colony, religious freedom—with the sole exception of Papism—is guaranteed by the laws. When you assaulted this man, 'twas you, not he, who were guilty of a criminal act. The Moravians want peace, and are willing to suffer for it. I call that—heroic. What you've done is its opposite. And not only now. When they tried to emigrate to Pennsylvania, you held them here until they could pay back into the common fund the price of their passage here. The only reason why this man hasn't gone is because he's poor. So now, my fine patriots, form ranks!"

"Form ranks?" Henry spat. "Why the devil should we?"

"Because I say so," James snapped; "and I'm the devil's son! Tim, form them up. We're going to march in proud formation to the recruiting office, where these sterling patriots will be most happy to put down their names. Detail a couple to help the German to his home. And Tim—"

"Yes, boy?"

"Shoot the first man who breaks formation, no matter who he is!"

In truth he needed not his pistols; their shame in itself would have been enough. Watching them bending over the book on Hugh Mac-Kay's desk, he shook his head sadly.

"Aye, how cheap a thing is patriotism by my lights, Tim," he said.

Still, cheap as he held it, he bade his whitefaced, trembling Mary farewell, and marched overland with the Second Regiment of the Highlanders to the mouth of the Saint John's River. Engaged in the senseless harrying of the all but empty countryside, the burning of houses, farms. . . .

Engaged, too, in the first real battle of the War, the attack on Forts Picolata and San Francisco de Papa, west of San Augustin, where the Spaniards beat them soundly. Took part in the successful second attack on those same forts on New Year's Day of 1740, their forces led by General Oglethorpe, himself; fought bravely, albeit his effectiveness was somewhat hampered by the necessity of having to watch Henry Knox as well as the Spaniards, to see that that cowardly would-be assassin did not take advantage of the matchless opportunities the heat of battle offered a man bent on murder.

Camped with the Colonial forces before Saint Augustine during those weary weeks it took a man as stubborn as General Oglethorpe to become convinced they couldn't carry that grim stone pile.

And, finally, marched gloomily home with the retreating English forces, painfully aware they had accomplished nothing at all to recompense the young men they had left behind them for their gallantly given lives.

There to remain until the middle of April, when the General, his forces reenforced by South Carolina's reluctantly given troops, set out again. But the night before James left, still another thing happened to him.

He was lying on his bed, staring at the ceiling. What difference does it make? he was thinking. Aye, this time we must take San Augustin—and in that attack, half our men must die. The last Jarrett with them, mayhap—what's the difference? Between the life I lead and sudden death, the choice is but a meager one—and weighted on the side of death. The dead don't suffer—while I, while I—

Then he heard the creaking of his door. He whirled, and stared into Mary's face, white in the moonlight, her pale lips trembling.

"James—" she whispered.

"Lord God, Lass!" he got out; but already she was in his arms.

He lay there very quietly, holding her. Between the long, slow kisses, salt with her tears, he fought his silent fight. But he was a Jarrett, with a Jarrett's heated blood. His arms tightened about her; his heart was a drumroll in his own ears; then—

A vagrant ray of moonlight came through the window and fell upon the inverted bowl in which he had eaten his frugal supper. In that pale glow, it looked exactly like a skull.

She felt him stiffen.

"James!" she wailed, "what's wrong?"

"I can't, Mary," he groaned; "God help me, but I can't!"

And all that silent night he lay there inert, holding her in his arms, his nightshirt soaked through by her tears. . . .

Their chances were somewhat better now. The General had nine hundred regulars and provincials with him. One thousand, one hundred Indians. Nine naval craft. The Highlanders and the South Carolina troops marched overland, while the General and the rest went by sea.

It began well enough. On May 9th, the Highlanders, with James Jarrett in the van, stormed Fort San Diego, and took it, along with some forty prisoners. On the nineteenth, they marched into Fort Moosa, which the Spanish had abandoned to retreat behind San Augustin's stronger walls. Then it went wrong—all wrong.

General Oglethorpe attacked the Fortress, and was repulsed bloodily. His little fleet, upon whose guns he had pinned his hopes, proved far too heavily laden to cross the bar. So there they sat, in Forts Moosa and San Diego, trying to starve the Spaniards out. But, in the middle of the month, one dark and moonless night, the Spanish fleet swept lightly over the sandbars and supplied their beleaguered compatriots with food and ammunition for a year.

In the captured forts, bitter quarrels broke out. The Georgians accused the Carolinians of cowardice, pointing out the incontestable fact that the forces of the neighboring colony had not lost one man in all the fighting. And James Jarrett's life was not sweetened by the presence of Henry Knox like a grim, silent shadow at his side.

Fever decimated their ranks. Their food supplies ran low. The General had to suppress duels between the officers of the Carolina troops, and those of Georgia. Finally, on June 20th, he gave up the obviously hopeless task. Saint Augustine was as strong as Porto Bello, nearly as strong as Cartagena—and the whole British Fleet had failed before those two, while his nine pitiful craft with their light guns lay outside the bar, their crews growing daily more mutinous . . . On the night of the 19th, he gave his orders for a general retreat. And in Fort Moosa, the Highlanders and the South Carolinians lay down with dreams of home filling up their minds.

But, just before dawn, the thunder of cannon wakened them. James leaped to his feet, his broadsword ready in his hand. Heard the cries of *"Viva el Rey! Por Dios y España! Adelante, Chicos!"* "Kill the heretical dogs!" as the Spaniards swept over them.

It was slaughter. They were quite literally hacked to pieces. The Carolinians prudently beat a retreat; and Tim Higgins and Cromwell Knox wisely went with them. But, to James' astonishment, Henry Knox held out, fighting in what seemed to be a curiously feminine combination of hysterical rage and fear, until long after both Tim and Cromwell had gone. Then he, too, fled. Out of the corner of his eye, James saw Henry disappearing into a nearby growth of underbrush. A moment later, the last of the Georgia troops broke, throwing away their arms, running pell mell into the swamps.

But the Highlanders were made of sterner stuff. They fought to the last man. Who, be it said, was Laird James Jarrett, Marquis of Argyll, the sole survivor of his Clan. Which now, he bitterly knew, was going to die with him. He held his ground for all that, blood streaming from a dozen wounds, all of them so far slight, and cut the Spaniards down like a berserker.

Their commander, a tall man, clad in cuirass and helmet, came forward through the ranks. As he approached, James saw his beard was golden blond, and his eyes a kindly blue. A Don had no right to look like that, but this one clearly did. When he was close enough, he called out, in English as perfect as James' own, bearing even, a trace of an Irish accent:

"Surrender, Lad! Ye're too brave a man to die! I promise ye we'll treat ye well. By'r Lady, ye've my word on that!"

"Take me if you can!" James snarled; and met a giant Negro's sabre stroke, making sparks in the cool dawn air.

Sadly the Spanish Commander nodded; and a dozen muskets were leveled at James' chest.

"I give ye a count of three," the Commander said. "One!"

"Shoot and be damned!" James howled. "You heard me, shoot!"

"Two!" the Commander boomed.

Wearily James shook his head. A sardonic grin crossed his somber face. What was he trying to prove? That he was brave? He'd proved that already. The pile of mutilated cadavers around him was proof enough for any man. And dying would arrange nothing. Was, in a way, a betrayal, a species of cowardice. Living was harder; took, actually, far more courage. The thing was a cheat. He could go out gloriously in the eyes of men, making this infantile show of valor; leave Mary, depart a world that was too much with him; end Clan Jarrett forever—by this easy out, this mock of intrepidity; this showy dying in a war he didn't believe in; in which he knew his enemies were morally right.

"Thr—" the Commander began; but James lifted his hand.

"Wait!" he called peacefully. "You win! I'll try the justly celebrated hospitality of your dungeons!"

"Good!" the Commander laughed. "Spoken like a man of sense. Now drop your arms, and come forward, hands raised. . . ."

James did as he was told. But he never reached the spot where the Spanish Musketeers stood. For, from the thicket in which he was hid, Henry Knox dashed out, and buried his knife to the hilt in James' back.

"Kill me that treacherous dog!" the Commander roared. "You hear me, boys—*matale!*"

All the muskets crashed at once. Henry went down, rolled, came up again, running with a bad limp. Plunged into the underbrush.

"Find him!" the Commander thundered. "I'll see how English honor withstands the thumbscrews and the rack!"

The helmeted and armed Spanish troops plunged into the thicket after Henry Knox. A group of Spanish officers bent over James.

"Santa Maria!" one of them breathed. "Yet he lives!"

"Call me the Padre," the Commander said.

"For a heretic?" a young lieutenant said in astonishment.

"The soul of so brave a man should not go to hell," the Commander said quietly. "I'll have him baptized and shriven. For Dios will surely pardon such a man as this even the errors of his beliefs. . . ."

The Padre came, went about the solemn business of the rites of baptism. *"En nombre del Padre, Hijo y Spiritu Sanctus,"* he murmured gently. "Now I must administer Extreme Unction before he dies, poor boy. . . ."

Which, being what he was, James stubbornly refused to do. They took that knife out of his back. The Spanish surgeon cauterized the wound with a hot iron. Mercifully, James was far beyond even feeling it. Then they put him on a stretcher, and bore him, along with their own wounded into San Augustin. He was the only Englishman they brought back. The rest were fled—or dead.

So it was, that two weeks later, James opened his eyes to stare into the face of an angel. Her eyes were a deep, soft blue; her brows and lashes that color the Spanish call *castaña,* a shade between auburn and blonde. He guessed that her hair must be the same color, but he couldn't see it—because she was clad in the robes and veils of a nun.

"So," James whispered wonderingly, "I missed hell after all!"

"Quiet," she said gently, in very slightly accented English. "Your wound is grave, Ingles. Now lie you still while I go to seek my father who wishes to speak with you. . . ."

James lay there very still, feeling the weakness in him unto death. Then the nun came back with the blond Commander.

"My thanks," James murmured, "for sparing my life. . . ."

"I did not spare it," the Commander said gravely. "That was God's own grace. And, incidentally, lest ye think ill of Spanish honor, 'twas no man of mine who struck you down, but a treacherous swine from your own ranks!"

"Henry—Knox!" James gasped.

"Then ye know who your assailant was? A pity we could not find him. But no matter; wounded as he was, he's likely dead by now. . . ."

James was staring at the nun. She was very young; no more than nineteen, he guessed.

"Your—your daughter?" he got out.

"Aye," the Commander said sadly; "my daughter Nieves, now Sor Asunción, of la Hermanidad de Nuestra Señora de la Misericordia."

"You—you speak English well—" James whispered.

"I learned it at my sainted mother's knee," the Commander said. "Permit me to introduce myself: Don José Garcia Jimenez O'Rourke, at your service, Don Diego!"

"So you're Irish! I—I thought you could not be Spanish by your looks. . . ."

"Father," the girl said sharply, her Castilian like dark music in James' ears, "for one whose hurt is of the gravest, he speaks too much, I think!"

"Nieves says you're talking overmuch, and she's right. But ye may listen well enough, I'm sure. First of all, I am not Irish, but Spanish.

'Tis our way with names that confuses ye, I think. We always put our mother's name after our father's. . . ."

"Then your mother was—"

"Irish, yes. Lady Maureen O'Rourke, daughter of the Irish Ambassador to Spain. And an angel both on this earth and in heaven where she is now, rest her soul. A woman of great piety, and of considerable learning. I spoke your tongue, Don Diego, before my own, and read Shakespeare through ere I came to Cervantes. . . ."

"Father, leave him, for God," Sor Asunción said. "Seest thou not that he is terribly tired?"

"What a lovely language," James whispered. "Though in a voice like yours, Sister, all tongues take on celestial music. . . ."

Sor Asunción colored vividly.

"You must not flatter me, Don James," she said gently, "for I have forsworn all vanities. . . ."

"Yet ye retain a bit, I think," her father laughed. "I see ye've not forgot how to blush!"

"So young," James sighed, "and so very lovely. Forgive me Don José, but it seems such a waste. . . ."

"Her Novio—her fiancé was killed at Fort Picolata," Don José said; "so Nieves here, believing like the young always do in such a case that there is not his like on earth, took the veil. She is, of course, within her novitiate, so there is yet time for her to change her mind. . . ."

"*Nunca!*" Sor Asunción said.

"Never? That's what she said, isn't it?" James whispered. "Tell me, what did she say—before?"

"That I should leave you, that you're terribly tired. Again she's right. Rest well, Don Diego. . . ."

"Don Diego?" James said.

"Spanish for James. You see, I know your name. Ye raved a bit—mostly about a lass called Mary, and another—an Indian, I have no doubt—Loosaponakee. . . ."

"Oh God!" James groaned.

"Ye spoke not clearly, nor overmuch. I have no idea who they are. But of one thing I am sure: ye love them both. A complicated way to live, Don James!"

"Aye, so it is," James sighed. He thought: And now, God help me, I'm going to complicate it even more!

Or simplify it, through the additional complications. Which was, very definitely, a possibility. Because, lying there, after they had gone, turning the matter over in his mind, it came to him that Henry's murderous knife thrust had offered him that opportunity. Before, there had been no chance. A man with one dim remaining spark of decency in him did not leave a lass like Mary, not even for the worthy purpose of preserving his clan. But—if she believed him dead—as Mary, by now, surely must?

That grief was acceptable. She'd mourn long and deeply for a husband heroically fallen in defense of his country. She'd weep, but time dries all tears. Knowing Mary, he realized that she could get used to the idea that he was dead; perhaps she'd even wed again. But never in this life could she support the idea that he was alive and with another. Only she wouldn't have to support it. He could bow out, close the curtains on that part of his life—and with a certain kindness . . .

And Nieves—Nieves! What a woman this one was! Her dignity was absolutely shattering, her serenity beyond compare. She was lovely, yes. But it was not that which held him. Rather it was something else: something in her bearing, a certain mastery of self, an almost awesome purity of soul. Which now, she was proposing to bury in a nunnery! By heaven and hell, no! What mattered it that the way out offered him was in itself a dishonor and a betrayal, as long as she, no more than Mary, would know it was?

What I offer thee, Lass, is life, he thought; tall sons and endless joy. Based upon lies, and deceit, yes—but without malice, Nieves, rather with all that's good, despite this ugly way. My sons will grow up speaking an alien tongue, practicing a faith strange to me—for, by all the Saints, you're worth a mass! One day, when we're very old, mayhap I'll tell you and you'll understand, for I—I cannot let Clan Jarrett die!

So, lying there, he planned it out, calmly contemplating still another sin to add to those with which his soul was burdened now. He studied his campaign—a maid who could blush like that had not yet lost her feminine weaknesses. He'd appeal to them—go slow, deal with her gently, until she surrendered to the promptings of her heart.

Thinking that, he sighed with complacent satisfaction. He'd always had a way with the lassies, and no veils and uncompleted vows would stand in his way. No, by heaven, he'd—

But one thing stood in his way, though yet he knew it not: The sure and awful Hand of God. . . .

For, sometime during the night, he waked in dreadful pain. It stabbed upward in fiery waves, reaching for his heart. He opened his mouth to call for help, then closed it again, grimly. No. It was very late, and the pain was too bad for him to be dying. He'd shift his weight a bit and—

He tried to move his right leg. It did not budge. Furiously he concentrated upon it, upon his left as well. They lay there, his long, slim fencer's legs, like two pieces of butchered meat. The sweat stood out on his forehead. He put down his hand, and pinched his own flesh savagely. It was as if he had pinched a cut of beef. Those legs were alien, apart from him. They had neither life nor feeling.

Wildly he turned. In the glow of the candle that Sor Asunción had left burning, he saw the knife and fork left for his supper—the supper he had been too weary to eat. Well, he was not weary now. He seized the knife, pressed the point into the muscle of his thigh. Kept on pressing until he saw his blood well up around the blade. Lay there staring at it, feeling only the black doom in his heart.

Then, for all his twenty-five years, he put down his head and cried.

Not loudly, but with the deep and terrible whispered spasms of far too bitter grief. But softly as he wept, she heard him. Came sweeping into that room with matchless grace. Bent over his bed.

"Don James!" she murmured; "what's wrong?"

"My legs!" he croaked; "they—they're paralyzed!"

"I know," she said gently. "The Doctor believes that this will pass, with time. There has been some damage to the spinal cord; but it is not severed, or else you'd be dead. When it heals, you'll regain use of your limbs—at least in part. . . ."

"In part!" he howled. "So I'll be a useless cripple! Oh God, why did You not let me die!"

She sat down beside him on the bed.

"That is an impiety, Don James," she said. "My loss is far greater than yours, and yet I bear it. . . ."

He stared at her.

" 'Twas because of you I wept," he said softly; "for I meant to make you forget that loss, give up this folly of a solitary life. . . ."

Her eyes were deep and sad.

"That was beyond you, well or not," she said; "aside from the fact that my vows are sacred to me, think you, Don James, that I could consent to wed one of the men responsible for my Paco's death?"

"Yet," James said bitterly, "you've treated this particular murderer with most tender care!"

"It was my duty," Sor Asunción said simply. "I asked the Mother Superior for this post. You see, she had some doubts about the verity of my vocation. So, if I can proceed with charity toward our enemies, it seems to me that you—"

"Should be able to endure being half a man. Mayhap less than half. Nay, Sister, I cannot bear it. I have not that kind of courage, nor even the consolation of a sure faith. . . ."

"You will have," she said serenely; "I cannot permit you to remain a heretic, Don James. Thy soul, as well as thy body is my concern. Father told me how you fought—one man against an army. We Spanish respect courage. Even courage of that base sort. What I must do now is to teach you a higher, purer kind—"

"What you must do now," James growled, "is to love me, and pray your God to make me well again. . . ."

"I do love you," she said with that immense and shattering dignity; "for it is written that we should love our enemies. And I have prayed to God to restore you, that you may serve Him well. . . ."

" 'Tis not that sort of love I meant," James rasped, "as well you know. I'm sorry if this offends you, Nieves. But, truly, can you expect a man to look upon you and not love you?"

"All men henceforth must do just that," she said quietly; "For, at Fort Picolata, your soldiers buried my heart as well. . . ."

Then she got up and left him there, moving so softly she made no sound at all.

So began for James Jarrett a thing he needed badly, though he knew it not: a quiet time. He recovered his strength, though his legs remained unmoving still. But he had some grounds for hope. Feeling had returned to them; he could twitch his toes. Don José, Doña Isabel, his wife, and, indeed, all the Jimenez family accepted him as one of them.

To pass the weary hours, James offered to teach Don José's three young sons, Juan, Xavier, and Miguel the subjects of English, Latin, and mathematics. His offer was gladly accepted. And though those merry, mischievous lads proved but indifferent scholars, James enjoyed their company. They served him rather better than he served them, for, in those three years that the War of Jenkins' Ear wore on, their careless way with English forced him to learn Spanish very well indeed.

From Don José and Doña Isabel, he got another thing: a comprehension of, and a respect for people whose religion, ideas, way of

life, differed widely from his own. And from Sor Asunción, the sad
lesson of how true and binding a thing a devout faith is.

She came to see him often, still bent upon converting him. But
James resisted all her efforts. He had been willing enough to make a
show of conversion for the purpose of winning her; but now that the
chance was gone, he would not deny the belief of his fathers merely
because she believed it a heresy and a sin.

The boys took him out daily for airings, mounted in a comfortable
chair which was lifted into a pony cart. He was, perhaps, the most
tenderly cared for prisoner of war this world has ever seen.

But it was a troublesome thing to sit helpless among this brave,
gallant, kindly people, and watch their preparations to destroy his
own—equally brave and gallant, and, at bottom, kindly, too. Throughout 1741, Spanish privateers raided the coast of North America from
Georgia to Maine, sacked plantations, brought back loot and prisoners. And, in July of 1742, they made their grand attack upon Georgia.

Only to return, late in August, defeated by dissension among their
own commanders, disloyalty among their Indian Allies and their Negro
slave troops, storms at sea, and James Oglethorpe's masterly strategy.

All this James learned from Don José upon his return. He listened
quietly, and made no comment, his heart filled with a double joy—that
his side had won, and that on yesterday, he had discovered he could
straighten his legs, even lift them. . . .

For hours on end now, he massaged his wasted muscles, exercised
them until the ache in his limbs was pure agony. His progress was so
slow that for what seemed to him an age he could see no sign of it at
all. Three months later, in November, he stood erect for the first
time. Took a trembling step, and crashed full length to the floor.
Forced himself upright, tried again; fell once more.

Days of that. Weeks. Months. The winter of 1742–1743 was cold
and wet. His legs hurt like the very devil. But by the eighth of March,
1743, two full years from the time that Henry had tried to murder
him, he could get out of his chair, take a few tottering steps around
the room. He concealed his recovery from the Jimenez, because, a
week before, on the third of March, 1743, General Oglethorpe had
once more appeared before San Augustin. Better that they did not
know. With everyone believing him still crippled, his chances for
escape were that much better.

During the days and weeks that the siege wore on, he practiced walking assiduously. He was still too slow, too awkward; but given time, time—

Which he was not to be given. During a long quiet spell, the boys, bored with their enforced confinement, took him for a ride. Evaded the sleepy guards, and whipped the pony up into a gallop on the side of Saint Augustine away from the river. They had no sooner entered the woods when they heard a cry.

"*Niños!*" Sor Asunción called. "What are you doing out here?"

"I might ask you the same thing, Sister," James laughed. "We felt the need for freer air."

"Ah, Sister," Miguel wailed; "you aren't going to send us back, are you?"

"Well," Sor Asunción hesitated; "there really isn't much serious danger, is there?"

"None," James said stoutly, "else I shouldn't have let them come. Up with you, Fair Daughter of the Church!"

As it turned out, he was wrong. They hadn't gone more than a mile into the woods, when a villainous looking Englishman stepped out of the brush, and seized the bridle of the pony.

A second later, they were surrounded. And the leader of the band, James saw, was Cromwell Knox. . . .

"Ah ha!" Cromwell said, "my damned traitor of a brother-in-law! Henry said you'd turned coat, but I didn't believe him. Look at you— Grandee of Spain—with wife, family, pony cart and all! Get you down, you wretch, so I can deal with you!"

"He cannot," Sor Asunción said softly. "He is crippled. And I am not his wife, as these robes should be enough to show you. . . ."

Cromwell grinned at her.

" 'Tis what you've got beneath 'em I aim to see," he mocked; "to see and to fondle right tenderly. Look boys, a prize! A Papist nun—think you she comes equipped like other women?"

"Crom—" James said grimly.

"Hold your tongue, you crippled beggar! Henry told me how you ordered your friends to fire on him. Cost him his leg. And useless though they be, I see you've both of yours!"

"Nieves!" Juan croaked, in his uncertain voice, "they'll not touch you! I'll fight—"

"Tie those brats up, and leave them here," Cromwell ordered.

"And him?" the villainous looking soldier growled.

"No. Bring him along as he is. I want him to watch the sport we'll have of her. An edifying sight, eh, Brother James?"

They left the weeping boys tied to the trees, and plunged deeper into the woods. James did not move. He had not so much as a pen knife; so he'd have to wait until—

Dark. That is, if this goatish band of ugly villains would hold off that long. As, it appeared, they would. They seemed to be searching for a likely spot, where no Spanish patrol could come upon them. And it was already dusk. A few stars dusted the heavens, palely. Oh, God, James prayed, give me time—time!

They came to an open glade. Cromwell had James lifted roughly down, and propped up against a tree, with Sor Asunción at his side. He didn't bother to tie them up. For that, there was no obvious need. Instead, he set the bewhiskered scoundrel who had seized them over them as a guard.

James sat there in the brooding darkness, watching them drinking and carousing some yards away. At his side, Sor Asunción prayed very quietly.

"Don't fear, Lass," he whispered. "I'll see that you come to no harm. . . ."

"How can you?" she wept. "Besides, you're as bad as they! You were going to pay court to me, knowing all the time you have a wife!"

"For which, forgive me," he said sadly. "I had my reasons, which seemed to me good—"

"No reasons on earth," she began, but Cromwell called backward over his shoulder:

"Josh! Come here a minute!"

Their guard approached the fire. Cromwell, sprawled lazily on the ground, said something to him. In the red glow, they could see his teeth flash in a wolfish grin. Then he turned and came back to them. Put out his hand, and jerked Sor Asunción roughly to her feet.

"Come Bride of Christ!" he mocked. "Let's see how much a bride you are!"

And that was all. Those were the last conscious words he uttered. For James Jarrett came up in one long tiger's leap, his two hands gripping the man's throat, his iron fingers biting in until the soldier's face purpled, and he slumped heavily to the ground.

"Fly, Lass!" James whispered. "I'll keep these beggars entertained!"

"But, James, your legs!" she gasped.

"Do you not believe in miracles?" James said, not entirely with mockery, "or in the efficacy of prayer?"

"Josh!" Cromwell roared drunkenly from the fireside. "What's keeping you, boy! Bring her on!"

James gave her a shove. Bent and possessed himself of the unconscious soldier's sabre, pistols, muskets. Saw her disappearing through the trees. Looked toward the firelight. Saw a fat lout bent over double, snatching a cut of beef from the embers. Lifted the musket, sighted it upon that most inviting target. Touched the trigger. . . .

The flash of the priming in the flintlock's pan all but blinded him. But the fat one clapped both hands to his rump with a most satisfying howl.

"*Adelante, Chicos!*" James roared in Spanish. "Kill the heretics! *Viva el Rey! Por Dios y España! Adelante!* Forward, men, and kill the English dogs!"

What happened next was sadly comical. Cromwell and his fellows made a mad dash for the woods. Seeing them go, James fired first one pistol then the other to speed them, knowing he would not need his weapons now.

So it was that James Jarrett won the last battle of the War of Jenkins' Ear—for Spain. He walked slowly back to where his three pupils were tied, his heart filled with joy at the fact that he no longer even limped. His steps were painful and slow, but they were entirely normal. In time, he'd walk as well as ever.

Two days later, Don José took him across the river to the English camp, under a flag of truce.

The General received him grimly.

"You'll face a courtmartial, Jarrett," he growled. "For desertion, and for the attempted murder of your brother-in-law! I thought better of you than that; but, unless you can produce evidence justifying your behavior, you'll hang!"

"Which," Don José said quietly, "he can, Your Excellency. I witnessed that fight. It was I who took him prisoner. He was the last man on his feet and still he would not surrender. I did all I could to take him alive, for I wanted not to kill so brave a man. But even I should not have been able to capture him, had not this brother-in-law of whom you speak stabbed him in the back, while he, and he alone, was facing us!"

"I see," the General said; "You speak the truth, Sir?"

"Upon my mother's grave, and before the Holy Virgin, I do, Sir," Don José said stiffly. "I am a Grandee of Spain, and a gentleman. Such men as I have scant need to lie!"

"My apologies," said General Oglethorpe. "Will you and your men stay for supper?"

So it was, that a week later, when the General's siege proved as fruitless as his first, James Jarrett sailed back to Frederica and his home. To be met by a wife as white-faced and trembling with joy, as she had been before from grief.

"Ah, James, James!" was all she said.

"I'm back, Lass," he said sadly; "though what good it is, I'm sure I don't see—"

She looked at him, then, her eyes filled with light, with joy, with a thing he could not know was—determination.

"All the good, my husband," she whispered, her voice throaty, warm. "You see—I saw Doctor Fergurson the other day—"

"And?" he growled.

"I—I went to see him on purpose! I felt so much better that—that I hoped—"

"Then you knew I was alive?" James said.

"Yes. A prisoner escaped and told us. And even though you were crippled, I thought—Anyhow, I insisted that the doctor examine me. And, James, darling, I'm well! I can so have a child! There—there's nothing wrong with me at all!"

He stood there, holding her, almost afraid to release the riptide of his joy. Then, very slowly, he bent and kissed her mouth, having no words to say what thundered in his heart.

For he had no way of knowing that she lied.

CHAPTER EIGHTEEN

THROUGHOUT HER SECOND pregnancy, Mary's health was wondrously good. She accompanied James to Savannah to say his sad farewells to General Oglethorpe, who, on July 23rd of that year, 1743, sailed away from Georgia forever. The parting was touching; the General gripped James' hand convulsively, not trusting himself to speak. James was equally moved. He had broken the General's laws, argued furiously with him, openly defied him on more than one occasion. But, very truly, he loved this shaggy old lion of a man. He took what comfort he could from the fact that he had once saved the General's life, had served him well and gallantly in War.

"We'll miss you, General," he said gruffly. "I know not how we'll manage without you, Sir—"

"Well enough, I think," the General said. "Perhaps, now, you can commence to be practical!"

"Still remember that, Sir?" James smiled. "Well, I was wrong. I doubt that a practical man would have been able to beat the Dons and save the colony with only five hundred men, and no fleet, fighting against five times your numbers. I, for one, wouldn't even have tried. . . ."

"War's a most impractical business," the General said. "If men were not fools, we'd have perpetual peace. But now the future's yours, Sir James—to do with it what you will. Only, if you'll take the advice of an old and tired man, never put this practicality of yours above— simple decency. You'll regret it if you do. But with you, fair Mistress, to take him in hand, I need have no fear of that, I know. . . ."

"I'm sorry you're going, Sir," Mary whispered. "I realize it's presumptuous of me, but I had hoped—"

"What, Mistress Jarrett?" the General said. "With me you're free to speak your mind—"

"That you'd stand as Godfather for our son. We're going to name him James—after you. . . ."

"And likewise after his father," the General smiled, "since we both bear the same name. I'm sorry, Lass, but my work here is done. There'll be peace now, which can be better managed by civils. But when you send him to Oxford, have him look me up. I'll be around; we Oglethorpes are a long lived race. . . ."

"God grant you many more years, Sir!" James said.

The year wore itself out with waiting. James experimented with the planting of cotton, with but poor results. His plantation, operated by white labor, simply was not geared to the production of the fiber. With rice and tobacco, he did a little better. But the plantation could not be called successful. Had it not been for the cattle, and the fur trade, they would have been poor indeed.

His planting was not helped by the fact that ten or twelve times a day, he went back to the house to see how Mary fared. She'd told him there was no danger, but he worried still. Reassured by the sight of her serene and lovely face, he'd return to the fields to find the indentured servants, as often as not, sleeping in the shade. He damned them roundly; but there was nothing more he could do, because, by now, the fur trade was taking all Tim Higgins' time.

Late in September, Tim reappeared, after an absence of some three months. And, by the end of three minutes of halting talk, James saw that his old friend was deeply troubled—more so than at any time during the years he had known him.

"Out with it, Tim," he growled. "Tell me what's on your mind. You've done nothing but sit and stare at me as though I were some rare beastie. Since, obviously, what you're thinking concerns me, I want to know what it is. . . ."

"Nothing," Tim said.

"Hell's fire, Tim! Don't lie to me! A man would think I'd done you some grave harm. Between friends, the truth. What is it?"

"I don't know—" Tim said; "not truly. And I don't think I want to know. For, as far as I'm concerned, of all the maids upon this earth, your Mary's the fairest and the best—"

James stared at him.

"Tell me, Tim," he said very quietly, "where did you go, this time?"

"Up North," Tim growled; "to the section round about Stone Mountain—among the Cherokees. . . ."

James sat there a long time, staring at the ground. When he looked up, his eyes were bleak.

"Loosa," he said softly. "That's it, isn't it, Tim?"

"Aye," Tim said flatly. "That's it."

There was a silence between them, stretching itself out, wire fine.

"Tell me, Tim," James whispered; "how is she?"

"Just fine," Tim said dryly. "Sent you her love."

"Has she—has she wed?" James said.

"No. You know better than that. Interpreted for me—and when I mentioned I came from this section, her eyes lit up—like candles in a church. A good lass, that, and very sweet. You seem to know how to pick 'em, boy. . . ."

"Aye," James said bitterly, "for all the good it does. . . ."

"Mary looks all right to me," Tim said.

"I know. But I can't help worrying. About Loosa, Tim—did she seem sad or—"

"Nope. Calm. Composed. Resigned to her lot. Hell of a thing to wish on a woman!"

"Tim, I don't follow you. What happened between Loosaponakee and me—had its reasons. I could make you see them, but I won't. I have no need to explain my behavior, even to you. But it's over and done with; and, since nobody knows about it, I don't see—"

"Nobody knows!" Tim roared; "why with—"

And, at that moment, Mary came heavily down the stairs.

"With what, Tim?" James said.

"Nothing," Tim whispered hoarsely. "I was about to talk too much. Good morning, Mistress Mary, how do you fare?"

"Quite well, thank you," Mary smiled. "From the size of me, you'd think I were going to present James with a complete family all at once, wouldn't you?"

Persistently James tried, in the days that followed, to make Tim break his stubborn silence. But Tim kept his jaw clamped shut.

"Don't know what you think I was about to say," he growled. "Fact is, I've quite forgot, myself. . . ."

"You lie!" James spat.

"Look, Jim, you're taking on over nothing. All I could have told you was that I had a feeling that Loosa's father, and mayhap other folks, do know. She must have talked. Women have a plagued hard time holding their tongues, now don't they?"

"Not about that," James said. "Tim, there's something else, something more—"

"Word of honor, boy," Tim said, keeping his fingers crossed behind his back, like a child.

It was not until Tim had gone on still another trip that it hit James—all at once and completely. He sat bolt upright in bed, remembering Loosa's words:

"All my life long, I'll think of you, and the very thought will comfort me. Besides—"

That one word. "Besides—"

And his own voice, gruffly:

"Besides what, Loosa?"

"Nothing," she had whispered.

Only she had lied. For it had been something. Very much something. The final, bitter touch of life's irony. For Clan Jarrett would go on now. But how? Clad in feathers and beads. Prancing around campfires. Whooping warcries. His son—his son!—must grow up a painted savage, lost in the wilderness, knowing nothing of his proud heritage, counting coups, taking scalps—a savage!

No! he thought. I'll go! Find him, bring him back—

"James," Mary whispered sleepily, "what ails you?"

And he was lost. The thing was—impossible. To bring home Loosa's son, he must wound unto death this sleepy angel at his side. This gallant creature prepared to descend into the valley of the shadow to give him—in honor—the son he craved.

"Nothing," he groaned; "Just a—a nightmare, Lass. . . ."

The phrase rang true. It was. And one that would haunt his sleep life long.

Winter came in with driving rains, which was good for the crops, but played havoc with James' mood. During those cold, grey days of January, 1744, when the sea never stopped its thundering, and all the winds sang dirges, he had only one thing to be thankful for: that in the daily rides he took despite the weather, coming home soaked to the skin, and acquiring a deep-seated chest cold, that, though he dismissed it as unimportant, nevertheless hung on stubbornly, neither Henry nor

Cromwell Knox crossed his path. Both of them, he'd heard, now that the population of Georgia had passed three thousand, were busily courting two fair and buxom maids.

"God grant the lassies tame them down a bit," he growled to Mary. "Were they not your brothers, I'd know how to deal with them; but, since they are—"

"Oh, James, you promised!" Mary wailed.

"I know. And I'll keep my word. But the next time you see Henry, you might remind him that a knife in the back doesn't cement family relations at all. . . ."

"I mean to," Mary said furiously. "After the child comes, I'll pay him a call. Because he won't call on me, you can be sure of that! James—"

"Yes, Lass?"

"Why don't you go for another ride, or something?"

"Lord God, Mary, it's pouring!"

"I know it is," Mary said tartly; "but since you're made of neither sugar nor salt, I don't think it'll hurt you at all. Besides, since when has the weather bothered you? You've ridden out on days worse than this. And sitting there fidgeting like a scared cat, you get on my nerves!"

"Sorry, Lass," James said. "Guess I am in a state. I keep remembering the last time—"

"James, promise me one thing—"

"Anything you say, Lass. No, wait! You've some plagued silly notions in your head. So, first, what d'you want me to promise you?"

"Doctor Fergurson said," Mary whispered, "that there was—at least some choice between saving me—or the baby, before. He put it up to you. James, this time, if it comes to that—save my baby, please!"

He came up out of his chair, and stood before her. Even in the wintry gloom, she could see him trembling.

"James!" she said sharply, "don't look at me like that!"

His two hands bit into her soft shoulders. He shook her, furiously.

"You told me it was safe!" he grated. "You told me! Damn your soul to bitter hell, Mary, you had no right—"

"James, you're hurting me!" she wailed.

He released her, instantly contrite.

"Sorry," he said gruffly. "But plague take it, Lass, you do get me wild!"

Then he saw she was smiling, though her eyes were suspiciously wet.

"James," she whispered, her voice vibrant with wonder; "do you love me that much?"

"Aye," he growled. "I love you that much. So if you die because of this monstrous folly, take what comfort you can from knowing that I'll spend what's left to me of life in chains—"

"James!"

"Baying the absent moon, like lunatics always do. And upon your head be it!"

"James, you come here!"

He came over to where she sat.

"Now bend down," she said. "I'm far too heavy to get up. . . ."

He bent to her, and she wrapped her arms about his neck.

"Don't worry about me, darling," she said softly. "I'm quite all right, just as I told you. I—I only said that to test you—"

"Goddamnit, Mary! You know how I feel about you!"

"Yes, I do know. But a woman likes to be told, James. Over and over again. 'I love you' isn't a phrase that grows tiresome—especially from the man who is my life, all my life. So be a good boy, and say it, please!"

"Hell's foaming brimstone, Mary!"

"Please, James. . . ."

"All right. I love the silly little goose whom I had to carry off by main force before she'd marry me—"

"That isn't all you did by main force!" Mary giggled.

"Will you shut up, Mistress Jarrett? I was about to make you a declaration. Where was I? Ah, yes. I love her because she is as sweet as she is brainless; I love her eyes that make summer lightnings when they move, her hair that's moonsilver touched with gold, her mouth—"

"Oh, James, don't be so artificial!"

He dropped down beside her, rested his dark head upon her lap.

"And I love the years I'll have with her, now," he said gravely; "those years in which, to my eyes, she'll never change. I'll be blind to greying hair and wrinkles, deaf to the cracked quaver that age puts in every voice. For me, stooped, bent, halting, dim of sight, she'll always be my Mary, and the only woman in the world. And, when, as it must, time comes to an end for us, I ask only to be laid beside her in the dark—until, God willing, and the Word men call His being true—I wake to find her radiant beside me, granted the joy of loving her throughout eternity. . . ."

"Oh, James!" she sobbed. "You mustn't say those things to me! I'm not fit—"

"If you're not, I don't know who is," he growled. "Now I'll go take that ride. . . ."

On the 5th of February, he woke up from a deep and dreamless sleep, to find her shaking him.

"James!" she whispered, "it—it's come! You'd better send somebody for Doctor Ferg—Oh! Oh, God! Oh Jesus! I—"

"Send?" he roared; "I'll go myself!"

"No," she whispered. "I want you here. I—I want to see your face while yet I can—"

He stared at her, his eyes wild.

"While yet—you can!" he got out. "Mary! For God's love—"

"I—I'm being morbid," she laughed nervously. "I'm perfectly all right, dearest. Now go send one of the boys—"

He yanked his kilts up over his slim flanks, hurled a coat over his naked trunk, and dashed out into the rain.

When he came back, she was moaning piteously; but, seeing his face, she stopped her cries at once, and held out her hand to him.

"Hold me, darling," she whispered. "I'll be good. I promise not to cry . . . ."

He took her in his arms, held her like that, death in his heart, for all those four hours before the doctor came. Hearing Major Fergurson's heavy footsteps on the stair, he started to get up, but she clung to him. The Army surgeon marched into the room, his beet-red face working. He stared at James a long, slow time. Then he said it, his voice choked with fury:

"You get out of here, you selfish swine!"

James came upright, then. Even his lips were white. The wound that Henry had given him had taken out of him more than he knew. And the stubborn chest cold he had been nursing for weeks now hadn't helped. Both of which explained it, in part. In very small part. Perhaps not at all.

"You mean," he croaked, "that she's not all right? You didn't tell her—?"

"I told her," Major Fergurson said grimly, "that if she tried to have another child, she'd die!"

James took a step forward. The lamplight seemed curiously dim. It flickered fitfully. He put out a groping hand. Leaned forward, on empty air, went on down, down into a roaring blackness that had no end.

Through it, he could hear Mary screaming. Her voice came from a thousand miles, and ten thousand years, away:

"He didn't know! I lied to him, Doctor! He would have never—Oh, God, I've killed him!"

"I think not," Thomas Fergurson said. "Funny how often husbands faint at a time like this. Even the bravest and the best—"

"Especially the bravest and the best," Mary whispered. "Oh, Doctor, look to him, please!"

Doctor Fergurson bent over James, slapped his face smartly. James did not move, or even groan. The Doctor laid a heavy hand on his brow. It was like touching a stove lid.

Major Fergurson looked up at Mary.

"Tell me," he growled, "has he ridden out in the rain, these days?"

"I—I sent him out," she whispered. "He was so nervous and jumpy, so worried about me that—"

"Well, Mistress Jarrett, you've laid out my chores for me, for fair! He's got pneumonia—double from the sound of it. Probably's been sick for days. Didn't you notice anything?"

"No!" Mary wailed. "He hid it from me! Didn't want me to worry and—Oh, Doctor, he won't die, will he?"

"Hardly," Tom Fergurson said with a conviction he was far from feeling. "It's you I'm worried about. Though, damn it all, I must say you look well!"

"I feel fine," Mary said wonderingly; "Oh, Doctor, wouldn't it be funny if the tale I told James were the truth, after all?"

"You've the smallest pelvic girdle I've ever seen in an adult woman," Tom Fergurson growled. "But now I'd better see after your man. You'll be in labor for six or eight hours yet, or I miss my guess. And what he's got wants attending to, right now. Where's the bell cord? I need those louts of yours to carry him off to bed. . . ."

Mary reached up and yanked the cord with all her strength. While they waited, the Doctor stared at her.

"Mary," he said heavily, "don't lie to me. Did you really tell James you were fit for childbearing?"

"Of course! What do you think he is? Why he slept in another room from the time I lost my first baby until he came home from the war. . . ."

"Mary, you're a fool! I know how badly this lad wanted to save his Clan; but, damn it all, you could have gone down to Bethseda Orphanage and adopted a child!"

Mary smiled then, softly, tenderly.

"It wouldn't have been—a Jarrett, Doctor," she said.

For fourteen days and nights, James Jarrett lay and choked, or tossed and raved. Mrs. Stephens scarcely left his side. Major Fergurson called daily, pitting his considerable science—for even then the men of Edinburgh University were one hundred years above the quackery in which their age was sunk—in skillful defense against this ugly way of death. On the fifteenth day, quite abruptly, the fever broke. James sank into a deep and healing sleep.

"Thank God!" Tom Fergurson said feelingly. "He'll be all right, now. One thing, though, Mistress Stephens—see that he's not alone when he wakes. With what he's got on his mind—"

"I'll be here," Mistress Stephens said grimly. "Poor boy! How he loves her!"

"Aye, that he does," the Doctor said; "and far better than I knew. A good night to you, Mistress Stephens—at last I can get some rest!"

But, as it turned out, Mistress Stephens was not in the room when James awoke. Her husband came into the sickchamber, and grumpily demanded that she make his coffee. She looked toward the bed. James lay there, sunk in slumber, still.

"All right, all right!" she said; "but I'll have to hurry. I must be here when he wakes—"

"If he ever does," Stephens said gloomily; "Come on!"

So it was that James awakened in that empty room. He lay there a long time, blinking, until it came to him, until he remembered.

Alone, he thought; alone. She'd never leave me if she were—

He pushed down with all his strength, trying to get up from that bed. He could not. He was far too weak. He tried again, straining. The sweat beaded on his forehead, despite the cold. He came up inch by inch; fell back again. Lay there, panting, feeling the weakness in him unto death.

Then, because there was nothing else he could do, he put down his head and cried. Terribly, hoarsely, the great animal sobs tearing up out of his throat, weeping out his anguish and his despair.

"Can't live!" he choked; "can't live! Without her, I can't—"

Then he felt a gentle touch upon his arm. Lifted his shaggy head like a wounded beast. Turned over, wildly, with the newborn strength of joy.

And sweetly, softly, the tears trembling on the upturned corners of her mouth, Mary bent and laid the bundle in his arms.

He lifted a big hand, pushed back the blankets, stared at that wizened, tiny countenance, at that head covered by a bristling mop of jet black hair. At that wisp of brow that soared across that red, wrinkled monkey's face without a break. Saw that tiny mouth come open, heard that angry howl. . . .

"I give you—the son I promised you, James," Mary said.

CHAPTER NINETEEN

NO ONE WHO had known James Jarrett before would have believed he was the same man now. In those eleven years between 1744 and 1755, between his twenty-ninth birthday and his fortieth he changed completely. Even physically. He put on weight, he who had always been as lean as a broadaxe blade. Not much, of course, for he was not of the kind who would ever grow fat; but enough to give him a certain aspect of dignity, to lessen his look of hard rapacity.

He smiled often. He was gentle with his fellows. Pleasant. He busied himself with the affairs of the Colony; rose to positions of command; gained the universal respect of the settlers. Most surprising of all was the fact that he managed to maintain an unbroken peace with his brothers-in-law, despite not infrequent provocation on their part. Calmly he avoided them, ignored their thinly veiled insults with total complacency. . . .

It was in the nature of things that his affairs should prosper during this period. He retired Tim Higgins from the fur trade; and the two of them set up a commercial house in Savannah, the second in the Colony. Within a year, they were rivaling Francis Harris and James Habersham, who had established Georgia's original mercantile business. In that field, be it said, James' canny Scotch shrewdness fitted him far better for success than in his original venture into planting. Yet, even in farming, his luck was good, if not remarkable. After July 7th, 1749, when the prohibitions against rum and slavery were finally withdrawn, the plantation, worked by gangs of Negroes whom Tim bought for him in Carolina, began, for the first time, truly to flourish. He built a fine frame house in Savannah—because, sadly, Frederica, which had been born of war, died with the peace. Besides, he wanted James, Second, to have the company of other boys of his own age, the advantages of Savannah's academies.

They led, therefore, a divided life: summers on Saint Simon's Island at the Plantation, and winters in Savannah. Heeding Mary's plea, James sported the tartan and the kilt but rarely now. Instead, he returned to the splendor of his youth: powdered bagwig and smallsword, embroidered waistcoats, habits *à la française,* silk stockings, buckled shoes—the whole ensemble worn with such grace that many a maid and many an aging spinster, too, cursed Mary Jarrett in their hearts. . . .

"Nothing," Tim Higgins said to his wife, Beth—for that worthy, in his early fifties, had repented of his lonely state and married a comely widow—"changes a man like happiness. And Gol Blimey if Jim Jarrett ain't the happiest man on the face o' creation!"

"Too much so," Beth said quietly; "and upon far too slender a foundation. . . ."

Tim stared at her. Staring at Beth was a pleasure, even though she was in her forty-second year. She was round and rosy, a peaceable soul. And she had made him happier than he had believed possible.

"What the devil do you mean, Beth?" he growled.

"His whole life is wrapped up in that boy. And they've but that one. If anything happened to little Jim—"

"Which God forbid!" Tim said fervently.

"Amen," Beth sighed. "I love Jimmy as though he were my own. Tim, didn't you tell me that Tom Fergurson said it was perfectly safe for Mary to have more children if she wanted to?"

"Yep," Tim said. "And she wants to. Were it left with her, they'd have ten by now. . . ."

"Then James—"

"No. He'd gladly sire a dozen. Blame it on the Lord, Beth. They've tried and tried, but—"

Beth laughed then, merrily.

"Hardly a troublesome task, what, Tim?" she said.

His whole life. Which was, perhaps, an understatement. James, Second, was brought up like a prince. His only suffering during his boyhood was from the rigor of the education his father imposed upon him. James rode up to Highgate, the village that had been settled by twelve French Huguenot families some years before, and brought home

Madame Gerard, a widow in her fifties, to instruct his son in that language, for he had all but forgotten the precise and bookish French Gaspard had taught him at the Andrews'. The circumstance is worth noting, because James sat in on all his son's lessons, and thereby rapidly recovered and surpassed his own youthful fluency—which, strangely, was to affect his own future, albeit he knew it not. Latin, Greek, and Mathematics were at the charge of Doctor Briggs, a somewhat alcoholic Oxford Don who headed an academy for boys. James, himself, inflicted Spanish upon his son's helpless head.

The boy was not a remarkable scholar, but he made up for a certain slowness by intense effort, because his adoration of his father was total. What James felt, of course, for his own image in miniature, was nothing short of sinful idolatry. Only to the councils of the Colony, and the parties and balls to which he squired his Mary, did he go unaccompanied by his son. Even in those realms of adulthood, he fidgeted miserably, anxious to rush home to see how James, Second, fared; though, in sober truth, he had no cause for concern: for all his Jarrett's slenderness, young Jim was both tough and wiry. He learned to ride at six years of age, to swim at five. Daily he exercised with the foils with his father; at nine, he was already a polished wingshot, far better with a gun than his father would ever be.

"I don't see why you fuss so over the lad," Mary sighed. "Can't you see he's quite all right?"

"Aye," James growled, "and that's precisely why I worry. Things go well—too well, Lass. Remember the year we lost our first born?"

"Yes," Mary said sadly. "To think that she'd be all of seventeen, now—ready to wed and make me a grandmother! Still I don't see—"

"I know you don't. That was a good year, Lass. One of the best I'd had up until then. Since Jimmy was born, it's been even better. Everything I set my hand to, prospers—"

"And you worry about that?" Mary said.

"Aye, I do. Is not happiness nearly always a fool's paradise? Justice is a man-made word. In life, it doesn't exist. We are but the sports of chance, the creatures of blind accidentality; the playthings of mocking, ribald Gods who love us not. Our faith's a sentimental thing, hardly justified by the slightest evidence of our eyes. Who has done more for England than General Oglethorpe—and look what happened to him after that second Jacobite rising in 1745! Courtmartialed, all but disgraced—"

"James, you said yourself that he had Jacobite leanings. . . ."

"He did, but he was not a fool. I'm sure he served our fat Germanic King as well as he could. He was punished for the wayward errors of his youth, for the memories of the Rising of Fifteen, not for the actuality. . . ."

"So, thinking the way you do, you fear—"

"Happiness? Aye, Lass. I fear and distrust it. The Fates permit it to a man only to make his subsequent sufferings the keener—"

"They've granted it to you a good long time now, James."

"Yes. The old Gods are sometimes forgetful. I pray that they never remember!"

But they did.

April was fair in all the land that Spring of 1755. The sunlight changed the streamers of Spanish moss in the oaks into filigrees of gold. The light lay warmly on the green slope of lawns surrounding the house. Mary's beloved flowers, pansies, phloxes, hyacinths, roses, nodded in the gentle breeze. A little way from James' clumsily built manor, the cows grazed. The sea showed no white at all, lying before them like a mirror, reflecting a sky where only the wheeling gulls broke the sweep of blue. A lazy day, a day of peace. James sat there with Mary on the little stoop, gazing at his world—the world he had made, created, earned—

And young Jim came flying down the stairs, calling: "Father! Father!"

James turned, smiling.

"What now, lad?" he said.

"Just don't sit there like a lazybones!" Jim laughed. "On a day like this—let's ride! Prince Charlie's fretting. He wants a gallop. What say you, father? Race me to the South fields?"

James looked at Mary.

"Go with him, James," she said gently. "He's been at his books all morning. Dr. Briggs is mightily content with his progress. And Madame Gerard says he could enter any lycée in Paris. Seems to me he deserves an outing—"

"Very well," James said; "but have some respect for my old bones, lad. No racing! The last time we raced, I was swathed in liniments for a week. . . ."

"What a fib!" Jim laughed. "You're the best horseman in Georgia, father. You beat me handily that time, and I want revenge. Besides, ever since I took a fall last June, you've been fretting. Everybody falls once in a while. And it was only that once. Now I know better than to give Prince Charlie a slack rein—"

"All the same, son," Mary whispered, "I'd rather you didn't race. You're all I've got, you know. . . ."

"Oh, Mummie!" Jim wailed, "don't be an old poke! I can ride as well as father—almost. . . ."

"I know," Mary said tartly, "so you don't have to prove it. You wouldn't want my hair to turn white, would you?"

"No—" Jim said soberly. "All right, we won't race. We'll go for a long, long ride instead. Clear down to that old Fort on the other end of the Island. All right, father? And you can show me where you beat the Spanish—"

"Didn't beat them," James chuckled. "When the Battle of Bloody Marsh occurred, I was a prisoner of war in San Augustin—"

"And paralyzed," Mary shuddered.

"Good thing I was. Those Spanish lassies are deuced winsome. Mayhap, if I had had use of my limbs, I'd have never come back. . . ."

"Then," Mary said serenely, "you'd never have had your son, James—"

"Oh, I'd have had him, all right—or a reasonable replica. Only he'd have been called Diego, then, and been a Papist!"

"And I," Mary said half seriously, "I counted nothing for you, then?"

James looked at her. He was endlessly sensitive to the slightest nuance in her tone.

"You counted everything, Lass," he said gravely. "I'd come back, e'en if I'd had to crawl. . . ."

"Oh, stop talking mush!" Jim said; "C'mon, father!"

They cantered out through that wash of light, that sweep of moving air. It had, now, a certain tingle to it—a hint of electricity. Going to storm, James thought. My back aches, and that's a sure sign. But on a day like this? And whoever heard of a storm in April? Rubbish. Growing old, that's all. Forty, by God! A man travels far in this world—and not only in miles. That trip to England and Scotland I've been trying to talk Mary out of—is possible, physically; but what man can swim backwards against the current of time?

A bad thing, that. She wants to see the Highlands—and Edinburgh. The town in which the gallows awaits me, still—Small chance. By now, folks have quite forgot Squire Pitcairn Hogg. But Maebelle, Maebelle—

aye, that would be scanned. By now, thirty-eight or nine—if she lives. And Hogg's bastard, a man grown. That, more than any fear of hanging. Edinburgh, and London—where Sue is surely still. Dear God, is there not an inch of earth untroubled by my sins?

They could see the Negroes, now, at work in the cane fields. Hear them singing. Always, when they sang, James could feel a little knot of unease forming at the pit of his stomach. There was no sadness in this world equal to that in the blacks' songs. The thing was not right, not right—still—

'In the corrupt courts of this world,' he quoted bitterly in his mind, 'offense's gilded hand can shove by justice. But 'tis not so above. . . .'

As always, young Jim seemed to share his mood.

"The poor niggers," he sighed. "I shouldn't like to belong to another man—"

"You belong to me and your mother," James said.

"That's different. I belong to you, because I *am* yours. I look like you. I have your blood in me. But they—"

" 'Twill not always be thus, lad," James said gravely. "One day they will be free . . . ."

As they cantered by the cane field, the Negroes waved to them, gaily. One and all they worshipped little Jim. The boy was always down at the quarters, playing with the black children, bringing them sweetmeats, toys, listening to the old blacks as they talked. Nodding his dark head sagely. Cheerfully accepting their advice, and, what was more, acting upon it.

Which is why, James mused, they love him. He gives them a sense of importance, they who are the mudsill of this life. Mayhap that's the deepest of all hungers: this curious desire to matter to someone, to be listened to, heeded. Men can stand any fate better than that of being disregarded. . . .

They trotted on, down the Island. They had gone perhaps half way when James noticed the sudden change in the sunlight. He pulled the Arab up, and sat there, staring seaward. Over the water, to the southeast, fantastic pinnacles and spires of cloud were piling up. They peaked, domed, darkening very, very rapidly into an angry purple. Below them, as he watched, the mirrorlike surface of the ocean broke, lifted, showed crests of white. Where they were, it was still. But he could see that wind racing in before the clouds, silent, destructive, intent.

"Jim," he growled; "we'd better—"

"Ah, father!" Jim wailed, "it'll blow over! Whoever heard of a storm in April?"

James looked behind him. The Island lay bathed in sunlight, peaceful, lovely. He shrugged. Perhaps the boy was right. In any event, they were closer to the deserted fort than they were to the house, now. And, if this tempest struck, their chances of reaching shelter were better if they went on.

"Come on, lad!" he said sharply. "You wanted to race; now here's your chance!"

Little Jim leaned forward over his gelding's neck. Brought his crop down smartly. Shot ahead like an arrow. James thundered after him, reining in the Arab a bit so that the boy could have the joy of winning the race to Fort Saint Simon.

But no horse ever foaled could outrace that storm. In minutes the saplings were bent over horizontally before the wind. The sea rose up to meet the sky, booming as though every cannon on earth had been fired at the same time. They were a considerable distance inland, but, even so, the sea spray lashed their faces, leaving the taste upon their lips.

Then the rains came.

In sheets. The visible world disappeared, cut through by that broadsword blade of water that came not down but straight in from the sea, in one steady, undiminishing roar. It was impossible for James to even see his horse's head, much less his son.

"Jim!" he cried. "Jim!"

The wind snatched the name from his opened mouth, buried it in that wild tumult of angry sound. He bent over, belaboring the Arab with whip and spur. The wind was harder now. It seemed incredible for that force to increase, but it did.

James saw something huge and dark arching down before him. He yanked the Arab to a halt, sawing savagely at the bit. And a two hundred year old oak crashed to earth not fifty feet before him, with a sodden, rumbling thunder far louder than the storm. He lifted his mount over the huge bole of its trunk in a jump that would have gained him a prize in any equestrian meet on earth, pounding on, shrieking: "Jim! Jim! Jim!"

Then the Arab shied, reared, his forefeet pawing the angry sky. James fought him down again, saw—

The gelding lying on its side, its neck doubled at an angle that left no room for doubt. And beyond it, far, far beyond it that small and sodden bundle. So small in all that world of water. So small—and so unmoving.

James climbed down. Picked up his son. Felt him loll, boneless as a rag doll. Lifted high his own craggy head.

And outhowled the winds. Outroared the thunder.

CHAPTER TWENTY

THERE WERE NO words. There were not, now, even tears. What remained was—silence.

No man, nor any woman either, heard living sound pass James Jarrett's lips between April, 1755, and January, 1756—save for a harsh, "Aye," or "Nay." Beyond that, nothing.

Because grief cannot be spoken. Nor wept away. Not when it is total—As James Jarrett's was.

Nor could Mary find time for crying. She was too busy trying, quite literally, to save her husband's life. She wore herself into trembling exhaustion trying to get him to eat. For the first three months after Jimmy's death, she managed to force a bowl of soup down his throat every two or three days. Even then, as often as not, his grief-constricted stomach refused it; and up it came again. Just looking at him made her want to cry. He was gaunt, skeletal; his eyes peering out of cavernous hollows; his lips a taut, grim line. He spent untold hours before that tiny tomb, staring at it in silence. A silence that drowned life, ended time.

After those first three months, he was somewhat better, but not much. His temper became absolutely fiendish. The indentured servants and the Negroes learned to ask their Mistress whether it was safe to speak to him before asking instructions about their daily tasks. He met John Filbert, a crony of the Knoxes, on the streets of Savannah, and in response to some real or fancied insult, sent that worthy to bed for six months. John's right arm was broken, three of his ribs crushed in, and his face a mess, both from the hammer blows of James' fists, and the grinding of his heels as he stamped his fallen foe into the ground.

After that, men gave him a wide berth—even his brothers-in-law. Mayhap especially them. And five months passed before he was calm enough to even attempt the obvious solution: that of trying to sire another child.

But, as well he knew, his hopes were slight. Mary and he had had nearly ten years of normal, happy marriage since little Jim's birth, with no results at all. And his deep conviction of the blind malignity of fate did not let him believe that state of affairs was going to suddenly change.

Yet change it did. For in January, 1756, the Acadians came.

For, during those years, the colonies were again at war, this time with France. Which made little or no difference to Georgia, for the battles of the French and Indian War were waged in far away Canada. Georgia's military resources depleted, its tiny fleet gone, without artillery, there was nothing the southernmost English colony could do but maintain guard against the French in Mobile and New Orleans, and their Indian allies, who were everywhere. That guard was successfully maintained. Not one Georgia musket was fired in anger, nor a single life lost. As far as Georgia was concerned, the War might as well not have existed.

But, far to the North, Governor Charles Lawrence of Nova Scotia was preparing to bring it home to them. The Governor didn't trust the Acadians who made up the bulk of the populace of his province, and who, having become English subjects against their will, stubbornly refused to learn English, give up practicing Catholicism, or be aught but simply, piously, devoutly French.

And now that war was flaring in Canada, the Governor didn't know what the Acadians would do if the French invaded Nova Scotia. And he jolly well wasn't going to wait to find out. Being a military man, he acted with characteristic military directness. He packed six thousand Acadians—men, women, and children, aboard ships and dumped them upon the colonies to the South. Each of the thirteen colonies received its quota; but nowhere did this good, simple, pious people find refuge except in the French Province of Louisiana.

And, in January, 1756, two ships dropped anchor before Savannah, bearing four hundred Acadian exiles, four hundred suffering witnesses of man's inhumanity to man.

Among them, a girl of twenty named Simone Duclos.

James walked through the streets of Savannah with Tim.

"Foul thing, Jim," Tim growled. "They're Papists, so we can't let 'em stay. They could be kept on as indenturers 'til they learned English, and accepted conversion; but they won't have any of that!"

"Don't blame them," James said dryly.

"Me, neither. A man can't help what belief he was brought up in—and he oughtn't to be forced to change it just because we think differently. Still Mobile and New Orleans are a sight too close for comfort. And them Frenchies have a way with the Indians. . . ."

"Treated them like human beings," James said, "which most of us didn't."

"Frenchies ain't squeamish about different colored hides. Nor over the smell of a squaw soaked in bear grease. . . ."

"They don't all use bear grease," James said.

"You should know!" Tim laughed. "But I wasn't talking about your Loosaponakee. She's damned near white, anyhow, and civilized. A pity—"

"What's a pity, Tim?"

"Nothing," Tim growled. "Heard tell we've decided to keep the Acadians here over the winter at public expense, and then send them down to Haiti and Sainte Dominique. . . ."

"Yes," James said.

"Some of their lassies are fetching, I've heard. The ladies are fair panting to acquire them as maids. Gives tone to a house, what? Having a French maid, I mean. . . ."

"I wouldn't know," James said.

"Damned if you ain't the hardest man to talk to!" Tim exploded. "Have to pick the words out of you!"

"Sorry," James said.

"No, it's me who's sorry. You were a good companion, before, boy. Now, just looking at you makes a body want to bawl. Come home and have supper with me and Beth?"

"All right," James said.

They were passing the slave market at that moment. Suddenly Tim stopped short, gripping James' arm.

"Blimey!" he croaked, "that maid's white!"

James looked.

"She is," he said quietly. "And French, or I miss my guess."

He stood there, staring at her over the heads of the crowd. Her hair was tawny blonde, her eyes, blue. There was no hint about her of the peasant stock from which she must have sprung. She was slender, graceful. She carried herself like a queen. Which was unusual enough. But more unusual still was—her face.

Not by any stretch of the imagination could she have been called pretty. But she could have walked into a room filled with the loveliest women on this earth and turned every man's head. Because her small, sad, gamine's face was the most exciting thing James had ever seen.

Those greenish blue eyes had a faintly Oriental slant. That mouth was born pouting an invitation that made sardonic sport of childishness. The sculpture of cheekbones, the slant of delicate jaw—

But it wasn't that, James decided. It was not exterior. To stare into those smoke-blue eyes was to look into—vacancy. That slim, lovely body was a deserted chateau, that face was the face of absence—the empty remainder of a soul blasted out of time by lightnings.

What happened to her? he thought. In the Name of God, what?

She was returning his gaze now, caught by the fixity of his stare. And the eyes of those compatriots whose country was death, locked, held. They moved toward each other, without moving, through the sombre, eternally wasted roads of sorrow.

"Jim—" Tim Higgins said uneasily.

James strode forward. The auctioneer was shouting, now.

"Look ye, lads!" he bawled. "What a lass! Alone of all them Frenchies, she's up for indentured service! Three years, gents! What a lady's maid she'll make—if your goodwives will countenance it!"

The men were laughing now—hoarsely, obscenely.

"Fifty pounds!" one of them sang out. Without looking, hearing that voice, James knew it was Cromwell Knox.

"One hundred," he answered quietly.

Cromwell turned upon him, his face furious.

"Goddamnit, James!" he roared, "you're a married man—and to my sister at that!"

"So are you," James said imperturbably, "and with five kids, to boot. I said one hundred, Auctioneer!"

"Hundred ten!" Cromwell shouted.

"One fifty," James said.

"Two!" Cromwell howled.

"Two fifty," James said.

"Two fifty-five!" Cromwell groaned.

James was close to the platform now, looking up at the girl.

"Thou," he said softly, "how calleth thou thyself?"

"Simone," the girl whispered. "You are, then, French, M'sieur?"

"No. But I was instructed in thy tongue as a child. Bonjour, Simone. Wouldst thou like to come home with me?"

"'Tain't fair!" Cromwell growled. "Just because he can speak this heathen palaver. . . ."

"No," Simone said, "not with thee, nor with any *Anglais*. But since I have to—I think—"

"What do you think, Simone?"

"That it is better to go with a man with whom I can at least talk. . . ."

"Done!" James said crisply. "Two seventy-five, Auctioneer!"

"How about it, Mister Knox?" the Auctioneer said greedily. "Do I hear three hundred?"

"No!" Cromwell spat; "let him take her and be damned!"

"Jim," Tim Higgins groaned, "you're fair asking for trouble!"

"I know," James said; "but since it comes bid or no, what are the odds? *Viens, donc,* Simone—come. . . ."

She walked with him through the streets. He did not even notice how every head turned as they passed. She stared at him, openly, frankly, and what was in her eyes was—fear.

"Thou must not have fear, Simone," he said harshly. "I am not a beast. . . ."

"You are *Anglais*," she whispered; "and all *Anglais* are animals!"

He turned then, and looked at her.

"Tell me," he said, "what was it that passed with you?"

"Les Anglais," she said bitterly, "they invited *mon père* and my brother to the church—for a conference, they said. Then they seized them. *Moi,* I fled the camp, and hid in the woods. After four days the soldiers found me. They were drunk as beasts and—"

"I see," James said gravely. "I'm sorry, Simone. . . ."

"Tu regrets!" she stormed. "Of what? That your countrymen took me, ripped the clothes from my body in the snow? Committed upon me *toutes sortes de vacheries?"*

James smiled dryly. Each nation had its ways. That the French called bestiality "cowishness" had no rational explanation; but then, what did?

"The fortunes of war, Simone," he said. "To the victor belongs the spoils. . . ."

"And thou—thou art a conqueror, art thou not? Too bad—to me

that puts all things equal. For I—I am no longer *française.* . . ."

"And why are you no longer French?" James said.

"Because—my own people treated me even worse. You see, M'sieur, those species of pigs left me—*enceinte*—"

"And the child?" James whispered.

"Was born before its time during a storm at sea. It died—*au bon Dieu toute merci* . . . They have heaved it over the side without even a prayer. And from then on—"

"They treated you badly?"

"*Comme une putaine*—like a whore. *Les* Acadians are a pious people, and very strict. To them it did not occur to think that what a maid does, and what is done to her, are not at all the same!"

"The results often are," James said flatly. "But enough of this—come. . . ."

As always, when he came into the house, Mary stared at him a little fearfully, trying to gauge his mood. Then she saw Simone behind him. She looked from him to the girl and back again, her eyes widening in her face.

"Mary," he said mockingly, "I've brought you a maid—a French maid. According to Tim, that gives tone to a house. . . ."

"But, James!" Mary gasped, "I don't need—"

"I know you don't. But she needs us, Lass. She was being auctioned off like a nigger slave wench when I passed. That was one thing. Another was that I had one of my rare impulses toward—pity. Look at her face, Mary."

Mary stared at Simone.

"Oh, the poor thing!" she whispered. "What on earth has happened to her?"

"The precise word for it," James said dryly, "is rape. Decorated with a few other indignities which have no names. And at the hands of Englishmen. It seems to me that she needs to be taught that all men are not beasts, and that people of our race can be kind. Beyond that, she had nowhere to go. Her own folk—ruddy straightlaced beggars they are—threw her out."

"Why?" Mary said.

"She was with child, as the result of the tender attentions of some one among fifteen British soldiers. The Acadians, in their curious way, felt that it was somehow her fault. The child died at sea, but they've made her see hell for awe that. . . ."

"Oh, the poor thing!" Mary said again. "What's her name?"

"Simone," James said.

"Simone, come here," Mary said kindly.

Simone stared at James, her eyes filled with questioning.

"Here is thy mistress, Simone, and my wife," James said in French. "Come, then, and say *bonjour*. . . ."

"Oh, James," Mary wailed, "how will I ever talk to her?"

"She'll learn English quickly enough. And I'll relay your orders until she does. . . ."

"*Ta femme*—your wife?" Simone whispered. "*Par la sainte Veirge,* but she is beautiful!"

"Aye, that she is," James said; "and what's more—very gentle. See that you serve her well. . . ."

"I think," Simone said seriously, "that it will be a pleasure!"

"James, what *is* she saying?" Mary cried.

"That you are beautiful and she thinks 'twill be a pleasure to serve you. But tell me, what d'you want her to do, first?"

"James—she looks hungry. Ask her if she's had breakfast."

"Thy mistress wishes to know if you are hungry," James said; "and if you've eaten anything this morning. . . ."

"No, nor yesterday, nor the day before," Simone whispered. "And she is extremely gentle, is she not, your wife?"

"Extremely," James said dryly; "*les Anglaises* sometimes are."

At supper that night, Simone served the table. She did it quickly, neatly, and well. But between James and Mary the silence lay fathoms deep.

"James," Mary said suddenly, "d'you know, she—she isn't really ugly at all!"

James looked at Simone as though he were considering the matter for the first time.

"Nay," he said at last, "not ugly—but odd, don't you think?"

"Yes, but it's an attractive oddness, I'd say. Of course, I'm not a man, but—"

"A man," James said easily, "would look at you, and forget she existed. How are you making out with her?"

"Just fine. She's very intelligent. She guesses what I mean through gestures. And she's already learned five or six words of English. . . ."

"Good," James said. "Ye Gods, but I'm sleepy! Come, Lass—"

"James—I—I'm glad you brought her home!"

"Good. I'm glad you're glad. But might I ask why?"

"You haven't been so pleasant in months. If she has that effect upon you, bless her, I say. . . ."

"Put it down to time, Lass," James said gravely; "which heals all wounds. So come . . . ."

That danger has passed smoothly enough. Mary was a woman, with all a woman's unshakeable belief in the importance of feminine beauty. She had no way of knowing that once a man has grown up, he puts other things far above it. Sometimes even things he cannot give a name to—the things that Simone Duclos had in superabundance: a certain electric quality; the trimmed-down fineness of a thoroughbred; a slow and slumberous sensuousness, that—

But these, Mary Knox Jarrett could not see. She saw only the plainness, the near ugliness of Simone's face. The sorrow written large across that ravished countenance. Did not see, in the nature of things could not see, what there was about this abused child that could interest such a man as James. So she put his action down to pity. She should have known better. The fact was, that she didn't.

Worse, she disregarded a thing she knew full well: that the preservation of Clan Jarrett was the nearest thing to a religion that James had. He had tried to do so openly and honorably; and the ribald gods of fate and chance had made mock of his efforts. He was not such a man as to submit tamely to outrageous fortune. Rather he would lift his craggy head against the heavens, defy the lightnings, hurl down his gauge in titanic anger before the very throne of God, Himself.

Which was blasphemy. And would cost him his immortal soul. But he wasn't counting costs any more. When the time came, he'd pay the forfeit. To him, Clan Jarrett was worth his soul and more.

He had to wait a week before Mary left the house upon a shopping trip. Then, as soon as the carriage had borne her out of sight, he went to Simone's room.

She stood up as he entered. Looked at him. She didn't say anything. The silence between them stretched itself out, out, out, quivering upon a violin note just below the level of sound. The room was alive with that tension; the very air crackled with unseen lightnings. Simone's eyes were the blue green of the sea, far out, darkening, darkening. Then she sighed.

"It will not be necessary for you to tear my things," she whispered. "What now have I to struggle for?"

But they had come together along those eternally sombre roads.

Entered, hand in hand, that country whose name is death. They were both children of sorrow, and by that sorrow mated. So what occurred between them was very different from the things they had both expected: for Simone, cold, disdainful surrender; for James the carrying of this bleak, deserted chateau by storm. . . .

No. Not those things. Nor ever those things.

He, who waged cruel war, who had embarked upon this shameful expedition without pity, was wounded by pity, by tenderness slain. He, who wanted to destroy her maddening image, still the night of her voice, blast out of time desire and form and memory, take upon her indifferently the liberties of war, did none of those things. Instead, he cupped between his two hands, trembling—with pity, with tenderness—the chalice of her face, no longer obscure, perverse, absent; but vibrant, stormlit, a silver flame in an antique goblet, flickering before the gale winds that bore them both into that country whose name is death, that country which, with anguished longing, they both loved. . . .

And she, who had meant to surrender only the outer ramparts of her flesh, preserving inviolate the inner fortress of her grief, learned the meaning of surrender, saw it transformed into—

What? What were the words?

"Thou. Oh, thou. Eternally thou. . . ."

Night that voice. Stormlit that visage. Dark anguished. By the lightnings of nothingness illuminated. By wave thunder shaken.

"*Tu*. Thou. *Tu et moi*. Thou and I. We, two. Thou art me, and I am thee. And we are—one!"

Indivisible along those sombre roads. Entered together into the country which is death. Saw and knew and understood that that fire standing tall in the midst of its desolation was life. Found together. Taken. And questions of warfare, of surrender, had nothing to do with it at all.

She lay there in his arms, crying very quietly.

"Why do you weep, Simone?" he said.

"Because I love thee. And because of thy wife who is so good, so gentle—"

"*Ta femme, si bonne, si gentile*—" who did not matter now. Who had no passport to cross the frontiers of that country into which they had entered; that country whose name was no longer death, but life.

Still, he would play out his tragi-comedy of deceit as long as he could, spare his gentle Mary all pain as long as he was able.

Until the very last. But not forever. Within two months, that was no longer possible.

Late in the Fall he came down the stairs to meet her eyes become those of a doe stricken unto death.

"James—" she whispered.

"Yes, Lass?" he croaked, already knowing.

"Simone is—with child. And you—"

He did not answer her. There was no need.

She stood up very slowly. Behind her eyes something died—screaming. Her face whitened, whitened—

"Mary!" he said.

"No, James. Don't touch me. Not ever again in this life. You had to save your Clan, didn't you? But here—in my house, beneath my roof, and with my maidservant—oh, James!"

"Mary, Lass," he groaned.

"No, James. Mary is—dead. Her body will live on for yet a little while; but she is—dead. I think you can say that she died well, and with dignity. That should be some comfort to you."

Then very quietly, she turned and left him there. Went up those stairs. Entered her bedroom. Locked the door behind her.

It was to be ten long years before she came out again.

On Christmas Day of 1756, James Jarrett's son was born. Like all men of that Clan, he was a Jarrett through and through, though his hair was blond, his eyes, blue. James named him Jarl, which, in old Gaelic, means a liegeman.

Which was the last thing upon this earth that Jarl Jarrett was. . . .

CHAPTER TWENTY-ONE

RATHER JARL WAS one of the gentle people; the first, and perhaps the last Jarrett who ever was.

His childhood was shadowed, and that marked him. Beyond the fact that, unlike little Jim, who had been a sturdy shoot of the primordial oak, he was physically delicate, falling easy prey to every illness known to infancy and childhood, as well as a few that James had never heard of, a child of his deep brooding sensitivity and vivid imagination could not help being scarred internally by the life he led, by the things he saw and heard, and, being a child, could not understand. . . .

For even his birth was heralded by war. Learning of it, Henry and Cromwell Knox came riding down upon James to punish this outrage inflicted upon their sister. Seeing them coming, James picked up the Kentucky long rifle that Tim Higgins had brought back from Pennsylvania—where, in sober fact, and by Dutchmen, Kentucky rifles were made—and shot the horses out from under both of them. Henry had to be dragged off with a broken leg. Fortunately for him, it was his wooden one; for Major Fergurson had sawed off that gangrenous mess Henry had brought home with him as a souvenir of the day he had tried and failed to kill James Jarrett. And Cromwell's retreat was sped by a load of birdshot in his seat from one of James' fine, imported fowling pieces.

Which confirmed all Savannah in its conviction that James Jarrett was a mad man who had best be left alone.

But, if the men proved craven, the women of Savannah were not to be daunted by that fierce scowl, that angry jut of nose and brow. And they had subtler, feminine weapons—arms before which James Jarrett was powerless. They simply closed their purses, yanked the drawstrings tight.

"Jim, they're fair ruining us!" Tim Higgins groaned. "I sit and sit, and not a soul enters the store! The perishable goods are spoiling; and nobody brings in hides, or tallow, or pitch, or—"

"I see," James said quietly. "Well, Tim, Lad—there's but one thing to do—we must part company. What d'you offer me for my share of the business?"

"You could stay on as a silent partner," Tim said.

"No. The break's got to be public, or they'll never believe it. There must be papers, signed and sealed before the Magistrate. They've got to *know* that I'm no longer a part of Higgins & Jarrett, or they'll ruin you, too. Incidentally, you'd better have a new sign painted: T. Higgins & Company, Limited, say. . . ."

"All right," Tim growled; "but I'm damned sorry, boy—"

"And I," James said softly. "But there it is—"

So it was that Jarl Jarrett grew up in a house where his father sat scowling, a house his mother no longer ever left, even to take a stroll.

"*J'ai honte!*" Simone stormed; "I have shame, *mon* James! When they see me coming they descend from the *trottoir,* sweep aside their skirts as though I were *quelquechose sale*—a dirty thing of *mauvais ordures.* I cannot support it! *Je ne suis pas une mauvaise fille!* I love thee, and this is not a crime. Cannot they comprehend that she—that she—was not a proper wife for thee? That such a man as thou had need of sons?"

"They comprehend nothing," James growled; "be quiet, *ma belle*—this is not worth thy tears. . . ."

These were the things Jarl Jarrett heard, and this the life he led.

That silent house. That house which was—haunted. Often, in the night, he awoke to hear the whisper of footsteps above his head. They went on and on, back and forth, far into the dawn. But when he questioned his mother about them, she screamed at him.

"*Fermez ta gueule!* Close thy trap! Pose me not the questions! *Ce n'est pas de toute ton affaire!*"

But it was his affair, because it troubled gravely the years that should have been without troubles. He soon observed the Negro maids going upstairs with trays of food—and bringing them down again, as often as not untouched. In his unease, he turned to that silent, brooding giant of a man he feared with all his gentle heart.

"Papa," he quavered, *"dites moi, qui est ce qui vive en haut?"*

"Speak English!" James growled at him. "You'll never learn if you don't!"

Jarl made the attempt. His father's tongue was alien to him still.

"Who is it," he stammered, "who lives upstairs? This person whom one never sees?"

"That does not concern you," James said coldly. "Go get your books. I'll hear your lessons, now—"

Jarl scampered off. In that, at least, he pleased his father. Though he knew it not, he was a far better scholar than his dead half brother had ever been. Jim had done almost as well as he, but through great effort; while Jarl soared through his books with tranquil ease. For Jim had loved his father, and worked hard to please him; while Jarl loved the books themselves, adored the high vaulting world of the spirit. The pages of his notebook were filled with verses, hymns to Spring, to the birds, the flowers. And those verses were not half bad. Other pages were covered with drawings, done with verve and skill. But it was not until he was eight years old that he found the love that was to last him all his life.

He was passing through the streets in which the Saltzburgers lived. And Pastor Martin Zuhlbuber was standing by his window playing the violin, while his daughter, Maria, accompanied him upon the clavichord. Jarl stood there transfixed, struck by lightning. The good Pastor was running through a series of fugues and preludes from Bach's matchless "The Well Tempered Clavier." Jarl had, of course, heard music before: the pedestrian hymns of the church, the English drinking songs; but music like this, like this!

And all unbeknowingly, the tears started from his grave blue eyes.

From his window, Martin Zuhlbuber saw those tears. He arrested his bow in midflight.

"Why dost thou weep, my lad?" the good Pastor said kindly.

"Because—because," Jarl stammered, "it is—so beautiful! If only I—"

"Come in! Come in!" Pastor Zuhlbuber said jovially. "Won't hurt to have a try, now will it, my boy?"

Jarl entered that house. Sat there watching Maria's flying fingers on the keyboard with all the stars of heaven in his eyes. . . . Stared at Pastor Zuhlbuber's masterly way with the bow and the strings.

"Sit down, boy," Maria said kindly, "here beside me. I will show you how . . ."

Timidly Jarl sat down beside the plump and rosy *maedchen;* stretched out trembling fingers, caressed those keys with a lover's touch. Maria struck a chord. Instantly, Jarl duplicated it an octave higher. Wonderingly, Maria played a simple passage. His fair face flushed, his eyes alight, Jarl played it after her without fault or fumbling.

"Ach Gott!" the Pastor roared. *"Ein Wunderkind!* Something must be done about this! And at once!"

An hour later, James Jarrett stalked into the Pastor's home, brought by the message Martin Zuhlbuber had sent him by a manservant. The good Pastor had known that he would never be able to convince James Jarrett by any amount of talk. For that, a demonstration was necessary. And since it was obviously impossible to transport a clavichord to the Jarrett home, Reverend Zuhlbuber had depended upon wording his note vaguely enough to give the requested visit the import of extreme urgency.

"Look you, Sir!" he boomed, "I've been told you are a hard man; and I know you are a sinful one! But no sin you've ever committed can compare with the one you'll do, if you give this boy not the thing he needs!"

"And what, pray, is that?" James said dryly.

Without a word, the Pastor turned toward where Jarl sat before the clavichord.

"Play!" he thundered.

And wonderingly, fearfully, Jarl Jarrett played. Badly at first, for, as always, his stern and silent father frightened him. But the music took hold; he forgot his father quite, forgot the Pastor, the dim and silent room, forgot all else but what was in his heart, what he was made for, born to do.

James listened very quietly. Then he smiled.

"The lad plays well, does he not?" he said.

"Well!" Martin Zuhlbuber roared. "You, Sir, are one of the most privileged men on earth! He has had no lessons; he has never seen a clavichord before today; and yet—"

"You're saying that he's a born musician?" James said. "I'd much rather that he learned to shoot. . . ."

"God in Heaven!" Martin Zuhlbuber almost wept. "To shoot! With those hands—with those God-given miracles of hands! Have you neither eyes nor ears? He is *ein wunderkind*—a genius! One like him is born every hundred years! And you'd consign him to killing little birds! *Ach Gott! Ach Du Lieber Gott!"*

James stretched out a big hand, let it rest upon Jarl's fair head. It was the first caress that Jarl had had from his father in all his life.

"You want this thing, son?" he said kindly.

"*Oui, papa!*" Jarl whispered, his voice almost inaudible.

"Then you'll have it," James said. He turned to Martin Zuhlbuber. "You'll undertake his lessons, Reverend? I'll gladly pay—"

"Pay me? To teach him? Do not insult me, Sir!" the Pastor growled, "I should be paid for this privilege, this opportunity, this—"

Six months later, a bulky object swung down from a ship come from Hamburg. It was a curious new instrument called a pianoforte, that is, a softloud, because unlike the clavichords, and harpsichords, it could thunder as well as sing. It would be many years yet before natural human laziness would shorten that name to piano, and forget completely what the word originally meant. Jarl's treasure had been built by no less than Gottfried Silbermann, himself, that master designer who had made the first such instrument to be heard in Germany for Johann Sebastian Bach.

And Jarl, whose efforts had been confined to the violin and the puny clavichord, lived in the seventh heaven of delight.

In his gratitude, he tried harder than ever to please his father—a difficult, if not impossible task. Because, all unknowingly, little Jarl, in his father's eyes, was guilty of an unpardonable sin: he was not his dead brother. To James, it seemed, quite often, that he was not a Jarrett at all.

James had believed that the realization of his ambitions, the preservation of Clan Jarrett would make him perfectly happy; in practice, however, it proved another thing. He had realized his ambitions, saved his clan—but, at what a price! Above his head, those endless, nightlong footsteps whispering; eight years of that now, by God! Steady and slow, treading away the nights, the weeks, the months, the years, grinding into his ears his anguish and his shame. Around him, the teeming world of his fellows with everyman's hand against him; and he, an outcast and a rebel still, at the age when a man has lived beyond rebellion, come to value peace, the respect of other men, a sober, decent place among his kind.

Underfoot, this pallid, delicate, artistic caricature of a Jarrett, with his maddeningly Frenchified manners, his shrinking from sports, from bloodshed, from all the rough and tumble ways of men.

And worse, far worse, at James' side, this bitter wasted woman turned shrew by sorrow; that electric, alive gamine's face turned ugly by neglect, by shame. For a woman, even a basically good and gentle woman like Simone does not live the life of a convicted felon without suffering a certain degeneration of temper. She quarrelled with James violently; screamed insults, naming him every conceivable species of a pig for the thing he had done to her. She threatened to leave him—to go to Mobile, New Orleans, France. . . .

But in the night she almost destroyed him with love, which, besides her fits of temper, was the only outlet she had.

All this, while above James' head, those footsteps went on wearing away the years. And strangers stood gaping before that house of brooding horror, listening to the natives' garbled tales of what was believed to occur within. . . .

Jarl learned to ride and shoot. To speak English without a French accent, though for years he continued to fall helplessly back into his mother's tongue whenever he was upset or afraid. But his heart was not in any of these things. The first time he went duck hunting with his father, he lead the first blue headed teal just as James had instructed him, touched the trigger of his fowling piece with those delicate, pianist's fingers and exploded the duck into a mass of broken feathers drifting down the wind further off than James had believed it possible for birdshot to carry.

But, when the water spaniel came up to him dripping, with that limp and bloody bundle in his mouth, Jarl wept.

Worse, that night, when Cindy served up his prize, golden brown, surrounded with candied yams, he took one look at it and fled the table. Outside in the yard, Simone and James could hear the ugly noise of his retching.

"That goddamned, sniveling little fiddler!" James Jarrett said.

It was shortly after this, that James began to note a change in Simone. She seemed, oddly, to be getting younger. That gamine's face came back, sparkling with mischief, enchanting and alive. She was gay, playful. Sang the songs of her childhood all the time. Treated him with a grave tenderness so different from her former savage moods that it had in it something strangely akin to—pity.

She started going out again. The first time she disappeared, James met her upon her return, his black brow a thundercloud, his lips a taut, grim line. His rage was all the worse because he knew it unworthy. He had believed himself above such petty emotions as jealousy; but now, clearly, he found he wasn't. For the matter had been tested but once before; and then he had had the excuse of being only nineteen years old. After Maebelle, and that aching debacle with Pitcairn Hogg, neither Sue, nor Loosa, nor Mary had given him cause to test his growth, his coming into man's estate.

But, living the way he did, his life had become entwined with Simone. Without her, the things he had to bear: the hatred and contempt of his fellows, the slow, creeping years of silence, of loneliness, those ten full years of listening to his Mary's anguished footsteps in the night, would have been beyond even his endurance. He needed Simone. He didn't know truly whether or not he loved her; but he needed her—God, how he needed her!

So he faced her now, so sick with rage, with fear, that despite himself, he trembled.

"Where the devil have you been?" he snarled.

Gaily she put out her arms to him.

"*Sois pas bête!*" she laughed; "don't be stupid, my heart. I—I simply felt the need for air."

But her disappearances became more frequent. James found himself reduced to the miserably knavish temptation to follow her. He resisted it. There were things beneath a Jarrett's pride. He told himself her excursions were innocent; that he had nothing to fear; but still—but still—

The war was over now, and had been ever since 1763. England, victorious, had gained Florida as a prize, for the Spanish had made the mistake of coming to the aid of the French too late, when the fight was already lost. So, now and again, French vessels once more put into Savannah. One of them, *Le Cygne,* out of Le Havre, was hove to for nearly three months, repairing the grave damage done to her by a storm.

How, when, and where Simone met her fellow countryman, James never knew. But afterwards, he was able to pinpoint the time almost to the hour. For returning from one of her "walks," Simone turned her mouth from his so that his abrupt, angry kiss slid along her cheek. Whispered, that same night, when he tried to take her in his arms:

"*Pas cette nuit, mon coeur; je suis trop, trop fatigué.* . . . Not tonight, my heart. I am too, too tired. . . ."

He had stared at her in astonishment, in anger, in deep and bitter pain. Then, his pride vanquished by his fear, he said it, put it into words:

"What is it that passes with thee, Simone? Tell me, is it that—that there is someone else?"

"Quelqu'un d'autre?" she chuckled. "Since you think that, *mon coeur,* I find I am not too tired after all!"

So, by wiles as old as female faithlessness, she lulled the doubting in his heart, stilled the festering rage, the blank despair. Lulled them, stilled them, until the day—

He picked up her note and read.

*"Mon cher—mon pauvre, pauvre cher—pardonez moi, mais—*my dear—my poor, poor dear, forgive me, but—"

Then he was gone, roaring from that house. He caught them on the quai, just as Simone was preparing to embark with a tall, lean son of Gascogny. Sailed into the Frenchman, his big fists flying. Which was a mistake. For he had never heard of La Savate, that curious French art of fighting with one's feet. And of that art, Jule le Grand, Big Jules, was a past master. He evaded James' bull-like rush with ease, and caught him on the point of the chin with a kick that would have done credit to a ballet dancer. James went down like a poleaxed steer. Came up, shaking his shaggy head and howling like a maddened timber wolf, to be met with a left jab to the face, a right cross to the jaw with one hundred seventy pounds, and twenty-five years of youth behind them; reeled back, and a hobnailed seaboot smashed into his chin again.

He lay there, face down upon the rough, tarred planks of the quai. Put down his hands and forced himself halfway up again, the blood streaming from his mouth and nose, in time to see Simone stepping into the long boat with all the pride of the warrior's woman, the conqueror's bride, glowing in her eyes.

"You Jade!" he whispered. "You goddamned fickle Jade!"

Then he sank back again, into a darkness deeper than the night.

Jarl was playing the pianoforte when they brought him home. He stood up, his blue eyes wide and frightened. Heard the Negro servants babbling:

"Oh, Lawd, he's kilt! Somebody done kilt Marse James!"

Heard, too, through the aching silence, suddenly fallen, the whispered footsteps on those stairs. Turned and saw—

An angel. Pale and wan, but an angel still.

"Carry him up to bed. I'll attend to him," Mary Jarrett said.

CHAPTER TWENTY-TWO

THEY CARRIED JAMES up to bed. When, a few minutes later, he opened his eyes it was to stare into Mary's face. He didn't say anything. He lay there, looking at her. And what was in his eyes was beyond any woman's endurance. That look would have been bad enough in any man, but in James Jarrett—this utter defeat, this piteous, dog-like searching of her face, this prostrated, wordless, grovelling abasement—no! By heaven and hell—no!

"James," she said, her voice low, taut, trembling, "will you forgive me, please?"

That hedgerow of a brow leaped upward, crowding against his greying hair.

"Forgive—you!" he croaked. "Dear God, Mary, Lass—'tis I who—"

"No," she whispered. "I—I failed you, James. I was old enough, woman enough, even then, to know all men remain boys until the day they die. Even such a man—as you. I shouldn't have given you up, knowing your worth—"

"What worth?" he groaned. "The worth of a blackguard, a despoiler of serving wenches? Such a—a thing as can be deserted by a heartless Jade, beaten by a lout of a sailor? I ask you, Mary, what worth?"

"The worth of the man you were, and are. The worth of a Jarrett. Lift up your head, James! For if you have lost your pride, I will give it back to you again. I'll—"

"How?" he growled. "In God's Name, Mary, how?"

"Perhaps," she smiled, tears trembling on her lashes, "by telling you this: I have endured ten years, James—ten centuries, it seemed to

me—of silence, of loneliness, even of sleeplessness. Ten years of knowing that—that *she*—lay nightly in your arms. Yet, James, there was not
one instant in all that time, not one interval between two beats of my
heart, that I—ever stopped loving you. I—I forgave you long ago, so
far as I may presume upon God's power to forgive. I lived on in hope
that one day, one blessed day, you'd mount those stairs. You didn't—
so I've come down them. I am here, at your side, almost, but not quite
in the place, where I belong. . . ."

"Almost?" he whispered wonderingly, "not quite?"

"Not quite," she said gently, her voice a flute note, warm, dark
toned. "For where I belong, my husband, is—in your arms. . . ."

"Mary, Lass," he groaned. "I—I can't! I'm not fit—"

"Oh, stop talking rubbish!" she said crisply. "And kiss me. After
all, it has been ten years."

It was, fortunately, nearly an hour later before Jarl summoned up
enough courage to knock upon that door. Mary was sitting before the
mirror, arranging her hair. Despite her years, she had the look of—
a bride.

"Now who the devil?" James growled; but Mary smiled.

"Come in!" she called.

And Jarl Jarrett pushed open that door, and stood there, staring at
her.

James saw her stiffen. He could almost see the thoughts flaming with
bitter fire behind her eyes: Her son—hers! The fruits of James' faithlessness. The living reminder I'll have to endure until the day I
die. . . .

"Papa," Jarl quavered; then his voice deserted him.

"Speak up, speak up!" James snapped. The English words wouldn't
come. "Thou—" Jarl whispered in his mother's tongue—"thou art not
too gravely hurt, art thou, Papa? Never have I had so much of fear!"

"Nonsense," James said curtly. "Now mind your manners. Say good
day to—to the lady. . . ."

"*Bonjour,* Madame," Jarl murmured.

"Oh, James!" Mary wailed, "doesn't he speak English at all?"

"Yes, Madame," Jarl said gravely; "but not well. It is sometimes
difficile—difficult—for me to say the things I think. . . ."

"And what are you thinking now, my boy?" Mary said gently.

"That—that—*jamais j'ai vu dans toute ma vie aucune femme si belle
comme toi, ni si gentile, j'en pense. Ta voix, elle est si douce—comme
la musique. Tes yeux sont si jolis, et—*"

Mary stared at James helplessly. His voice came over to her, deep and tender.

"'That never in my life have I seen any woman so beautiful as you, nor so gentle, I think. Your voice is so sweet, like music. Your eyes are so lovely, and'—Which means, my dear, either that he is a glib rogue like every Jarrett born, or that he is beginning to display some glimmerings of sense. . . .'"

"James, you wrong him, I think. Come here, my boy."

Timidly Jarl came to her. She laid gentle hands on his arms.

"How handsome you are!" she whispered. "And this face so—so sensitive. That I did not expect in a son of yours, James. . . .'"

"You thought he'd be a savage brute like his father?" James mocked. "Well, he's not. Rather too refined for my tastes. Accomplished musician. Plays like a master. He can ride and shoot, but he hates both. The only thing he really loves is that ruddy piano."

"Then," Mary said, "it was he I heard? Oh, James! I did not know such music existed, nor that anyone could play like that!"

"*Si tu resterais avec nous,*" Jarl whispered, "I will play for you every day, all day long!"

"Then," Mary said, catching the sense of that word, 'rester' to remain, "you want me to stay, Jarl?"

"With all my heart," Jarl said gravely, in English; "for I shall love you very much; of that I am sure, Madame!"

"And," Mary said, her voice quavering a bit, "you'd like for me to be—your—your mother?"

"Yes," Jarl said, sure of himself, now, no longer groping for the English words; "for you are—kind. And *Mamam* often—wasn't. One does not scream, and say cruel things in a voice like yours, Madame. I should—I should be most happy, if you stayed. . . .'"

Wordlessly, Mary swept him into her arms. He was Simone's son— or he had been. Now, he was hers. Born, at that moment, of her pity, of her starved longing for such a son as this; of, finally, her boundless capacity for love.

So James and his Mary slipped back into marriage, uneasily at first, but gradually becoming accustomed, sure, warm. For James realized what a treasure he had as a wife; but, sadly, that only intensified his brooding sense of shame.

But poor little Jarl was shocked to find his father's occasional, gruff demonstrations of tenderness abruptly withdrawn. Jarl looked like a

Jarrett, except for his blondness—perhaps even in that, for there had been blond and redhaired Jarretts before, such as his grandfather, Jonathan, whose hair and beard had been fiery red—but in almost every other way, he was his mother's son. His speech, precise, completely unaccented, remained curiously French in a sense it was hard to put one's finger upon. Perhaps in its very clarity and precision, its beautiful enunciation, its way of crisply pronouncing letters that natives usually slurred. Speaking, the boy gave the effect of a perfectly educated foreigner, because, like such foreigners, he spoke English too well, far better than those born to the tongue ever do.

And his gestures were, to James, embarrassingly Gallic. He used his hands when he talked, just like a Frenchman. Daily, hourly, he committed what were to James unpardonable sins: he reminded his father of "that fickle Jade" as James always referred to Simone; and he was an artist, a musician to the core of his gentle soul. To his great, craggy bear of a father, scion of a race of warriors, nothing was harder to bear.

Yet, to James' credit, be it said that he did endure these things. He was far too intelligent to play the heavy father, forbid young Jarl the music that he loved. Often he would sit by the hour listening to his son play—for this music spoke to him, too; but always without uttering a word of comment or the praise that Jarl longed to hear.

Constantly the boy increased his repertoire. And in this, he was particularly fortunate. For Martin Zuhlbuber corresponded frequently with Germany, and every ship brought him new scores. Jarl played everything that Johann Bach had written; extended his range to Stamitz, Scarlatti, Couperin le Grand, Rameau, Handel, Haydn, and Carl Philip Emanuel Bach, Johann's brilliant son. But he never succeeded in obtaining more than a grunt from his father—and to a boy whose soul was naked in its sensitivity, that was bitter, indeed.

The day after his fifteenth birthday, he was sitting at the piano, playing for Mary. She listened raptly, her eyes closed, marking the beat with a slight and graceful movement of her right hand. Then, abruptly, the music stopped. Mary opened her eyes to see Jarl disappearing through one of the room's two doors. Then, turning her head, she saw her husband standing in the other.

"That," James said, "is the third time he's done that. Does he think I dislike music?"

"No," Mary said quietly; "he thinks you dislike him, I guess. What I know is that you're making him dislike you."

"Name of God, Mary," James growled, "what did I ever do to the lad?"

"Nothing. It's what you don't do that causes all the trouble. Not to mention some of your mistaken kindnesses."

"Mistaken?" James said. "For instance?"

"For instance, yesterday was his birthday, and you bought him a fine English fowling piece. *I* bought him a new violin."

"I see," James said soberly. "And he resents my trying to make a man of him. That's it, isn't it, Lass?"

"James, at times, you're positively dense! He *is* a man. There's nothing cowardly about him. He's actually far braver than you are!"

James laughed then.

"He has one bloody poor way of showing it, then," he chuckled.

"James, you sit down! You give me a crook in the neck looking up at you this way. That's it. Now just you sit still like a good boy— or rather like a nice shaggy tame bear, and listen to me. Don't you open your mouth. If you do, I swear I'll smack you!"

"Lord, but aren't we fierce!" James grinned. "Tell me, Lass, what brought all this on?"

"You. Your thick-headed want of imagination. That boy rides like a centaur now, doesn't he? You've taught him to, despite the fact that wild riding has cost you one son already—"

"No," James said. "Jim didn't die of recklessness, Mary—neither his nor mine. That was an act of God. Punishment for my many sins, I suspect."

"Have it as you like. But Jarl does ride well, doesn't he?"

"He does," James admitted. "I've never seen a finer horseman, nor anything like as good a shot. Only, when I see him doing either, with his face white to the gills, that look of desperation in his eyes, it damned well drives me wild. Hell's bells, Mary! A body ought to enjoy the things he does well. And Jarl does most things well—even a few superbly. So I don't see—"

"I know you don't," Mary said tartly; "not even that you've just proved my point."

"Proved your point?" James growled. "How?"

"That he's brave. How much courage, James Jarrett, does it take to do a thing you're not afraid of? And how much more does it take to do something you are afraid of? Not only to do it; but, to do it, as you've just said—superbly?"

James stared at her.

"You may be right," he said; "but what has that got to do with his stopping playing everytime I enter the room? Plague take it, Lass, I *like* music! Listening to that boy play has been one of the greatest pleasures of my life. . . ."

She leaned forward then, laid a gentle hand upon her husband's arm.

"James," she said softly, "have you ever *told* him that?"

"No," James growled. "I'm not one for mouthing things over, Lass. But I thought the boy knew—"

"Well, he doesn't. He's gone through life aching for a kind word, a mere sign of approval from the father he worships and adores. He comes to you like a puppy—or he used to—his eyes alight after having risked his neck—no, not his neck, because he doesn't care about that—having risked those matchless, God-given hands, as Pastor Zuhlbuber calls them, justly, I think, taking the watercourse jump, and you grunt at him just like the bear you are! Never, 'Well done, son! I'm proud of you!' never any of the things he's longing to hear from you—only from you—"

"Dear God, Mary," James whispered, "I never thought—"

"Well, think now. Have you ever shown him that drawing of that lovely English house you carry with you always? Told him that you now plan to have it built on the spot he chooses, and give it to him and the girl he'll marry, as a wedding present? Ever shown him, even slightly, how much you love him, as I know you do?"

James stood up.

"James, where are you going?" Mary cried.

"To look for him," James said simply. "To tell him a few of those things. You see, Lass—you're right. But then, you always are. . . ."

Unfortunately, James did not find his son then. In fact, when, hours later, he did find him—physically—he came close to losing him—spiritually—forever.

For Jarl was at the last place James would have thought to look for him. He was down on the docks with a crowd of his fellows, watching a ship come in. Opposite them was still another crowd of youths, Jarl's own age and older. But there, the similarity ended.

For the second group was composed of the sons of notables, led by Cromwell Knox's three sons, Preston, Foster and Philip, and Henry's two, Roger and Tyler, for the Knoxes' growing wealth had provided their offsprings with the training of the best academies, of which they took but dubious profit; fine clothes, and insufferable manners of that peculiar badness often found in the spoiled sons of self-made men. But the Knoxes were part of Savannah's aristocracy now—a place Jarl normally would have had better right to than they, being, as he was, the son of a Lord. Ordinarily, Jarl wouldn't have given a fig about the title or the position in life he could never hold; but, being denied them by the widely known circumstances of his birth, he quite humanly desired both with all his heart. And matters weren't helped by the endless taunts his cousins only by courtesy flung at his head: "Jarrett's unlawful get," they called him. "The fiddling bastard. That sniveling little frog-eating son of a French whore."

Which, being after all a Jarrett, Jarl didn't take in silence. He sailed into them like a young tiger, forgetting his precious hands. Outnumbered by lads far bigger and stronger than he, he invariably got the living hell beaten out of him. Which did not stop him from attacking them again, as often as the Knoxes insulted him, which was every time they met.

He never told his father about these encounters, avoided him for days until his bruises no longer showed. In a way, he should have, for James overvalued physical courage. But, in another way, he was wise to keep silent. For the taunts of the boys who under normal conditions would have been his natural companions, drove Jarl to seek friendship among youths far further down the social scale than he. Which was why the boys with him on the docks that day were for the most part sons of those same Liberty Boys, who, on October 26, 1765, when Jarl was not quite eight years old, had celebrated the Anniversary of George Third's Accession to the Throne, that is the fifth anniversary of the crowning of the Third George of the House of Hanover as King of England, by burning in effigy Governor Wright and all the others who had favored the Stamp Act.

Jarl was, therefore, surrounded by lads whose company his father had expressly forbidden him. Considered coldly, James' point of view was not strange, although it threw him into the Tory camp, made him a reluctant ally of the Knoxes. For all his wild and checkered life, James Jarrett had never rebelled against the order of things. From the days when, as a child, he had forced his tenants' sons to accord him his due respect as the future Marquis of Argyll, until he had turned highwayman and rumrunner, his motives had always been the same: to win back the high place in life his father's folly had cost him. James Jarrett wanted not to turn the world upside down as the Liberty

Boys did, but rather to set it right, with him and his kind on top, where he serenely believed they belonged.

And this, be it said, Laird James had now all but accomplished. It hadn't been easy, but he had done it. Under Mary's gentle urging, he had made his peace with the people of Savannah. He went to church now, not because of any sudden conversion, but because it pleased her. He contributed to charity, preserved a dignified mien; entered again into business with Tim Higgins. And with the public outrage of Simone vanished from their sight, his grave charm had its effect upon the ladies of Savannah. Mistress Wright broke the ice by inviting him to an official ball. There, he listened attentively to female chatter, concealed his boredom, paid a few studied compliments with a grace that no other man in the city could match, and the thing was done. His plantation and his business flourished in those ten fateful years between 1765 and the outbreak of the Revolution. Nothing so inclines a man to conservatism as increasing years and growing wealth. James Jarrett was no exception to the rule.

But Jarl, his son, by nature and temperament, one of the most unlikely revolutionaries anyone could possibly imagine, stood on the quai, a rebel among rebels, prepared to turn upside down a world that had rejected him, and by so doing, earned his undying hate.

"What's all this ruddy muck about?" he said to Edward Telfair, one of the leading young firebrands. Among his friends, Jarl talked tough. He didn't want them to think him a hothouse plant.

"Sir Benson Tyson," Edward growled. "A real Lord High Chief Pooh Bah. Oh, veddy, veddy, and also quite too, too. Jolly, what? In from the Mother Country—to teach us oafs our manners. Permanent assignment. Official mission, only nobody's saying what it is. Veddy top drawer. Buttoned lips, old boy. . . ."

"Deah me!" Jarl quipped, replying with a fake London accent as bad as Edward's own. For even then the speech of the colonists had varied widely from Standard English, especially among the new generation born in the colonies. "But what, pray tell, are all the *jeunesse dorée* turned out in parade formation for? Surely not to bow to His Lordship?"

"Now look, Frenchy," Noble Wymberly Jones snapped, "we like not the taste of frog, nor the sound of that whining you call a language. What the devil does *jeunesse dorée* mean?" Of them all, Noble W. Jones was most nearly on a footing with Jarl. He always used his middle name to distinguish himself from his father. Noble Jones,

Senior, was one of Georgia's richest men, and perhaps its stoutest Tory. Which didn't prevent his son from being as ardent a rebel as Jarl, though with less reason.

Jarl colored. He dearly wanted their respect; and now he had made the tomfool mistake of slipping back into French. He couldn't afford such mistakes, and he knew it.

"It means gilded youth," he said slowly. "Sorry, Noble, I didn't mean—"

"Gilded youth, eh?" Noble grinned. "I say, Jarl, that's good! Fits the ruddy beggars to a T. Look at 'em, in their gold braid and lace. The popinjays! I'd dearly love to treat the lot to a whiff of grape-shot. . . ."

Jarl sighed with pure relief.

"But I still don't see—" he began.

"Simple, old boy," Joseph Habersham, son of that same James Habersham who had deserted the cloth to become a businessman, said. "Not His Nibs—his daughters, one of them at least. You know that your so called cousin, Preston Knox, was at Oxford last year for a stretch, before he was sent down for introducing a tavern wench into his diggings—"

"Yes," Jarl said dolefully. Tavern wenches in one's diggings were beginning to seem a jolly good idea to him by then. He was growing up fast, and he was James Jarrett's son. One of the reasons he hated Preston Knox so was that at bottom he envied him.

"Seems he met the Tyson girls at a ball. Mightily smitten of the eldest—Gertrude, he says her name is. Eyes like the heaven's own blue; hair like fine spun gold, and—Cripes! Here they come!"

They craned forward, watching the canopied longboat being lowered. They were too far away to make out anything more than the billow of skirts, the white gleam of powdered wigs. But that was enough. They hung there, staring.

The longboat crawled toward the quai.

"Lord God!" William Gibbons whispered. "Old Pres didn't lie!"

Jarl didn't say anything. He was lost. Never in all his life had he seen anything quite so delectable as Gertrude Tyson. She was sitting behind her father, Sir Benson, and her mother, Lady Sybil, with her younger sister and a boy Jarl took to be her brother, but who was actually, her orphaned cousin, Tarleton, at her side. She was a big girl, of the type who, before she was out of her twenties, would be nothing short of fat. But she wasn't fat now. What she was, Jarl hadn't the words for. But Joseph Clay, another of his band, had.

"A woman!" he exulted; "all woman—with all the natural equipment in the right places and some left over to give away!"

"The waiting line for grateful receivers of such donations forms on the right," Noble W. Jones laughed. "And I, friends, am going to be at the head of it!"

"Brother Friends of Liberty," John Milledge said dolefully, "I feel my convictions slipping. Hold me before I turn Tory and make peace with England!"

"Look at her sister," Ed Telfair hooted. "Skinny little wench, isn't she?"

Jarl looked. Millicent Tyson was skinny—but—he leaned over the rail, staring into the longboat. The intensity of his gaze caught Millicent's gaze. She looked up, and her penny-brown eyes widened into wonder. Light flooded them. Her thin, childish face lit with sudden illumination, became—lovely. Jarl didn't know how or why, but it did. She was, at thirteen, an elfin sprite. A merry, mischievous fairy of a lass. And she was pretty, though none of them could see that, then. Not even Jarl. With all his sensitivity and imagination, he could not discern that Gertrude's overblown charms would early become gross, her pink and healthy face sink into bovine dullness, while Millicent would only grow more taut and sculptured, more achingly, excitingly alive with the years. If he had had sense enough to look at Lady Sybil, he would have seen the wire-fine gentlewoman that Milly would become. Or at Sir Benson, the archetype of Blimpishness that lay ahead for Gert.

But, even so, that matchless face of Millicent's held him.

"You know, Chaps," he said soberly, "the little one's really not half bad. . . ."

And as if in answer to his words, Milly spoke up. Her high, clear soprano carried easily to the bluff.

"Oh, I say, Gert," she piped, "look at that perfectly stunning boy up there!"

"My dear Milly," Tarleton Tyson growled, "must you always behave like a scullery wench?"

"Yes," Milly said crisply. "They have more fun, Tarl. But isn't he just too perfect, Gert?"

"Milly," Gert snapped, "you'll disgrace us, quite!" Then, in a lower tone: "Which one?"

"The blond one," Millicent said; "the one who's leaning over staring at us. Oh, Gertie, isn't he just too beautiful for words?"

"That's quite enough, Milly!" Lady Sybil said with icy calm. But she was too late; for his companions had already laid rough hands on Jarl.

"Come here and kiss me, you beautiful, beautiful thing!" Noble Jones roared. "I say, chaps—old Jarlie's stunning, d'you know that? Got it on the best authority—Lord Pooh Bah's daughter!"

"Tell us how you do it, Jarl, boy?" Ed Telfair groaned. "Damned best shooting I ever did see—knocks 'em dead at forty yards!"

"That's 'cause he's bootiful," Bill Gibbons grinned. "Now you, Ed, ain't bootiful. You look like the south end of a northbound cow. But Jarl's bootiful. You heard what the lady said!"

"Oh, come off it, you chaps," Jarl said. He was blushing furiously. "Mind your manners! Here they come up the stairs!"

Preston Knox sauntered forward, the perfect young Oxonian, a smile on his handsome face. He slipped gracefully around the Governor and the other dignitaries come to greet the Tysons, and, taking Gert's hand boldly, conveyed it to his lips.

"Now 'at 'ere's wot they teaches a bloke at Oxbow—I mean ford," Noble Jones jeered, trying hard to sound as Cockney as possible. "But we aighn't niver learned how, 'ave we chaps?"

Tarleton Tyson glared at him. He was entirely unaccustomed to such a want of respect on the part of his inferiors.

"Why, Preston, how nice!" Gert said archly. "I hardly thought you'd trouble to come to meet us. . . ." She had, of course, thought precisely the opposite. And the gesture fed her overpowering vanity, even, coming as it did, from a boy she privately described as "a backwoods lout."

"Wild Indians couldn't have kept me away," Preston said fervently. "You honor our rude colony by your presence, Milady. . . ."

"Quite the courtier, isn't he?" Bill Gibbons said, loud enough for Preston to hear. "Bet he practiced that pretty speech while he was out on a cowhunt, chasing one of his old man's steers!"

Preston flushed; but held his peace; he had no intention of being drawn into a vulgar brawl before his princess' eyes.

"A very good day to you, too, Sir Tarleton. And to you, Lady Millicent," he said. "Now, if you don't mind, I'd like to present my brothers, and my cousins. . . ."

"That includes you, Jarl," Noble Jones grinned. He caught Jarl by the arm, propelled him forward with a powerful shove. "Go and join the band!" he laughed.

Millicent was standing there smiling, like the little minx she was.

"And this one," she said, "is he also a cousin, Preston? He doesn't seem a brother of yours; he's far too goodlooking!"

"He is neither," Preston growled, "and what's more, I haven't the slightest intention of presenting him, Milly!"

"Then you're horrid," Millicent said succinctly. She stepped aside, crossed to where Jarl stood, his face white.

"I'm Millicent Tyson," she said easily. "And I think you're awf'ly nice. What's your name?"

"Jarl," Jarl muttered.

"Jarl what?" Milly said.

"Jarl Jarrett," Jarl whispered.

"How d'you do, Jarl Jarrett?" Milly gurgled, and put out her hand.

Jarl took it, stood there holding it. He hadn't the faintest idea of what to do with it.

"Kiss her, you oaf!" Ed Telfair howled.

Jarl misunderstood the command. What Edward meant, of course, was that he should kiss Milly's hand. But Jarl, his soul a seething broil of confusion, bent and kissed that soft, pink mouth.

"Milly!" Gertrude screamed.

Milly didn't hear her. She was too busy kissing Jarl back with real fervor and evident pleasure.

Preston got there first, though Tarleton was right behind him. Sir Benson. Governor Wright. Lady Sybil. All the welcoming dignitaries.

"Listen, you nameless bastard!" Preston roared, "just who the blazes d'you think you are?"

"I don't think," Jarl said icily. "I know. I'm Jarl Jarrett, the future Marquis of Argyll; and you'd better stand back, you cow chaser!"

Preston hit him, then; a wild right-handed swing. Jarl went down like a sack of chaff.

"Boys!" Noble Jones thundered, "are we going to stand by and let that bloody toff get away with this?"

The question was purely rhetorical. The riot was already joined. The Junior Liberty Boys swarmed all over the young Tories. Judge Blount got his wig knocked off in the first rush, revealing a head that resembled an ostrich's egg. Sir Benson got an elbow in the stomach and sat down in the dirt with a loud "oof!" But the Knox boys and Tarleton Tyson, charging at the head of the young Tories, acquitted themselves nobly. Eyes were blackened and noses bloodied on both sides.

Jarl took no part. He was lying on the ground, with his head pillowed on Milly's silken knee. Even sick and hurt as he was, the sensation was deuced agreeable. Milly was stroking his bloody face, occasionally bending to kiss his grimy cheek, and cheering on the battlers.

"Give it to them, boys!" she was crying, gaily. "Hurrah for the bluecoats! That's it! Rip some lace off those blinking country toffs! That's it! How jolly! What a perfectly ripping brawl!"

For Millicent Tyson, lady though she was, was at heart an earthy little plebeian.

Lady Sybil's fine, blue-veined hand closed over her daughter's wrist. She yanked Milly to her feet, and boxed her ears with icy, aristocratic fury.

"You shameless little baggage!" she snapped. "You'll pay for this, d'you heah?"

Jarl staggered to his feet, joined the fight. Tarleton Tyson sent him down again with one hard left. Groggily, Jarl came up again, went on fighting.

It was then that the city Guard arrived.

So it was that James Jarrett, come on an errand of understanding and conciliation, found his son, gorgeous black eyes, bloody nose and all, securely lodged in the city gaol.

And understanding and conciliation vanished.

"You little whelp!" James howled. "How many times have I told you to stay away from those Liberty Idiots! You've disgraced me forever. And I'm jolly well going to have your hide!"

And, despite all Mary's entreaties, he did.

Jarl seldom saw the Tyson girls after that. The lordly Tysons had been fully informed of the circumstances surrounding his birth. And, somehow, out of his thin-skinned sensitivity, he blamed Milly for the whole debacle. Besides, there was another thing. Milly was one of those girls who develop late. At the moment her silhouette was the exact replica of a fence post. While Gert—Gert! Jarl dreamed of that round and rosy blondness day and night. His fellows made it worse by teasing him unmercifully about Milly, who on quite a few occasions managed to evade the vigilance of her parents and waylay him.

Jarl, himself, put a stop to that.

"Look, Milly," he snapped, "I have no interest in a creature who looks like a boy in skirts. If you must know, I'm in love with Gert. I mean to marry her when I can. . . ."

"Oh!" Milly gasped. "That proves two things, Jarl Jarrett! Or maybe three. One, that you don't know my stupid sister. Two, that you're an idiot. And last, but not least, you're horrid. So, goodbye!"

Jarl turned homeward again. He was amazed at the sudden, bitter ache in his heart. Milly was a skinny little thing, but—

But he missed her. His dreams got more than a trifle mixed up. He sometimes saw Milly's elfin face atop Gert's opulent body. But, during the next two years, he never got a chance to speak to either of them. When finally, in April of 1774, he did find the opportunity, the encounter proved disastrous.

"Look, Gert," he said plaintively, "what have I ever done to you? It seems to me that we could at least be friends. . . ."

"Now, really, Jarl Jarrett," Gert sniffed; "you can't expect a Tyson to be interested in a chap whose bar sinister blots out his whole escutcheon, can you, now?"

"Oh, Gert, I think you're positively horrid!" Milly cried.

"You take him, then," Gertrude mocked, "since you seem willing to have your future family sired by a natural child!"

"Gert!" Milly gasped; but in her heart, she thought: if I only could! Oh, God, if I only could!

And, on June 8th of that year, 1774, the news that the British Parliament had closed the Port of Boston to commerce in reprisal for the Boston Tea Party, reached Savannah. Noble Wymberly Jones, the leader of Jarl's band, called a meeting at the Liberty Pole before Peter Tondee's Tavern. And, as a duly inscribed Son of Liberty, seventeen-year-old Jarl Jarrett went.

To return to find his father waiting for him, a riding crop in his hand.

"I've told you, and told you!" James roared. "I won't have a son of mine involved with this rabble scum!"

"Hardly scum, father," Jarl said icily. "Noble Jones is as rich as you are, and very nearly as well born—"

"Shut up!" James howled. "Look you, lad; no colonies in human history have been better treated than these ungrateful swine; none have enjoyed the tenth of our liberties! And who are your fiery patriots, I ask you? John Hancock, who'd have us fight so he can go on smuggling! Sam Adams, a trembling old wreck who's failed at everything he's tried! That dirty little scribbler, Tom Paine, who has been hungry all his life! A broken down silversmith called Revere! That blabbermouth, Patrick Henry! Misfits and cranks, the lot of them!"

"What about Boston, father?" Jarl snapped. "What say you to shooting innocent people down like dogs in the street?"

"Innocent! That howling mob who'd been stoning the troops for three days? That rabble of thieving scum—even niggers like Attucks? Hold your tongue, you whelp! You know not what you say!"

"I know, well enough," Jarl said slowly. "I know I have no wish to be the slavish minion of a foreign king; nor to be subjected to your good people, like Preston, Foster, Philip, Roger, and Tyler Knox! Or—for that matter—even to an insensitive blackguard—like you!"

"Blackguard, am I?" James whispered between set teeth.

"Yes! You who bought my mother like a slave. Shamed your house and outraged my poor Aunt Mary to get me! Made of me such a thing as no decent maid will speak to! Blackguard, yes! Bloody, bloody blackguard!"

It was then that James brought that crop whistling across Jarl's face.

Jarl was a gentle lad; but some things are too much. And, at bottom, he was a Jarrett. He doubled his fist, swung. Put all his wiry strength behind that blow. Caught his father high on the cheek bone.

And the slender, delicate bones of his pianist's hand, broke like matchsticks under the impact.

It was then that Mary came downstairs and ended the affair, too late. For, a month later, when old Tom Fergurson removed the splints, Jarl's right hand was twisted into something that resembled a claw.

That night he sat before the piano. Put out his left hand and ran a scale. Turned it into a long *glissando* like a shower of silver sparks. Put out, trembling, that broken claw. Touched the keys. The sound he made, that wild discord, entered him like a blade. He kept on trying, desperately, pounding the keyboard until the whole house rocked with ugly thunder.

Upstairs in the bedroom, Mary heard him. She looked at her husband. But she didn't say anything. There was, at that moment, nothing to be said.

Then there was silence.

"James," Mary whispered, "I'd better go see—"

"Leave him alone, Lass," James said quietly. "He's a Jarrett—and he won't want or accept your pity. And Lass—"

"Yes, James?"

"I'm sorry. You just don't know how sorry I am. What that boy had—is rare. Zuhlbuber says that he—"

Then they heard it. The wild crashing. The splintering of wood. The twanging snap of cords cut through.

They went down the stairs together. Saw Jarl Jarrett standing there, with the broadaxe in his hands, before the ruin of the piano. He wasn't even crying. And then they saw his eyes. They were as hard as death.

And as cold.

CHAPTER TWENTY-THREE

IT MIGHT WELL be said that Jarl Jarrett died that night. And that a new being was born, Phoenix-like out of his ashes. For nothing Mary knew about her foster son prepared her for his subsequent actions.

He met the three oldest Knox boys, Preston, Foster and Philip, on the street, and tearing a paling from the nearest fence, left Philip unconscious on the ground, and his brothers bloody and reeling. He rode his Arab, Grey Ghost, at breakneck speed, jumping obstacles that nobody in living memory had seen cleared before. He spent his nights in Peter Tondee's Tavern, tossing off drams of rum with the best of them. He stayed out all night whenever the notion struck him. He was seen in the company of disreputable women. And between him and his father, a wall of frozen silence towered up to the very stars.

He was in Tondee's Tavern on May 10th, 1775, when the news of the Battle of Lexington finally—for such was the state of communications in those days—reached Georgia. He seized the violin from the fiddler, leaped to the top of the bar—finding to his pleased, and drunken, amazement that his broken claw could draw a bow well enough, while his left hand could finger the strings with all its accustomed skill—and composed a Hymn to Liberty upon the spot.

Reeled from the Tavern in the full light of morning, for that drunken rabble whose female descendants would become The Daughters of the American Revolution kept him playing bawdy drinking songs all night, and encountered Gertrude and Millicent Tyson going to the market, accompanied by their slaves.

Jarl stopped before Gertrude, made her a deep and mocking bow.

"Milady," he said, "my fair, fair lady. Only, there aren't any ladies any more. Did y'know that? Only women, now—daughters of Mother Eve. Only various conditions and kinds of sluts. . . ."

"Why!" Gertrude gasped. "You're drunk, Jarl Jarrett! You're foully drunk!"

"Aye," Jarl laughed, "and upon the wine of Liberty! 'Tis enough to befuddle what wits your beauty has left me, Gertie, dear. . . ."

"Don't call me Gertie!" Gertrude cried. "I forbid you to speak to me, you drunken lout!"

"Gert—" Millicent began.

"You've insulted me, I think," Jarl said quietly, "and for that I demand recompense—right now!"

Thereupon he dragged Gertrude into his arms, and kissed her mouth with a practiced skill that where, how, and with whom, he had gained, are far better left unsaid.

Gert struggled free of him. Drew back her hand, and slapped his face, stingingly.

Jarl stood there, looking at her. At that moment, except for his blond fairness, he was his father's image.

"D'you know, Gert," he said, much too quietly, "one doesn't strike a Jarrett. Not ever."

Then he brought his left hand across her face in a slap that sounded like a musket's crack. Gertrude reeled back, would have fallen, if Millicent hadn't caught her.

"*Mister* Jarrett." Millicent's voice was a blade, ice-tipped and deadly. "Why don't you try slapping me, too? I'm sure you'd find the party lively enough to suit even a beast like you. For you are a beast, you know!"

"Aye," Jarl whispered; "and not such a one as to be trifled with, by any woman born!"

The Tyson girls had no brothers; but their cousin, Tarleton, was not one to allow a man to slap his kinswoman in a public street, after having kissed her first, just as publicly.

He encountered Jarl in Percival Square. Sat there looking at him, without even dismounting from his magnificent black horse.

"I do you too much honor," he said icily, "and myself too little, to soil my hands with the blood of a bastard. But will you be so kind as to meet me at dawn tomorrow, Jarrett? Or shall I have to send my niggers to cane you?"

Jarl stared at him. It was the stare of a young eagle. Tarleton felt a blade of chilling cold penetrate his shoulder blades.

"I'll meet you," Jarl said simply. "Should be interesting to see if you Tories bleed red, instead of blue, as you claim. I'm afraid I'll have to settle for pistols, as my right hand can't manage a blade any more. I'd refuse on the basis that this aristocratic custom is an obscenity, unworthy of a patriot; but I do my country a service, I think, to rid her of at least one of her foes. 'Til tomorrow, Tyson!"

As it turned out, he had no time to brood over the approaching duel, for that same night, Noble Wymberly Jones, that rebellious son of a stout Tory father, Edward Telfair, Joseph Habersham, William Gibbons, Joseph Clay, John Milledge, and a few other young firebrands, organized an attack upon the royal powder magazine. And Jarl Jarrett was in the van.

They seized six hundred pounds of powder, breaking the heads of three guards to get it. Scattered, dividing their loot among them to hide in their respective homes. Jarl ripped his mattress open, and stuffed the bags in among the feathers. Sewed up the mattress clumsily, grinning over the idea of sleeping on gunpowder, and sallied forth to meet Tarleton Tyson.

It was not yet dawn, so he had some hours to wait on the sandbar below the city. He sat there, staring broodingly at the river. And a soft hand stole out and touched his arm.

He whirled, and stared into the face of Millicent Tyson. Her face was white. Her lips were trembling.

"Jarl!" she said, her voice strained, a little hoarse; "you mustn't! It won't hurt you to apologize. Tarl will accept your excuses; I'll see to that!"

He gazed into those penny-brown eyes a long, slow time.

"And Tarleton," he said dryly; "it would hurt him, then, to apologize to me?"

"Don't be an utter idiot, Jarl. You know quite well he can't. He's his family's position to maintain and—"

"And I," Jarl said quietly, "have no position to maintain, except the dubious one of a natural child. So I can apologize. People will shrug, say: 'Jarrett's unlawful get showed the white feather. What else can one expect of a bastard?'"

"Men!" Milly said in purest exasperation. "Don't you realize he'll kill you, you fool! He's a good shot; and you'll have to use your left hand!"

Jarl went on looking at her. It was distinctly a pleasure.

"Tell me, Milly," he said flatly, "why should you care?"

She turned her face away. Stared out over the river.

"Don't ask me that," she said furiously. "Since you already know, why must you make me shame myself by saying it? Only, I do care, Jarl. I care terribly. So, for my sake—"

Jarl stood up then, his blue eyes bleak, his mouth twisted into that bitter, sardonic smile he had copied from his father.

"No," he said cruelly, "not for your sake, Milly. Not even for the sake of your sister, whom I love. Come, I'll help you to the shore. . . ."

She didn't say anything, as he waded through the shallow water, bearing her in his arms. In May of 1775, for a gently born girl to declare her love for a man who loved her not, was not only impossible, it was unthinkable. Which was a pity. For the next three years of Jarl Jarrett's life might have been very different if she had.

So it was, that when Tarleton Tyson, his seconds and the two sleepy louts who had offered to stand with Jarl, finally appeared, Jarl was alone. Or he thought he was. He did not know that Millicent had gone no further than the nearest clump of woods, and hid herself, there. Why she did so, she did not know. What it was that impelled her to stay and witness that horror was beyond anybody's comprehension, even her own. But she knew very well that she couldn't go. She had to see, to know—

So it was that she endured a full hour of terror. Because that duel was a reality, not romance. And all the legends of pistols for two, and coffee for one to the contrary, the man who could hit the side of a barn with a flintlock dueling pistol even at ten paces was rare indeed.

Jarl and Tarleton exchanged fire five times without either of them getting a scratch. Between each exchange, their seconds tried to get them to shake hands and make their peace. Each time, stubbornly, they refused. All this consumed time. Millicent crouched there, trembling.

But, on the sixth exchange, Jarl was hit. It was characteristic of the marksmanship possible with the weapons of that day, that the ball raked a furrow across his left thigh, six inches above his knee. Still, its impact was enough to spin him around. His foot skidded on the loose sand, and he fell.

Which was enough for Millicent Tyson. She came plunging through the waters, screaming:

"Stop it! Stop it! Oh, Tarl, you've killed him!"

Jarl got slowly to his feet, in time to be almost knocked down again by the force with which she hurled herself into his arms.

"It's nothing, Milly," he growled, "only a scratch, not more. . . ."

"This must stop!" she wept, "this instant! Do you hear me, Tarleton!"

"I hear you, all right," Tarleton grated. "And what's worse, I see you, you shameless baggage! You come away from there!"

"No!" Millicent screamed; "you'll kill him, and—"

But Tarleton crossed to them on the run. Put out his hand and jerked his cousin from Jarl's arms. Hard. So hard that she fell.

"I don't know whether you know it or not," Jarl whispered; "but you've just signed your death warrant, Tarleton!"

The seconds bore Milly away. Jarl and Tarleton took their places again. Raised those long-barrelled pistols. Sighted down them.

"Fire!" the seconds sang out.

And Tarleton Tyson bent over, gripping his middle, inclined ever more steeply forward. Went down, striking the ground with a thud curiously loud in the echoing silence.

The seconds turned Millicent loose. She raced to her fallen cousin. Dropped on her knees beside him. Jarl hobbled over to her. Stretched out his hand, let it rest on her shoulder.

She whirled, her eyes light-filled, blind.

"Don't touch me, you murderer!" she cried.

"He's not dead," Bill Fordly, one of Jarl's seconds, said.

"Nay," Forsythe Rayford, Tarleton's second, growled; "but he's gut shot. And with the heat coming on—"

Then he turned to stare at Jarl.

"You'll swing for this, Jarrett!" he said.

But Jarl didn't wait to put the matter to the test. He left that same night, the blood soaking through the clumsy bandage, mounted on Grey Ghost, a seething broil of trouble in his soul. Where he went might have been expected of him. He headed north to join the forces of General Washington.

And he forgot completely the gunpowder hidden in his mattress. Which had tragic consequences.

For, as he left his native Georgia, the first American Civil War was under way. It was fought without quarter, with an absolute disregard for the rights of civilians that distinguished it unhappily even from the second, which was bad enough. Only the colonists didn't call it a civil war, which it was. They called it a Revolution.

James Jarrett kept out of it as long as he could. He might have been able to keep out of it forever, but for Jarl Jarrett's gunpowder.

Only, as he soon found out, nobody was going to be allowed to remain neutral in this struggle. The Liberty Boys had taken over. Governor Wright was under house arrest. And everybody even suspected of being a Tory was already beginning to see purest hell.

In their defense, be it said that Jarl's friends didn't move at once against his father. In the first place, they were afraid of him. In the second, several of them, such as Noble W. Jones, and Joe Habersham, couldn't afford to, because their own fathers were as stout Tories as James Jarrett. So they limited themselves to appearing before the door of his town house in Savannah, and ordering him to remove his cattle from the plantation on Saint Simon's Island, where the danger existed that they might fall into British hands, and thus give aid and comfort to the enemy.

James stared at them a long, slow time. When he spoke, he didn't even raise his voice. But there was the crackle of lightning in it, the boom of sudden thunder.

"You insolent young whelps," he snarled. "Get out of here while yet you're able to walk!"

An hour later, he had all but forgotten the incident. But the Sons of Liberty hadn't.

As always, he slept soundly that night. But a shower of glass from a window blasted in by a volley of musket fire, is enough to waken the soundest sleeper.

James leaped from the bed.

"James!" Mary shrilled, "what's happened? The window—oh my God!"

"Lie down on the floor, Lass," James said calmly; "roll under the bed. That way you won't be hit. Those sniveling young bastards are attacking the house. . . ."

"No!" Mary cried. "I'll go with you! I know how to load a gun! And I can shoot, too, if need be—"

James stared at her. He was a gnarled grey oak of sixty; but his eyes filled up with the same tenderness then as they had the first time she crossed his sight.

"Mary," he said, "while there's time, I want to tell you that no man has ever been so blessed as I—"

"Rubbish!" Mary snapped; but the whine of a musket ball cut her off.

"Come on!" James roared.

They raced down the stairs to his study, where he kept his rack of firearms. The hall was alive with the frightened babble of the Negro house servants.

"Jupiter, Cassius, Jonas!" James thundered. "Come here!"

Trembling and grey with fear, the blacks came.

"Load for me," James said kindly. "Keep down and you won't be hit. I'll give these beggars a good show!"

He did. He was reluctant to kill boys so young; friends, moreover, of his son; but with his first three shots, he wounded three of them.

"That'll hold them for a while," he said.

But it didn't. They were too well fortified with patriotic rum.

"Look out, James!" Mary cried.

James hurled himself down and to one side. As he did so, he saw the flash of the priming, heard the flintlock in Mary's hands buck and roar.

"Game lass!" he exulted. "Give 'em hell!"

"Oh, James!" Mary faltered; "I—I'm afraid I've killed him!"

James raised his head.

"No, you haven't," he said; "the beggar's crawling off. . . ."

They went on firing. There was a lull—a suspicious lull. Then a voice rang out:

"All right, Jarrett—you win, for now! But we'll get you, you Tory bastard! Just you wait!"

And the street outside echoed with running feet.

For half an hour longer, James and Mary stood guard. The silence crawled along their nerves. But nothing happened. Nothing at all.

"Come, Lass," James said tiredly. "Let's totter off to bed. Jonas will keep watch. I can trust him. . . ."

"Oh, James, I'll never sleep a wink!" Mary wailed.

"Oh, yes, you will," James chuckled; "come along. . . ."

He was wrong; she didn't sleep. An hour later, she shook him.

"James, wake up!" she hissed. "I smell smoke!"

James opened one sleepy eye. Sniffed the air.

"Don't smell a thing," he growled. "Go back to sleep, Mary; you've got the vapors for a fact. . . ."

"James—" Mary quavered.

"Oh, leave me in peace, Lass; I'm tired!" James said.

The next time she shook him, twenty minutes later, there was no room for argument or doubt. He woke up choking and gasping, hearing already the crackle of flames.

He stumbled from the bed, picked Mary up as though she were weightless, raced down stairs firelicked, and already beginning to give. He reached the downstairs hall. But he never got to the front door. He was still a yard away from it when Jarl's hidden store of powder split the night apart with hell's own thunder.

Three of the Liberty Boys were killed outright by the flying timbers. James never knew what hit him. He regained consciousness three full weeks later, to learn that Mary was still in a coma.

For four weeks more, he watched beside her bed. She began to recover. Smiled, talked to him. But one cold Fall night, she caught cold. Developed, within hours, double pneumonia.

Died, sweetly, softly, gently, as she had lived—with her hands growing cold in his.

For the last time in his life, James Jarrett wept. Then he got up from there. Stripped off his clothes. Put on his ancestral kilt and tartan. Picked up his arms, never to lay them down again while yet he lived.

Within months, Patriots and Tories alike were speaking of Jarrett's Raiders in whispers. Murmuring fearfully about the Revolutionists chained in their houses and burned alive. About the wholesale slaughter of livestock; the trampling of canefields. The coldblooded pistoling of men who had already surrendered.

They called him the Scotch Devil.

Which was, if anything, an understatement.

CHAPTER TWENTY-FOUR

JARL DIDN'T GET to Cambridge, Massachusetts, where that wild band of backwoods bushwhackers who called themselves the American Army were, until after the Battle of Breed's Hill—to give it its right name, for it wasn't fought on Bunker's Hill at all—was over. But he did reach the camp a day or two before General George Washington arrived to take command. And, almost immediately, he incurred his general's displeasure.

For Jarl Jarrett, a buck private in the rear ranks, was being shaved by his own commanding officer, Captain Thomas Wynn, when the imposing figure of the great Virginian, splendid in his spotless regimentals—the only complete uniform in all of Cambridge—came marching through the filthy cluster of huts and tents whose stench was an offense in the nostrils of the Almighty. For a private to be shaved by an officer was usual, especially when the officer was a professional barber, which Captain Wynn was. The American forces were like that: nobody saluted, drilled, presented arms, or did aught else but chaw terbaccy, get drunk whenever rum was available, and consort with the whores who outnumbered the soldiers.

But now General Washington was here. And he had two more years to go before he would discover he was the Father of His Country. At the moment, he was still a Virginia Planter, and an Aristocrat. This rag tag and bobtail collection of profane Yankee scum looked like poor whites to him. The General didn't like poor whites. On the whole, he rather preferred his Negro slaves, to whom, considering his temper which overmatched the devil's own, he was remarkably kind. And he had a deep seated sense of the fitness of things. These rapscallions were jolly well going to be taught to respect their betters. To salute. To drill. To be turned into soldiers. So Jarl's having chosen that moment to get a shave was, to say the very least, slightly unfortunate.

The General stopped. His steel-grey eyes went smoky with rage. Jarl Jarrett leaped to his feet, one side of his face still covered with lather. He had sense enough to salute right smartly.

The General ignored him completely.

"Captain," he said icily, "what is this man's rank?"

"Private, Sir," Captain Wynn said uneasily.

"And you were shaving him!" the General roared.

Captain Wynn quailed before that steel-blue gaze. He had sense enough to keep his mouth shut. But young Jarl Jarrett didn't.

"You see, Sir," he began; "it was like this—"

"Who in the name of the forty-seven unspeakable varieties of unholy hell ever asked you, soldier!" the General thundered. Which was a sample, suitably deodorized, of one of his greatest talents. The one that didn't get mentioned in the history books. George Washington, every man who served under him was prepared to take his Bible oath, was the undisputed heavyweight champion of the universe when it came to profane language.

Jarl was young enough, foolish enough to try again.

"But, Sir," he protested, "I thought—"

"You thought! Goddamnit, soldier, privates don't think! They take orders! Why, you—" And for five full minutes the General proceeded to dress Jarl Jarrett down with a masterly command of language which left that worthy white and shaking, and completely awed. The grinning soldiers who witnessed it swore that the grass turned brown in a circle fifty feet in diameter around the General. The leaves shriveled, turned brown, and dropped as though it were Fall. Lightnings crackled. Thunder crashed. And there was a suspicious aroma of brimstone in the air.

All in all, with every side of the matter considered, Jarl got off lightly. The General marched away. But two days later, Jarl came within inches of losing a square yard of his hide. He went to a party given by a group of his new-found companions. The party was a rollicking one, well supplied with rum and "laundresses" which was the military euphemism for whores. A glass in one hand, and a lass tucked beneath his other arm, Jarl was roaring out a stanza of the song that one Francis Hopkinson, who later made the first American flag—the

one that Betsy Ross didn't make, but got the credit for anyhow—had
written.

> "Sir William, he, snug as a flea
> Lay all this time asnoring,
> Nor dreamed of harm, as he lay warm
> In bed with Mrs. Loring!"

"Three cheers for Mrs. Loring!" he howled. "May her dewy charms
last forever!"

"Why?" the little dark-haired snip of a girl he was holding said, her
voice blurred with rum, "what's she got that I haven't?"

Jarl grinned at her.

"She's got Sir William Howe," he said thickly. "Commander in
Chief of the Brit—tiche forces. And as long as she's got him, we don't
have to fight. Sturdy ol' campaigner, Sir William. Fights th' blinkin'
war on interior lines. Deuced interior. Exact circum-circum-fer-rence
of Mrs. L's—boudoir. Wonder what Mr. Loring thinks about it all?"

"Ah, to hell with him!" a soldier growled, "long as he don't inter-
fere. For this kind of war suits me ruddy well!"

"Look, Bets," Jarl whispered, "what do you say we go for a stroll in
th' woods?"

"Now aren't you the forward one, though?" Bets giggled. "All right,
come on!"

"Now that," another of Jarl's companions roared, as they got up,
"is the damned fastest flanking movement I ever did see! Let us know
who wins the battle, Jarl!"

"Battle? You mean wrestling match, don't you?" a Connecticut
Yankee grinned. "Catch as catch can, 'n to the winner belongs the
spoils. Nice lil' spoils. . . ."

"Put your money on me, boys!" Jarl laughed and left the tent.

In good time. Not ten minutes later, his companions' drunken roars,
punctuated by shrieks of female laughter, awakened General Washington. Awakened that Virginia Aristocrat with a sense of the fitness of
things.

The next morning, drawn up in parade formation, Jarl witnessed
the punishment meted out to his companions. And though he was
doing his best to imitate his roaring old hell of a father, he hadn't yet
been hardened by warfare. His guts knotted from pure sickness.

"It's not right," he muttered. "I'm as guilty as they. More, because

I profited from the occasion, and they never got a chance to. I should confess—take my medicine along with them—"

He hung there watching it, and getting sicker all the time.

For General Washington had the ringleaders straddle a narrow board six feet off the ground. With stones weighing twenty pounds tied to their feet. The toughest of them slumped over unconscious after five minutes of that. The rest received sixty-nine lashes apiece on their bare backs. The nine-foot, leaded muleskinners' whip cut through their hides like a knife.

Coward! Jarl howled inside his head. Father's right. I'm a nogood sniveling sneak and a coward! Letting them take that while I—while I—had all the best of it. Sweet lass, Bets. Funny how much she looks like Milly. Dear God! Look at that! I won't hold back; I won't be a yellow bellied rat enough—

He took a step forward, so sick that the square danced before his eyes. Another. But at that moment, the sergeants hurled buckets of briny water over the victims. And Jarl Jarrett, gallant volunteer, crumpled to the ground in a dead faint. The screams of the soldiers when that salt water bit into their stripes were absolutely beyond his endurance.

For nobody had ever told George Washington that his favorite pastimes were supposed to be cutting down cherry trees, then. Or throwing silver coins across the Potomac. It would have been interesting to see what would have happened to them if they had dared.

Jarl came away from that exhibition with a curious confusion in his mind. He got General Washington mixed up with his father. And he knew well what fathers were like. He often thought about that dark and brooding giant whom, had he been allowed to, he would have loved. Wondered what James Jarrett was doing.

It was a mercy that he did not know.

For James, at that moment, was out at the McGerk brothers' farm. Sadly for them, the McGerks had gotten out of hand. Had taken advantage of the war to settle a long standing quarrel with James' in-laws, the Knoxes. On the face of things, he had no reason to love his late wife's family; but the McGerks had elevated a bucolic feud into what was for James a matter of principle.

That morning, Cromwell Knox came riding into James' camp, that is, if a man stark naked, his hands tied behind him, and facing his mount's tail—a tail which, incidentally, had been painted a gorgeous blue—can be said to ride.

James carefully folded the drawing of the Perkins' London house, which, for the ten thousandth time he had been studying with some care. Put it without haste into his pocket. Got up and seized the trailing bridle of Cromwell's horse. In spite of himself, he had to grin.

"Plague take it, Crom," he chuckled, "but you're downright fetching, I must say. Were you a mite younger—and female—I'd—"

"James," Cromwell wept, "the McGerks, they—they've killed Henry! God damn them—they—they tortured him to death!"

James sobered at once. Henry had been a sneak and a coward. Had tried to murder him. But that was long ago, now. And, with all his faults, Henry had done what he could for the Loyalists' cause. Besides, this filthy rabble could not be permitted to get away with killing King's men—not even such a crippled, palsied wreck of a King's man as Henry Knox.

He whirled, his bass a cannonade, rocking the quiet trees.

"To horse!" he thundered. Then, whipping out his dirk, he cut Cromwell loose.

"Give this man a blanket," he commanded. "Then, damn it, follow me!"

They found Henry soon enough. The branch the McGerks had chosen to hang him from was so low and so limber, that the stump of his wooden leg, and his toes had traced convulsive spirals in the dust; his toes, bare like all the rest of him. There was a splatter of droplets all around him—blood from the hundreds of knife wounds they had inflicted upon him. Henry had looked like Mary; had had a truly handsome face. But it wasn't any more. Purple is hardly a becoming color.

James sat there on his Arab, looking at him. Then he turned to the Raiders.

"Cut him down," he said softly.

Cromwell got down from his horse. Covered his brother's body with the blanket James had given him. Stood there, crying. James dismounted. Threw an arm across his brother-in-law's shoulder. And that, finally, and forever, was the end of the war between him and the Knoxes.

"Come, Crom," he said.

They swept down upon the McGerks like the wrath of God. Killed Tobias and his eldest son, William, outright. Captured the other three

of them. Bound them to a rail fence while they burned the house and
the barns. Pistoled the cattle. Rounded up the horses for their own
use. Sabered the pigs. Set the hen houses afire with the chickens in
them. Rode through the fields, trampling the crops flat.

Then they dealt with the other McGerks.

Molly, Tobias' wife, was, at fifty-five, and one hundred and sixty
pounds, hardly a fit subject for Jarrett's Raiders to have sport of. But
they shaved her head. Painted one half of the crown of it red, the
other blue. Put her on a horse, in the same position, and in the same
costume that the McGerks had placed Cromwell, and sent her into
town like that.

After that, they tied the McGerk brothers two by two, face to face,
and lowered them down the well by their feet on leather thongs. Green
leather thongs, cut from the hides of the slaughtered cattle. Left them
there, their faces inches above the water, knowing at what rate those
thongs would stretch under their combined weights. And how much
the McGerks' struggles would increase those thongs' tendency to give.

Then, like ghosts, they disappeared into the woods.

Four days later, James had visitors. All of the Knox boys: Preston,
Foster, Philip, Roger, and Tyler. With them, a fat man—a strangely
familiar fat man, splendid in British Regimentals.

"Look, Sir," Preston said, "we've come to join your Raiders—if
you'll have us. We can all ride and shoot and—"

"And you've all good reasons for wanting to join," James growled.
"He was your father—or your uncle. Good enough. I'll give you a trial.
Now who, pray, is this?"

"My sister Mathilda's fiancé," Foster said, "though the marriage
will have to be postponed a bit, now. Hardly fitting to have a wedding
with our father not yet cold under ground. . . ."

"Permit me to introduce myself," the fat Britisher said; "the name
is Haig, Major Geoffrey Haig, of the Fifth Royal Edinburghers on
detached service—"

"I see," James said. "Might I ask what that detached service is?"

"Liaison with the Irregulars who support the Crown," Major Haig
smiled. "Such as yours, Sir James. They, I'm told, are by far the most
effective. . . ."

James stood there, staring at him. At that round face, so full of
calculated cordiality. At those little pig's eyes that were strangely—

hypnotic. At those pudgy hands. At time turned back. At black and bitter memories.

"Haig?" he growled. "Are you sure it is not—Hogg?"

The Major shrugged.

"Hardly an attractive name, what?" he said. "I had it changed legally. Petition before Parliament. So you're *that* Jarrett. I rather thought you were. . . ."

"And your—mother?" James whispered.

"Dead. These many years. But father's well enough, though sunk in age and gout. Told me to look you up, give you his regards. Deuced insistent about it. Seemed to take an unholy pleasure at the thought of my conveying to you the information that your ball failed to penetrate that tub of lard we Hoggs wear before us. So, now, you know—"

"The Devil takes care of his own," James said evenly. "And Trudy?"

"I suppose you mean my grandmother? My father's first wife. Bit thick, all that, what? I didn't know her. She was in a madhouse when I was born, and died there shortly afterwards. Any more questions, Sir James?"

"Yes," James said; "one. Do you come as friend or foe, Major?"

"As a friend. My father's ancient quarrels are of no interest to me. Rum old chappie, anyhow. Besides, I'm under orders to tie in your sterling efforts with ours. A damned sight more important, that, than discussing your rivalry with my pater over various females, or what a rotten marksman you used to be. Right, Sir James?"

James stared at him. A long time. A very long time.

"Very well," he said at last. "Upon your head be it. . . ."

Which was another thing that Jarl Jarrett didn't know: that his enemies had been reenforced. And worthily. Because, in themselves, the Knoxes were nothing much. But now they had—and down through the years would have—a leader. Brute force, animal ferocity, they were born with; but, now, those qualities were going to be led, directed, put to use by the Machiavellian intelligence, the serpentine indirection, the subtle cunning—even the mesmeristic powers of—a Hogg. The difference was vast.

And the long chronicles of Clan Jarrett would be forever changed by that meeting in a Georgia wood.

But Jarl didn't know that. He was too busy running from the British.

Fighting, bleeding, starving. Even occasionally winning, as at Trenton. As at Princeton. But most of the time they lost.

The Jarl Jarrett, who, on August 23rd, 1777, marched through Philadelphia with his comrades in arms, their rags fluttering jauntily, green sprigs in their battered hats, was a vastly different lad from the stripling who had fled north two years before, to escape hanging. He was as lean as a rapier's blade. As hard, as fine tempered. James would have been proud of him, now. Every bit of the softness of his boyhood had been marched and beaten and starved out of him. A considerable portion of his sensitivity, his delicacy.

The Jarl Jarrett who marched through the silent crowd who stared at these pitiful scarecrows who called themselves an army, in horrified pity, was another thing altogether. He was, at long last, a man.

Marching, unafraid, ready to face hell, if need be. Only hell wasn't his destination as Fall decorated the trees in the lovely Pennsylvania valleys they marched through. But it was a good enough replica.

For its name was Valley Forge.

When Spring came at last, Jarl could hardly believe it. Seeing the flowers budding along the sparkling little stream that ran through the valley, he wanted to cry. Because just being alive was a miracle. A gift from God.

He turned his eyes away from General van Steuben's pock-marked face, and stared out over the rows of graves. So many graves. The flower of the American Army lay buried there. He had seen General Washington weep as they laid those pitiful heaps of skin and bone in the frozen earth. Seen the proud, icy Virginian, who had once had men whipped bloody for failing to salute, turned human by suffering, turned great by care, treating lowly privates for the ugly itch they were inflicted with, smearing on the salve over their filthy sores with his own strong and tender hands.

Seeing the General coming down the lines with the Marquis de la Fayette at his side, Jarl's heart leaped. He loved his General now. Poured out upon him, silently, all the pent up need to love, worship, adore, that James Jarrett had never accepted from him.

Astonishingly, General Washington stopped directly before him.

"Jarrett," he growled, "you're a Georgian, aren't you?"

It wasn't strange that George Washington knew his name. By the Spring of 1778, they were so few that the commander could probably call roll of the entire Army without a list in his hands.

"Yes, Sir!" Jarl whispered.

"And the Marquis tells me you speak French—"

"Perfectly," de la Fayette said.

"Good. You are hereby detached, Jarrett. I'm ordering you back to Georgia. Some time this Fall, or perhaps next Spring, our beloved allies are going to launch a naval attack against the British in Florida, then move north through Georgia. I want you there as liaison officer to coordinate our efforts with theirs—"

"Officer, Sir?" Jarl gasped.

The great Virginian's smile was frosty.

"Hardly do to conduct our conversations with the French through a buck private in the rear ranks; now would it, son? I hereby commission you First Lieutenant. You're to leave at once. Anything you want to say?"

Jarl stood there, visions of the gallows he'd swing from for young Tarleton's death filling up his mind. But he didn't tell his General that. For George Washington could have from him now what his father always might have had for the asking, and had endlessly denied. His life.

"Nothing, Sir!" he said, and saluted smartly.

CHAPTER TWENTY-FIVE

IT TOOK HIM until the fifteenth of June to get home again, living off the country, blessing James at last for having made him learn to shoot. He had a Pennsylvania long rifle he had taken off the body of a fallen companion. And he could shoot it about one tenth as well as frontier braggarts claimed a man ought to be able to with the celebrated long rifle. Which was well enough. Because the misnamed Kentucky rifle wouldn't shoot as accurately as its exponents claimed it would, even locked down in a bench vise. He didn't bark any squirrels, or shoot them through the right eye to leave their fur unmarked. He hit them anywhere he could, and cursed the waste of powder and ball when he missed them altogether—as he frequently did. Like every other rifleman. Only he didn't lie about it. He had a deep and reverent respect for the truth. And he still hadn't become uncivilized enough to give a damn about his prowess at murdering small animals. In fact, he hated it. But he had to eat.

He rode into Savannah at last, his Arab, Grey Ghost, once more sleek and fat from the fine grazing along that journey. Which made the contrast between mount and rider all the more marked. For Jarl Jarrett looked like an ancient barbarian from the North—a Vandal, or a Viking. Except that it is to be doubted that those old seafarers ever managed to get quite that dirty. He sported a sunburst of a blond beard, and his yellow hair hung over his shoulders. His rags fluttered out behind him as he rode, right jauntily.

To get to his father's townhouse, he had to pass the Tysons'. He stared hard at their windows, hoping for a sight of Gertrude—or even of Millicent. Because his memories of Milly were confusingly warm.

Skinny little thing, he thought, but—sweet. . . .

He didn't see either of them. But they saw him. Standing behind the curtains, Milly cried out, her voice vibrant with joy:

"Gert! That's—that's Jarl! He's come back! Oh, I—"

"You're all set to rush out and embrace that filthy rebel beggar," Gertrude said mockingly, "rags and all. Control yourself, Milly. Don't disgrace us, I beg you. . . ."

"Oh, you!" Millicent began; then she stopped. And what was in her eyes was horror.

"Gert!" she whispered. "He doesn't know!"

"What doesn't he know?" Gert said indifferently; "not that I care. . . ."

"He's going home—to a house that isn't there anymore. To those ruins—in which his stepmother died. . . ."

"She didn't die in the ruins," Gertrude pointed out flatly. "She died in the hospital. And the rebels will rue that day forever. A pity Jarl isn't the man his father is. . . ."

"I'm glad he's not," Milly snapped. "I wouldn't want him to be such a beast! But now I've got to go—"

"Go? Where?" Gertrude said.

"To stop him. To—to warn him. Even to ease the blow a little. You know how Jarl felt about his stepmother. . . ."

"He should have. Not many women would have taken their husband's natural child to their bosom the way she did. I'd have kicked the little bastard out in the street to starve. But I must say, Milly; father isn't going to like this when I tell him. He won't approve of your being such a forward baggage!"

"I don't care," Milly whispered; "these are modern times and I—"

"You love him with all your plebeian heart," Gertrude sneered. "Go, then; I wouldn't give a fig for you, or him!"

But the argument, slight as it was, had taken too much time. Millicent found Jarl standing before that jumble of broken, charred timbers, his face grey under all the grime.

"Jarl—" she said gently.

He turned. Looked at her. His blue eyes widened, darkened. He hadn't seen her in three years. Perhaps he had never really seen her before. She wasn't skinny any more. Slender, yes—even willowy. But that tight bodice was not broken into planes and angles now. It curved in, lifted up, rounded with devilish provocation. Her waist was still a twohands' span; but her hips were wide and feminine at last. And her face, her face arching upon the swan-slender column of her neck, bending toward him, those penny-brown eyes filled with grave concern—

"My God, Milly!" he croaked. "You—you're lovely!"

"Thank you, Jarl," she whispered, forgetting what she had come for, the day sinking out of time and mind for her, the noise of the busy, bustling street dying into bee-drone, into far, sweet murmuring.

He took an involuntary step towards her. Then he stopped.

"Milly," he got out. "Tell me—where are my folks?"

"Your—your stepmother is dead," Millicent said sadly. "She was—injured in—*that,* and died of pneumonia. And your father—"

"My father?" Jarl said.

"I don't know where he is. He's off fighting—for the Crown. You see, the Liberty Boys blew up your house the night after you left and—"

Jarl took a backward step. Let his knees buckle the way they wanted to. Sat there in the dirt, his young head bowed, the great tears ploughing streaks of white through the dirt on his face.

"Jarl!" Millicent cried; "I'm sorry! I didn't mean to upset you so—"

He lifted his head. The sunlight caught in his golden lion's mane and blazed. Millicent thought she had never seen anything so wonderful as his face then, nor anything so—terrible.

"They didn't blow it up, Milly," he choked. "I did!"

"You!" Milly gasped. "Oh, Jarl!"

"Aye, me. I was one of those who raided the powder magazine. I hid twenty-odd pounds of gunpowder in my mattress. Forgot about it, what with the duel. I suppose a ball must have hit it and—"

"No," she whispered. "Your fine friends threw in a torch . . ."

He came upright then, his eyes a blue blaze.

"I'll get them!" he snarled. "I won't rest until—"

"You don't have to," Millicent said dryly. "Your father already has. . . ."

He stared at her.

"All of them?" he croaked.

"All. One of them was dragged back into town, tied to the tail of his own horse—with his throat cut, Jarl. Three others were chained inside their house, and burned alive. The rest shot, stabbed, bludgeoned to death. He—he's not human, your father! People call him the Devil's Spawn. Even though he's on our side, I can't see—"

"You mean," Jarl said, "he's still doing things like that?"

"Yes," Millicent said.

"Then I'll get him," Jarl said quietly. "Bring him in, lock him up. Because he's mad, Milly, dangerously mad. . . ."

"Very likely," Millicent said. "Jarl, would you like to come home with me and clean up a bit?"

"Come home with you?" Jarl said wonderingly, "even though I killed your cousin?"

"You didn't kill him. He's recovered. In fact, he's riding with Banastre Tarleton, now. So there's no reason why—"

"Does," Jarl said quietly, "Gertrude share your point of view?"

Millicent's brown eyes clouded.

"Jarl," she whispered, "do you still—love her—so very much?"

"I don't know," Jarl mocked. "Tell you that after I see her. But you haven't answered my question. Am I still persona non grata with Gert?"

"Yes," Millicent said simply. "I'm afraid you are."

"Then no, thanks," Jarl said flatly. "I'll go out to the island and find some of my old clothes. That is, if they haven't burned the plantation, too. . . ."

"No, it's still there. Mr. Higgins has been looking after it for your father. . . ."

"Good," Jarl said. "You know, Milly—you've changed. You used to be the absolutely worst nuisance upon this earth. As pert and forward a little baggage as I ever laid eyes on. . . ."

"I—grew up, Jarl," Millicent said tartly. "One does, you know. And I can be forward, even now, when the occasion seems to warrant it."

"Fine," Jarl said. "I shall have to seek such an occasion—such a rarely delightful occasion—as soon as possible. Tell me, Milly, will you come for a ride with me tomorrow night?"

She looked at him then, and her heart was in her eyes.

"Me?" she said bitterly, "and not Gert?"

"You, and not Gert," Jarl said. "I hardly think she can compare with you, now, Millicent."

"She can, though," Millicent said sadly. "She's prettier than ever. Much more than I'll ever be. . . ."

"That," Jarl grinned, "depends upon tastes. And, right now, you suit mine. . . ."

"Jarl, don't plague me . . ." Millicent said. "It's not fair!"

"Everything is, in love and war," Jarl mocked; "and this looks like a bit of both, at the moment. Come on, Milly, will you ride with me, or have you something else of earth-shaking importance to do?"

"No," Millicent whispered, "I haven't anything to do. Or I hadn't. But now—I have. Something of—earth-shaking importance, just as you said. At least—to me. . . ."

"And what may that be, milady?" Jarl said.

"Waiting for you—at the foot of the landing," Millicent said. "This one more time. Just as I've waited for you—all my life. . . ."

"Milly!" he bassed.

But she turned then, and fled, wildly, down that sunlit street.

When he stepped out of the boat rowed by his father's slaves, he had been transformed. His hair had been cut, clubbed softly into a queue on the back of his neck. He was clean shaven. Lace spilled out at his throat and wrists. He wore a sky blue habit *à la française,* that made him look like a prince. Wore it in a way he had never worn clothes before. Because he had broadened, hardened into lithe and vibrant steel. The gentle, over sensitive lad of before was gone, and in his place—

"Oh, Jarl!" Millicent got out, "I think you're the handsomest man in all the world!"

Then her face flamed scarlet, though he couldn't see that. It was already too dark.

"Thank you, Milady," he said, and took her arm. "I suppose there are still horses for hire? I mean to take you for a long, long ride—"

"Yes," Milly whispered, "but I have my own. I'll go home and—"

"No!" he thundered. "I don't mean to let you out of my sight! Come on—"

They rode through the moonlit fields, become for Jarl flowing seas, undulating under his Arab's hooves, until they came to a bluff above the river. Jarl pulled Grey Ghost up.

"Here," he said; "this will do—"

Millicent looked out over the water, moonwashed and silver. Saw the black shapes of the trees on the Carolina side. Heard the whippoorwills crying. The mocking bird chanting a hymn to the night.

"It—it's too perfect for words, Jarl!" she said.

He helped her down. But when her dainty feet touched earth, he did not let her go. Instead he raised that broken claw of a right hand, and touched her cheek, lightly as a breath. Murmured something under his breath.

"What did you say, Jarl!" she whispered.

"I said, Praise God from Whom all blessings flow!" Jarl said fervently.

"Jarl, don't say things you don't mean!" Millicent got out; "I know how you feel about Gert and—"

That was as far as she got. He bent and kissed her. Softly, sweetly, tenderly. With aching desire. With tenderness. With something akin to worship.

"Oh, Jarl!" she sobbed. "Oh, Jarl, Jarl, I—"

"You what?" he growled.

"I—I love you so!" Millicent wailed.

"And for that you're crying?" he said wonderingly.

"Yes! Because I—I'm too happy; and I'm afraid!" she wept.

"Don't be, little Milly," he said quietly; "there's nothing to be afraid of—"

"Oh, yes there is!" she moaned; "there are so many things between us!"

"Then," Jarl whispered, his voice deep, grave, tender, amazingly like his father's, "a link to bind us together, Milly—forever. Give me your left hand—"

"My left hand?" Milly got out. "Why, Jarl?"

He didn't answer her. He stretched out his own and took it. Then, clumsily, his broken hand impeding his efforts, he slipped a ring upon her finger.

"It was—my foster mother's," he said quietly. "She'd want you to have it, I know. . . ."

Millicent didn't say anything. She couldn't. She simply lifted her face to meet his kiss, all heaven's glory in her eyes.

But, about those many, many things between them, it turned out she was right. Such as the British and the Tories, who, after allowing Jarl Jarrett the happiest seven months he had known in all his life, descended upon Savannah the morning of December 29th, 1778, arriving long before the French Jarl was supposed to conduct liaison with, and gave the Georgians an object lesson that slavery was an unworkable proposition. For a disgruntled Black led British Colonel Campbell through the swamps, so he was able to fall upon Savannah like a thunderbolt.

Jarl took part in that melancholy debacle in which the British lost six killed, and nine wounded, while driving the American General Howe—no relation to Sir William—and his forces before him like cattle.

More than half of the Continental Troops were shot and sabered, drowned in the swamps, or ran away so fast that nobody ever heard of them again.

And, for the first time in three years, Jarl saw his father. Saw that white-maned, kilted giant, in the vanguard of the Tory forces, swinging his broadsword with both hands, cutting down the fleeing rebels like a berserker.

It was then that Jarl got out of there. He paused only long enough to pistol a fat British Major. Unfortunately for him, his ball caught his foe in the shoulder. Which, for all future Jarretts, was a pity. For his victim was Major Geoffrey Haig—alias, or ex—Hogg. Then Jarl Jarrett fled. He knew better than to try to face James Jarrett. Knew that one of them would have to kill the other. Which was too much.

So he fled. Organized, within the next two months, an irregular company of horse, composed of those among his old companions who had taken no part in the assault upon his father's house. Took the field against the enemies of his country.

Among them, his father.

In August of 1779, Jarl Jarrett and his Irregulars were once more encamped near Savannah, completely surrounded by the British and the Tories, which, to that hardbitten crew, mattered not a damn. The reason why they were there had plagued little to do with the war, though they served their cause right nobly, harassing the Tory forces. Jarl had led them so far south, in the forlorn hope of seeing Milly again, though he didn't tell them that. Not that it mattered, in one way. By then, they would have followed Jarl Jarrett into hell itself, swimming their mounts through the boiling brimstone and out again, as long as he rode in their van.

But, in another way, it did matter. Because, if he had told them, what happened next probably wouldn't have occurred.

For, on one moonlit night that August of 1779, Gertrude and Millicent Tyson went riding with two young British officers. Gertrude rode happily, joyously, because Lieutenant Bruce Forbes, of His Majesty's Fifth Light Horse, was the kind of a man she had been dreaming of all her life. Bruce was tall and dark. Handsome enough to turn any maiden's head, Tory or not. He was gay, charming. He had a wonderful baritone voice, and he knew all the hit songs of the day. He sang tender love songs to Gert. Rollicking camp ditties, taking care to clean them up so that she would not be offended. But Milly went reluctantly.

She felt that what she was doing was in some obscure way a betrayal of her love for Jarl Jarrett. The more so because Lieutenant Peter Tyburn was every bit as handsome as his friend. As gay, as charming, and could sing almost as well. The trouble was that Milly, being human, liked him very much. Since she'd already promised to marry Jarl once the War was over, the way she felt about Peter disturbed her. She needn't have worried. That night, Jarl's Irregulars ended her confusion forever.

Jarl wasn't with them. In his desperation, he had stolen into Savannah itself. Made his way to the Tyson house. A *mulata* serving wench told him where Milly was. And Jarl, who was growing more like his father every passing day, roared out of Savannah on Grey Ghost, with blood in his eye.

Too late. For, by then, Peter Tyburn was already dead, shot from the saddle by Tom Morrison, Jarl's Second in Command. Bruce Forbes, crawled away through the darkness, stabbed through the body. Fortunately for Gertrude, he lived.

Now, in the history books, those fine, clean living, upright young patriots never took advantage of the helpless women who fell into their hands. In actuality, the grimy, unwashed, louse-infested crew of brigands who did most of the real fighting, were soldiers. And rape has always been one of the favorite pastimes of a conquering army. They committed it upon every conceivable opportunity, and made opportunities when none presented themselves.

In a strange way, when life is reduced to its ultimates, anything that happens to a person boils down to a matter of choice. There are many levels of guilt. Even the business of submitting to superior force involves the sin of putting the fear of death above other things. Which was what the five men who had captured the Tyson girls were up against when it came to Milly. She had promised herself, Jarl Jarrett, and her God, that she would come to him in the same state in which she had been born. And she'd come to him like that, or die.

She had certain advantages. She was as quick as a cat. Utterly fearless. And Tom Morrison's crew made an unwise division of forces: Because Gertrude was both bigger and stronger, three of them held her, leaving the other two to attend to Milly. By then, in the state of cold fury she had reached, no two men could have held her—nor any ten.

She tore her hands free from Reuben Tyler's grasp. Raked his face bloody. Almost blinded him. Snatched the horse pistol from his belt, and shot Dick Meadows through the leg. Dashed off through the woods for help.

Which was where Jarl Jarrett found her. He had been guided in the right direction by the sound of her shot. He leaped down from his horse, took her in his arms.

Her clothes were torn. Her shoulders were bare. Her hair was loose and wild. She was sobbing, hysterically.

"Fine friends you've got, Milly!" Jarl snarled. "If this is how British officers treat women—"

"Not British!" Millicent stormed. "Your men, Jarl! Your own company! Tom Morrison, Reuben Tyler, Dick Meadows! Two others I don't know! And they've got Gert! They mean to—"

Even under the stress of her emotion, that was a word she couldn't say.

"Dear God!" Jarl whispered. Then, very quietly, he looked to the priming of his pistols. He had four of them: two great horse pistols, and two smaller, pocket arms. Then he lifted Milly up onto the Arab's back. Mounted. Thundered through the night, with her clinging to him, and crying.

What he did, when he got to that clearing, made Millicent fear and respect him all her life. His Irregulars were quite expert at their warriors' sport. Two of them held Gertrude's arms; two her legs, while the fifth—

Jarl pulled Grey Ghost up. Drew his pistols. Shot three of his old companions dead upon the spot. What saved the fourth was the fact that the last weapon missed fire. Then he was down from his horse, sabre in hand. Crowded Tom Morrison and Reuben Tyler up against a tree. Made them throw down their arms.

Reuben was the Troop's bugler, which, now, was unfortunate for him.

"Sound the call!" Jarl whispered. "Damn you, Reuben, sound it!"

White with fear, Reuben sent that silvery call soaring through the night. Within minutes, the others were there. They sat on their horses, staring at their leader. At the three dead men on the ground. He didn't have to explain. Just looking at the shivering, weeping, completely hysterical Gertrude, they knew.

"Parade formation!" Jarl barked. "Gentlemen, I don't think I need to tell you that Jarrett's Irregulars don't commit rape. Nor see I any need for a formal courtmartial. Take these two swine to that oak over there, and hang them!"

Watching it, Gertrude slumped to the ground in a dead faint. And Millicent buried her face against his coat, sobbing helplessly.

But when Jarl helped her and Gertrude down, just outside the British lines, Millicent looked at him with eyes he had never seen before.

"Goodbye, Jarl," she whispered.

"Not goodbye," Jarl said softly. *"Au 'voir,* Milly. Because we're going to take Savannah one of these days—and when we do—"

"It will do you no good," Millicent said. "You and I are finished, Jarl."

"Milly, for God's love! I did what I could! I'm sorry that happened. I think I've proved to you—"

"You've only proved what company you keep," Millicent said. "And one thing worse—"

"Worse?" Jarl croaked.

"Far worse. You've proved, Jarl Jarrett, that you're as cruel as your father! So, now, goodbye!"

Then she turned and left him there, putting one arm about her sister's shaking shoulders.

"Come, Gert," she said bitterly, "there's nothing more to cry for—now."

Some hours later, it occurred to Jarl that she hadn't given him back his ring. He took what comfort he could from that fact.

On the night of October Eighth, that fateful year of 1779, Jarl spent hours rehearsing the speeches he'd make to her on the morrow. Going over his pleas, his explanations. Because Savannah's fall was certain. Count d'Estaing was there, with the whole French Fleet, enabling Jarl to obey his General's orders at long last. Three weeks ago, they'd pounded the Fort of Tybee Island to powder. Captured four British Men O' War. Sent in a demand for the surrender of the city. Waited for General Prevost to consider the demand during the twelve hours respite the Englishman had asked for—that twelve hours during which Prevost managed to transport all his troops to the mainland. To dig in. To send, at the end of that time, a note couched in polite, diplomatic language to the gentle, trusting old Auvergnat. The import of that note was that Monsieur le Comte could go to hell.

But they would take the city, all right. Gallant Count Pulaski was there with his Light Horse Dragoons. General Lincoln, fat as a hog, with the American Troops. Six thousand, five hundred men to the Britishers' twenty-five hundred. They'd roll over them—

Jarl moved away from the campfire. He was praying, begging God to keep Milly safe from harm. By tomorrow, she'd be safe all right. Safe forever in his arms.

He wandered off into the woods, his mind busy with his plans, his fears. Almost stepped upon a couple on the ground. The man leaped to his feet, towering above Jarl Jarrett. In the moonlight, Jarl saw he was blacker than original sin. While the woman—

Jarl froze. He was a born Southerner. And this slender, snowy creature—He jerked out his pistol.

"Goddamn you, you black ape!" he roared; "I'll—"

But the black man moved like a ghost. Fingers of inky steel closed over Jarl's wrist. Twisted cruelly. A half heart beat later, Jarl was imprisoned in the arms of the strongest man he had ever met in all his life.

"What is it that passes with you, white?" the Negro growled.

French. One of those blacks from Haiti whom le Comte d'Estaing had brought with him.

"Leave him, Chris," the girl said in soft Creole patois; "he thinks I'm white—"

"*Eh bien, quoi, donc?*" the black rumbled. "*Quelle importe?*"

"I'll show you what importance it has, you ape!" Jarl howled in the French he had learned at his mother's knee. "This is Georgia! And here, we don't let niggers touch—"

"I," the black man said softly, "am not one of *votre sale negres*, M'sieur. Yours, nor anybody's. I came not to this country of yours to save your cowardly hides, but to learn to fight. To instruct myself in tactics, in strategy. And when I have, I shall hurl the last French dog into the sea, and make all Haiti mine! *Tu comprehends tout ça, petit blanc?*"

"You're mad!" Jarl whispered.

"Yes. I have the madness of glory. One day you will hear of me, little white. And you'll say: 'I—and I alone, tried to kill Henri Christophe, the Emperor of all the Blacks!' And that will be your glory, little white—*peut'être* the sole glory you'll ever know. . . ."

"Master," the girl said in English, "don't take on. Henri's a little crazy for a fact. 'Sides, you's gitting riled over nothing. I'm Dulcie Sallette, one o' Marse Bob Sallette's yard chillun. I only looks white, Suh. . . ."

"Too white to be consorting with this animal!" Jarl howled.

"No, now, Master, you's wrong," Dulcie laughed. "If I makes Henri turn you loose, you promise not to fight?"

"All right," Jarl growled.

"Let him go, Henri," Dulcie said.

The black released Jarl, stood back.

"You know Master," the girl said, "Henri ain't all crazy. Proud, yes. Strong. Don't even start to know how to bow his head. Black or no, I like that. A gal can really cotton to a man what's a man, no matter what color he is. And you know another thing, Suh? I'm betting he'll do jes what he said. . . ."

Jarl stared at the Negro. That long, heathen mask was endlessly intelligent. Curiosity overcame him.

"Tell me, Henri," he said, "just how do you propose to beat the French?"

"I'll take to the hills, me," Henri Christophe said: "raid them in the night. Burn the cane fields, the houses. Never attack them from the front, which is a brutishness, a sottishness, a folly, considering their arms. No, little white, I shall bleed them to death by inches. Then, when they are weak enough, I shall push them into the sea!"

Leaving them, half an hour later, Jarl's mind was filled with wonder. He'd never dreamed there were blacks like this one. In his middle years, of course, he would remember that brief encounter, remember it as he read of Henri Christophe, Jean Jacques Dessalines, and Toussaint L'Ouverture whipping the armies of Napoleon, driving them into the sea, setting up a black empire. Which was, really, but of scant importance to him, or to Clan Jarrett. What was important in that strange meeting, he could not know. Later, and bitterly, he would learn.

They stormed into Savannah that next morning. Stormed into hell. The British were firing shrapnel: broken bayonets, rusty nails, old belt buckles, scrap iron. All around Jarl Jarrett, men were going down, vomiting blood. He saw a whirling chain shot take brave Count Pulaski in the middle, bearing him to the ground, horribly mangled. The Count lay there and screamed in Polish until he died. The average life of a man under that hail of death was five minutes. The ground under foot turned into red mud, slippery with human blood. Count d'Estaing was crying, tottering forward on his short legs, his great tun of a belly heaving. The screams of the wounded rose above the cannons' roar.

Then the raw American Troops broke. Ran like sheep from the battlefield, throwing down their arms. Sixty-five hundred men, running from less than three thousand. Papa d'Estaing tried to stop them. He could not. His gallant French troops held, and were slaughtered. More than one thousand men lay dead upon that field when it was over. And the British had beaten the Rebels again.

As always, when they failed to cover up their shins.

Georgia sank back into a savagery blacker than the pit. Men no longer said James Jarrett's name aloud. Nor the McGerk brothers'. Nor Thomas Brown's. Nor Colonel Gierson's.

Augusta was in Tory hands once more. Andrew Williamson turned traitor in May of 1780, and handed it over to the British. And the citizens of that town had made the mistake of tarring and feathering Thomas Brown, and dragging him through the streets behind a cart for his Tory sympathies. Now he was in charge. And what he did to the people of Augusta, made even James Jarrett call his hand.

Jim Dooly harried the Tories, who cut his throat in bed one dark night. His son took the field, rounded up a group of Tories and murdered nine of them. Nobody stopped him, not even his officers. The war in Georgia was like that.

Jarl's Irregulars left fire and destruction in their wake. But they never touched a woman again. In September, they rode with Colonel Clarke to attack Augusta. They got the living hell beaten out of them. They left thirty prisoners behind. Tom Brown hanged thirteen of the wounded men from his stairway. Turned the rest over to his Indians. Spent a pleasant three hours watching the redskins torture them to death.

A man could read a newspaper all over Georgia by the light of blazing Tory houses. No Tory maid, were she as ugly as homemade sin, was safe by day or night. Which was the aspect of this civil war between brothers, between fathers and their sons, that was not set down upon the noble pages of the chroniclers. Which was entirely understandable: murder, looting, torture and rapine don't make inspiring reading.

Jarl and his Irregulars struck like sudden lightning. In the driving rains of that Fall and Winter, they slashed their enemies without letup. They could scent victory now. As the air warmed into that Spring of 1781, they caught the heady smell of it, in every lilting breeze.

In May, at long, long last, they stormed into long sought Augusta again, with the Army commanded by Light Horse Harry Lee and Andrew Pickens. Jarl's Irregulars were directly under Colonel Clarke's

command. They captured Colonel Gierson the first day, and an in-
fantryman pistoled him after he had surrendered. Everybody knew who
had done it, but no one would tell. And cruel as Gierson was, his
death was unfortunate. It stiffened the Tories' will to resist. They holed
up in Fort Cornwallis. Light Horse Harry built a tower. Put his cannon
upon it. Blasted Fort Cornwallis to kingdom come.

Tradition has it that James Jarrett was shot down by a foot-soldier
while in hand to hand combat with his own son. Tradition, as usual,
was a mite mixed up. It wasn't his father that Jarl fought. Very likely,
it was—his brother.

For, in the midst of the fight, he found himself facing a Cherokee
Brave. He was out of ammunition by then, so he drew his hunting
knife. The brave swung a fearsome looking tomahawk. They locked,
gripping each other's wrists, straining silently, the sweat beading on
fair forehead and on dark. Stared into each other's eyes and—stopped
fighting. Stood back, gazing at each other. At those identical axeblade
noses, at that single brow which swept across their faces without a
break. At faces, which, except for coloring, and the trifles of hair
dress were mirror images.

"Your name is—Jarrett?" the Cherokee said in perfect, accentless
English.

"Yes," Jarl whispered.

"Then go in peace," the redskin said. "I soil not my hands with
mine own blood. . . ."

Jarl saw now that the brave's skin was very light for an Indian's.

"I—I don't understand," he got out.

The Cherokee smiled.

"I know you don't, Pale Brother," he said. "Ask thy father. When
you see him—ask him of Loosaponakee and her son. Mayhap, he will
tell thee. And now, farewell. The Great Spirit guide and guard
thee. . . ."

Then, silent as a ghost, he was gone.

Jarl found his father in the ruins of the fort, bleeding to death of
his wounds. He bent to staunch them.

"Too late, boy," James growled feebly. "I'm past help, now. Besides,
you cure me, and I'll hang. Hell of an end for a Jarrett. . . ."

"Father," Jarl whispered, his voice thick with choked back tears,
"I—"

"You," James croaked, "are a man and a soldier, son. I'm proud of you. And here's my hand on it. . . ."

Jarl took that great hand. It was already growing cold.

"Tell me boy," James whispered, "have you a lass?"

"Aye, father," Jarl murmured; "only—"

"Only, nothing!" James thundered, his voice booming out, deep and strong. "Wed her, lad! Get sons! Many, many sons! You hear me, boy? Sons!"

"Aye, father," Jarl wept.

"Don't cry, boy," James said gruffly; "I've been a rum father to you. I've done things that—but no matter. Here. Put your hand in my coat pocket. . . ."

Wonderingly, Jarl did so. Drew out a folded, creased, dirty, blood-stained paper. Saw, as he opened it, the drawing of a house. That matchless Georgian Mansion in which the Perkinses lived. In far off London. In Bloomsbury Square.

"Drew that before you were born," James said tiredly. "Before I'd dreamed of coming here. So, boy—"

"Yes, father?" Jarl whispered.

"Build me that house! I—I never could. But you can. Clan Jarrett's ancestral seat. The home of countless generations of—men. . . ."

"Father, please! You're too weak, and—"

"I'm dying, lad. So heed me. Build me that house. Bring your lass home to it. Get sons—"

"Yes, father," Jarl choked. "And father—"

"Yes, lad?"

"Would you mind—if I—if I kissed you—goodbye? I never have, you know. Not in all my life. . . ."

"Still Frenchified, aren't you?" James growled. "Englishmen don't kiss each other. Still—"

Then, for the first time, he stretched out his great arms to his son. And the last.

CHAPTER TWENTY-SIX

THEY DROVE THE British before them, after that. Pinned them down in Savannah. Colonel James Jackson and the Georgia Legion carried flaming war to the banks of the Ogeechee. Colonel Twiggs pushed the redcoats into Ebenezer.

And Jarl Jarrett hovered about Savannah, waiting for the all out attack that would carry him into Milly's arms.

Perhaps.

But that attack never came. Betimes there was Cowpens where brave Tarleton Tyson died. Guilford Courthouse where Earl Cornwallis beat Nat Greene in an indecisive battle, losing twice as many men as the Americans, leaving the flower of the British Army upon the field.

And, finally, there was Yorktown, where Cornwallis' troops marched out to stack their arms to the tune of "The World Turned Upside Down."

As it damned well was.

In July of 1782, the British evacuated Savannah. Gertrude Tyson, who had married Lieutenant Bruce Forbes, went with them. But Millicent Tyson stayed.

To stand there looking at her tall, dirty, sweaty, ill-shaven warrior. All the impassioned speeches he had composed inside his mind died on Jarl Jarrett's lips. He stood there, trembling a little, unable to speak.

Then, very softly, slowly, sweetly, Milly stretched out her arms to him. And with a sound curiously like a sob, Jarl came to them. Came home to his haven, and his refuge.

In September of 1783, they came to that place, with their firstborn,

Jeremy, sleeping in Milly's arms. Because they couldn't stay in Savannah where heated arguments raged over whether the property confiscated from the estate of Tory James Jarrett could be legally restored to his patriot son. Where Milly's father and mother had both died in their shell wrecked home during the ill-fated American attack. Where Mary Jarrett had been blasted out of life. Where all their common memories were bitter.

Nor could they go to Augusta, where the very name Jarrett was anathema. So they went northwest of that town for one hundred and sixty-five miles. Drew their Conestoga wagon to a halt near the spot where Atlanta now stands. Sat there looking at that endless sweep of green under the giant oaks. That place, their hearts told them both, was home.

"How green it is, Love!" Millicent whispered. "As green as Jade!"

Jarl's face twisted into the expression of brooding mockery that had become characteristic of him. Inside his heart, he could hear his father howl: "That Jade! That goddamned fickle Jade!"

"You've given me a name for it, Milly," he said. "Jade—Jarrett's Jade. Like it?"

"No," Millicent said. "Let's call it—Jadewood, Love. . . ."

"All right," Jarl said absently. Then he got down and began handing out the axes and the saws to the Negroes.

But he never called it that, not even after he had built that brick Georgian mansion he had promised his father he would. Sired his roaring brood of sons. Risen to power and influence in the state.

Nor did any other Jarrett—except rarely. As when, perchance they were talking to strangers.

Among themselves—never.

The End

Madrid, Spain   July 17th, 1959